I Took Soul to Church Today

I Took Soul to Church Today

DENNIS RAY 'COACH' CLIFTON

Dennis Clifton

Latest Revision Year: 2015

ISBN: 069247031X
ISBN 13: 9780692470312
Library of Congress Control Number: 2015911393
Dennis Clifton, Union, KY

Disclaimer

This book is fiction, and the events are for the enjoyment of my reading audience. The book is for entertainment purposes only. Some of the events in this book are real events that did occur, but many stories are fictional to meet the needs of the story. I do strive to provide useful, accurate, and complete information. However, no person(s) or organization contributing to the preparation or presentation of this material makes *any* such claims. Any resemblance to locations, landmarks, people, animations, or depictions are strictly incidental and may or may not be real.

Send all questions, comments, or concerns relating to the content of this publication to P.O. Box 1139 Union, Kentucky 41091.

All information provided herein is for informational purposes only. The user assumes all risk and responsibility for the proper use and translation of the contents of this book. The author assumes no responsibility for the improper use of the information.

This book has been self-published and copyright protected by the laws of the United States of America and its government.

Dedication
To My Oldest Grandson
Noah Gayhart

While we were playing baseball in my backyard one summer day, Noah said, "Coach, I love to hear stories about our family and your way of telling them. It makes me feel like I was there when the events were actually taking place. In some strange way, I guess I really was." Some of my grandchildren call me coach, and some refer to me as Grandpa; both make me smile inside. He asked me to write down the stories describing our past so someday he could share them with his family. He said he understood that every story might not be told exactly the way it happened. Then he smiled and said it would be close enough for our family and future generations of families to remember the past.

Thank You, Noah
I love you,
Coach/Grandpa

Introduction

The first few chapters of this book explain my relationship with Soul. It reveals a moment in church services one Sunday that set the stage in motion for the entire series of life events for Soul and me.

The next several chapters describe the events that earned the bull the front cover. It covers a series of tragic events that could have very likely occurred during the nineteen sixties and seventies and introduces you to a number of the characters who were around at the time the events were taking place; they too will have their own version of what happened.

The Clifton family is a real family, and most of the members of the original family are still living as of the writing of this book. They continue to live in the area where the stories took place.

My family moved to Carroll County, Kentucky in the early fifties from Owen County, Kentucky. My father accepted a position with a highway construction company named Ohio Valley Paving Company. The paving company owner was a very kind, smart and generous man. He and his family lived in the town of Carrollton, Kentucky. The company plant site was located near Milton, Kentucky. The money my father earned was used to improve the quality of life for his family. My family lived off the land for five generations; we grew tobacco, grain, and hay. We raised cattle and horses, sheep, hogs, and chickens. Many of my family members were expert hunters. My father served in the United States Military shortly after the attack on Pearl Harbor.

Something happened to my father when he jumped off his watercraft and waded to shore during a Japanese ground invasion in the Philippine Islands. He learned that if you want something bad enough, you have to be willing to go get it, work hard to keep it, and protect it with every ounce of life you have left in your body.

Just days before we moved to Carroll County, my father met with the president of the local Farmers Bank of Milton. The bank president asked my father for collateral to secure the loan. My dad presented him with a beautiful, pearl-handled pistol. The president said, "Wow, what a gorgeous weapon," and handed the pistol back to my dad. My father told the president he could be trusted, and if he would lend him the money to purchase a farm he would be forever grateful. The bank president loaned my dad the money, and my father remained a customer of the bank until the day he died.

My dad purchased a ridge farm not far from his employer's business. Our family cleared the land to make room for several garden plots, pasture for the few cattle we owned, and two plow-horses named Jerry and Jim. It did not take long for us to clear the trees and till much of the 250 acres needed to plant tobacco, corn, and hay to feed our growing herd of livestock. The money earned from the sale of tobacco paid our farm mortgage, purchased new and better farm equipment, and increased the size of our herds.

Our original house was located on a half-acre lot at the point where five small streams met to form the main waterway to the Ohio River. The old house we lived in was named the Old Locust Bridge Tollhouse. The tollhouse, built by local farmers, was used to collect money needed to build Locust Road and the bridges over several large creeks known as the East and West Prongs. Once the community had enough money to complete the project, they gave the house to the previous owner. The house was move from Locust to the area were we found it when we purchased the farm.

My family added on several rooms and a large stone patio during the five years we lived in the house. The patio was built from large stones we collected from the five creeks, loaded on a two-rail sled, and then pulled to the house by our team horses. We called the tollhouse home until we purchased the adjoining farmland, which also included a big farmhouse.

The farm became available when the owner died. She was well into her nineties, and we considered her a member of our family. As a young child, I mowed her lawn with a mechanical push mower and helped her weed the garden and harvest her crops from time to time. I think my dearest memories were of the freshly baked apple and cherry pies she would share with me when our day's work was finished. Her death deeply touched me. It was my first encounter with the grieving process, and I hated it. My heart was broken, and I missed her so much. My father explained to me what it meant to go live in Heaven and be with God. He knew that was where she went and that she was happy.

The new Clifton house was much closer to the main road, State Highway 36. The house was located on a two-acre lot in the valley and surrounded by two enormous creeks. The creek on the left side of our house was named Clifton Creek, after our family. The creek on the right side of the house was Mills Creek, named after the previous owners. The two creeks joined about one-hundred feet from our house to form Conway's Creek. Conway's Creek was fast flowing and spent more time out of its banks during the rainy season than inside its boundaries. It traveled along Conway's Bottoms and around the base of Cedar Point for about five miles before emptying into the Ohio River. The mighty Ohio River flows along the edge of the farm fields and serves as a boundary between Kentucky and Indiana.

A giant northern pine tree stood at the most northern point in our yard and just inside the yard fence. According to Indian legend, the tree served as a marker to indicate the level of the two creeks during the rainy season. Once the water flowing in the creeks got to a certain point on the tree, the Indians living nearby knew it was time to run for the hills to safety from the rushing water.

The story, handed down through the generations, was that the cedar tree was transplanted there from the top of a ridge named Cedar Point. Cedar Point was a unique landmass, covering about 60 areas of land. It was located behind our house, just across from the tobacco patch.

An elderly man once told me the Indians who lived in the valley several hundred years ago named the ridge Cedar Point. Cedar Point was a sacred burial ground because of its elliptical shape that pointed to the heavens. It served as the final resting place for leaders in the tribe. I am not sure if the man was correct, but I can tell you I spent a lot of time in my early childhood years climbing to the top of Cedar Point. It is a place where the earth appears to touch the sky, and the clouds could almost be touched by my bare hands.

Many times, I would climb to the top of a large hickory tree that served as a home for wildlife, including raccoons and squirrels. It was also the resting point for some of the most beautiful birds on earth. The tree seemed out of place, but it was much easier to climb than dealing with the sap from the large cedar trees surrounding it. The branches of the tree were large from the bottom to the top. I remember the days, especially in the spring and early fall seasons, when I would climb to the tree's highest point. I would brace my body between the branches and the trunk of the tree and fell fast asleep, a light breeze causing the tree to sway gently from side to side. Other times I would just sit and enjoy the beautiful colors that transformed the scenery in the valley below, which was adorned with fertile farmland, stretching as far as the eye could see. I know other members of my family spent hours on top of Cedar Point talking to God and seeking help in making important decisions about their life. Even today, I still think God himself uses Cedar Point to find peace on earth. He probably has a vacation home up there; I just never could find it.

The cattle barn in the upcoming bull story, where Mom runs into the barn to hide from the mad bull, is located on the banks of Clifton Creek.

Our farm had four gardens, and the ridge where the first bull attack took place was several miles from the house. The garden was at the end of a very long stretch of ridge land. The fence I attempted to jump was located at the end of the ridge next to the real pond in the story.

The great northern pine tree must have lost its powers to control the flooding associated with the two creeks. I can remember at least three rain events in my lifetime when the creeks ran so fast and deep my family had to run for the hills to keep from being washed away. Whoever chose the site to build the house and outhouse had the wisdom to locate the structures as close to the hill as possible and as far as possible from the creeks.

Okay Noah here is the answer to your question about the outhouse. Why was the outhouse a two-seater? The answer is simple: girls on the left and boys on the right, but not at the same time, and yes, the door did have a lock on it.

Consultants and Credits

Gretchen Akers: Marketing and Management, Northern Kentucky University; Elementary Education, Murray State University; Earlier Age Reading Specialist, Murray State University

Jason Akers: Author & Technical Assistance, Author of: Hunt, Gather, Grow, Eat; The Self Sufficient Gardner. Amazon.com, Jason Akers

Janet Clifton, Melanie Gayhart, Tim Gayhart, Jay Louden, Adam Clifton: Research Story Development Events Sequencing and Design

Ben Murrell: Artist: www.createmeadrawing.com email: Murrell.artwork@yahoo.com

Special Recognition: Jackson Akers, Ava Malynn Akers, Alexander Akers, Kate Gayhart, Noah Gayhart, Abby Louden, and Sydney Louden

 # About the Author

I am one of those people who never figured out when it was time to quit. Many of my stories in this book are from actual events that took place during my lifetime.

I am now a grandfather, and as most grandfathers sometimes do, I have a tendency to embellish the actual events just a little bit. All of my books are family friendly and contain appropriate language. I do everything possible to write stories for all ages that can be shared and enjoyed by the entire family. Some of my stories have surprise endings and will probably make you cry happy tears. Some will make you laugh and relieved to find it ends the way we all hoped it would. A few will likely make you want to hold your family a little closer.

I thank God every day for allowing me to live in America, where citizens have the freedom to choose the path they want to travel from start to finish.

I spend many of my Sundays telling stories to my children and grandchildren. We talk a lot about family history and how those events led us to where we are today. They love to hear stories about moms and dads, grandparents, aunts and uncles and others who made a lasting impression on the family history. They seem to be interested in where the people I talk about lived and how they died. Many of the stories in my books are true events, with a little added drama to help keep the reader's interest. These stories always seem to wake up the past and allow it to live at least one more generation.

The main character in my books is Soul. God, on my birthday, Saturday January 2, 1954, assigned Soul to me: he is my guardian angel. As you will see in the first story, we got off to a bit of a rocky start, and our relationship had a lot of room for improvement.

Soul spent too much time making excuses and feeling sorry for himself; he was a *big fat chicken*. What God was thinking when he placed this prima-donna in the middle of nowhere? As it turns out, God was right all along.

One Sunday morning at church, all of our bickering and disagreements abruptly ended. Soul's boss unexpectedly dropped by at the beginning of the church service and held a private session at the altar with the two of us. All I can say is we both certainly changed after that day. If it were not for Soul doing what guardian angels do, I would not be here today to tell these stories. Soul has stepped in and gotten me through some difficult situations.

The first story takes place inside a small church in North Central Kentucky. The weather was sunny, and there was not a cloud in the sky. Many things happen to people inside a church, and when I admired the beautiful stained glass window, I noticed it was suddenly pitch black outside. I had a feeling someone was about to get a visit from you know who. I looked around the congregation to see if I could figure out who was in *trouble*.

One

I am indeed convinced Soul is a real guardian angel. I think you will be too once you finish reading this book. He has to be or there is no way I could have survived some of the disasters that I made it through in my life. Actually, I would not have made it past the age of seven if not for him. I believe Soul is actually about ten-thousand years old. This is based on some very complicated theories to prove scientifically, of course. I think God assigns guardian angels to people purely on heaven's future needs—he needs to helps us understand him and his angels need understand how to keep up with an ever-changing world. You will get a better idea why I feel that way later in the story.

Somehow, God discovered Soul was a *big fat chicken*. When I got him, he had no courage whatsoever. In fact, early on in my life, Soul would conveniently disappear when I needed him most. I think God knew Soul had to find more courage to stand and defend himself when threatened or when his assignment on earth was in harm's way. This all happened about the same time I was due to make an appearance in this big old world. God had reached the end of his patience with Soul. He had made enough observations to know he had to take some action. The time had come, and God had to find out if Soul would ever find his courage.

I know God is kind and thoughtful and he wanted to protect Soul as much as he could. After all of these years together, I have a superb idea about how things went down between God and Soul prior to him being assigned to me.

I think God met with Soul at heaven's gate when he made his last delivery from earth one day. He told Soul he needed to take a vacation and rest up for a few days. He promised him his next assignment would be his most exciting and by far the most challenging assignment ever.

Knowing Soul as well as I do, he probably told God it did not matter what the assignment was because he was the best of the best and the boss could count on him. God likely just smiled and told him he would see him in a few weeks.

As you can tell, Soul had built up a lot of personal pride and confidence over the years. It is hard to say how many times God had to cut Soul off from bragging to keep him from breaking his arm from patting himself on the back. I think his arrogance stemmed from the fact Soul had been assigned to a series of some of the most prominent and wealthy people to ever walk the earth. You will also see how I came to that conclusion later in the story.

Soul was likely a little tired from his last assignment and decided to take God up on his offer to let him rest.

A couple of weeks went by, and one of God's messengers informed Soul he needed to meet with God at heaven's gate. Soul was likely growing impatient because he likes to work, and let's face it folks, he has the greatest boss in the universe.

By then he was well rested and ready for his next assignment. If he only knew what God had in store for him, he would have likely taken a leave-of-absence for about a hundred years.

I am sure Soul assumed his next assignment would be another prominent person on earth as it had been in the past. He reported to work dressed in his best attire and wearing his most precious jewels. Soul's jewels were made of the purest quality gold and lined with perfectly shaped diamonds—sounds like a high-maintenance guardian angel to me!

He felt it was important to make a good first impression for his new assignment. God handed him the address and told him he had three hours to get to his next destination. His new assignment would be a boy child, and he would be born on Saturday January 2, 1954 at precisely 12:05 AM. Soul told God in his arrogant tone of voice, "If you had moved it up one day, I could have enjoyed the New Year's night celebration and fireworks displays." God just shook his head in disgust and said, "No. It is time for you to be off, my son."

Just as Soul was getting ready to depart through heaven's gate, God informed him he would not need to wear his precious jewels to impress his next assignment. Soul took it to mean he was actually under-dressed and could not imagine the treasures or wealth of his next assignment.

Soul took a quick look at the address and saw the word Kentucky. One of the more senior angels awaiting transfer offered to trade assignments, but Soul insisted he would keep his appointment. Soul told God he would be fine and Kentucky would be great for him and he just had a good feeling about this. God ordered the gates to open and sent Soul on his way.

The address did not ring a bell, but Soul was an experienced angel and thought nothing else about it until he made a left turn and headed straight for the new world. He was so excited. It was his first assignment in the new world. He had heard other angels talk about places like New York and San Francisco and the opportunities they had to visit some of God's greatest creations in that part of the world. As he approached earth and headed for the United States of America, he looked up to God in heaven and said, "Thank you master. I deserve this." God replied, "Yes you do, my son."

As Soul streaked towards his new assignment, one could hear him humming bars from popular American songs. "New York-New York," "I left my heart in San Francisco," and the original "What a Wonderful World" were the ones most prevalent at the time. Somehow he knew a few lines from some good old southern songs: "I wish I were in the Land of Dixie" and then heaven forbid a few lines from "My Old Kentucky Home." He suddenly slowed down and said, "Stop. not Dixie—and for God sakes, not the South. I am a big city boy and that is where I belong. I love the big city lights and sipping expensive wines. I know I will enjoy America's most excellent cuisine prepared and served at some of America's best restaurants."

God checks in on Soul's journey, and after a few minutes of observing his attitude, he probably thought to himself, "What have I done?"

Soul took a quick peek at his timepiece and realized he was running short on time and had to pick up his speed. He focused his attention on the address, which just read "Hunters Bottom Kentucky and right near Locust Creek." He thought to himself, *Wow, maybe Kentucky is not so bad after all,* and he felt confident God had rewarded him for all of his great work from the past.

It sure was a strange address, but again, he saw earth as his personal playground. He knew he would find the house. He finally arrived in the area and started circling the hills. He was trying to locate his chariot, which, of course, would carry to the palace by the royal guard of the parents of his next assignment. He could not quite find the chariot, so he decided to listen for the trumpets announcing his arrival and alerting the servants to prepare the master suite. He did not hear the trumpets, but he did see a farmhouse below. He did not want to be late and disappoint his boss, so he decided to drop in and asks for directions from another guardian angel.

When he walked into the house, he heard the cries of a mother giving birth to a baby. Then he heard the midwife smack my behind, and I blurted out my first cry. This cry hit Soul like a ton of bricks. As best I can remember, he opened his arms wide, spread his fingers wide on both hands, and placed his palms in an upward position, facing the heavens. He slowly raised his head, looked up to the heavens, and said, "Oh my God, you have got to be kidding me?" God looked down at Soul and said, "Make me proud, my son. Not all of my children are blessed with the riches of the earth, but they are all my children."

Soul's new assignment was the seventh child in a family that would eventually grow to fourteen children (seven-boys and seven-girls). My mother wanted to name me Eddie, but at the last second Soul intervened and I was named Dennis.

The first few years of my life passed by and, to be honest with you, I do not think Soul was awake. On the other hand, it could have taken God that long to convince him I was all he was getting.

Two

Time to Wake up Soul, Break's Over

I took Soul to church. It seemed like the thing to do since we had not been to church for a while due to the lack of wedding invites or funerals to attend.

But, who is counting? God is, and Soul and I were about to find out the score.

I could tell Soul was a little nervous as we drove from our house in the country to the church. Keep in mind my family did in fact live in a gated-community.

I still remember the disagreements between my brothers and sister about whose turn it was to manually open and close the three gates between my house and the main road. Soul is the name I gave that little voice in my head who seems to make his presence known when I'm about to make a foolish decision. He is also there when I find myself needing him to comfort me and when I am lonely, confused, afraid, or in need of a little courage to move on.

You likely have a similar little voice inside your head who talks to you from time to time. If you do and it does for you what it has done for me, you may want to pay a little more attention to it when you are about to do something you will regret.

As with most Sunday mornings in a small church, the only seat available once the rest of my family sat down was in the front row next to the altar. At the time, I was one of the youngest and smallest members of the family. It seems I was always the one picked to make the long journey to the front row. Most of the time, Soul was asleep by the time we got out of our driveway. He did not appear to have a concern on earth or in heaven.

The scariest thing about having to sit in the front row was the direct dialogue with the minister, and I was eyeball to eyeball with the church elders. I remember the elders were always dressed alike and focused on something I could not see. They never smiled or stood when the rest of the congregation stood. I decided one Sunday I was going to stare directly at one of the elders just to see if he knew I was there. He never blinked or moved a muscle the entire church service.

The only people sitting in the front row were me, Soul (which no one else could see), and some woman staring at the left side of my face. She appeared to be dressed in her best black dress.

I continued to watch the woman out of the corner of my left eye, which has excellent peripheral vision. I could not take my mind off her:

What did this woman want?
Did she know me from the past?
Did she just want to talk or need a friendly hug?

Finally, the music started, and it was time to relax and take part in the service. Soul and I both loved to sing; unfortunately, we also liked to play baseball, football, and basketball—I think you get the point. Over time, we missed every single music appreciation and voice class the church ever sponsored purely due to our love of games.

Picture below of the family church in the early days that served as the home of many saved souls, funerals, weddings, and eighth-grade graduations.

Three

I had noticed for several weeks that something was weighing heavy on Soul's mind. He was more silent than normal and seemed to be carrying the burdens of the world on his shoulders.

Frankly, he really let me down on numerous occasions. At times, he has just been downright mentally *hurtful.*

I am not saying he had not put in any effort. He just seemed to be satisfied with putting in mediocre effort, especially when what I needed was for him to increase the tone of his voice, take control of the moment, and ask me questions like:

"What are you doing?"

"Why are you doing this?"

"How could you hurt the people depending on you to make the right choice?"

"Why can't you delay, postpone, or leave?"

"Is it really worth it to you?"

"Can you please ask yourself what the right thing to do is?"

I had been praying for months for God to provide more guidance in my life to help me become a better and wiser person. On Wednesday nights, a woman and her family from the church would visit my family's house. She was a great person and spoke about her relationship with God. I was young and did not understand most of what she was describing to us. Nevertheless, I knew it was good, and if I applied it to my day-to-day routine, my life would turn out okay. She always closed the visit with an individual prayer, so powerful it would make my mother cry. To be honest, I think she really was one of God's special angels.

I had a feeling God would, in time take care of the motivation issues lurking in Soul's mind and spirit. I think by now it should be apparent something or someone with much greater powers than normal, helped me make the decision to bring Soul to church that Sunday.

We needed desperately to straighten our behavior before we really screwed something up. I felt those special feelings of peace, comfort, and forgiveness one feels when they enter through the vast corridors of a place of worship. When I walked into the church, I immediately felt all of my troubles and burdens lift from my shoulders. I guess it's part of the promise when you allow your savior into your heart. He will help carry you through the bad times and help you learn to appreciate the good times a little more. With the burdens placed temporarily on the shelf, I felt rested and my mind opened up to the real me. It gave me a chance to see that not everything I allowed to build up in my mind was as bad as it seemed. It provided me the time I needed to put things into the proper order before the service was over and God had to hand my burdens back to me.

I went in ready to accept my punishment from God. I knew in my heart I had not lived up to God's expectations up to this point in my life. I also knew not all of the blame should rest on the shoulders of Soul alone!

The minister started to deliver his message, and I suddenly felt something take control of my body. I was still awake and could hear everything going on around me, but it was as if time was just standing still. Later, I wanted to believe I had simply fallen into a very deep sleep and had dreamed the entire event I am about to share with you.

The event seemed real, and I can remember every word spoken to this day. I remember seeing beautiful colors surrounding me, and the feeling of peace was like nothing else I had ever felt before. I knew I was in a safe, faraway place and I was not going to return until God was satisfied I was back on track to fulfill my destiny.

I could instantly feel a change in Soul, which made me very nervous. Soul seemed to know exactly what was going on around the two of us. He whispered into my ear to try not to be afraid that God was in the church. God wanted to talk to both of us. I said okay and felt at peace but very nervous.

God spoke to me first in a very quiet and peaceful voice, but he got right to the point.

He said, "My son, you need to learn to give forgiveness and seek forgiveness, and I would suggest you start with Soul." I knew God was not actually suggesting I just work on this problem when I got around to it. Fortunately, I recalled what my mother had taught me about God: God is good and kind, and if I gave him a chance, he would without hesitation help me rise up and do the right thing.

God smiled and said, "Your mother is right. Shall we continue?"

Four

My Best Moment

I realized when God referenced my mother, he was trying to help me relax before we went on with our discussion. My mother will be one of the main characters in many of my stories. You will get a chance to see how amazing she was and why we miss her so much.

Regardless of your religious or spiritual beliefs, the thing about talking to God is that he already knows what you are going to say before you say it. Therefore, you never catch him off guard or find him surprised by what you say to him. You do not need to search for just the right words or tell him half of what is on your mind in fear that he will get mad or be upset with you.

God reminds me I am solely responsible for the body and mind he created for me. The network of people he surrounds me with help nurture and prepare me for the life he planned for me on earth. Ultimately, I am responsible for completing a plan that took thousands of years to develop just for me as it does for every person on earth. The plan will prepare my mind, heart, and soul for my future assignments in heaven.

God then paused for what seemed like an eternity. Without speaking a word, I could tell he was about to share with me a message I needed to take back with me—a message he expected me to deliver to all his children, including kings and queens, emperors, and presidents of countries.

11

His message was to those who have never believed in him or found their true spirit on earth. He wanted them to come and sit with him—to allow him the chance to lift their troubles and feel the incredible feelings of peace that surpass anything they have experienced during their life on earth. My job is to spread his message to those who live in the valleys and the ones who have made it to the mountaintops and had the privilege to peek over the other side.

Most of all I must deliver this message to those who do believe and have lost their way. I was to let them know he is still there for them. I was to remind them he will never give up on them. If they want, he will lift their burdens and provide them a chance to cleanse their body and seek a new path.

I was so young, but to this day, I can recite his message to me titled "Sometimes." Why he chose me to have this honor will be forever a mystery. Maybe he picked me because of whom I had as a guardian angel and Soul incredible drive to represent heaven in God's name just as it is supposed to be. God spoke directly to my heart and shared his wisdom with me:

God Said To Me

"My son, sometimes terrible things will happen on earth for what appears at the time to make little or no sense at all to you. Never forget, everything that happens has a true purpose. It may not be revealed today, next week, next year, or possibly not even in your lifetime, but it has a purpose and it will come to light the second it is supposed to, and nothing will ever change that."

God Said To Me

"Sometimes in life, the path you will need to follow will not always be a clear path with simple directions. You will be required to create your path using what you have learned and experienced up to that point in your life about what you know is right and what you know is wrong."

God Said To Me

"Sometimes you will make decisions that will lead you down the wrong path and you will seek forgiveness. You know what you should do, but sometimes we all have bad days and make mistakes. We let our emotions do the thinking instead of our brain. It is your time on earth that teaches you to make better decisions when you get to heaven.

I will always forgive you as long as I know it comes from your mind, heart, and soul."

God Said To Me

"Sometimes you will face danger or be in harm's way to test your true faith in me and the courage you have gained to help you get past the danger. Fear is a natural emotion that continuously tests your faith in yourself to have the confidence to step up and handle conflict and confrontations. In other words, it a test to see if you are willing to fight to defend what you believe in or run and hide and accept defeat."

God Said To Me

"Sometimes overcoming losses is life's biggest challenge. Losses come in all shapes and sizes. It can be your job, a serious health issue that may take years to overcome, not making the team, losing a sporting event, failing a class in school, being turned down for a date by someone you really care about, a financial loss, a loss of a friend or companion, and the list can go on and on.

Losses are a test of your faith in yourself and in me. You will forever be tested on earth and in heaven. I promise the sadness you feel in your heart today because of a loss will heal as time moves on. It gets better when you can accept the fact you are still here and your life is not defined by one single event or point in time. It is a journey that has no defined boundaries or limits. This means you will always have within yourself what it takes to turn losses into victories if you choose. I know that you have won when at the pearly gates of heaven I hear the statement: "I wouldn't have changed a thing, I have no regrets. Thank you God, for everything.""

God Said To Me

"Sometimes you will suffer grief and loneliness and ask how I could allow this to happen. The loss of a loved one is never easy to accept or understand. My only advice to you is if you truly love someone, make sure you appreciate the time you have with him or her every day. Make sure they know how much you care about them in whatever way is appropriate. For every person born on earth, there is a plan for his or her eternal life in heaven with me. The love you have in your heart and the love you share is my gift to you. It has a place and a time and a purpose on earth and in heaven."

God Said To Me

"Sometimes when you think you have messed up as bad as you can mess something up, all you need to do is open your heart, look to the heavens, and let me come into your heart. I will help you learn from your mistakes and help clear another path for you to seek forgiveness. After all, it took me thousands of years to plan your time on earth and in heaven and a few mistakes won't change that if you continue to believe."

God Said To Me

"Sometimes the people you trust and even love with all your heart may at times break your heart. They can betray you, lie to you, or violate the vows that formed your bond. These actions will leave you lonely, disappointed, and confused. Nevertheless, if you turn to me, I will help you find the path to recovery."

Five

Hurtful Words from Soul

With that, I said to God, "Thank for your kindness and beautiful words of encouragement. I know I have disappointed you and I will do better." I said "God, you know everything about my life up to this point and the journey I still have to travel. However, you had to feel the hurt in my heart the day Soul told me about how he was assigned to me. He said you made a mistake and he deserves and had earned a much better person than I could ever hope to become. He said I was not worthy of him and asked to be assigned to another human being.

"God, you know he shared this message with me. It was hurtful and unfair but I will forgive him and we will move on. Now that I think about it, in fairness to Soul, there had been times when he tried to throw everything at me but the kitchen sink as a sign I needed to stop and think before I moved ahead."

Six

Soul You Are Up to Bat

I do not think Soul was expecting God to be in church. Finally, I heard God whisper to Soul it was time for his performance review. God got right to the point with Soul just as he did with me. However, I had a feeling the message he had for Soul was not going to start out in the form of a suggestion as it did with me.

I was obviously not on the right track toward preparing for my first assignment in heaven, and I think the boss was a little upset with the both of us.

God said, "Soul, I hope you know you have to pick-up the pace and perform better than you have so far." The tone of his voice, which remained very low and non-threatening to Soul, clearly indicated to me that this was serious business. He offered some very direct words of encouragement not be taken lightly. He said, "It's time, Soul, for you to do better or expect to be pulled off of this assignment. Soul, it is your choice. You know very well this is too important to him and his future assignments in heaven for me to allow you to fail with him."

God immediately switched to what I call the coaching mode, as he looks straight into Soul's eyes. He said, "You know I only send guys like you to teach guys like him. Your assignments on earth are not up to you. I send the best of the best angels I have in heaven. The ones you prepare and who have the courage to complete their mission on earth will likewise be assigned the toughest of the toughest future situations on earth. You have to get him ready for his first assignment. Soul, bottom line is, I will do this with you or without you."

I know this conversation was supposed to be between God and Soul. I could tell they had been in many of these types of discussions in the past. One could also say God was undefeated, and he was trying to decide if it was time to re-assign Soul to someone else. I immediately spoke to God and begged him to keep Soul with me. Between the two of us, we would work together to fix what was broken. In retrospect, I must have sounded to him like a person who swam a couple of miles out into the ocean and then realized they did not really want to die and promises God everything he can think of if God would give him the strength to make it back to shore.

He said, "My son, each of those twenty times (Oh I told you earlier he keeps good records) you have strayed from my word, you have, in just the nick of time, prayed for my forgiveness. You showed me in your heart you were still a good person and deserved another chance. What you just did by sticking up for Soul clearly demonstrates to me you genuinely care about Soul. Who knows (rhetorical of course) you two may finally start to work together. You know Soul is not just an average angel, and I knew you would be a hard and frustrating challenge for even an experienced angel like him.

"Soul has tried to help lead down the right path each of the twenty or so times (let's see, 1, 2, 3, 4, 5, 6, 7...I started to think about which ones he was counting and if there was a limit) you have strayed off course in your young life. Has done everything an angel could do and say to keep you from making the choices you made. You also know Soul is only the quarterback, and once he tells you what to do, it is up to you what you do with it.

God then turned to Soul and began to speak. As soon as he said Soul's name, Soul dropped his head, and tears poured down his face for several minutes. I could feel the sadness in his heart and see the disappointment in his eyes as he listened to what God was saying. He was not crying because of his poor performance; he felt in his heart that he had let God down. He knew he was out of bounds when he said what he had said to me. He had not met God's expectations and he allowed his personal feelings to cloud his judgment.

I must admit I was scared to death. My heart was pounding, and I was suddenly hoping the congregation would break into another hymnal just to clear the air and get me through this moment.

Seven

SOUL'S BEST MOMENT

God did not come all this way to stop now. Then I witnessed something beautiful and very inspirational. I just cannot find the words to describe the excitement I was feeling and the range of emotions filling my body from head to toe. I never thought much about the actual role angels play in all of our lives. Just think, the only people on earth who get the opportunity to call God their boss are the ones who believe in him and have confessed their sins and allowed God to come into their life.

I am not sure how all of God's angels got there or how they knew something like this was about to take place, but they did. I guess when your boss is the greatest communicator in the universe you really do not need a letter, a text message on your cell phone, an E-mail, or even a meeting request; you just know.

It was like being at a pep-rally in high school, and everyone there knew their role and was willing to do what it took to get the victory. God spoke to the masses first and reaffirmed his love and commitment to them as he was about to do for Soul.

At first, you could have heard a pin drop among the billions in attendance. Then God lifted his arms, and the place went crazy. It was total bedlam, with angels hugging and giving high and low fives, and then a chant broke out—Soul, Soul, Soul—until God lowered his arms.

It was a life-changing moment for Soul and me. Then God delivered what I would consider the greatest message of all time.

His voice was soft but very firm as he asked Soul to lift up his head and look into his eyes. I knew Soul and I were not the only ones raising our heads and listening to God. God said, "Let us pray," as he bowed his head. He prayed, "I hope my children on earth will never fight another battle caused by their religious beliefs. My hope is my children can learn to respect one another's beliefs and never pass judgment or commit harm on each other again. Regardless of their beliefs or the faith they chose to follow, I pray my children can somehow understand the intent of the religious doctrines. I have sent many miracles and glowing signs to my children on earth that were appreciated and revered and have helped get individuals and families back on the right track. However, some documents were misunderstood or fell in the hands of sinners who intentionally led my people astray. The doctrines never should have caused wars or justified the killing of innocent people. Somewhere along the path, someone mistakenly or intentionally led my people to believe their path was the only path. They somehow felt I was putting them in charge and those who do not follow their path would be condemned and turned away at the gates of heaven. I pray those who do cause harm will someday know the path to heaven lies in the heart and soul of every single individual human being. One day soon, they will realize that there are just as many paths for each individual to follow back to heaven as there are stars in the sky."

He said, "As long as individuals on earth have faith in their God, I will continue to protect the kingdom of heaven for them and you." He said, "Soul, you have stood the test of time and have proven your love for me. You have supported everything the kingdom of heaven has stood by since the beginning of time. I know you have what it takes to complete your mission. Nevertheless, it doesn't matter what I think at this point, it matters what you believe and feel in your heart." As long as my angels and children on earth have faith and believe in me, they will always have a path to heaven. They will forever fall under the protection of my love. I will do for you, my son, the same thing I will do for any person who asks for forgiveness or needs my hand."

Then God took Soul's hands and said, "Soul, you are forgiven, my son." It was a very touching movement. I think it poured down rain from the heavens that day. I know I contributed my part. The speech was over and the angels dried their eyes, thanked the boss, hugged Soul, and got back to work doing what angels do.

Then God looked toward me while he whispered something into Soul's ear. I watched Soul shake his head in the affirmative direction, but that could be good or bad, depending on what God was saying. I could hear Soul talking to God and asking him for another chance to help me lift up my eyes and realize how precious the gift of life really is.

Soul told God he had gained some of his courage and learned a lot about life he never knew. Soul said, "As always God, you were right in assigning me to him, and I thank you for the opportunity."

God asked Soul to explain to him what he meant. Soul explained, "Well, you see boss, it's like this. Every assignment I have experienced in the past involved some of the wealthiest and most influential people on earth. My people were sheltered in the most secure structures money could buy. The best-trained defense people on earth protected them. Many were, in fact, God-loving, honest, and kind people who knew exactly how they would be judged once their time on earth was over."

"You won't believe this boss, but there are many people on earth who believe money will buy them love and peace of mind. They are willing to steal it, kill for it, beat others up to get it, lie for it, and deceive God-loving people to be as rich as possible. Money is their God, and they think they can use it to buy happiness and force people to respect them. It is very sad for me to think any person on earth would be willing to take the risk or could possibly believe money would somehow get them preferential treatment on judgment day."

God said to Soul that he was impressed and wanted to know what had happened to him since the last time they had talked (like he really didn't already know). So Soul clarified "God, as you know, this person you assigned to me lives in the country on a farm, way back in the hills of Kentucky, with his mom, dad, and thirteen brothers and sisters. I have experienced many emotional times with him. I have felt his tears and enjoyed his victories. He is helping me find the courage you sent me down here to gain. I know you are the only one who knows his plan once he gets to heaven. Whatever it is, I think he will be ready to handle it and he will not disappoint you.

Eight

SOUL MAKES A SPECIAL REQUEST

"God. I know this is an unusual request, but do you mind if the two of us we write short stories about our life together?"

Soul elaborated, "There have been numerous ups and downs in his lifetime, and I can only imagine what's to come. So far, he has found a way to never really waiver too far from his faith. When he did stray off the path, he asked for forgiveness and you forgave him. My point is, he could serve as a good example for others to follow who are dealing with similar crises in their lives. They need to know that if they can find a way to trust and believe in you things will be all right. They have the power and the means to do it if they just give your love a chance."

"Soul I think you have an excellent idea, and I am so proud of you for hanging in there with him and getting yourself ready for your next assignment." He said, "I have witnessed a lot of changes in you guys."

I saw God smile for the first time in what seemed like an eternity to me. Then just as quickly as he had appeared, he was gone.

I am still not sure what happened to me in church, but I must say it was my best day. I woke up just as the sermon was ending. It was time for the final hymnal of the day. This time I immediately located a songbook, moved closer to the woman still staring at the left side of my face, and began to sing at the top of my voice.

I looked to my right to see how Soul was doing, and he was not there, which made my heart almost stop. It was like being in a big department store and realizing one of your children has wondered off, and you immediately shift into panic-mode. In a matter of seconds, I was able to locate Soul. He was hanging out at the altar with his angel friends, all of which were laughing their butts off and begging me to stop singing.

It was the first time I had witnessed Soul happy and ready to get on with his destiny with me. Soul told me God had given us permission to write about the events we would experience in our lifetime together.

The first story takes place in my hometown in Carrollton, Kentucky. The exact location is in Hunter Bottom near Locust Creek in Carroll County, Kentucky.

Nine

Smile, You are Being Watched

Okay kids, what story would you like to hear today? "The *bull* story Coach. Tell us about the bull." "Yeah, tell us about the bull Grandpa, it is a great one," said my youngest grandson Jackson. The oldest grandson, Noah, told the others he had heard this story many times and it had gotten better each time. "Ok people, settle down and get your game faces on because you are about to hear the bull story."

"Yea!" said the next to the oldest Granddaughter.

"Quiet down now. All of you need to find a seat and settle down. I know I have shared the story about the bull with many of you over the years, but today I feel it is important you hear the entire story from the beginning."

I dropped my voice to almost a whisper and said, "Okay, this is important. Let me see your eyes." Then I said, in a little louder voice, "Just let me remind you I was only seven when this bull attack took place. What I'm about to tell you *really happened*."

My oldest grandson asked me to raise my pant leg up and show the kids the scar on the inside of my right leg. He told them in a very sincere voice that the scar was all of the proof he needed to convince him this really happened. "Coach was attacked not once but twice by the biggest meanest ugliest animal on earth. He is lucky to be alive."

As I started to tell the story, I looked at my oldest grandson and made it clear to him this time I was not going to leave anything out of the event. I was going to tell them the whole story.

I could tell Soul loved the time we spent with the children and enjoyed remembering the events leading up to the stories like the bull story. However, he apparently sensed some of the younger children might get scared if I told them all of the details leading up to this event.

He whispered into my ear and asked, "Are you going to include the part where the bull saved our life at the old cattle crossing? Remember the situation on one cold rainy-night when we were walking home from basketball practice? The white wolf attacked us and the bull came out of nowhere and saved our lives. Man, it was one dark night; ball game or no ball game, you should have never been walking back on that old country road in the middle of nowhere that late at night."

"Soul, please calm down. Who is telling this story, you or me? That is another story for another day." Soul stopped talking and said, "The floor is yours."

Ten

Dad's Home From Work

In the 1960s and 1970s, the evening meal was always a special time for families to pray and to appreciate each other. Our family was no exception but was a little larger than most. The fourteen of us could not wait each night to see what our mother had prepared for the evening meal.

Just as it was in most homes back then, there were a few rules in our house seldom broken.

First Rule: the evening mealtime is 6:00 PM sharp with few exceptions.

Second Rule: the first rule would not apply if Dad were not home from work by 6:00 PM.

I cannot remember a time while growing up when anyone actually sat down to our mother's table without Dad first taking his rightful place at the head of the table.

Some dads demand respect from their children, but ours earned it every day. We respected him for his attributes more than anyone could imagine.

When I think back about the reception our father received when he got home from work each day, it must have been incredible for him. For most men, it would have been overwhelming, but he was an extraordinary person.

Dad always seemed to have the ability to assess the range of emotions and feelings he would be walking into each night. He knew once he turned off the main highway onto our road that he would need to stop his truck and pick up the first group of children, typically consisting of two boys and three girls. The group was usually so excited to see Dad each day they would race each other from the house to where our drive lane met the main road. The first group usually would jump up into the back of the truck and enjoy the fresh summer breeze on the ride back to the house.

The lane was about two miles long and was constructed of gravel and small rocks from Conway's creek. His second stop would be to pick up our little sister, who could not run as fast or as far as the rest of us. Mom knew she could not keep up with the rest of us and each night she would issue the same warning to not run off and leave our little sister behind. We always replied "Okay Mom," and we all agreed that if she could stay within a mile of us she was close enough.

She sure got special attention, as dad would stop the truck, open the door, step out, and pick her up in his massive arms. Then he would sit her in the seat beside him.

I know she enjoyed the special treatment as she demonstrated many times by looking out the back glass of the truck and sticking her tongue out at the rest of us in the back.

Now that I think about it, our mother likely directed him to pick her up. You will read later in the bull story about how far she would go to protect her children from harm's way. I know most mothers will take many risks to protect their children, but this event may have been like the Super Bowl of courage on her part.

Once Dad arrived at the house, we would jump out of the truck and yell to our mom, "Dad's *home*! This was also like the two-minute warning, notifying her we were hungry and could not wait to eat supper. Once dad stepped out of the truck, he seemed to be an expert at sizing up what the older children were thinking. In addition, he sensed the range of emotions he knew he would need to deal with after supper. As he approached the house, he always stopped to hoist the youngest member of the family to his shoulders for a ride.

I can only imagine the beautiful feelings he would conjure up each night with 14 children tackling him the second he got out of the truck with hugs and kisses and to see his wife meet him at the door with a warm smile and a look in her eyes that seemed to say, "I love you" without saying a word. Now that I think back on it, he was a very lucky man.

Although the work he did each day as a highway construction manager was a very difficult and many times a very dangerous job, he knew he was living and supporting God's plan for him. And what a great plan it was!

Oh yes, back to the rules.

The Third Rule was that no one could enter the dining room until Mom and her four oldest daughters had prepared the table for the meal. I will always remember the excitement and the anticipation that filled each of our bodies each night just before Mom announced the meal was ready and it was time to eat.

The mouthwatering aroma comings from our dining room each night was amazing. She made everything: organic vegetables grown in her garden, meat cocked perfectly to please anyone's palate, homemade biscuits served hot straight from her oven, and the desert waiting for us to finish the main courses.

Mom's cooking would have added another star to any five-star restaurant you could possibly find today anywhere in the world.

The Fourth Rule was that Dad would bless the meal before anyone touched anything on the table. I do not think most of us at the time really understood the importance of this simple family tradition until much later in life when some of the children started leaving the nest.

It was the same prayer each night, and it was simple and to the point. The prayer seems to have meant something different to each of us depending on our circumstance at the time and our need to be with God. Once the prayer was over, Dad would start the process of passing the food around the table.

This was my favorite time of the day. The entire family would talk about the events of the day.

My mom was the facilitator. She made sure she and dad heard what was on each of our minds each day. You could hear the pride in the voices of the older children as they reported to dad about the farm work they had completed and what was on the schedule for the next day.

Soul, along with everyone else at the table, always enjoyed the farm animal report, especially the part about the new baby farm animals born during the day and the ones expected to be born later in the night. They discussed with Dad the difficulties encountered (mostly from the mothers attempting to protect their new babies) in relocating the babies and their mothers into particular lots and pins so their mothers could nurse, feed, and protect the babies from harms-way. Every person at the table took turns naming the new babies. Back in those days, every single animal received a name, which helped identify it for however long it was a part of the family.

The middle-aged children would report on their progress at school and ask for the help they would need after supper to finish their homework assignments. The younger children would talk about new games they had learned to play during playtime at home. For some strange reason, the younger group always seemed to say everything that they perceived the others had done wrong or the rules broken. Maybe it was just their way of searching out the boundaries of what was right and wrong. Nevertheless, at times, things got a little spirited. Occasionally a disagreement would occur when one of the younger children struck a chord with one of the older children. Phrases like "Did not!" "Did so!" "Not me!" "No Way!" "That's not what happened!" "You got it all wrong!" and "Excuse me I don't think so!" would ring out around the table. Once Dad or Mom had heard enough, they would let us know that if we could not work it out, they would be happy to meet with us after supper. I do not remember attending any of those after-dinner meetings. In fact, I do not think there was ever an after-dinner meeting. Once this process was over the real excitement began.

My dad was a great storyteller. He could turn the most inconsequential things into the most important events happening on earth. When he started to tell us about his day, you could usually hear a pin drop around the table. I can honestly tell you his stories, if possible, ended with reassurance;

someone or something turned what could have been a disaster into a unique situation with a very positive ending.

I think if you could today ask every member of my family what they remember most about our childhood, it would be our father's stories told around our old dining room table. Even though Dad was our hero, he never saw himself in that light. He never asked for such a label; he earned it.

Several years back, a famous basketball player said he was not a hero during an interview with the press. The television media and the press went crazy with the story and criticized him unmercifully. They could not believe a professional with everything to lose would make such a statement.

I must admit I was a little surprised by his statement. However, I think he was saying that he was just a man with a very special talent. He worked hard and was fortunate to play a very popular sport for a living. I think deep down he was also sending a message to his family about how much he appreciated the sacrifices they made for him so he could enjoy the life he had earned.

It reminded me of a time in my life when Mom and Dad made a huge sacrifice for me. You will read about what Mom and Dad did for me later in my short stories about my life. In my opinion, the professional athlete was right! Heroes are those people in your life who make personal sacrifices each day and help you make the right decisions. It is your mom, dad, and others who give you advice, love, and guidance. They are the people you should appreciate and revere as your heroes.

I have been very fortunate to be associated with some wonderful people in my life who have advised and coach me.

I was in the office one day meeting with a very famous college basketball coach at the University of Kentucky. He is at the top in wins among all college basketball coaches in history still today. I was young and a bit overwhelmed by the incredible number of awards and accommodations filling the gigantic room. When he walked into the room, he caught my eye and told me not to pay a bit of attention to all of the awards. He said, "What really matters in life is what you feel in your heart and the care you take of those," and he pointed to a picture of his family hanging on the wall.

"However, the most important of all is your love and commitment to Him," he said as he pointed to a picture of the Lord hanging on the wall directly in front of his desk.

Because of my respect for the coach and appreciation for his successes, I have used his advice to help me through many good and bad times. He also told me that great achievements or accomplishments are to celebrate and be immediately forgotten. You are only as good as your next victory.

My father and the coach's stories were right in line with how my dad lived his life. He was his family's hero and will retain that respect and honor on earth and in heaven. I shared this information about my mom and dad with you because of the 'role they are about to play in the next story that saved the family. By the time you finish reading the next story, they will be the mom and dad you wish or hope you could have had and the ones you will want to be for your children.

Eleven

Folks Try Not To Panic 'Yet'

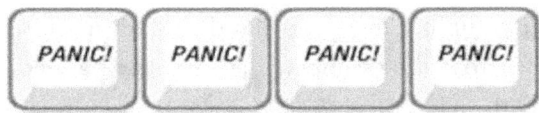

It was a hot early August night when, right after supper, we heard a knock at the front door. My oldest sister answered the door and immediately summoned my Dad to come quick. You could tell from the shakiness of her voice something terrible had happened. The sheriff stuck his head in the door and asked Mom and Dad if they could step outside with the others. This single event would, for the first time, help Soul understand he was no longer living in Safeville. He would not be under the protection of a wealthy family, surrounded by knights riding beautiful horses, waving their weapons and wearing shiny armor.

My brothers and sisters immediately gathered at the nearest window to see or to hear what we could about what was going on outside. We could see the sheriff and all of our adult neighbors who lived within 15 miles of our farm gathered in our front yard. Nothing had ever happen in our community to raise such a response from so many people. It was apparently severe enough that the intent for everyone meeting outside was to protect the children. Soul was the first one to climb under the bed and cover his head with a pillow, which was no surprise to me.

Once the meeting was over, our parents walked back into the house as the neighbors disbanded. We could all see the concern in Dad's face. Our poor mother immediately kicked into mother-mode. She started to worry about everything surrounding what the sheriff and several of our neighbors, who had witnessed the incident, had just shared with them.

Dad decided this was news the older kids needed to hear about, and the rest of us just needed to go to bed. He knew overreacting would not be sagacious, but not being prepared would be stupid on his part.

Once the younger children had gone to bed, Dad calls the rest into the dining room. He closed the French doors and instructed them to sit down and pay close attention to what they were about to be told. My oldest brother told me later he had never seen such a look on Dad's face. It did somewhat frighten him. He could not imagine what they were about to be told.

Dad explained that the neighbors had witnessed a wild, out-of-control, colossal animal with the features of an oversized bull. The animal had broken through fences, seriously injured livestock, and attacked and severely injured one of the neighbor's workhorses. The animal was a black and white stripped animal. It looks a lot like a Holstein bull. It had horns and the face of a brown-faced Herford breed of cattle. It was approximately 6 feet 2 inches tall and weighed between 2500-3000 pounds. Its most distinctive feature was the length of its Texas style long horns. The tips of his sturdy horns were as sharp as razor blades. The attacks had happened several days back, and no one had seen the animal since.

My oldest brother asked, "Dad, if it is a bull, where did it come from and who are the owners?" Dad explained that no one in a 50-mile radius, which included the areas between Louisville, Kentucky and Cincinnati, Ohio, was missing any livestock—or was at least willing to admit they had brought such a dangerous animal into the area. One theory was the animal had actually swum across the Ohio River from Indiana into the Hunters Bottom Kentucky area. Dad said that in his opinion, the idea seemed unlikely since the river is close to a mile wide, even during the dry season. The river is very deep in that stretch, especially since they built the dams upstream near Warsaw and downstream just past Louisville.

Dad told the older children to be on the lookout and not allow the younger children to stray too far from the house without someone with them at all times. He instructed them to not work in the fields without their guns loaded and ready to defend themselves. He made them promise not to share this information or talk openly about the situation with the rest of the children.

Once the meeting was over, my second oldest brother could no longer keep from laughing. He was one of the bravest people I knew at the time, and he could not imagine what all of the fuss was about. I mean, he was not afraid of *anything*. I am sure most of you have heard the old question "If you were under fire and pinned down behind enemy lines, would you want this person in a foxhole protecting your back?" You will read later in the book about his heroics. However, the answer to the question in his case would be an astounding "Hell yes" from the men he was pinned down with, twenty miles on the wrong side of the DMZ (Vietnamese Demilitarized Zone) between Vietnam and Cambodia during the Vietnam War.

Even at his young age, dad's information about the bull did not bother him in the least. He asked Dad if he honestly thought he was going to be afraid of a cow. My dad realized this son was unique and actually laughed along with him after Mom had gone to bed. He explained to my brother he had to play along, and he expected him to do the same. There's not much a man can do when Mom whips her old "mother's Intuition" thing on him. She had an atrocious feeling about this and felt her children were in danger. The other thing to keep in mind was it might not have been a cow. It really could have been a wild animal that escaped from a traveling circus setup over in the Trimble County fairgrounds the month before. Trimble County is the neighboring county between Oldham and Carroll. I was very surprised my brother did not load his gun and go looking for the beast.

I realize in today's world with most families it is not necessary to teach your children, how to use a firearms to protect themselves. However, in the sixties and seventies, it was common for country children to know how to safely handle a gun by the age of ten or twelve. Most shotguns in those days were used for hunting but sometimes for protection. It was still a very unsettled and potentially violent time to live on a farm in the country. This was true especially for those who lived on farms located 10-20 miles from any form of law-enforcement like the one my family lived on.

Twelve

HARVEST TIME: WHERE'S THE BEEF

Several weeks passed by without a sighting or an incident relating to the wild animal. Therefore, everyone assumed the bull had found his way back home. The crisis was over. We were all relieved and ready to put this incident behind us. We needed to settle down and get back to doing our routine chores.

It was in the heart of harvest time, and the crops needed to be gathered. There was tobacco to cut and move inside the tobacco barns for curing. The hay needed to be bailed and stored in the barns for the animals to survive the winter. Most importantly, food needed to be harvested and canned for the family to eat. This was necessary before the cold winter months were upon us.

The food harvest for the family involved washing and drying several thousand glass-jars and lids used for canning food. The glass jars were carefully lowered into near-boiling hot water to kill bacteria or germs that may have been present on the insides of the jars. Each jar then went through inspection, looking for breaks in the glass, chips, and hairline cracks. This investigation was paramount. If we missed a defect in a jar, severe injuries could happen to my mom or older sisters if one of the jars were to explode during the canning process. The canning process required heating the jars and the contents to near boiling before allowing the jars to quickly cool to form a seal on the top of the container. The seal prevented air from entering the jar that would cause the food inside to spoil. Every child above the age of six had responsibilities that had to be completed with the precision of a Swiss watch for the canning process to be safe and effective.

Immediately following the harvest, we gathered the thousands of pieces of firewood we would need to burn in the wood-burning stove to heat our home.

These jobs on the farm meant long days and very short nights for all farm families in the area. Our family was always well organized, and all of the children would participate in the tasks they were physically capable of performing. Dad and my older brothers and sisters did the most technical tasks requiring the use of farm equipment.

There were only three more weeks before school was to begin again. Even though the work was hard, it also meant once the harvest was over it was time to celebrate. We had lots to look forward to, including family reunions, community celebrations, and the 4-H fair, which were always lots of fun.

One of the most exciting things to do for all of the school age children was to sit down with the mail-order catalogs from Sears-Roebuck, Montgomery Ward, and Penney's and pick out shoes and clothes for the following school year. Yes, children, things, were much different back then than they are today. There were no big-box stores or malls to shop in for back to school specials or for the latest styles and trends. Once each child picked out what to order, mom took the proper measurement to make sure the fit was exact. She would then put the order forms together and give them to the man who delivered our mail each day. Once the process was complete, all the children could do was wait for the order to come to our house. This normally showed up a few weeks before school started.

I know now we must have stressed Mom out with the daily question, "Are our school supplies and clothes here yet?"

The post-man usually dropped our mail off at the mailbox located just off the main highway. The day the order arrived, the mail carrier made a special trip all the way to the house. He carried the large boxes in the house. I know now this was not normal behavior, and he would have gotten in serious trouble if caught by his postmaster. Nevertheless, I think he was willing to take a chance just to have the opportunity to sit back and enjoy the looks on our faces as we opened the packages. It truly was like having Christmas in August each year.

The school-age children tried on their new clothes and shoes for fit and immediately removed them once Mom gave the final approval. Once we finished trying everything on for fit, the children carefully put them away until the first day of school.

Mom reminded the kids it was time to prepare for the canning season.

The night before the harvest was to begin, Dad did one last inspection to make sure we had all correctly completed our tasks. He made sure everything was in its place for the harvest to begin the next day. The crates, baskets, and other containers used to put fresh vegetables and fruit in when harvested had to be clean and placed on the large hay wagon.

The jars were sorted into sizes: one-gallon jars up front and half-gallon jars next, all the way down to half-pints. The smaller volume jars were for canning jellies and jams for the thousands of peanut butter sandwiches we would eat over the next year.

Financial rewards and incentives were rare back in those days. However, hugs, compliments, and recognition were not. Dad would go down the list and call out our names as he inspected our work. Words from him like "Fantastic," "Incredible," and "I am proud of you" brought smiles to our faces. As he recognized each one of us for our accomplishments, he would give each one of us candy from a bag he had purchased from the penny-candy store on his way home from work. As I said, it does not sound like much to most people today, but for children back then it was very special and appreciated. I can remember my mom stating that the candy would ruin our teeth. My dad told my mom we had earned a treat, and with a big smile on his face and a quick wink to us, he said we would just need to brush a little harder that night.

Once the day was done, I could see the worry in my dad's face. He knew if the harvest were not plentiful, it would mean a very difficult year for him and my mother to put the good nutritious meals on the table we were accustomed to eating.

Even though the talk about the bull had stopped, Dad had spent countless hours hunting and searching for signs to determine if he was still out there. The gardens and blackberry patch we would travel to each day were several miles from the safety of the house. Dad had walked the trail at least 50 times and found absolutely no signs of a bull. Mom and Dad met with all of the children to talk about the bull and the actions taken to ensure our safety. It was a unanimous decision to move on with the harvest. It was time for us to suck it up and get things done without any more delays.

The next day came and the harvest was on. The oldest son got the tractor out of the barn and backed it up to the wagon so the next oldest son could hook the wagon tongue to the drawbar on the tractor. The older children would wash and put away the morning breakfast dishes while the next oldest group made all of the beds. Once these tasks were finished, it was time to take the long-journey to the family garden.

My mother would take the final inventory and make sure all of the children were safely sitting on the bed of the wagon. Then she would deliver the same message every day cautioning us to stay seated and to hold on. She would double-check to make sure we had plenty of drinking water and an ample supply of homemade peanut butter and jelly sandwiches to hold us over until lunchtime.

The farm was several hundred acres. Its boundaries were protected by one continuous fence, made of barbed wire. The farm was separated into several 30-40 acre plots to allow us to move the livestock from one pin to the next for summer grazing. The road between our houses and the gardens had five gates. Each gate had to be opened and reclosed during the trip. The trips to the fields were never boring. All of the children along the way filled the hills and valleys with songs and laughter. I even remember Soul one day climbing out on my shoulder and doing some crazy looking dance. He said he had learned the dance steps from a man who walked around with his hand in his coat. He said he thought the man's name was Napoleon. I kept my laughter to myself with the thought that some mother somewhere would name a child Napoleon.

The first and second day of the harvest went very well, but on the third day, things start to change. We made our way through the valley and up the one long and extremely steep hill to the ridge area. We found two of the five gates open and lying down on the ground. The code of the land back in those days was you were welcome to travel from one farm to another. However, if you opened a gate, you had to close the gate to keep the cows from getting out of the pin.

When Dad got home from work, we told him about the gates being down. He explained in a very cool and calm voice that someone apparently failed to follow the code. On the other hand, maybe they just did not properly latch and lock the gates. My oldest brother told Dad after supper he did not think two of the five gates was a mistake. My father gave him the hold-up sign, meaning they would talk about it later. Once they were alone, he said, "Dad, these were some of the largest hoof prints I have ever seen in the ground in front of the gates."

I remember Soul always seemed to listen to everything Dad said, and most of the time he was in awe or in full agreement with his explanations. However, this time I could sense the tension building inside him, which in turn made me a little nervous. Since he was my angel from God, I guess he was just trying to do his job. He sensed or maybe even knew danger was just around the bend for him and me.

Remember I told you earlier he was the biggest chicken I had ever met? His level of courage when measured on a scale of one to ten was still around a two. Okay, maybe a little harsh, but you will see in a few minutes why I scored him so low.

Thirteen

RUN BROTHER, RUN!

I did not know until my oldest brother told me months later that Dad had already made his mind up to investigate the incident with the two gates. He did not want to scare the children any more than necessary, so he waited until all of the children had gone to bed and were fast asleep. He woke up my two oldest brothers and told them the plan. They fired-up the portable-kerosene lanterns to light the trail. Then the three of them loaded their guns and filled their pockets with ammunition. They were off into the dark night following the same route the family had traveled the first two days of the harvest. The hunt turned up nothing, and everything seemed to be just as left earlier in the day. It was getting very frustrating for the people in the community and for Dad. This dangerous animal was out there running wild and out of control and no one could find him. Many thought he was a ghost. It was the only explanation for how this vast and destructive beast could do what it had done. He did not even leave a scent that expert-hunters and trackers could follow to his hideout.

The unusual thing about the trip was the conservation between Dad and the two oldest boys. It seemed to them that Dad decided it was time to let them take the next step to manhood. My brother said they turned off the lanterns and sat in total darkness. They sat in complete stillness for what seemed to be hours. They were listening and waiting for a sign the bull was back and on the move. Dad apparently started to have flashbacks to a time in his life filled with danger and uncertainty.

He broke the night silence and talked. He spoke about a subject seldom talked about by anyone in our family. Up to that point all the children really knew about Dad's war background was he had malaria and almost died. The only reason we knew about the disease was our oldest sister remembered asking our mother why she was crying one day. Mom had told her the military had notified her that dad was very sick and may not survive.

Dad told the boy's he and his brother-in-law had been rabbit hunting out on the old Gibson place in Owen County.

They decided to stop hunting early one morning so they could replace the shoes on one of his brother-in-law's best plow horses. Once they finished that task, dad decided to stick around for a few minutes to watch one of the tricks his brother-in-law had taught one of his show horses to perform. His brother-in-law said he had watched a man and his horse perform several tricks a few weeks earlier on an old TV set down at the general store in Sparta, Kentucky.

His brother-in-law spotted the show horse in the north pasture. He yelled out "Here Silver," and the horse sprinted up to him as he had done many times in the past. Dad really was not sure if it was because the horse liked the owner or the taste of the little sugar-cube he always received when he correctly completed a command.

Then, quicker than 'two shakes of a lamb's tail' the horse removed the hat from his brother-in-law's head with his mouth. The horse dropped down to one knee as if to perform a courtesy. Without receiving a command, he rose back to his feet and stood perfectly still, as if ordered to do so by a commanding officer in the army. His brother-in-law stepped up in front of the horse and bowed at the waist. The horse placed the hat back on the brother-in-law's head in a perfect position. Dad admitted it was impressive to watch but said he could not resist but to tell his brother-in-law he was watching far too much TV.

Just as they were saying their goodbyes, suddenly dad's sister bolted from the house. She ran up to him and her husband with tears streaming down her face. She said she had just come from her friend's house in Glencoe. Several men had come up onto the front porch and told her she needed to get home immediately and that the country was under attack by the Japanese. They decide to go to the house and turn on the radio. If it were true, the two of them would need to make a plan to protect their families. Just as they got the radio tuned into the station, a man interrupted the usual broadcast. He stated that the President of the United States was about to make a very urgent announcement to the American people. Then, after a brief pause, President Roosevelt announced the Empire of Japan had just attacked the United States of America naval base in Pearl Harbor, Hawaii. Many lives had been lost and damages to our Navy vessels were extensive. Our men were trapped inside the USS Arizona, which took a direct hit. The war vessel was slowly sinking into the Pacific. A frantic effort was underway by the survivors on the ground to help those men escape the sinking ship.

Dad knew in his heart it would not be long before he would join in the battle. He would consider it an honor to protect his family and the country he loved almost as much as he did our mother. He said it was difficult to describe the degree of urgency he felt to return home and be with his wife and family. Many Americans were disappointed our leaders had not anticipated the United States would somehow be dragged into a war. The war had been going on in Europe and Asia for several years. It was as if our leaders were asleep at the wheel until it was too late. The leaders of many nations believed at the time that the people of the United States had grown lazy and were afraid to defend our country. We would not fight a war 9,000 miles from our homeland. Twenty years had passed since World War I.

It would not take long for the world to find out how wrong it was. Rumor has it the Emperor of Japan stated, after the attack on Pearl Harbor, that his empire had made a mistake. They did not defeat a nation but woke up an angry giant. He was about to find out just how America felt about his sneaking and unprovoked attack on our 50th state that Sunday morning December 7, 1941—how this giant, as he described us, would not only deal with his country but the message it would also send to the rest of the world.

Dad said within minutes after the announcement by the president it felt like the mainland was already under attack. Every visible airplane in the sky looked like an enemy plane, and people ran to their bomb shelters. Even though our president tried to reassure us that the homeland was safe, we knew our navy had been severely damage during the attack. Could we actually protect our borders without a navy? Most people were anticipating the Japanese would move from Pearl Harbor to the West coast and bring the fight to American soil. Dad said it was difficult to describe the feelings and deal with the range of emotions sweeping the country.

For the first time in his life, documents like the Gettysburg Address and the Constitutions of the United States took on a new meaning. It was time to defend what we stood for or surrender the very soil we had fought and died to keep safe and free for more than two-hundred years. He said every American with a gun kept it loaded. They maintained a good inventory of ammunition and were ready to fight if necessary. Communities formed volunteer military type training-response centers. These facilities were designed to train the men to fight and protect their family if an attack took place.

Fourteen

I Am In the Army Now,
Not Behind a Plow

It turns out Dad was right and his orders came within a few days from
Uncle Sam. He was to report to basic training, and he would receive his
assignment upon completion of the training.

The training was over in eight-weeks. He returned home for a scheduled
two-week vacation before going back to his base. One week into his leave,
the military police came to our house. They had orders for him to report to
the station the next day. His leave was officially canceled due to the intense
fighting in the South Pacific. He kissed his wife and tucked his daughter
in bed one last time before catching a military bus set to leave Owenton,
Kentucky at 4:00 AM sharp. The canceling of his leave was the first of a
string of bad news.

Once he got to the base, he received the dreaded news. He had been
assigned to the infantry division of the United States Army. He would travel
by train from Cincinnati, Ohio to the west coast and board a ship in San
Francisco. His unit would receive their orders before the ship left the harbor. Six weeks later, he landed in the Philippine Islands in the middle of
an invasion by the Empire of Japan. When they landed on the beach, he
got his first taste of what war was all about. During basic training, the only
weapon issued in boot camp was a stick gun. They made noise with their

voice indicating they were shooting at the target; similar to when they were kids playing war games.

Two of the men in his camp had made friends with him during the voyage. They were from Cincinnati, Ohio and did not have a clue how to load or fire a gun. He told them he would teach them how to load and fire their weapon once they received them. Unfortunately, their guns were given to the men just a few minutes before they landed on the beach. With no time to teach the men how to load their weapons, both men lost their lives before they made it to shore. Their weapons had never been loaded. Even through several hundred American soldiers were lost during the invasion, Dad felt responsible for their deaths.

Three months went by before he could get permission to send his first letter home. It only said, "I am okay." The letter had been opened, indicating the military censored the letter. At least mom knew he was still alive. The Japanese made it clear their intentions were to become the largest empire on earth. They would continue to fight until they had complete control of all of Southeast Asia. They would fight to their death to accomplish the mission. Surrendering was not an option for Japanese's soldiers.

After several months of intense fighting, it became difficult to figure out why they were fighting. He missed his wife and child more than anyone could possibly imagine. He said he cried himself to sleep many nights wishing he could reach out and touch his wife's soft face. He held her picture in his arms every night while he slept. He longed to hold her in his arms for just a few minutes and hear the words "I love you" one more time. He said he prayed to God and all of the angels in heavens above one night that if he made it through the war alive, he would love God and all the angels in heaven for the rest of his life.

At one point, morale dropped to an all-time low. Supplies, including food, water, and even ammunition, were apparently being cut-off at the ports by the Japanese. The officers later learned it was not just Japan cutting off the supplies; they were simply not available in ample amounts to sustain the American soldiers. At one point, over half the men and women in his regiment, including him, were sick with malaria. Many of the men and women died from the dreaded illness. For several weeks at a time, they ate one meal a day due to the lack of shipments from the mainland. This was just another example of poor planning by the commander in chief and his staff. While the rest of the world was manufacturing bombs, equipment, ships, airplanes, guns, ammunition, and MREs, the United States was making refrigerators.

After he had recovered from the sickness, he was returned back to the front lines. One night during supper, he saw a Japanese soldier near the camp. He knew the man was the same soldier he had been shooting at all day and had been shooting back at him. Dad said he pulled up his rifle and had every right to pull the trigger. At the last second, he could see through his gun sight that the man was unarmed and defenseless. Dad knew he had no choice but to fire his gun due to earlier orders from his commanding officer. He fired his gun well above the Japanese soldier's head, which alerted the rest of the troops. The man escaped unharmed.

He said the soldier was unbelievably thin and was apparently starving to death from a lack of food. The Japanese soldier appeared to have made what must have been a difficult decision. He looked straight into my dad's eye and down the barrel of his gun. He needed food to sustain his body or a bullet to put him out of his misery.

Dad learned a lesson at that moment he would never forget about how fragile life really is. Both my brothers learned a lesson from dad and fortunately shared it with the rest of us. When you think things are bad and you are feeling sorry for yourself, just look around and you will likely find someone in a worse condition. You may suddenly feel very blessed and appreciative to have what you have. However, the real test is whether you are willing to share it. My dad said he recalled a lesson he had learned in church one Sunday about a man who shared his bread with some hungry and even starving people and how it changed his life forever.

Dad decided he would share half of his MREs with the man. He waited for all of the men sharing a tent with him to go to sleep. Then he placed the food outside his tent for the soldier to eat. He decided that even though the man was supposed to be his enemy he was still one of God's children and he needed food. Later in the night, the man somehow made his way into the camp unnoticed and took the food. The next morning dad witnessed the food was gone. He looked up on the hill where he had last seen the starving Japanese soldier. He witnesses a couple of flashes from a mirror, which he assumed meant the soldier was safe and could fight another day.

The alarm sounded, alerting the troupes it was time for breakfast. They all knew this was just a smoke screen and no fighting men would be served breakfast. The only meal they would receive would come much later in the day. It was time for the daily ritual of breaking camp and moving to a new location.

As he was rolling up his sleeping bag to break camp, he felt something inside the bag. The odd-shape item was wrapped in a very high-quality silk scarf with a small clasp holding the scarf in place. He carefully unrolled the scarf to see what was inside. First he found a note written in Japanese. Fortunately, Dad had taken an essential translation class on the ship during the trip from San Francisco to the Philippines. He was very intelligent and many felt he had a photographic memory.

The note said, *"Take this gift as a token of appreciation for saving my life. I may have to shoot you tomorrow, but I would rather take the bullet myself if it were not for my country and my family which I must defend with my life and at all costs. I know you will understand, as you will also do the same for your country and your family with the same honor and allegiance as I do. This gift passed to my father by his father who received it from his father. When I was leaving home to report to active duty, my mother and father gave it to me with the instructions to protect it with my life. This is the only thing of value I have left in the world and I cannot think of a more noble use than to give it to the man who saved my life.*

When he finished removing the cloth from the gift, he found a Japanese pistol with solid pearl handles. It was a beautiful gun with beautiful inscriptions and spiritual symbols carved into the grip. Dad knew right away this was not a fair exchange and he could not keep the gun. He was proud to receive the gift but was saddened by what must have been going through the Japanese soldier's heart to part with such a beautiful weapon and heirloom. He hoped someday when the world stops being so crazy he could return the gun to its rightful owner.

It was unusual for Dad to share much detail about anything related to the war. Mom said the day he returned home he told her to never mention the war again. He took off his uniform and never put it on again. He apparently had not talked about it until that night with the boys.

He said in his opinion it was the darkest time in not only American history but in the history of the world. It was the perfect storm. Countries with powerful leaders joined to attack and kill hundreds of thousands of people because of their religion. Other countries wanted to conquer land and overthrow governments, killing millions of innocent people in their quest. One leader was even so deranged that when he realized his country was about to lose the war, he ordered his own troops to destroy every building and asset in his country. His other order was unconscionable: he said to murder anyone in his or her way.

The oldest son said he now understood why he had protected and treasured the pearl-handled pistol for all of these years. Dad has rejoiced many times for not following through with his decision to toss the gun into the sea on his return trip home. Something just kept him from doing it. The reason why will be disclosed at the end of this story. It will turn out later that no one could have anticipated the true value of this gun. A gift of compassion from an enemy soldier located halfway across the globe would turn out to be the sword that changed the life of our entire family.

Soul seemed to experience a number of different mood swings when anyone mentioned World War II. At times I could feel excitement and other times total sadness.

It was as if Soul was somehow involved in or a part of the three most disappointing and disturbing events surrounding World War II. The first was the failed peace negotiations apparently held in the United States between Japan and the United States on the very day the Japanese attacked Pearl Harbor. The second was the Holocaust carried out by Nazi Germany and the torture and murder of millions of other innocent people by the Axis nations. The third was the day the United States decided enough lives had been lost in the war; it was time to stop the killing and mass murder of innocent people by those countries not willing to stop. The United States was the only country on earth with the weapon needed to send a message they would understand. The weapon, when used, would be destructive and heard around the world. It was obvious to all Americans that this war was not going to end until we used it.

Our president and congress finally decided it was time to send the final message to the Japanese, Germans, Italians, Hungarians, Romanians, and Bulgarians in the form of the most destructive force on earth.

Dad said millions of leaflets were dropped from planes to citizens in Japan and the surrounding islands. He, along with thousands of Americans troops, made a pilgrimage across the island warning the locals about the bombs and saying they needed to leave the islands immediately. The leaflets warned that the United States would drop two atomic bombs and the blast would kill thousands of people and would destroy their country. The Axis nation's leaders were given written notice to end the war immediately or the Americans would write the final chapter. The dropping of those two atomic bombs, which landed squarely on Hiroshima and a few days later on Nagasaki, caused the entire world to wake up and force their leaders to peace meetings. It only took a few months to shut down the war.

When the word 'nuclear' is mentioned around Soul, I feel a heightened sense of concern. I think his message is for us to never forget the day those bombs dropped on their targets—to always remember how the pain and suffering caused people from all nations to cry out once they saw the true devastation. Soul prays every day that the civilized nations of the world and its leaders will never use nuclear weapons to settle their differences again. Nations should always control nuclear production and never allow nations who share the same ideas as their predecessors to have access to such horrible weapons.

The evening was over. Dad and my two oldest brother's returned home empty handed. They reported to Mom that they found nothing out of the ordinary.

The only way to explain the gates being down and laid-back as found is if someone or something intentionally opened the gates. They forgot or lacked the strength or coordination needed to close them when they exited the lot.

Fifteen

The First Attack on the Children

The next morning the routine was the same, and by 9:00 AM, it was time for the children to receive their assignments for the day. The assignments would be a little different today. The blackberries were ready to harvest, and I drew the unlucky straw. Picking blackberries is a hot, miserable job! Long sleeves and jeans were the required attire to avoid painful scratches and even cuts from the briers. Each movement had to be carefully planned to prevent damaging the berries or dropping the container holding the blackberries. A keen eye was required before taking each step to avoid stepping on snakes lying and waiting to strike their target.

The wagon was loaded, and the long journey to the garden was complete without incident. The blackberry patch was located about a mile and a half from the garden. Mom stopped the tractor and wagon in the middle of the road. I got off the wagon to begin the long journey on the ridge to the blackberry patch. I had to pass through one of the gates left open the day before. I made sure the gate was closed and the latch securely in the proper location. I walked down the hill to the valley below. She reminded me to be extremely careful, and as with most moms, her final message was, "Don't get hurt." I have concluded the only reason mom's leave you with that thought is if you do get hurt, they can say, "I thought I told you not to get hurt."

By 10:30 AM, the temperature had increased to near 90 degrees. Soul finally woke up. As usual, he started to complain about everything. Within the first ten minutes, he complained he was too hot and too thirsty. Then he said, "I am tired." Then, "Ouch, a briar just stuck me in the butt." I could not help but chuckle when he said he had been stuck in the butt. His eyes drifted down to the container holding the blackberries. I knew he was hungry and he even suggested I eat some of the berries instead of put them into the pot. This was a violation of one of the cardinal rules of blackberries picking. He said, "Go ahead and eat some! No one will ever know." I asked him if he had changed his name to Eve, and he knew exactly what I meant. I think I heard God chuckle as Soul just folded his arms in disgust.

You know how sometimes you get a strange feeling something is behind you, but when you look around there is nothing there? For me on this day, that feeling just would not seem to go away. I had been feeling uneasy for about 20 minutes. I started to hear strange noises—limbs breaking and footsteps—as I worked my way deeper and deeper into the blackberry patch. If you have ever found yourself at the bottom of a hill in the middle of a blackberry patch you already know that your visibility is at best about 3-4 feet. I felt like something was just maneuvering itself into position so it could attack me. Just as suddenly as the feeling appeared, it went away. I got my composure back and told myself to stop being silly.

I continue to do my work, and Soul continued to complain, which was very typical for him. Soul was apparently several thousand years old and had never picked a blackberry in his life. He sure must have lived a very protected and pampered life. Even at the ripe old age of seven, I was more mature than he was. This was about to become more evident than ever.

I remember thinking how proud Mom would be once she saw the size of the berries I had found in the patch this season. Some years the berries were small and it seemed to take several hours to fill up a five-gallon bucket. Nevertheless, this year they were even larger than normal. I had finished filling up the containers with berries and started working my way up the hill to return to the garden.

I could hear my younger brother and sister yelling for me from up on the ridge next to the old tobacco barn. Mom had sent them to find me and remind me it was rapidly approaching lunchtime, which was music to my ears. I could feel my stomach growling as I had worked up a big appetite. I heard the message about food, and it was music to Souls ears.

I was envisioning the smile on my mother's face when she saw my harvest. As I was walking along the dirt path up the hill, I was thinking about my mother. My mother could never be characterized as a good loser. In her mind if you came in second it meant you were the last loser. Just a few weeks prior, I witnessed her shoot a penny off the top of a fence post from 50 yards with a 22–Remington rifle. The shooting competition was between the women and the men in the community. My dad won the competition, and my Mom finished second, which in her mind meant she lost. She was not happy and still to this day claims he somehow cheated.

All of those thoughts about my mother smiling about my harvest quickly dashed. The look I saw on my mother face instead was pure panic when suddenly all hell broke loose. I heard my younger brother and sister screaming. They were yelling at the top of their lungs "HELP, HELP, HELP, HELP US! HE'S GOING TO GET US!" I could not see them, but I could tell from the panic in their voice something was after them.

I put the berries down and started to run up the hill as fast as my legs would carry me to find out what was going on. From the garden, I heard my brothers, sisters, and mother screaming "RUN, RUN! OH MY GOD RUN!" When I reached the top of the hill, I could see the panic in my little brother's face. He and my sister were in a dead sprint around the top of the ridge. They were running back toward the garden to the safety of our mom. I saw my mother turn to retrieve her gun from the rack on the tractor. She pointed it in the direction of her two youngest children. I was not quite in a position to see what was chasing them, but I could feel my heart pounding in my chest. I could not believe my mother was pointing a gun in the direction of my brother and sister. I knew somehow I had to move faster, and by the grace of God, I did find a new gear. I remember yelling at my Mom not to shoot my brother and sister.

I think she just could not let her children die such a terrible death. The tears started to flow down her face as she realized the animal chasing her babies was too close to them and she did not have a clear shot. The older kids were screaming "Shoot, Shoot! Mom, take a shot!" I could hear my oldest brother screaming at my mother, "TAKE THE SHOT, PULL THE TRIGGER MOM!" Then my second oldest brother walked over to my mother and put his hand on the barrel of the gun, lowering it to a safe position. He realized the only person he knew with even a chance at the shot was our dad. He was an expert sharpshooter, and his skills had earned numerous awards while in the military. He knew Dad did not cheat during the shooting competition. I think the boys in the family who had been out hunting with my dad knew just how good he was with any type of gun. Nevertheless, I saw for the first time in my young life a look of complete hopelessness in my mother's eyes.

She had to make a terrible choice between leaving the other children or staying and trying to save the rest from this horrible monster who was about to end the life of two of her children. All Mom could do was watch and pray for a miracle.

In the meantime, the neighboring farmer was working in his fields. He heard the screaming and yelling and the cry for someone to help the children. He heard in my mother's voice the desperation from the already grieving mother trying to cope with what at the time looked hopeless to everyone involved.

He had known my mom, dad, and all of the children for many years. He knew he needed to respond and do what he could to help. He shifted his John Deere into high gear and headed in their direction. When he rounded the corner of the tobacco barn, he got a very clear picture of what was going on. He could not believe the tragedy unfolding in front of him. He stopped his tractor and pulled up his high-powered rifle, which was more than capable of bringing this monster down from several thousand feet. He had been a sharpshooter in the Battle of Normandy, which was one of the battles fought to end Adolf Hitler's Germany. He would have no problem dropping this animal in his tracks. After several attempts to adjust the scope on his rifle, he realized a clear shot would be impossible from his vantage point without the bullet hitting one of the children.

He knew the only thing he could do was to drive his tractor to the garden and then take up a position to take a shot if the animal got any closer to the others in the garden.

I finally worked my way out of the blackberry patch and reached the top of the hill. I suddenly realize why the sheriff and the neighboring farmers had summoned my mother and father from the house earlier in the month. I also realized what was causing my feelings of anxiety earlier in the day. I should have followed my instincts and gotten out of the blackberry patch.

I saw my sister and brother running as fast as their short legs would allow then to run. They were no match for the ugliest, nastiest, largest animal chasing them stride for stride around the top of the ridge. Fortunately, my little brother saw the bull when he broke the plane of the hill. He and my sister had a seventy-five foot lead when the chase started. Soul was not paying much attention until he realized what all of the screaming and yelling was about.

It was the mystery bull, and apparently had been making its home in the blackberry patch for weeks. The thick cover had provided the protection the bull needed to hide from the farmers who had spent weeks looking for him. I had apparently worked my way very close to where he had been hiding. He was very upset I had unintentionally exposed his hiding place.

I felt I was responsible for everything happening at that moment. The only chance my brother and sister would have was for me to, somehow, distract the bull. I needed to get his attention away from my little brother and sister. I decided to run as fast as possible in the direction of the bull. Once I got close enough for him to hear me I started yelling and screaming at him.

Soul was excited to see I was running. He was encouraging me to run even faster. Once he realized I was running toward the bull instead of away from the animal, panic set in. Soul spoke up in a small shaky voice. He said, "Hey dude I know you are young, and I must add not too smart, but the idea is to run away from danger not into it." As I got closer to the bull, Soul started to scream at the top of his lungs. He sounded like a little girl attending a teen idol concert for the first time.

"Why, why, why," he said, "are you doing this to me God? We are going to die. God prepare this fool a place in the kingdom of heaven because his life is about to end ugly and painfully."

Soul made one last appeal to me. He said in his little squeaky voice that I was making a very poor choice. He said he understood it did not look good for my brother and sister, but my mother would still have twelve more children. Twelve should be plenty for any family these days. As usual, I did everything I could to ignore Soul. I knew he was still a chicken and I just could not let my mother down.

My plan worked well, and the bull must have seen me out of the corner of his eye, which caused him to slow down. I am guessing, but it was likely the first time a seven-year-old child had outrun him. The distance between the bull and my brother and sister lengthened. The bull had a look on his face of disbelief and could not understand why I was actually chasing him. I think the bull was thinking the same thing Soul had tried to convince me of earlier. Soul was so scared he could no longer talk. His eyes were about to pop-out of his head, and all he could do was point.

The farmer repositioned his gun. He was attempting to get a bead on the bull when the bull quickly refocused his attention on my little brother and sister. The bull appeared to have made his decision to finish the job he started and take care of me later. He immediately closed the distance on my sister as she was exhausted and was now in terrible trouble.

The bull was so focused on his target he did not realize nor did not care I had veered off the original path. I took a shortcut to where my brother and sister were heading. I hid in the tall grass, and as the bull approached me, I jumped up and started to run with my little brother and sister. My plan was to take another route and hope the bull chased me instead of continuing to chase my brother and sister. My little sister slowed down and started to hold her aching side. I knew she had done all she could do and she just could not run another step. She located her mom in the garden and screams for her to come and help her. I saw my mother reach out her hand and then my oldest sister held her back and told her it was too late. At the last second, I decided the only way she was going to make it was for me to pick her up and let my legs become her legs. As I ran up to her, she jumped up into my arms. She buried her face into my chest and said, "Save me, I do not want to die." I told her to swing to my back and hang on.

My brother was running fast and was still holding his own in the pursuit. I knew our only chance was to make it to the farm pond located beside the road. It was only approximately fifty yards ahead. I yelled to my brother to dive as far out into the pond as he could and I would toss our sister out to him. "Once you get to her, go underwater and stay as long as you can." Dad had taught them both to be excellent swimmers. I knew they would out swim the bull even if he went in after them instead of continuing to pursue me. The plan worked to perfection. The sister closest in age to me told me later they both looked like Olympic swimmers as they crossed to the other side of the pond. They jumped out of the pond and sprinted across the field to the safety of our mother's arms. She said mother looked into the heaven and thanked God for his miracle. However, it was not over, and she knew she had to refocus. She knew things had turned in her favor. She needed to find a way to save her other little hero.

By now the bull was so mad his nostrils flared outward. His head was low to the ground, and his horns looked like razor blades. He was moving into position to jam his horns into the middle of my back. Soul finally realized he had been of absolutely no help to me up to this point. He also sensed God was watching. He failed God's mission for him to find the courage at a time when I desperately needed his help. God was disappointed with Soul as he watched him fail the first test to conquer his fears. The other thing God knew that Soul apparently did not was he would have many more opportunities down the road to get it right.

I continued to sprint around the ridge toward my mother. I could hear my brothers and sisters yelling and cheering for me to outrun the bull.

In the meantime, my mother realized Gods works in mysterious ways. She was just handed another opportunity for another miracle. She had to move quickly to seize the moment. She knew how fast I could run, and if she could get to me quickly, she could take control of the situation. She ordered my oldest brother to disconnect the wagon from the draw bar on the tractor. She was about to get in the game, and no one was going to get in her way.

The farmer started to shake his head in disbelief. He realized what she was about to do. My oldest sister said the farmer stated under his breath, "It might be time to start feeling sorry for the bull." He offered to help her, but he could see this bull had already pissed her off and things were about to change. Therefore, he decided to just stay with the rest of the children and enjoy the moment.

Once my oldest brother disconnected the wagon from the tractor, she ordered all of the children to climb up onto the wagon. It was no surprise to me when my next to oldest brother told Mom he was going with her. She said, "No son, this is between the bull and me. I do not plan on losing!" She looked at the farmer and told him to protect her babies. She said, "I'll be back," and he just shook his head and said, "Okay, good luck."

She started up the tractor and pulled the fuel-throttle located on the column next to the dash panel all the way to the bottom. The engine roared as it approached maximum RPM's.

Even I could hear the loudness of the engine, but more importantly, I could hear the message delivered by my mother: just hold on for a few more minutes and I will take over your battle. You know how mothers sometimes get.

The unburned diesel fuel from the engine bellowed out of the stack as she shifted the tractor into low gear and popped the clutch. This action caused the front wheels of the tractor to jump off the ground. She started winding her way around the ridge toward me. Later, the older children said she was popping the clutch and shifting gears in perfect harmony. She looked like she belonged in the Indianapolis 500. If she had been in a race-car, the other drivers would have been eating her dust.

In the meantime, Soul calmed down and positioned himself on my shoulder. He was starting to demonstrate a little courage. I know this got God's attention and caused him to raise an eyebrow. I think God was doing for Soul the same thing my mom was doing for me. Soul sounded like he was announcing the Kentucky Derby at Churchill Downs in Louisville, Kentucky. He got very excited when he noticed the distance increasing between the bull and me. He even started teasing and making fun of the bull's speed. He was growing confident by the moment as he also saw my mother getting closer.

What Soul did not realize was the danger was not over. Although I was much faster than a bull and I had the stamina to run in front of him for hours, I was about to run out of room to move. Remember I told you earlier in the story: many farmers divided off their fields into smaller plots to allow rotation of the livestock. Well, unfortunately, we were in one of those pins. The only way out was to go over the fence or exit through the gate.

Soul finally realized I had started to slow down. The bull was closing fast. Soul turned his head to get a better idea about why I was slowing down. He screamed out as loud as he could to me, "Watch out! FENCE, FENCE, LOOK OUT, FENCE!" Then he looked back at the bull, which by had closed to within a few feet of us. We could both feel and smell his bad breath. Soul yelled, "We are going to die!" He did not realize my plan was to attempt to jump the gate. We did not have time to climb over the gate. Soul had been with me now for seven years. He knew I was a splendid athlete for my age and size. I was the fastest runner and best jumper in the spring games at our school for all ages. Once he understood the idea, he starts yelling, you can do it! He looked back at the bull and said "WATCH THIS BIG BOY!"

As I approach the gate, I began to get my steps in perfect timing. My plan was to place my foot on the second rung of the metal gate. From there I would use the rung as a springboard to reach the maximum height needed to clear the gate.

At the last instance, I jumped and cleared the barbwire runner located at the top of the gate. The barbwire runner later measured to be a little over six feet high from the point I left the ground.

The bull was ready to make his final lunge at me and apparently did not see the gate. He hit the gate at full speed. He was too late to do his intended damage to my body. I hit the ground on the other side of the gate as the shattered pieces from the gate where striking my legs. I quickly got to my feet and ran to my mother. She caught me and I jumped up onto the tractor to safety.

As I was on my descent back to the ground, I did not realize Soul was eyeball to eyeball with this disgusting beast. He closed his eyes, bowed his head, and told God this was it. He would be making another delivery shortly, as we were on the way home.

The second thing Soul and the bull did not know was my mother was great at multitasking. She was making her plan as she was jamming gears on our old Ford tractor. She knew I could jump the gate as she had seen me do it several weeks back. Nevertheless, she also knew the gate would not be strong enough to even slow-down a 3000-pound bull charging into it running full speed. She had a big surprise for the bull waiting on the other side of the gate. I told you earlier it was never a good idea to attempt to come between a mother and her children.

She had perfectly aligned the tractor directly where she anticipated; the bull's head would hit the gate.

Did I forget to mention earlier in the story the front end of the tractor had an upgrade to include a hydraulically controlled front-end loader? Dad constructed it with 6-inch thick solid-steel beams.

Her plan worked to perfection. The bull did not have a clue what was about to happen. His head hit the beam squarely in the center of the beam so hard it dazed him. He drops to his knees. The impact literally pushed the 6000-pound tractor backward approximately 10 feet. The beam did bend, but it did not break.

The bull was now on his knees. He fought with all of his strength not to go down to the ground. He simply could not let this little boy and a woman beat him. He finally got back to his feet. He turns his head and looks at my mother and me with a bone-chilling expression on his face.

Soul was so terrified I thought his eyes were going to pop out of his head. The return expression on my mom's face was also sending a message to the bull. Her message was to get his butt back around the ridge and not mess with her or her family. However, I could tell in her heart she knew it was not over. Someday they would meet again. Mothers know these types of things. I do not know how, but they do, and boy was she right!

My second oldest brother wanted to shoot the bull right there and then, but my mother told him no. She had sent the animal the proper message, and in time, we would know the rest of his story.

Even though the bull was dazed by the blow to his head, he was still an impressive animal. We had better not let our guard down even for a minute with him still out there.

The bull, visibly injured, staggered back around the ridge and over the hill. He quickly disappeared as he entered the blackberry patch.

The celebration was on. No one could believe we had survived such an ordeal. Most of the kids could not wait to tell Dad about what had happened and the heroics demonstrated. The farmer dropped his lanky 6' 9" tall frame to his knees. He thanked God above for the miracle he had just witnessed. The farmer climbed back up on his John Deere tractor and sat in the seat without moving a muscle. He was visibly shaken as he placed his hands over his face. He could not erase the memory of what he saw through the scope of his rifle. Then he looked back to the heavens and realized this miracle could have only been the work of God.

He suddenly could not wait to get back around the ridge to his house and tell his wife about what he had witnessed. He also knew he had the inside scoop on what would be the wildest story to tell his friends the following Saturday. The men in the community would always congregate to talk about the events of the week at the old Yocum general store. The store is located where the east and west prongs of Locust Creek met. It is still standing today, forty years later.

After things had calmed down, my oldest sister looked down at my leg and noticed my blood-soaked shoe. She summoned Mom to come to the back of the wagon to examine my leg. Mom immediately took a harvesting knife and cut the leg of my jeans up to my knee. She asked me if I was in pain, and I told her no.

From the size of the cut in my leg, she knew right away that I was in shock. If she could not get the bleeding to stop quickly, I would bleed to death within a matter of a few minutes. She took a clean cloth from one of the unused crates, rolled it up, and tied it around my leg just above my knee. This seemed to work, and the bleeding did slow down.

She turned to my oldest brother and sister and told them to run as fast as they could to our neighbor's house. She said to have the neighbor contact the doctor and have him meet her at our house. My right leg had a severe cut from just above my ankle to the top of my knee.

Apparently, a barb from the broken barbwire on top of the gate was driven into my leg by the bulls head. All the damage had happened on the way down to the ground during the jump.

My oldest brother checked his gun to make sure it was fully loaded and ready to fire, and then he and my sister were off like a flash to make the five-mile journey to deliver the message to a neighbor.

My mother had my next oldest brother stand guard with his gun. She loaded me onto the wagon. She told my little brother and sister to run ahead of the tractor and open the gates. The neighbor farmer asked if he could be of help. My mom told him to come down to the house later and be prepared to join the search party to hunt down and kill the animal. She was willing to let the animal live until she saw the damage he had inflicted on one of her children.

She knew time was of the essence if I was going to survive. She starts the engine on the tractor and began the long trip on the ridge past the blackberry patch and down the hill to the house.

The two oldest children completed their mission and delivered the message to our neighbor. The neighbor called the doctor and then the local sheriff's office to report the attack. The sheriff could not believe what he was hearing from the caller. He had investigated the previous attack and personally witnessed the damage the bull had done to an animal the size of a horse. He did not even want to think about what he could do to a seven-year-old child. The sheriff immediately raced from his office to his vehicle. He went through town with his lights flashing and sirens blasting. This was his way of letting the townspeople know something serious had happened. He meets the doctor just west of town and escorted him to our house.

By the time the doctor had arrived, my mother had carried me to the house from the wagon and placed me on the bed. The doctor chased everyone out of the room and removed the bandage my mother had placed on my wound at the garden. He told my mother my fever was already 102 degrees and my life was in grave danger.

He said my heart rate was good and I was in excellent shape but that my leg was very swollen. He could see a piece of barbwire about three inches in length embed deep into the cut. The only chance to save the leg was to immediately cut the barbwire out and clean the wound. He said he would need to leave the wound open for several days to make sure gangrene did not set in. I was not sure at the time what gangrene was or what would happen if it did set in. It was clear from the expression on my mother's face though that it was not going to turn out very good for me if it did.

The doctor took my mother off to the side of the room where I could not hear him explain the procedure for removing the barbwire from my leg.

I could tell by the expression on my mother's face this was going to hurt. He asked my mother to get some hot water. She told him she knew he would need the water and it was already hot and waiting in the kitchen.

The doctor told me what he had to do. More importantly, he said it was going to hurt. He had no time to numb the area were the barbwire was lodged, nor did he have the medication needed to numb the leg in his travel case. If he did not get the wire removed in the next five minutes, I would likely lose my leg from the knee down. I told him to get on with it. My mother leaned over me, gave me a hug, and assured me it would be over soon.

The doctor asked my mother to go tell the rest what was happening. He said to ask for prayers as he was going to need all the help he could get. He said to tell them to be quiet. She left the room, and within a few seconds, you could have heard a pin drop outside my room. She returned with the water and told the doctor she would assist him in the surgery. Mom did not intend to leave me alone in the room.

The doctor looked at me and said, "It is time to operate. Any questions?" He handed me a piece of leather strap and told me to bite down on it when he told me to. I told him I had seen a scene like this on television, but I had no idea it was real. I was scared, sweating, and I remember thinking about Soul. It was the first time I can remember missing Soul and wishing he were there by my side. I was wondering if he were still alive or if the bull had literally scared him to his death.

The doctor told me he had to pour something into the wound to sterilize it. He said it would burn but was necessary to clean the wound. He told me it was all right to cry if I needed to and that most grown men cry. I told him I would not cry; crying would mean the bull won. I could feel him pulling on the barbwire, and finally the wire was out of my leg. The doctor asked me if I wanted to see what was causing all of my pain.

I told him, "No, all I wanted is my mother and a T-bone steak for Sunday dinner." The doctor just laughed and told my mother, "This kid is funny.. My mother assured me my dad would find the bull; he would pay for what he had done to me with his life.

The doctor asked my mother to step out of the room so he could talk to her. When he was outside my room, I heard my brothers and sisters jump to their feet. They were asking the same questions all at the same time. He told them the surgery was over but my life was still in danger. He told my mother he was very concerned about my injury, but the swelling would need to go down before he could do any more. He stated I would need to stay off the leg for at least two weeks. She needed to watch out for infections and pray my fever went down within a few days.

He explained that cuts from rusted barbwire were the most damaging and dangerous types of cuts. Many people and animals had lost body parts and some had died because of their injuries.

The neighbor had called my dad's employer, who immediately went to the job site and personally drove my dad to the house. The news of the attack spread through the valley like a flash flood.

People came from miles away to help our family and hear the story about the attack. The neighbor farmer elegantly told the entire story in great in detail.

The concerns for my injuries were heartfelt, but the overwhelming concern was that the bull was still out there. He could attack again at any time. The sheriff explained to the crowd this was a wounded animal, and only God knew what he planned to do next!

The next biggest challenge for my mom and dad was convincing my two oldest brothers not to go out on their own to hunt and kill the bull. They had already put the bridles on old Jim and Jerry and had enough ammunition to kill an elephant.

The sheriff helped convince the boys to stand down. He said, "Let the men take care of this." He probably did not realize it, but my second oldest brother mumbled under his breath, "If you had taken care of this, my little brother would not be in there fighting for his life." The sheriff immediately started organizing a hunting party to go find and kill the bull.

Sixteen

STRANGERS IN TOWN

Out of nowhere, a group of strangers showed up at the house driving an old pickup truck. The license plate on the back of the truck listed Middlesboro, Kentucky as it official registration. The words on the frame around the plate were "The Great Smoky Mountains." They had cages in the back of the truck that housed dogs, ready to be released to do the tracking. The hunters had heard the sirens in town and followed the neighbors to the house. They told the sheriff they were expert hunters from the Smoky Mountains. They told a story about an encounter with a monster bull. The story sent chills down the spines of even the bravest of the men volunteering for the mission to find the bull. The mountain men told the group they had been black bear hunting in the Great Smoky Mountains when they came under attack late one night. The attack on their hunting party was by a gigantic Holstein bull with a brown face and white neck. The animal described in the police bulletin posted in their area a few weeks back sounded a lot like the one who attacked and killed one of their packhorses used in the hunt.

The sheriff commented, "We now know a little about the bull and the owner." He called the sheriff in eastern Kentucky and asked for any information he could share about this bull and his owner.

The Smoky Mountain hunters were unaware of the attack that had taken place earlier in the day. A stranger in town told them about what all of the urgency was when the sheriff went racing out of town with his sirens blasting. They told us they had tracked the bull to our area of the state, which was several hundred miles from the Smoky Mountains. The reason they were so determined to find and kill the bull was that one of the men in the hunting party was a very close friend to all of them and was still in the hospital recovering from the injuries inflicted by the bull's razor-sharp horns. One of the men in the hunting party told the crowd around him that the bull just came out of nowhere. It all happen so fast there was nothing they could do to stop the attack.

The hunters ask if they could speak to me about the attack. They wanted me to describe some of the features on the bull's forehead. I have no doubt Soul could have provided a better description of the bull. He was the one staring at its terrifying eyes straight on. I was proud of Soul. He had showed some courage for the first time in my young life. I knew he was scared out of his mind with fear. He was babbling something I could not understand to someone name Caesar, who was trying to get a date with some Egyptian Queen named Cleopatra. This bull really screwed up my "brave" guardian angel's mind. I think he was convinced we were on our way to heaven. It is a miracle we had actually survived the attack.

My mother and doctor approved for the men in the hunting party to speak to me about the attack. My dad and two oldest brothers, the sheriff and his deputies, and a local reporter entered my room for a few minutes. I could tell from the expressions on their faces the men appeared to be upset when they saw the damage to my leg. One of the men had to excuse himself and left the room. I think he was the brother of the man in the hospital. The doctor told them I had lost a lot of blood. My leg was in bad shape, and I was still in shock.

One of the men told me he was proud to have met me and that it took a tremendous amount of courage to save my brother and sister. The hunters ask me a few questions about the bull's features. I could tell from their reactions that they were convinced this was definitely the animal they were pursuing.

I described the location of the blackberry patch I was picking blackberries from just before the attack. My dad told the hunters he knew exactly where the patch was and that he would lead the search party. As the men left the room, one looked back at me. He said they were all experienced hunters and they would join the search party to bring this bull to justice.

Once all of the adults (except for Dad) had left the room, my oldest brother called me "Hollywood" and asked me in a joking way why I had slowed down. My second oldest brother told me he would do my chores for two weeks. Every day past that he planned to kick my butt if I did not do them myself. They both left the room, leaving my dad and me alone.

My dad dropped his head in shame. He told me he felt he had let me down and he was sorry. I told Dad that I knew in my heart he did everything possible to protect his children. "For seven years, you have been my hero and will be for the rest of my life." I think it was the first time I actually saw tears in my dad's eyes.

I heard the man that could not stand to be in the room tell my dad he would pray for my recovery. The reporter asked for permission to publish the story in the next edition of the newspaper. He said what I did to protect my brother and sister was likely the bravest thing he had ever heard and that he would be proud to have a son like me.

My dad told the hunters it was time to take care of some unfinished business.

Seventeen

THE HUNT

O nce the stories spread about how dangerous this beast was, many of the men who previously volunteered to join the search party dropped out. The sheriff decided he would only allow experienced hunters with excellent shooting skills to join in the hunt. Previous military experience was a plus.

My father told the sheriff he and my two oldest brothers would be in the hunting party. If not, they would go out on their own to find the bull. He assured the sheriff they knew what to do and they were determined to kill the bull. He told the sheriff that earlier, the two brothers had to stand and watch while this bull attempted to kill three of their siblings. The sheriff put his hand on my dad's shoulder and told him he understood and said okay.

The sheriff decided it was too late in the day to start the hunt. If the bull were as sneaky and dangerous as described by the mountain men, it would not be safe to be in those woods after dark. The hunting party agreed to meet at the front entrance of the barn across Clifton Creek the next morning at 7:30 AM sharp. The sheriff went over the list of supplies they would need to bring to the hunt. He ordered each man to bring his best high-powered rifle with a full round of ammunition.

My dad met my two oldest brothers about midnight at the front door of the house. He asked them where they had been for the past six hours.

They explained they were guarding the blackberry patch to make sure the bull did not escape. I think it was the first time my father realized these two boys were becoming men. He knew their courage would lead them through tough times someday.

The full team met the next morning as scheduled. They decided to walk to the blackberry patch to avoid alerting the bull. Once they arrived at the blackberry patch, they all moved into their assigned position. The plan was to surround the perimeter of the field. The decision was to start shooting into the air in an attempt to bring the bull out into the open. The berry patch covers approximately 20 acres. It would have been impossible for the bull to slip past the 50 men in the hunting party. A few minutes into the hunt, the sheriff realized the plan was not working and ordered everyone to stop. He asks the Smoky Mountain Hunters to release their dogs to go into the berry patch and chase the bull out. The hunters refused to allow their dogs to be in harm's way. They loved their dogs and treated them like members of the family. They told the sheriff the briers would hurt the dog's paws and cause injuries to their bodies. The sheriff shook his head in disbelief.

The sheriff told half of the men to enter the south half of the patch and the rest would come in from the north side. The sheriff's order was simple: "Shoot to kill and do not stop shooting until you know he is finished!"

The search went on for several hours. Dark was rapidly approaching when the sheriff felt it was no longer safe to continue the hunt.

The next day was a non-work day. The entire team agreed to meet at daybreak and continue the hunt. The news reports for the day stated simply that the hunt was unsuccessful and that folks in the area should stay inside their homes until further notice.

The sheriff started to get information that clearly indicated that people in the community and the state were very concerned. TV crews from Louisville and Cincinnati were on location within a few hours from when the story broke. Late Saturday night, the sheriff got a call from the one of the highest-ranking county official. The official was getting pressure from the state house in Frankfort. It was a little hard to imagine this situation had not been resolved. The sheriff needed to put a stop to all of the rumors and find and kill the bull. He had to make sure the news media had photos to prove the beast was no longer a threat to me and the community. We needed to get things to return to normal; after all, it was an election year.

The men met again on Sunday morning with a new plan. In desperation, the sheriff asked my father if he would approve setting small fires throughout the blackberry patch in an effort to smoke the bull out. My dad agreed, and by the time the day was over, 30-acres had been burn to the ground. The hunt ended late Sunday night. After a meeting with county and state officials, the sheriff declared that the beast had left the community and folks should go back to living an ordinary life. This statement did not sit well with the press or the TV reporters. However, this was the least of the sheriff's problems. Every person in the community had serious doubts about the sheriff's ability to protect them.

Eighteen

SHERIFF, NEXT TIME TELL THE BULL
IT IS OVER THE SECOND ATTACK

Approximately two weeks after the sheriff had declared the community safe, my mother was awakened one night around 2:00 AM. A series of loud knocking sounds were coming from just outside her bedroom window. She alerted Dad and told him the bull was looking through the bedroom window. The message on the bull's face was, "I'm back and you and that kid are going to pay for what you did to me." My father immediately grabbed his gun from the gun case. Within minutes, he was on the trail and looking for the bull. Within five hundred feet from the house, the tracks disappeared. It was as if the bull had grown wings and flew away without leaving any sign he was ever there. Dad stayed out the rest of the night, but could not find the bull. However, he did find several massive tracks in the yard just under the bedroom windows of both my room and Mom's room. When he returned to the house, my mother told him she was not surprised he could not find the bull. This bull was very smart, and she had felt his presence for several days. She told dad the beast was doing his surveillance of the area. He was looking for just the right time to carry out the attack he had promised her he would at the gate immediately following the first attack.

My dad wanted my mother to leave the farm and take me with her to spend some time at her aunt's house in Lawrenceburg, Indiana. She said she would have nothing to do with something so ridiculous, saying, "I am not afraid of the beast, so take that thought out of your head." In her heart, she knew this was about over. Soul had fully recovered, and I am not sure how I knew, but I did. He woke up with more confidence and courage than he had demonstrated any time in his life with me. He did not want me to leave the farm. Mom just prayed God would protect her and her family. She felt the bull was underestimating her will to protect her family. He failed to consider the fact that he was not the only one making a plan. My father and older brothers spent the next several nights hunting for the bull. The farm at the time had numerous places the bull could hide, and it was like trying to find a sewing needle in a haystack.

School Days, School Days, Good Old Fashion School Days. Reading and Writing and Arithmetic, Taught by the Tune of a Hickory Stick!

The first official school event had finally arrived. Traditionally, the entire family would visit the school, talk to the teachers, and meet new classmates the Friday night before the first day, which was always on Monday. As it happens, my doctor had refused to allow me to attend the event because of my leg. The session typically only lasted a couple of hours, and the school was only a few miles from the house. What could possibly go wrong? My mother decided she would stay behind with me. She asked my dad to be home early from work so he could take the rest of the children with him to the event. He reluctantly agreed, but only if my mother agreed to stay in the house and keep the doors locked until his return. She obliged, and the family loaded in the Ford station wagon and left for the meeting.

I did not know my mother had made an agreement to stay in the house while the family was away. I decided to walk outside for a few minutes. I wanted to get some fresh air, which my doctor had agreed to during his last visit. I was a little upset because I wanted to go with the rest of the family to the event. I really wanted to see my friends, who I had not seen since school ended in the early spring.

I was standing on the side porch and facing the driveway when I noticed the gate to the front yard was open. I just figured one of my brothers forgot to close it in the excitement of heading off to school. My oldest brother's head had been in the gutter for the past several weeks; he suddenly seems to like girls better than baseball. At that point in my life, I could not even imagine something as stupid in a million years. Girls over baseball? What was it all coming to?

I went over to the gate, closed it, and made sure this time the sturdy latch locked into the proper position. As I was walking back to the house, suddenly the same strange tingling feeling I had felt in the blackberry patch shot up the center of my spine. Soul warned me we were in danger, and I needed to walk back to the house very slowly and shut and lock the door behind me. For the first time in seven years, I felt Soul was there to help me. He was helping me ease my pain in my leg and keep me calm. I had felt that over several weeks, both Soul and I had recovered from the first attack: Soul emotionally and me physically. I was hoping he brought some kick-butt courage back with him.

I went into the house and told my mom about the gate and the feeling that had come out of nowhere. She told me the same feeling had just come over her and she knew why!

She could not believe she had let her guard down, and we were now in great danger. No sooner had she made the statement than we felt the house start to shake as if we were having an earthquake.

We were the only two people left at home. The bull knew this was his best shot at the two of us to follow through with his promise. He was not going to hold back. He had warned us he would have his chance and when he did we would pay with our lives. I ran to the back of the house to see if I could locate the bull. Just as I looked out the window at the back of the dining room, I saw the bull running toward the yard fence. This time he did not bother with the gate, he jumped the fence with the grace of a full-grown reindeer. He cleared the six-foot fence by four feet. I returned to the front of the house and told mom the bull was in the yard.

We heard him running down the front porch of our house as if he were intentionally torturing us. The porch ran the full length of the house. If it was his intent to torture us, it was working. We could hear the planks on the porch explode one at a time from the bull's massive weight.

Suddenly complete silence surrounded us. It was so quiet I could hear my mother's heart beating from across the room. I knew my mother was more scared for me than she was for herself. I told her I would get a shotgun and get it loaded. She knew I was not ready to take such a responsibility. She told me to leave it up to her to protect me. She said, "Son, you will just have to trust me on this. I have a plan."

I went to the front door to see what was happening. I look out the windowpane in the door and saw the bull in the front yard. He was setting up to get a running start at the front door of the house. I yelled to my mother to go out the back door. I would distract the bull long enough for her to run to safety.

It seemed to me it was taking my mom more time than I expected to exit the house. I called out to her twice and said I would be okay. "I love you and you need to go now!" I heard the back door close. I was relieved my mother listened and hopeful she would seek proper shelter from the bull.

I saw her out a side window as she ran towards the cattle barn located across the creek from the house.

I moved back to the front door to look out the window one last time to locate the bull. I wanted to make sure the bull was not going after my mother. When the beast saw me in the window, he began running as fast as he could toward the front door of the house. I quickly realized I would only have a few seconds to run up the stairs and climb into the attic. I knew he would literally need to tear down the house to get to me in the attic.

The bull crashed his head into the front door of the house, and the door turned to splinters on impact. I could feel the entire house shaking as if he were taking the house apart one board at a time.

He started maneuvering his way through the house. He seemed to know the layout of every room by heart. I knew he would know how to make his way to the upper level of the house if he had ever been loaded on a truck with a cattle-loading shoot. The loading shoot looks like a ramp with stairs. The answer to the question came very quickly, as I could hear him sneaking up the stairs one giant step at a time to the upper level of the house. The stairs, constructed out of solid oak, had no problem supporting the weight of a bull. His loud breathing clearly indicated to me that he was getting more upset by the second. Once he had completed the search of the upstairs bedrooms, he seemed a little disoriented in the house. I was hiding in the attic, and he stopped directly beneath me at the top of the stairs. He appeared to be listening for any movement and using his incredible sense of smell for any indicator to help him find his prey.

Unfortunately, when I jumped up to retrieve the ladder needed to climb into the attic, the stitches rip apart in my leg and opened my wound from the barbwire. I could feel the blood running down my leg. As I put my hands over my wound to try to stop the bleeding, Soul took charge and spoke to me in a very soft and gentle voice. He told me to stay quiet, be calm, and not move. Remember, he is my guarding angel, and only I can hear his voice or communicate with him.

Soul was helping me control my heart rate, which also helped slow down the bleeding. We both knew if the beast smelled the blood, he would go crazy. We would be in deep trouble with no place to run; I have no doubt Soul saved my life! The bull never noticed me above him. Finally, the bull gave up the hunt and started the descent back to the lower level of the house.

Within a few minutes, I could hear my mother yelling at the bull to come outside and settle the issue for the last time. She was not sure of my condition or if I was even still alive. Nevertheless, she knew this had to end one way or another.

The bull was now at the bottom of the staircase. He was making his way back to the area where the front door used to be. I crawled on my hands and knees across the rafters in the attic to get a better look at the bull. A window located at the end of the attic was small but provided an extensive panoramic view to where the bull had to exit the house. I heard the bull step out of the house and onto the wooden porch. He raised his enormous head high above his back. He used his incredible sense of hearing and eyesight to pinpoint my mother's location.

She had positioned herself in front of the cattle barn across the creek from the house. Once the bull made eye contact with her, she sprinted across the creek bed and quickly darted into the barn. She crawled into a secure birthing stall surrounded by heavy timbers. It turned out to be a huge mistake, as the bull apparently knew every inch of the barn and every escape route.

The bull sprinted across the creek and into the door of the barn. As soon as I saw him take off after my mother, I climbed out of the attic and went to retrieve one of my dad's guns we called 'Old Long Tom.' I could not find any shells for the gun, so I left it outside the case and sprinted to the barn. I located the bull through an opening between the boards on the side of the barn and observed the bull hunting for his prey. He went stall by stall, stopping at each door to listen for any noise he could to find my mother. He knew she was in the barn, and this was what he had been waiting for. I knew my mother's heart had to be pounding out of her chest. The bull's sense of hearing would have no problem tracking her down. He finally located the stall where she was hiding from him and gently positioned his horns into the latch and opened the door to the stall. My mother watched him open the latch and immediately knew he was the one that opened the gates just before the first attack. He stepped inside to block the exit. My mother removed the blanket she was hiding under to face her enemy. He was preparing for his final charge to use his razor-sharp horns and massive size and power to end her life. She slowly rose up from her hiding position. She realized her back was up against the wall of the barn and she had no place to run.

The bull began his ritual of pawing and digging the ground with his feet. Once he finished digging his launching pad deep enough into the dirt floor, he was ready to charge his target with maximum force. His body was full of rage.

Then for some unknown reason, he paused for a second. He raised his head and looked directly into my mom's eyes. It appeared he expected her to drop to her knees and beg him to spare her life. He obviously did not know my mom as well as he thought he did. What he found was a confident woman who had previously out-witted him and was determined to do it again.

My mom knew something the bull did not know. She had this bully right where she wanted him. Then she did what moms do best: she gave the beast the opportunity to explain why he was so angry. She wanted to know how any creature created by God could grow to have such hate and vengeance for everything and everyone crossing his path.

The bull obviously could not understand the words, but he did feel the emotions and the tenderness of her voice.

A few weeks later, we all learned from the bull's owners the whole story about this bull. My mother had struck the right chords to help him finally stop and think about what he was doing. It became much clearer to us why he did what he did. As he moved closer to my mother, he felt something in his heart he had not felt for many years.

The story goes: At one time, the bull had a wife and an enormous family proudly roaming the Great Smoky Mountains with pride and dignity. He was a great provider and the leader of the herd. Then one day everything he had worked for crumbled right before his eyes. Everything changed for him.

His wife and two children were out grazing one sunny afternoon on the side of the mountain with the rest of the herd as he stood watch. One of the children (a baby calf but not one of his children) in the herd had wandered away from the group. It was his turn to find the child and bring it back. He found the lost baby calf about a half-mile away from the herd. He scolded the calf and explained the dangers of not staying with the herd (it takes a village to raise a child and a big herd to raise a calf). He and the baby turned to walk back to the herd, which had moved up the mountain for better grazing. He heard loud screams, growls, and the sound of an attack coming from the area where his wife and children were eating. As he approached the top of the mountain, he saw a gigantic grizzle bear running off into the wood. The grizzle bears are normally located much deeper into the forest of the Great Smoky Mountains.

As he got closer to where his wife and children were grazing, he could see signs of the attack all over the place. Then complete silence and stillness filled the forest. All one could hear was the hopelessness of a broken heart echoing through the mountain. The other animals knew a great tragedy had just occurred. The mountain would likely never be the same.

The angry grizzle bear had brutally attacked and killed his wife and two babies. The bull had nothing to live for except the revenge fueling his heart. All of his plans and dreams for raising his family in peace were lost forever. His wife ambushed and killed by a bear for no apparent reason, and his children never had a prayer of survival with the size of a grizzle bear.

His owners said he disappeared shortly after the attack. However, he was seen numerous times running wildly in the night. His size had more than doubled. It was obvious he had revenge in his heart. He was determined to strike back on the bear responsible for killing his family. He was learning to hunt like a great stalker in the night. He was determined he would become an enemy of the bear. One day soon, he would hunt down the bear and seek revenge. This bear had to pay with his life for what he had done to the bull's wife and babies.

The owners did find the bear he felt killed the bull's wife and babies ripped to pieces one day, but the bull had altogether disappeared. Many felt he had jumped off the side of the mountain to his death. The drop was more than 5,000 feet straight down, and nothing could survive the fall. It was apparent to the bull's owners that the bull would likely never be able to recover from his loss. The grief he had in his heart for his wife and baby's was just too much for any animal to live with.

What the bull must have sensed in my mom was that he had met his match. He found someone just as determined as he was to defend her family. The bull decided it was time to end this nonsense. He went into a rage and was ready for an all-out attack on my mother.

I had climbed through an opening in the barn and into the loft above the stall my mother was sheltering in. I knew the bull did not know I was there, but I knew he was about to attack. I started yelling and screaming at the bull and dropped a 40-pound bale of hay directly onto his back from the loft. Then I removed two planks in the loft so I could drop down directly in front of my mother. This may sound crazy, but when you love someone as much as we love our mother, I strongly feel any of her children would have done the same thing in her defense. The drop from the loft was about fifteen feet, but the straw on the floor of the stall would help break my fall. As I climbed into position, I heard Soul say, "Father, please help us." Then Soul said to me, "We can do this. I will be by your side." The bull was surprised to see me, but he quickly realized he could get a two-for-one deal out of the attack. We were undoubtedly the two people he hated most in the world.

Without losing eye contact with the bull, my mom put me behind her as if to attempt to use her body as a shield. This is what good mothers do when their children are in danger. She told me she was very proud of me and no matter what the outcome, her feelings would never change.

What she said next took me by surprise. She told me this bull was about to be presented with his final two options. This mommy has a plan. Soul told me to listen to my mother because mothers always know best. He said in a calm but stern voice to stay behind her and stop talking so much. Soul said my mother knew exactly what she was doing.

This time I decided Soul was right as I felt the blood running down my leg, soaking my shoe. It was time to turn this over to Soul, my mother, and God.

The bull was within 10 feet of my mother when I witnessed a miracle. Maybe it was Soul doing what angels are supposed to do or God decided enough was enough. I noticed my Mom was wearing the apron our Aunt from Lawrenceburg had given her for Christmas the year before. I knew she was not wearing an apron when I last saw her in the house just before the bull attacked the front door.

My mother slowly moves her left hand toward the large front pocket of the apron. Then, as quick as the eye could see, she pulled the old Japanese pistol with the pearl handle given to dad by the Japanese soldier. I heard Soul say to God, "Boss, I think she is pissed." The revolver carried the same specifications as a modern day 44 Magnum. The power of a 44 Magnum would have no problem taking the bull down for good with one shot. Believe me, from that distance she would not miss, nor would she back down from this challenge.

The bull appeared to have a look on his face that questioned my mom's courage. He was having serious doubts that she would actually have the courage to follow through with her plan. When she set the hammer on the gun and points it straight at the bull's head, he appeared to have some other thoughts about her ability to complete the mission.

Soul punched out his chest and pointed at the bull and said, "Go ahead make my day, you big bully. Come on she's got this."

Now I knew what my mother meant when she said the bull would need to assess his options. The two options in my mind were:

Option One: Leave my family alone and disappear forever

Option Two: Die.

The bull seemed to calm down once he saw the pistol and the determination in my mom's face to defend her family.

For some reason, my mom started remembering the events surrounding the reason the gun was even available to her. She decided to lower her arm and give the bull a chance to live, just as my father had done twenty years earlier. He intentionally shot above the Japanese soldier's head who gave him the gun in the first place.

She was allowing the bull the opportunity to walk away with a clear understanding that this was over. He should end his hate and learn to love again. He must have had a flashback to a time in his life when he was happy and his wife and babies roamed the mountains free and safe.

The bull stood there for several minutes before making his choice. He dropped his head and turned to walk away only to turn back. He looked at my mom as if to say, "You are quite a lady and one a hell of a mother. You remind me of a lady I use to know and love a long time ago."

She could see the tears forming in the bull's eyes as he lowered his head in total defeat and turned to walk away. She felt the fear she had felt for so many weeks also end. She now knew her family was finally safe.

In the meantime, Dad had sensed we were in danger and had come home as quickly as possible. When he found the door shattered and 'Old Long Tom' lying on the floor, he knew something had gone terribly wrong. He picked up the gun, loaded it, and tracked us to the barn by following the blood trail I left on the ground just minutes before.

As the bull stepped through the large sliding door at the end of the barn, my dad met him face to face.

Dad pulled his gun into position and prepared to pull the trigger to shoot the bull. The bull did nothing to defend himself. He just stood there and watched. My mother asked my father to put the gun down and spare the bull's life. My dad apparently could tell by the tone of my mother's voice something very special had happened, and he honored her request. He lowered his gun and allowed the beast to escape. The bull lowered his head again even lower, walked slowly into the woods, and disappeared into the dark of night.

My dad picked me up with one arm and placed the other around my mom. As we stepped past the corner of the barn, I could see the full moon developing far above my head. The sky was full of stars. I felt the northern breeze touch my face with the chill of autumn drying the sweat from my brow. I suddenly felt all of my fears and anger for the bull replaced with sadness and a sense of grief for the bull. I ask my dad if we could go in the morning to find the bull and bring him home with us to live with our herd. My father said, "No son, I think the bull has learned a great lesson over these past several weeks. He now needs time alone to figure out what is next for him. I would not be surprised if someday we see this bull leading another herd somewhere with his wife and children by his side. Understand me son; he will never forget this experience. However, he will learn to appreciate the life he has created once he has accepted the fact life is what you make it. However, sometimes things do not always turn out as we plan. Son, I think you will see what I mean when you get older. Always appreciate what you have today because life is full of changes. Now let's get you to the house and take care of your leg." Mom said, "Amen!" My mother carefully placed the silk cloth around the pearl-handled pistol and put it back into the case.

I felt Soul take a deep sigh as if the pressure of the whole world had lifted off his shoulders, at least for the time being. I thanked Soul for his help. He replied in his normal tone of voice, "Whatever." Nevertheless, I could tell he had changed. For the first time, he helped me when I needed it most in the attic of the old house. I think he and God knew it was the beginning of Soul's training; he received an 'A-plus-plus' from the boss this time, but he still had a long way to go.

The next day, everyone in the valley was aware of what had happened at the Clifton's house the night before. They were relieved the emergency was over and had ended peacefully. Many felt my Mom should have taken the shot when she had the chance. She explains that she felt this bull had something left in his heart that was good. It was a part of God's plan for her and the bull. She did not know what the plan was or when it would happen; nevertheless, she had a feeling it would be significant and would affect the life of someone she loved very much.

You cannot imagine who it was, but she was right. I will cover that in a future story. Several of the neighbors helped my dad repair the house and put up a new front door before nightfall the next day.

My leg healed just fine, and I started to school a couple of weeks later. My teacher made sure she sent my homework home with my brother. He told me my teacher was just as mean as she was when I had her in the first grade. Keep in mind my school only had four classrooms, four teachers, and one cook, and grades 1-8 shared the four rooms. Each teacher had full authority to spank you with a paddle of their choice anytime they felt you needed it.

My second-grade teacher was a great example of how my losses sometimes turned into wins. You see, back in 1959 it was okay for teachers to spank their students when, in their opinion, the student had broken the rules. Judging by the number of spankings I received, my teacher apparently felt that I broke the rules a lot.

She reminded me the first day I returned to school that she was meaner than the bull, and if I messed with her, I would get the horn. Ironically, she gave me a spanking the next day for failing to turn in my homework.

Many years later, I witnessed her crying one day. I am not sure if she was crying because she felt sorry about all of those spankings or if it was because I was marrying her favorite niece.

Soul continued to find his courage. He would be my partner for the rest of my life thanks to the deal we made with God.

Nineteen

THE MAD BIRD

Okay Jackson, I will tell you children the story about the mad birds that attacked my little brother and me. It was on the same ridge and just a couple hundred feet to the south of the fence I jumped to save my brother's life a few years earlier.

We were both having a great summer. We had learned to use the tractor to do many of the regular chores on the farm, and Dad asked the two of us to mow down the hay on what we called "Short Ridge." Then we were supposed to clean out the barn, where we could stack the hay after it was allowed to cure out the moisture for a couple of days in the summer sun.

The morning started just like most mornings around the Clifton household: each of the children ate breakfast, and Mom told each of us about the expectations for the day.

I reminded her that Dad had asked my little brother and me to mow the short ridge and to clean out the barn. She said she knew all about it, but she felt we were too young to take on something as complicated as mowing hay. I assured her Dad had taught us both how to use the tractor and to mow hay.

First, we needed to connect the hay-cutting machine to the hydraulic system on the back of the tractor. The cutting machine weighed about one thousand pounds. My oldest brother was now working a public job but offered to hook up the mower to the tractor before he left for work. My second oldest brother backed the tractor into position so my oldest brother could hook up the machine to the tractor.

Soul had settled in, and even though he would not openly admit it, he seemed to like living on the farm. The task we were going to do today was his favorite. He loved to ride on the tractor and got very excited when we were on steep ground. He was even learning the lingo. He knew what "Keep on digging baby" meant. This is what we say to the tractor when we think it is about to be stuck in the mud. Naturally, the only thing keeping the tractor from being stuck was the action of the operator. Nevertheless, Soul thought the tractor could actually understand his commands.

My mother finally agreed to let us do the task. Dad had a lot of confidence in us and felt we could accomplish these two tasks without getting hurt or breaking something. I went to the gun case and pulled out my 22-rifle and loaded the chamber with a full round of bullets. Before the bull attack, Soul could not understand why we took guns with us when we traveled to the back part of the farm. After the bull attack, he reminded me every time we went out to take the gun. My little brother filled up a gallon jug with ice water, and we were off to perform the work. We got to the barn at about 9:00 AM and started cleaning it out. We had to wait until the dew dried off the hay before we could cut it.

My mother had sent a couple of peanut butter and jelly sandwiches each for both of us to eat for lunch. We were both hungry by ten o'clock and decided to eat the first two sandwiches and save the other two for lunch.

We finish cleaning two of the three sections in the barn before lunchtime. We were still both less than ten years old, and we did like to play while we worked. In those days, we made up games and spent hours playing when we probably should have been working.

My little brother told me about a game he had learned from our two older brothers and their friends.

Caution was the first thing to cross my mind when he mentioned my brother's friends. I could not help but have a flashback to the Fourth of July weekend. My brother's friends were mostly city boys and were a little ahead of the social teachings of farm boys. I think they all smoked cigarettes by the time they were twelve. In those days, we did not generally purchase cigarettes from the store. Most farm boys had access to the tobacco set aside from the previous year's crop, and they rolled their own smokes. The Fourth of July was the first time my brothers had been around any sort of fireworks. Late in the afternoon, six of my brother's friends show up at the house driving an old fifty-five Chevy. The Chevy sounded like it was running on four of the eight cylinders. When they turned off the engine, it backfired so loud, it causes the cattle in the neighbor's field to stampede. The neighbor was not jubilant to have to spend the rest of his holiday mending fences. As best I can remember, the boy's names were Bill, Dale, Eddie, Ronnie, Troy, and Herman.

The boys went directly into the barn on Clifton Creek. We assumed they were going to smoke some cigarettes. Within an hour, we heard an explosion in the barn that sounded like someone had dropped a bomb. The explosion was so loud our neighbors from several miles away heard it. My dad ran out of the house and sprinted to the barn. Just as he opened the sliding barn door, he saw my brothers trying to put out a fire. The rest of the boys were running out the back door. Once the fire was out, he asked the boys to meet him inside the barn. My little brother and I could not resist but join in with the rest of the boys in the barn. We knew somebody was in trouble, and for once, it was not us. My little brother always had a hard time keeping his mouth shut. He started out the meeting by asking my father if the hole in the top of the barn had always been there. My dad focused on the 18-inch round hole in the roof of the barn. He said, "I did not think so, but maybe we should ask the rest of the boys." My dad asked my oldest brother to explain what had happened. How did the hole end up in the roof? My oldest brother began to explain, but Dad interrupted him and said, "Never mind." I am not sure how dad figured it out, but he knew my oldest brother was about to spin a big one. Dad turned to my second oldest brother and asked him the same question. He knew he was not quite as good at spinning a story as my oldest brother was.

My second oldest brother told dad the hole was made in the roof by a pipe rocket. Dad asked him where they got a pipe rocket. My second oldest brother said, "Well sir, we built it. We built and launched a rocket with these," and he handed Dad about ten explosives called cherry bombs. He said, "It sounded like fun, but I guess we used to many." The remains of the homemade pipe bomb were found later about three hundred feet from the house. My father told the boys he expected them to repair the hole in the roof before sundown. He also expected all eight boys to help or he would share the entire incident with the other boys' fathers.

Now you can understand why I was a little skeptical when my little brother told me he learned the game from my brother's friends.

My little brother said the game was call splits. The way to play was to face your opponent, spread your legs about three feet wide, and stand six feet apart. Then you would take turns throwing your knife at your opponents feet as close as possible without hitting their foot. If you hit the opponents foot with your knife, they got to punch you in the arm with their fist without retaliation. Whoever got the closest on each throw won a point, and the first one to ten points would win the game. I said, "It sure sounds like a fun game." What I did not tell my little brother was my friends and I had been playing the game for two years during recess at the bottom of locust creek during the dry season. I was good and felt I could win. Therefore, I, asked him what the winner got. He could not come up with anything, so I suggest we bet on our sandwiches. The winner would take all. My little brother could never resist a bet and immediately jumped on it. This game with knives would have been considered dangerous if it had not been for the most popular television shows of our time. From the time we were three or four years old, we had been throwing knives at boards, trees, and into the ground. We were mimicking our television heroes like Daniel Boone and Dave Crocket. By the time most boys back in those days reached seven years old, we could throw and stick a knife where we wanted it to land ninety-five percent of the time.

I think Soul was glad the competition was over. I felt him flinch every time my little brother threw his knife at my feet. I won the game, and my little brother handed me his sandwich. I convinced my little brother I was full and could not eat his lunch. He just smiled and said thanks.

We decided to go take a dip in the pond before we started back to work. No Jackson, we did not wear swimming trunks, and we did not wear our underwear. We just went skinny-dipping.

Once the fun was over, it was time to get back to work and finish our assignments for the day. We agreed that my little brother would clean out the last section of the barn and I would mow the hay.

Soul was happy with the decision and could not wait to get going on the tractor. My little brother helped me drop the mowing sickle into position. I told him to stay in the barn once I started up the tractor and engaged the mower. This device was capable of cutting off any body part in a matter of a seconds. I did not want to take any chances that he would get hurt.

As I drove the tractor and mower around the first swath, I felt Soul leaning to the left as if he was trying to balance the tractor and keep it from flipping over on a steep incline. I had to laugh just thinking he felt he had enough weight to balance a six-thousand pound tractor and keep it from tipping over. I mowed a swath around the short ridge perimeter just as I had watched my father and older brothers do in the past. It took about 20 minutes to make one pass all the way around the field. It would take about three hours for me to finish cutting all of the hay my father wanted to be cut.

I made several passes around the field and was about eighty percent finished when I noticed some large birds fighting with each other in the thicket on the bottom side of Short Ridge. Soul took one look at the birds and became mesmerized by what he saw. I stopped the tractor to see if I could figure out why they were fighting. The birds were turkey buzzards. They are colossal birds, and their main diet is dead animals. I could feel Soul nudging me to restart the tractor. He was ready to get the heck out of there as the fight intensified between the two birds.

I can tell you now we both hated birds and for good reason. A flock of chickens in a coupe attacked me when I was about four years old. I never overcame my fear of roosters. I will always remember the look on Soul's face when I reached under a mother hen to get an egg. The roosters were waiting for me in the hen house and came at me from every direction. By the time, my mother rescued me, I had multiple cuts and scrapes all over my body. I swore I was never going back in the hen house again. Soul felt the same way and encouraged me to stick to my word. I did finally get my reward when it was harvest time. My job was to chop off the roosters' heads before we put them in the scalding hot water to pluck out their feathers.

Soul clearly understood these were God's creation and knew he needed to support them. Nevertheless, privately, he felt God must have been very tired when he created some birds and heaven would be just fine without these two.

The turkey buzzards were fighting with each other in a way I had not seen before. It was a violent fight to the death. I thought it might be a rogue bird trying to kill the other bird's babies. I did see a big nest high in a large hickory tree. The two adult birds dropped to the ground and continue to fight. I lost sight of the birds and decided to get back to mowing before it got too late to finish. Even though I had restarted the tractor, I noticed Soul was still keeping an eye out behind me. I made the next swath and was about one hundred feet from the barn when I heard my little brother screaming something and pointing at the sky. I saw the black winged buzzard with soft cold black feather lining his neck coming right at my head. We both knew the black-feathered buzzards were by nature the meanest birds in the sky. I estimate he was traveling about 30 miles per hour. Soul screamed, "Duck!" along with a few other descriptive words I cannot put into this story. I ducked down below the steering wheel of the tractor for protection just as the bird went for my head. He hit the large exhaust stack on the front of the tractor and fell to the ground. I turned the tractor around and head back toward the barn to retrieve my 22 rifle. By the time, I return to where the bird hit the ground, he was gone. I did not see him fly away, so I assumed he was still on the ground planning his next attack. Soul was in a conversation with God. I heard him say, "Please do not give me any future assignment involving birds. I will take on bears, hippos, mountain lions, snakes, gorillas, wildcats, and mad dogs, but please keep me away from birds."

We spent a few minutes in the barn to make sure the bird was gone before I went back to finish the last swath. The bird did not return. I decide to finish the mowing so we could head back to the house. Just as I finished the last cut, I caught sight of the buzzard, and this time he decided to attack me from the front. Just as he made his dive with his claws spread and clutched, I slammed on the brakes of the tractor, which caused the bird to hit the ground in front of me. I put my tractor in reverse and raised the mower to keep from hitting the bird. As I drove the tractor back to the safety of the barn, I saw the bird running along the ground behind me. He was literally chasing the tractor, and if he caught us, he would have finished what he started. He was too tired to keep up and disappeared into the woods. I drove the tractor as fast as I could to the barn. We closed the doors on both ends of the barn and kept an eye through the smaller doors located along each side of the barn. I was looking for a clean shot, but the shot never came. After about thirty minutes, I told my little brother we needed to get home before it got too dark to see to drive a tractor. I opened the door and start up the tractor, but the bird had apparently perched itself on top of the barn and was waiting for me to drive the tractor out of the barn. I saw him at the last second and was able to turn off the key on the tractor as I jumped to the ground to run back into the barn.

I spent the next ten minutes trying to get a clean shot off at the crazy bird. I tried to find out what had caused the bird to be so upset, but it was impossible. He was the aggressor and I was his meal. I convinced my little brother to open the front door of the barn. I would open the back door. He was reluctant at first, but he trusted me and agreed. I told him if the bird started to chase him to move toward the rear of the barn. As he ran out, I would slam the door shut and the bird would fly right into it. When he hit the ground, I would shoot him. Soul was all for my little brother putting himself in harm's way. He told me that I had learned a lot and it was an excellent plan. Soul was getting better but was still a bit of a chicken. Within five minutes, we saw the bird heading for the barn door opening. The bird chased my little brother to the other end of the barn, and as he went passed, I slammed the door and the bird crashed into it and fell to the ground. The plan worked well until my gun jammed and would not fire a single shot. This bird was lying on the ground and was attempting to get to his feet.

The bird started to chase my little brother. He cornered him in the left side of the barn. He had no place to run, and I knew I had to do something. I looked around and noticed a lathe tobacco stick (A lathe tobacco stick is much wider and is about half the width of a regularly shape tobacco stick) with a sharp flat edge lying in the debris my little brother had swept up in a pile while cleaning the barn. I picked up the stick and made an aggressive swing at the vultures head. It was a clean hit, and the bird fell over dead. My little brother told me that the next time, the bird could chase me through the barn and he would slam the door.

I guess we had lost track of time, and out of nowhere, my dad walked into the barn. My two older brothers were with him. He asked us what was going on. We showed him the dead bird, and he told us not to touch it. I told him I had a clean shot, but my gun had jammed and would not fire. He handed the gun to my next to oldest brother and told him to clear the jammed chamber. He told my oldest brother to retrieve a large bag from the back of the truck. We told him the rest of the story, and he asked us to show him where the birds were first fighting. As we walked around the ridge, he motioned for us to stop in our tracks. He placed his finger in front of his lips to signal us to not say another word or move another inch. Then he motioned to me to hand him my gun. He signaled to my oldest brother to get in front of us and to drop to the ground when he told us to do so.

He made eye contact with my next to oldest brother and pointed to the chamber of the gun. He gave him the thumbs up high sign, and the gun was ready to fire. Just as my father pulled the gun to his right shoulder, the second bird flew up from his cover and headed straight for his head. As I told you earlier, it was a big mistake on the bird's part if he thought my dad was going to miss. It took only one shot for my dad to hit the bird between the eyes.

My dad asked both of us if the birds had touched us or if we had injuries while fighting it with the bird in the barn. He checked us both and found no injuries. He told my oldest brother to take the tractor home. We could ride with him to the house in the back of the truck.

He carefully placed both of the birds into a bag. Once we got back to the house, he called the local wildlife officers. The officers came to the house and took the birds for testing. He told my father what to look for if the birds had actually scratched my little brother or me. He told dad that if the birds tested positive, he would need to take us both to the hospital for a series of rabies shots.

The officer and his partner returned the next day and asks us to take him to the tree where the nest was located. He found two baby birds flying around the nest and determined that they were old enough to survive on their own.

It took about five days for the officer come by the house to explain why the birds were so violent. The bird my dad shot tested positive for rabies and had apparently attacked the second bird. The second bird did not test positive, but he was sure the reason it attacked us was from fear and confusion once it escaped from the bird with rabies. The second bird was the mother, and she probably thought we were after her babies. Fortunately for the two of us, we never even got close to the sick bird and did not need to take the shots.

Twenty

THE END OF THE SIMPLE LIFE

Life as we knew it on Locust Creek was changing. The county was growing in population due to the surge of industry building up along the mighty Ohio River, and growth requires change. Most citizens were not willing to give up their way of life without a fight, and why should they? As it is in many small communities throughout the world, life revolves around the church and the school. Locust had one school, and it housed grades one through eight. In addition, we had two churches and one general store.

The school schedules and attendance of the students directly related to the seasons and the weather. Our community was no different from most rural communities in the state of Kentucky. People would spend their last dime to attend a school basketball game and support their boys. It did not matter if it was a good team or a not-so-good team; the fans always held out hope and knew on a given night anything could happen.

I caught the basketball bug watching my oldest brother score 49 points and single-handedly outscore the boys from Worthville in the old Locust gym in the county championship game. When I watched him walk off the floor, he was bigger than life to me. He was my brother and my hero. Frankly, he still is today. When I got home from the game, I spent the next two hours shooting baskets at my old hoop nailed to a power pole just off the left side of the garage. My mother flashed the porch light signaling to me it was time to hit the winning shot, finish the game, come into the house, and get ready for bed. My mother knew the highlight of my life was to watch both my older brothers play ball for the Locust Squirrels. She always made sure I had the 10 cents it cost to get into the game and 10 cents to buy a bottle of coke and candy between the seventh-grade game and the eighth-grade game. What she did not know was that I saved the second 10 cents. Even through the coke and candy would have been an amazing treat, I could not afford to take the chance that my mom would come up a little short on money and I would not be able to attend the next scheduled game.

The old gym is gone now, but I still remember exactly how the gym was laid out. It had an enormous wooden pull-up stage at one end, about two feet from the visitor's end line. An old wood-burning stove sat about three feet off the court at the mid-court line. The players' parents were responsible for keeping the stove fueled and red hot the entire night. The fathers were also responsible for catching any players chasing a loose ball near that old stove. I remember the fans for our team lining up around the stove at half time to warm up their freezing cold hands and feet. Most of the adult conversations related to what was going on in the communities and who would win the next county election.

Rivalries were at an all-time high back in those good old days. This meant the visiting fans were not welcome to the heat from the stove, and they certainly did not want to force their way up to the stove if any of the hometown fans were still getting warm.

Hey, Kate do not laugh; we were the Squirrels and very proud of it.

Kate jumped to her feet and performed her first official cheer.

"Give me an S" "S"

"Give me a Q" "Q"

"Give me a U" "U"

"Give me an I" "I"

"Give me an R" "R"

"Give me an "R" "R"

"Give me an "E" "E"

"Give me an "L" "L"
"Give me an "S" "S"
'What does that spell?"
"Squirrels! Go squirrels!"
Thank you Kate, your cheer was special and it warms my heart.

The Locust Squirrels were always able to put superb teams on the floor. When my two older brothers played, it took the team to an even a higher level. Letting up on the pressure and intentionally letting a team score just because we had them down by 35 points, was not an option. Our coach was one hell of a coach. She (that's right, she) liked to win. However, mostly she expected our players to perform in her classroom just as they did on the floor. She was a magnificent coach, but most of all she loved to teach. She did not need Title-9 to get what she wanted in sports. The players respected her, and she knew the players, students, and the fans had her back. She felt better about one of her students solving complicated algebra equations than she did for one of her players to hit a great shot to win the game.

Two incidents come to mind when I think about our Locust teams. In the middle of a blowout one night, I remember a little guard named Shorty, of all things, from Worthville ran into the stage full speed while attempting to shoot a layup, and the stage won. The coach of the Worthville team claimed my oldest brother had actually pushed Shorty into the stage from behind. He informed the referee that my brother needed to be ejected from the game. In addition, he also wanted my brother to not play in the next week's scheduled game. The next game just happened to be against Worthville at their place. The coach really wanted him out of the game since he had already scored 35 points. He would have likely hit for 60 that night if the game continued. The Worthville team was down 23 points at the time of the incident. Once the coach realized the referee was not going to buy his story, he went over to Shorty, who was still lying on the floor. Shorty somehow had miraculously managed to crawl from the front of the stage under the basket to out near the half-court line on the floor. Shorty was a terrific player but a bit of a crowd pleaser. Now that I am older, I can see why the folks from Worthville loved him so much. The coach whispered something into Shorty's ear. The next thing we knew, Shorty went limp as an old mop. His coach picked Shorty up off the floor and starts carrying him to the dressing room. Just before he exited the floor, several of the Locust squirrels fans witnessed Shorty go from acting as if he had been knocked unconscious to smiling at the coach. The victory went to the Squirrels because the coach walked off the floor. Nevertheless, the bad judgment by the coach was enough to justify the fight after the game.

A few weeks later, the fans from English orchestrated the ultimate attempt to pay back the Squirrels. It was near the end of the game, and the Squirrels were beating the English team something awful and were showing no sign of letting up. Suddenly, with about two minutes to go in the game, the doors to the school gym flew open. Undoubtedly, it was an inside job. The Sutherland and Short families decided to ride their motorcycles up the ramp and into the gym. Before the player's parents could get control, they were popping wheelies and burning rubber on the playing floor. This floor was like sacred ground to the Squirrels. The game was stopped, and the fight was on. Keep in mind not every game ended in a fight, and I cannot remember a time when anyone was actually hurt in any of those fights. Most were just a lot of yelling and screaming at each other. God what a great time it was to be a Locust Creek Squirrel.

My mother knew my older brothers liked to play basketball, but she knew I had to play ball to be myself. I know for many it is just an old wives tale, but I actually did sleep with my basketball. I went to sleep nearly every night imagining being in the championship game with my team down one point with six seconds to play and the ball in my hand for the winning basket. I spent hour after hour pretending I was one-on-one with some of the greatest basketball players in the world. I beat them all with some long distance shot described by the announcer at the time as a miracle shot never attempted before. Mom knew somehow that I would eventually become a top-level basketball player. No one would stand in my way. She would clear out my path and help me when she could.

She also knew I had spent my summer vacation prior to entering the 7th grade getting up at four o'clock in the morning. I had to finish my regular chores before noon each day, and I spent the rest of the day working for a local farmer to earn the money I needed to play basketball and cover my expenses once the season started.

The owner of the farm seemed to have kept track of my life ever since the bull attack. Somehow, he just knew I would make him proud someday. Many years later, I remember looking up in the stands before our biggest game ever and making eye contact with the farmer. Just before the tip-off, he clasped his hands tightly together and placed them over his heart as he bowed his head. I knew he was praying, but I was not sure if he was praying for us to win the game or if he was thanking God for giving him the privilege of being there for such an important game.

Twenty-One

The War Within

A referee was about to toss up the basketball at mid-court to start the second half of the 1972 Kentucky High School 8th Regional tournament game. As we broke the huddle, I realized for the first time this was it. We had made it, and now it was up to us to finish off the dream. We had committed seven years of our lives for this moment. Winning the regional championship meant we would be representing the Carroll County Panthers in the Boy's Kentucky High School State Basketball Tournament for the first time in the school's history. This tournament was one of the most elite basketball tournaments in the world. College basketball coaches from most major colleges attended the tournament in hopes of finding their next great player.

It may not sound like a big deal for a small school to set a goal to win the regionals instead of the state tournament as it is today. Keep one thing in mind: no small school had ever won the 8th regional end of the season tournament in modern history.

My mind, for a brief moment, slipped back in time. When I peeked up into the bleachers, I saw the people who provided the players on the floor the opportunity of a lifetime. I started thinking about all of the things this team had been through to get to this point. I remembered how the leaders in the community had pulled together to bring all of the super-small county schools together into one school system. The schools included in the merger were Worthville, Ghent, Sanders, Carrollton, English, Prestonsville, and Locust Creek. The transition to one county school was difficult for all of the students. The change meant only the best of the best players from each of the six communities could try out to play on the school basketball teams.

Many citizens in the community were concerned about the merger. The county seat was Carrollton, and the population of Carrollton was 10 times the population of the other six districts combined. Would the athletes in the small communities get a fair chance to make the teams? The county children, made up mostly of tobacco-farming families, had additional chores the city kids did not have. Would they be excused from practices when the tobacco crop needed to be planted, cut, and when it was time to strip the leaves from the stalk for sale in the middle of basketball season?

Keep in mind this small school is in North Central Kentucky, and in Kentucky, basketball is king, followed by beautiful horses and bluegrass. The state bird is the cardinal, and the flower is the goldenrod. The tree is the tulip popular. Kentuckians do not like change and will get disturbed when someone wants to change their way of life.

"My Old Kentucky Home" is a song that brings tears, laughter, and hope for millions of men, women, and children across the planet when played just before the most viewed sporting event in the world, the Kentucky Derby. For many, it is a song about hard times. It becomes easy to reflect on the words of the song as they relate to their personal lives. Nevertheless, when the gate opens and the caller says, "They're off!" people of all races, colors, and creed are able to set everything aside and cheer for our four-legged friends as if they were a member of their own family for the next two minutes.

For Kentuckians, the song makes us think of a small, long-legged foal trying to get up onto his wobbling legs for the first time. Instead of taking its first steps to nurse on its mother, it first takes a lap around the track. The owners dream that someday soon they might be watching the foal break from the gate and win the run for the roses at the Kentucky Derby.

In basketball, the song makes us think of our son or daughter attempting to take their first steps. Mom, dad, and grandparents scream and cheer,

"You can do it; I know you can do it!" Instead of the baby taking its first steps to Mom or Dad, the child goes over to the corner of the room and attempts to pick up a basketball. Within a few days following those first steps, a basketball backboard and goal is nailed to a structure directly in line of sight of the baby's crib. The backboard and goal will be the last thing the child sees every night before closing its eyes to sleep. For those of us who have been there, we know what causes those small smiles you see in the corner of his or her face as they sleep: it is the dream of hitting a thirty-foot shot to win the game. It really does not matter what game; it could be to beat a sibling or a last second shot to win the Thanksgiving Day family tournament in the backyard or even the final shot to win the regional or Kentucky state basketball tournament.

Every game to a ball player in his or her mind is the biggest game and their most amazing win of all time. You will find them playing on their court in a driving rainstorm—in weather conditions so cold, their hands get numb when they touch the ball. Sometimes when the snow gets deep enough, all a ball player can do is carry the ball around the court and catch it as it comes through the basket to prevent it from landing in the snow. The snow would stick to the ball, making it almost impossible to get a good grip for the next shot. I hate it when the snow sticks to my basketball even today at the age of sixty.

Moms want their kids to come in the house where it is safe, dads say, "Leave them alone," and coaches, well, coaches would stop traffic on a busy interstate in the middle of the day to watch a child hit his final shot of the day.. "My Old Kentucky Home" is a great state song, and you should consider looking it up on the internet and playing the lyrics.

The county school parents' concerns ended when the final list of players who made the team was display on the bulletin board next to the principal's office. The list included former players from all of the small communities.

Maybe it was luck or possibly it was good planning by the community leaders. However, most think it had everything to do with building a winning team to help establish a new school with a winning tradition. People who have never lived in the State of Kentucky will never understand why basketball is so important to our way of life.

Twenty-Two

Time to Practice

The schools hired new coaches for each of the teams in Carroll County. We had two school gyms to practice in, but we had to play all scheduled games in the high school gym. For most of the older groups, the first few practices did not go very well. Players spent more time arguing and fighting with each other than they did practicing. After all, these same players had been bitter opponents just the previous year playing for their small school teams.

Even through most of our 7th grade, team players had been playing ball since our first steps as a baby. We were the first group to have never played against each other. Our team consisted of the best athletes in the entire county. It became apparent this team was special when after only three weeks of practicing together, we scrimmage and beat the 8th-grade team. Two weeks after that game, we scrimmaged and beat the high school junior varsity team in front of a packed gymnasium. Many of the fans leaving the gym after the game sincerely felt we could have beaten the high school varsity team if it were not for their superior size.

The people in the community loved basketball. They became very excited to know that within a few years they would have a team that could likely compete and win the district and, who knows, maybe even the eighth region.

I still remember what our head coach told us during our last practice before the regular season was to begin. He was a good and honest man, and we believed in him. He told us if we played together and work as a team, we could easily go undefeated for the season. He had been coaching a long time. He had coached many gifted athletes in his time, but this group of players was without a doubt very special. He felt in his heart that our future was going to be exciting to watch.

He wished us all a happy thanksgiving weekend with our family and asks us to include our school, its leaders, and the team in our prayers. The team's first game was scheduled for the Monday night following the Thanksgiving holiday break.

We could not wait to get our first win toward an undefeated season. The team was to travel to Madison, Indiana and take on the Saint John's Knights. The scouting report pointed out that the Knights consisted of some of the most talented players recruited from all over the State of Indiana.

Twenty-Three

Our First Setback

The practice ended, and I was looking forward to a four-day weekend. I really needed some time away from the court for the blisters on the bottoms of my feet to heal up. Besides, I loved spending time with all of my brothers and sisters and our extended family. A number of my brothers and sisters were married, but all felt obligated to come home for the holidays due to an individual request by our mother. I finished my shower and prepared for the ten-mile walk home. I made the walk each day from the gym to my house located in Hunter Bottom near Locust Creek. I was hoping to have a peaceful journey, but I knew it would be difficult since practice ended late and darkness had already set in. Soul was not much help. Not only did he still have courage issues, he was afraid of the dark.

When I tried out for the team, my parents made it clear to me that this was an extracurricular activity. They would not be able to pick me up each day from practice. They also made it clear that the money needed to cover the expenses related to playing school sports was not in the family budget. I think my dad really wanted me to play ball. Some of his greatest pleasures came from watching his boys play ball at the small gym on Locust Creek. He was worried the city kids would somehow mistreat the country children and even possibly try to bully and make fun of us. My mother stepped in immediately and told my dad she was ashamed of him to think such a thing. She told him that in her eyes, all of his children were special. "This one has a gift to play ball, and he going to play ball. I think the kids at school are smart enough to know that when they mess with one Clifton child there are thirteen more waiting in line to defend the first."

Just to make the point clear to him, she reminded him of an incident earlier in the school year. The students riding the school bus consisted of children living in the Locust Creek-Hunters Bottom community. Several seniors rode the bus and all felt they had the right to bully the rest of the younger children every day. Many of the younger children would get off the bus at their homes each day in tears. They were scared to death due to the bullying going on during the trip home. To make matters worse, the bus driver's children were the ringleaders. One day, one of the biggest bullies of all decided it was time to pick on one of the Clifton children. Big mistake!

The Clifton children were, prior to the start of each school year instructed by our parents to get on the bus each day, find a seat next to each other, and keep our mouths shut except to talk to each other. The bully was a senior in high school with a gigantic and lean physique. One day he decides to get off the bus at our stop. He had told the other bullies he was going beat up my oldest brother while the bus driver held the bus so all the others bullies on the bus could watch. We were also taught to not to fight unless we were defending each other or ourselves. The bully walked up to my oldest brother and hit him in the eye with his big fist. Then he picks my brother up and attempted to throw him onto the highway into oncoming traffic.

I moved about 45 feet away, which was about the distance from home plate to the pitcher mound in the field next to our house where we all played baseball each day. I pick up a piece of round gravel about the shape and size of a regulation baseball from the gravel lane leading to our house. I told the bully to put my brother down and to leave us alone. The bully just laughed and put down my brother. He told the rest of the bullies on the bus to watch him punch my lights out. As he turned to walk toward me, I told him he was making a big mistake. I showed him the stone. I warned him if he took another step toward my family or me, I would hit him right between the eyes with the piece of gravel. All of my brothers and sisters were standing behind me and were out of harm's way. My oldest sister knew the bully's name. She advised him to get back on the bus before he got hurt. He just laughed and said to his audience that after he punched my lights out he was going to beat up my sister. Second big mistake! Our father taught my brothers and me at a very young age that we should never hit one of our sisters. Even if they were beating the heck out of us, we could never beat up a girl. Any male who hits a girl was really just a coward.

The bully felt he had to back up his words. He could not back down with all of his friends watching from the windows on the bus. My younger brother next to me in age told him, "He has the courage to do it and will not miss. Please do not take another step toward us." Final big mistake! When I saw him lift his left foot to lunge toward me, I released the stone. The stone hit him directly between the eyes, and he fell to the ground. I leaned over and picked up another stone as the bully got back to his feet. He looks at me and saw my arm was in a position and ready to deliver the next stone. He dropped his head and motioned he had had enough. He returned to the bus, and as the bus driver pulled away, we could all hear a silence on the bus, clearly indicated to us the bullying was over for good. We went directly home and told Mom what had happened. My little brother was the most excited when he was describing how I told the bully I was going to hit him right between the eyes and then did it. He told Mom I was going to be a great pitcher someday. What he did not know was my mother had as much to do with my ability to control a baseball as I did.

We had a standing rule that if I ever hit one of my sisters while at bat in the family games with a fastball, my next step would be to pick out a switch from our old hickory tree next to the garden that she would use to spank my butt. She did have her way of getting her point across when it came to disciplining the children. In most cases, it did not take a second time to get the point.

It did not take long for the news to circulate throughout the schools about what had happened on the bus. The message was clear: if you messed with one on the Clifton children, you would likely get a visit from the other thirteen. As it turned out, one of the parents of the younger children had already reported the bullying to the local sheriff. Once the police finished the investigation, the seniors were suspended from ever riding the bus again, and the bus driver was fired from the job. Mom had to instruct the rest of us to stop making fun of my oldest brother for using his eye to stop the bully's fist.

My dad listened to what my mother had to say about me playing ball. Nevertheless, he still knew it would be very difficult for me to balance my schedule. He had a hard time visualizing how I could go to practice every day, travel to away games two nights a week, maintain my good grades, and do my farm chores each day. Even though he never mentioned it again, I still believe he felt I should have stepped down and given my position to the city boys with families who could afford the expenses to play school sports.

My mother knew how much basketball meant to me. The basketball passion bug bit me when I was only three years old. The only cure for the bug was a new basketball every birthday and Christmas and watching my shot go through the hoop. At bedtime, my brothers and sisters would spend our last thoughts of the night talking to each other about what we thought we would be getting for Christmas each year. My oldest sister would always tell the group the only thing she knew for sure was I would be getting the same gift I got last year. The rest would chime in, "We know, a basketball." We would have a good laugh. After that, my next to oldest sister would send us into dreamland with her beautiful version of "Silent Night." She had a beautiful singing voice but could never overcome stage fright. Dad would tell her it was okay, as he was sure her best audience was the angels in heaven. When she sang, Soul seems to always stop and listen. He would follow up what my father said to her with an "Amen. Dad, you can take it to the bank." When she was older, she finally overcame her fear by singing in front of a packed house. She was the solo vocalist at the annual church Christmas play. I was so proud of her for sharing her talent with the congregation. They heard what all of her siblings had been enjoying for many years, and she received a standing ovation. To my knowledge, at least thirty years passed before she would again sing as a soloist in public. She always received a standing ovation regardless of what song she chose to sing.

Twenty-Four

NOT AGAIN

As I made my way through town from practice, I started to lose the lights from the streets as I reached the end of the Carrollton city limits. The moon was full and filled the sky with the light I needed to see my way across the bridge over the Big Kentucky River. It also lit the path well into the first major bend in the highway heading to the second bridge. The second bridge was over the Little Kentucky River and was a very difficult bridge to walk across in the daylight hours. It had no pedestrian walkway, and I had been a little afraid to cross the bridge for some time. A car had hit a man a few months earlier, and he landed in the river below. The man did not survive the fall. I always checked for headlamps from any oncoming traffic, and when the coast was clear, I did a hard sprint to the other end of the bridge. This seemed to be a safe procedure, and I had not had any narrow escapes with oncoming traffic. I had made this trip every day after school for six weeks, but this particular night things were very different.

Maybe it was because it was a holiday weekend, but for some reason, there was no traffic on Highway 36. I felt all alone, and Soul was already nervous and seemed to be more fidgety than normal. As I made my way past the last service station, which was already closed-down for the weekend, I started to hear noises. The sounds were different, and it took a while for me to figure out where the noises were coming from. Keep in mind I was a country boy; I had spent many nights out hunting and had even completed my farm chores well after dark. I was not afraid to work in the dark. As I walked toward the 'Y' that connected Highway 36 to Madison, Indiana and US-42 to Louisville, Kentucky, I found the source of the strange noise. The Little Kentucky River was flowing extremely fast. It was well out of its banks as it emptied into the mighty Ohio River. It had been raining steady for three days and nights. At the 'Y', I would take the Highway 36 route, which was a very narrow two-lane road. The road made its way through a carved out section at the bottom of a vast and steep wooded hillside on one side and the mighty Ohio River is on the other.

The Ohio River was also well outside of its banks. It was flowing fast and had an unusual roar as it flowed past me. The large hillside blocked the light from the moon, and as I walked along the edge of the road, the river appeared to get louder and louder. It sounded much closer to the road than I had remembered in the past. The river was already over a mile wide in that stretch of the road when it was running normally. At one point, I noticed the river was splashing up onto the highway. I found myself praying I could get past the lower elevations before the river went completely over the road. The real danger was if the river crossed the road behind me and in front of me; I would be a trapped without a good way to escape.

When I left town, the temperature was in the mid-thirties but it certainly felt like it was dropping fast. My ears and fingers were feeling the change in temperature. I was now completely in the dark and could barely see the road. At one point, I tripped over something lying in the road and fell very hard to the payment. I was able to drop my bare hands to the pavement and catch myself before my face hit the hard blacktop surface, but Soul was shaking uncontrollably. I decided I would need to pick up the pace. I was trying to get my body temperature up, even though it was difficult to see the road without the help of the light from the full moon. I kept telling myself I was fine and the journey would be over soon enough.

After about forty-five very scary minutes walking and at times running down the narrowest and darkest stretch of road, I reached the Locust Creek

Bridge. The bridge was the last of the three bridges on my route home. The bridge was just past the tallest peak of the hillsides blocking the light from the moon. The moon once again provided the light I needed to see the road. Once I reached the bridge, I knew I had only about four miles to go until I was home. I envisioned the warmth from the coal-burning stove in the family room. The Locust Creek Bridge was much shorter than the previous bridges, and again it did not have a sidewalk. I knew it would not be a problem since I had not seen a vehicle for almost ninety minutes. The roar of the Ohio River was getting quieter since it was moving away from the highway.

Locust Creek was also flowing fast and once the raging waters cleared the bridge it would empty into the Ohio River. I hear a loud crash near the center of the bridge. It was a large tree dislodged from a beaver dam upstream. It hit the bridge deck very hard and caused the water to splash over the side of the bridge up onto the road. I felt the bridge shake as the tree wedged itself into the bridge. It was just barely hanging onto the side rail of the bridge, and the water started to run up onto the highway on each end of the bridge. This meant the water was more than 25 feet deeper than normal. The Ohio River and Locust Creek finally crashed into each other, and the noise sounded like a loud clap of thunder. I was now surrounded by rushing floodwaters and had no choice but to wade through the water before the bridge became completely flooded. If I did not get on with it quickly before the bridge flooded, it would mean another 15 miles through the hills and backwoods to get home. As I stepped into the water, my shoes and socks were immediately soaked. Within a few seconds, I could feel the sting of the cold water on my feet. The water was about 18" deep, and by the time I reached the other side, it was up to my waist. My clothes were now soaked, and I must admit I could feel my heart pounding through my chest. It was a very freighting experience. I knew once I made it across the bridge and started up a steep grade known as Long's Hill, I would be out of danger.

At times when we were very young I could feel Soul's mental state of mind revert to being so scared he became motionless. I think God knew this was about to happen. He always seemed to come to our aid. As I walked down the other side of Longs Hill into a deep ravine and just before a river-bottom farm named Mother Farms, I felt a feeling I had not felt since the day in the Blackberry patch just before the first bull attack. The closer I got to the final turn onto Conway's Lanes, the sounds of the night seemed to get closer and more proncunced. Soul had felt the same feeling and was going crazy. I tried to settle him down. I know he was afraid, and he started questioning why we were out here in this much danger and if playing ball was really worth the dangers and the risks always present in a rural community.

When Soul finished his speech, I did my first of many coaching jobs. I said, "Soul, I need you to grow up and stop acting like a baby. Stop talking like a loser. Understand that anything I will achieve in life will probably require me to take chances—to go beyond the call of duty to get what others have handed to them. I am not a quitter, and you need to get used to the idea. We will make this journey hundreds of more times. I know I will need to develop as much courage as possible, and soon." I told him I was scared to, but I would not quit. I told him I wished he loved me as much as I loved him, and I told him I would take a bullet for him. I reminded him he was my guardian angel, personally assigned to me by the highest authority in the universe. "What I need most from you was during times like this is for you to tell me it is going to be okay—you have my back every time no matter what the dangers are ahead." I told him it was time for him to make a choice. He could be my guardian angel sent to me to find his courage or he could go on being a loser and excuse maker. It was time for him to stop feeling sorry for himself. I said, "Soul, I hope you can understand this: I am going to do this and I am going to be successful and take advantage of every opportunity as it presents itself to me. It will be with you or without you. It is your choice."

We walked for several minutes without saying a word to each other. I knew God was listening, but he never said a word. He never sent me a sign he was upset with what I said to Soul. I think what I shared with Soul might have been an example of tough love we all need to hear sometimes to get our attention.

Finally, Soul broke the silence and said, "You know the thing you said about loving me?" I said yes. "Would you really take a bullet for me?" Again

I said yes in a heartbeat. "Hum," he said, as he stroked the left side of his chin with his right hand. "It has been a long time since someone told me those words." There was another long pause before he said, "It feels good. I think you have always felt this way about me, haven't you?" I said yes, from day one. He said, "You know, sometimes those words needs to be said aloud to the ones you love. You should not just assume someone knows how much you care about him or her." There was another long pause. After several minutes of complete silence, Soul said, "Thank you coach." I could tell he wanted to say that he loved me, but the words just would not come out. I knew at the time I touched him deeper than he had been touched emotionally in a long time. I also knew Soul did not lightly, throw words around like "I love you." He was saving those words for a time when I would need to hear them to help me get through a tragic moment I will write about in future stories.

As we walked down the remaining stretch of Highway 36 to Conway's lane, the only prevailing noise was the sound of the water squishing inside my shoes. Soul broke out into a song he titled "Squish, Squish, Squishy, Squish, Squish." It sounds goofy, but it did have a good beat to it. It also took my mind off how cold my feet were getting. Soul finally stopped singing and went to sleep.

Once we turned onto Conway's Lane, I knew we would have a few more scary moments but that it would not take long to get home. Once we got past the clearing, we would walk past a family cemetery. The graveyard was spooky to walk past during the daylight hours and double as spooky at night. The next landmark was the last one but the most dangerous. Over the years, several wild animal attacks resulted in the death of numerous cattle and even a large Hampshire hog. The landmark was a cattle guard over Conway creek. This cattle guard was a manmade bridge, and its primary use is for vehicles and foot traffic to cross to the other side of the creek while not allowing a path for the cattle to cross the bridge.

The cattle guard was about 7-feet wide and 20-feet in length and spanned the creek below. The problem with walking across the bridge was that there was a narrow 10-inch walk path. It was very difficult to maintain your balance. Several people had fallen off the side of the cattle guard into the creek, and some had broken their legs by slipping between the 6-inch steel pipes. The design of the bridge/cattle guard was the last thing on my mind. Balance had never been an issue for me. I had spent years developing my leg muscles and could actually jump the bridge with a running start.

I was more concerned with what people had told us about seeing an albino wolf who had taken up residence under the cattle guard.

Then I happened to remember a conversation I had overheard between my dad and my sister's boyfriend. He said he saw a huge albino wolf run across the road in front of him on his way back down the lane from a date with my sister. I figured at the time that he was just saying what he said to try to scare me. I assumed he was just spinning another one of his wild stories as he had done in the past. Besides, he was an even bigger chicken than Soul. If he had seen the big bad wolf he was describing to my dad, he likely would have never come back down the lane again—or he would have insisted my sister meet him at the end of the drive near the main road for the next date...city boys.

I told myself to keep cool and ordered Soul to relax and told him we would be home soon. I reminded him we had made this trip more than thirty times in the past six weeks without incident. Soul did calm down until we had once again lost the light from the full moon. It was time to cross the cattle guard over Conway's Creek, which had several blind spots. It was also within a few feet of where the boyfriend had claimed to see the albino wolf. Due to the darkness, I decided it would be too dangerous to attempt to run and jump the bridge. I chose to walk across the concrete walk path on the right side of the bridge. This was the cattle-side of the lot, and if I were to slip and fall off the bridge, at least I would be dealing with cattle instead of swine. The swine under the bridge had mammoth tusk, and if they were to get a hold on me, they could easily crush anything they had in their mouths.

Once I reached the other side, I could feel the hair stand up on the back of my neck. Then all hell broke loose. I heard growling, and I could see the sharp teeth of the albino wolf. He crawled from beneath the bridge.

The wolf's body was snow white, but his eyes were ruby red. His eyes look like the eyes of the devil. Soul screamed at the top of his lungs, "Run! We are only a mile from the house! I am not ready to die yet!" As I started to sprint toward the light on the front porch of our house, I could feel the wolf getting closer. I knew I could not out run him, so I started looking for something to defend Soul and me with. I had my gym bag on my back, but I knew that would not defend us. The wolf was within five feet of us and was ready to make his final lunge on my back to take me down to the ground. As I ran, Soul asked, "What is that noise? And why is the ground shaking?" Then, out of nowhere, the bull was eyeball to eyeball with me, and I was out in the open and had no place to hide. For the first time, I felt Soul may be right—that our journey together was over. We had a wolf just a few feet away who wanted to devour us for supper and a mad bull ready to drive his sharp horns through my chest.

We had not seen or had heard anything about the bull since the night my dad pulled up his gun and let the bull surrender into the woods. It had been nearly five years since that incident. I could not imagine why the bull had been out of sight for so long. Why he had teamed up with the wolf was hard to understand. As the bull charged toward me, I knew it was over. All I could say was, "Sorry Soul," and I closed my eyes in preparation for the bull's horns and head to strike my body. I felt the bull brush my side on his way past me and could not understand how in the world he had missed me from that distance. Then I heard a bone-chilling scream from behind me. As I quickly turn in the direction of the bull, I could see the wolf flying through the air. Then I saw the bull pin the wolf between his head and the ground. The wolf appeared to be begging the bull to spare his life. The bull backed off the pressure and released the death hold he had on the wolf. He seemed to tell the wolf, "When you mess with him, you are messing with me, so do not ever let it happen again." The bull released the wolf's body and allowed him to limp off into the woods.

The bull turned and looked at me with contentment and appeared to smile. He gently pawed the ground as if he were sending a message to my mother. I think he was signaling that he had found peace in his heart. He had fulfilled his mission and now it was time to return to the mountain to start a new family. The bull suddenly let out a loud sound I had not heard in the past. He appeared to be saying, "Farewell to all; it is time for me to go home." He slowly moved his head across the field as if he were looking for someone to join him on his trip back to the mountain. Then he turned his head back toward me. We made eye contact, but there were no good-byes. Something told me it would not be the last time I would see the bull. I dropped to my knees and thank God for protecting Soul and me. I got back to my feet and walked the rest of the way home. I knew I could never tell anyone about what had happened to Soul and I on our journey home, and I never did.

My mother asked me when I walked through the door if I was okay and how I got so wet. She said she felt something was going on, but it was a peaceful feeling and she liked it. She told me to get next to a warm fire to allow my clothes to dry and that she had saved me some supper as I gave her a hug. Then, unexpectedly, she whispered in my ear that she knew it was finally over. I told her the bull was at peace and was going home.

She said she had asked dad to come out and find me, but he told her I was fine. I was twelve years old, and the next day I would join the annual Thanksgiving Day hunt. It was time for me to grow up, and he refused to come out and find me. My mother was 8 months and 3 weeks pregnant with one of my younger brothers. She did not have the strength to debate the issue with him. She also knew I was not looking forward to the hunt; I did not like to kill animals for any reason. My clothes did dry, and the meal was incredible as usual. I went to the barn and milked and fed the rest of the animals in the barn before turning in for the night.

Twenty-Five

Happy Holidays "Right"

The next morning was Thanksgiving. It meant we could sleep in a little late and do the chores later in the day than usual. I was excited for a number of reasons. My entire family and now our extended family would get to be together for the first time since Independence Day. In addition, once the weekend was over, I would finally get to wear my school uniform and play the first basketball game of my career. Thanksgiving in the sixties seemed more like a spiritual holiday than a day of fellowship as it was between the pilgrims and Native Americans in the beginning. The one similarity was the feast would be on the table at exactly twelve o-clock: high noon. Once the feast was over, my family would meet on the basketball court and the game was on for the next couple of hours. I learned quickly that it was less painful for me to shoot the ball from 25-30 feet from the basket. The first time I tried to drive to the basket for a short shot, my oldest brother hammered me to the court.

The next activity was the one I was dreading the most. It was a big celebration of me coming of age and joining the traditional family Thanksgiving Day hunt. My father was especially proud of the tradition and actually enjoyed his time with his kids. He was a great hunter and had taught all of us to be expert shooters by the age of twelve. My mother stepped up her level of concern when dad announced this year's hunt would be a little different from in the past. Normally it was just him and his sons that were twelve and older. This year he invited my brother-in-laws to join the hunt. This idea made my sisters a little nervous. You could tell this announcement was a big surprise to them. Most of my married sisters were not sure if their husbands were capable of handling a gun with a large group of hunters. My mother became very angry, but my dad was not finished with the announcements. When he announces the final change, my mother was so upset she just went into the house. She went into the house to avoid demeaning her husband in front of the family. You see, there is a thin line between love and support. Good marriages learn those boundaries quick.

My father announces we would be moving the hunt from our farm, which was about 400 acres, to a much smaller farm. The farm was about 5 miles from our house. We would need to walk about five miles off the main highway to get to the hunting area. My oldest brother told my father he preferred to stay closer to home; he really did not see the need to move the hunt. However, he too knew any additional words would be disrespectful of our father.

A few minutes passed, and dad announced it was time for all of us to meet him at the old Ford station wagon. In his mind, Ford was the only car made in America. He would not own any others manufacturer's car.

He went up to my mother to give her a goodbye kiss. This was apparently a requirement between the two of them even if they were upset with each other. We could tell she would have rather nailed his big toe to a stump and then set the stump on fire to keep him from following through with his plan. Nevertheless, all she said to him was "Please be overly cautious and bring my boys home alive and unharmed." He touched her belly and told her to calm down—to take care of their unborn child and everything was going to be all right. He would be in control of the hunt and no one was going to get hurt. Her last words were that she had a bad feeling about the hunt. Thank God he did not share with her the rest of the program.

Dad announces it was time for the hunt, and we placed our guns in the back of the station wagon and finished preparing for a trip to the farm. The route required us to drive past the old Locust schoolhouse. This brought back so many great basketball memories of my older brothers playing ball in the old gym. Then we traveled alongside Locust Creek, which had calmed down considerably since the night before. The creek had left piles of debris along the sides of the road but was now back in its banks. It was harmless compared to just 24 hours earlier. Dad pulled the station wagon onto the side of the road and into an open field. We carefully retrieved our guns from the back. We started the 5-mile walk up a steep hill and eventually to a clearing to an open ridge area. The peak seemed to run on forever. My father bent down and picked up a handful of black, fertile top soil. He told us he had an opportunity to buy this farm. We could tell he was excited about the possibilities. He envisioned us raising hay and tobacco on the land. He would build a new house to live in. He told us the land had never been touched by a plow and was still exactly the way the Native Americans had left it. As we continued to walk parallel to the ridge, we finally came upon a small cabin. We could smell the scent of firewood burning in the fireplace. I must admit I was a little chilled, and the thought of a fire to warm my hands was very appealing. As we approached the cabin, three men walked out to greet my father. My father introduced the rest of us to his friends and to the current owners of the farm. Then he made his final announcement of the day. The three of them would be joining the hunt.

My family was not an alcohol drinking family. One of my brothers smelled liquor on the men's breath, and the odor raised a red flag with my two older brothers. Our mother told us to be very cautious around people drinking. Alcohol and guns were never a good idea, and I could tell the men caught my dad off guard. We could tell he was disappointed that he would need to deal with this issue, especially on a holiday.

My mother and fathers families did allow alcohol to flow freely in their home. In their minds, it was the root of many family arguments and even fights. Several of their family members had divorced after abuse by their spouse while being drunk from drinking too much liquor. Both were determined not to drink alcohol or allow alcohol in their home.

Twenty-Six

Soul Where Are You? Why Can't I See You?

One of the men asked my father to join him inside the cabin. He needed dad to provide medical care for a female German shepherd and collie mixed breed. She was a mother dog with a little male puppy. The mother was apparently living under the cabin and had given birth to a small puppy. The puppy had the same marking as the mother. He appeared to be in good shape. My father had attended veterinarian school on the GI bill shortly after returning home from World War II. He had treated hundreds of animals in the past.

My father asked one of the hunters what had happened to the mother. The hunter told Dad that just as they were arriving the day before, they heard the animals fighting behind the cabin. He went to see what the fight was about when he saw a coyote on top of the mother. He felt the only chance the mother would have was for him to shoot the coyote before he killed the mother. She was apparently attempting to prevent the coyote from killing her baby puppy. The hunter said he shot above the coyote's head with the first shot to try to scare him off the mother but he refused to release the mother and continued biting her throat.

Then he yelled at the coyote and got his attention. The coyote was startled to see the men and appeared to be running away. For some reason, he turned and charges one of the other hunters. The coyote knocked the man to the ground, and the third man had no choice but to take a shot at the coyote. Dad asked to see the coyote. The man said he had gotten away, but he was sure he wounded the animal and it would not return.

The hunters had moved the mother into the cabin and managed to get the bleeding stopped. He was trying to comfort the mother as much as possible. Dad took one look at the mother's severe wounds and knew there was very little he could do for her. The hunter said the little pup had a lot of spunk. He was attempting to join the fight to help his mother. He sounded like he was growling like a bear but would have been no match for the coyote. He said the baby had been crying all night and was starving. The mother was in too much pain to allow him to feed on her milk. Dad knew the mother was fading fast. She suffered internal injuries and significant loss of blood during the attack.

I wrote earlier in one of the stories that God put some people on this earth with natural ability to communicate with animals. My dad was one of those people. He seemed to know exactly what the mother was trying to tell him. She realized her baby needed her milk soon or it would die. My dad looked around the cabin and locates a large burlap sack. Dad instructed my oldest brother to fold the bag into four folds.

My father found a piece of flat steel about 18" wide and 20" long. He placed the steel in the fireplace just above the flames. Then he placed the burlap bag on top of the hot piece of steel. The bag heated up quickly to the proper temperature. Dad removed the bag from the plate and opened up the first fold. He borrowed a hunting knife from one of the hunters to cut two openings in the bag so it would slide over the mother legs. The mother cried in pain from the movement. Nevertheless, she seems to know exactly what was going on. Then Dad cut holes in the other fold and slid the bag over her front legs. Once the bag was in place and wrapped around the rest of the mother's body she seemed to relax, as the heat generated by the wrap helps improve her circulation and took away some of her pain.

My father sat down beside the mother. He hummed a tune I had never heard before. It was a spiritual song my father had learned from his best friend while sharing a foxhole in Japan. The mother laid her head in his lap as he gently stroked her forehead. I could see a tear running down her face. I did not know if it was from the pain from her wounds or the sadness of leaving her new baby, but she and Dad knew her time was almost up. But dad had helped her gain enough power to perform her last motherly act for her baby. With what appeared to be her last ounce of strength, she managed to push her milk down into her milk sack. It was obvious she was determined to produce the milk needed to feed her baby one last time.

I was holding the baby puppy. I had already named it Little Bear in honor of his last act of courage to help his mother fight off the coyote. Dad asked me to hand the puppy to him, and he placed it in front of his mother's head. She opened her eyes, stroked the puppy's head with her mouth, and finally licked his face with her tongue as if she were saying goodbye. Then dad placed the puppy near the only part of the mother's body not enclosed inside the burlap bag. The baby puppy latched on and started to suck the fresh milk he needed from his mother's sack. About three-fourths of the way through the feeding, the mother opened her eyes. She looked straight into my dad's eyes as if to say, "Thank you, and take care of my baby." Dad stroked the mother's face and felt her heart stop beating. He continued to hold her head until the puppy finished drinking the last drop of milk. Little Bear lay down beside his mother and went fast to sleep.

I told my dad I would take the puppy home with us and we would make it the family pet. My older brothers said they would help take care of him. He would probably make an excellent family pet. We agreed to leave the puppy with his mother until after the hunt. We would come back to the cabin, have a funeral for the mother, and take the puppy home with us. The mystery of where this mother had come from would likely always remain unsolved. The cabin was located five miles from the nearest farmhouse. Little Bear turns out to be a large dog, and he lived for almost twenty years. He produced a long line of offspring, which allowed my family to maintain the bloodline for six generations of Little Bears.

Dad apparently decided he could control the hunt and decided to move forward. He met with the entire hunting party and explained the plan to set up a single line across the field. We would only shoot at rabbits out in front of the line as we moved across the field. The ten hunters in the party were carrying enough firepower to defend a small country. Within a few minutes, it became apparent that the plan was not going to work. Some of the hunters were obviously inexperienced hunters. They did not realize they would need to walk without talking or making too much noise and were scaring the rabbits out of their nests well out of range of the shotguns. Dad decided to keep everyone happy; he would break the large group into four smaller groups. Each group was assigned to a particular area. We all agreed we would start from a central point. Once we reached the boundary fence, we would follow the exact same route back to the starting point. My group included my father and my older brothers. This was the first time all day I actually felt safe. We had been hunting for about two hours, and everyone in my group had their quota of rabbits but me. My brothers and dad unloaded their guns. They told me they would just walk along with me until I got my first kill.

Within a few minutes, we jumped a rabbit and I took the shot. My dad knew I had intentionally shot over the rabbit's head. I acted as if I was excited and wanted to go to where I had shot at the rabbit. He told me to go ahead, but he knew I had missed my target. The spot was about 75 feet ahead, and I started to run toward the place.

Suddenly I heard my father and both brothers yelling something at the top of their lungs in my direction. I could not understand what they were saying. The wind had started to blow and the words distorted by the time they reached my ears. I finally reach the spot where I had shot at the rabbit. I bent down to make sure I had really missed the rabbit. As I rose to my feet and I turned back toward my father and brothers, I noticed they were running as fast as they could toward me. They were pointing at something behind me, and I turned to see what was happening. I saw another group of hunters who had apparently decided not to follow the same route back to the point where we started the hunt. They were clearly in our zone. I figured out very quickly why my dad was upset. He was by far the most skilled hunter in the group—maybe the best hunter in the State of Kentucky. When he was young, he did not kill for the sport of it. His family depended on him to bring home the game they would eat for their next meal. If he failed, his family would go without meat and would possibly even go hungry the day.

My father had apparently picked up a sign indicating some quail in the area. He then realized I was standing in the middle of the flock. One wrong move would cause the birds to become spooked and they would attempt to fly. I immediately froze and decided I would wait for my dad and brothers to get to my position. Soul was not paying much attention to what was going on around him. He had apparently decided Thanksgiving was a good day to rest.

My brothers were now about 50 feet away from me. They were still trying desperately to warn the hunters rapidly entering into our hunting zone of my whereabouts. My father was attempting to load his gun while running full speed toward me. He was planning to fire a warning shot in the air to alert the other hunters. I think dad knew from the angle and the difference in elevation from where I was that the men approaching me would not be able to see me.

Soul was finally awake and attempting to figure out what all of the yelling and screaming was about. Within a few seconds, I found out just how much danger I was really in. Apparently, I moved just enough to cause the flock of quail around me to lift. I heard my dad scream out at me to hit the ground. Before I could react, I felt something strike my face as if someone had punched me with a fist. My chest felt like it was going to cave in. My legs were screaming with pain. I remember my lips and mouth suddenly went numb. The world around me became pitch black. My body felt like it was on fire, and I could not figure out why I was laying on the ground. While I was on the ground, I remember asking Soul if he knew what had happened, but he was silent.

My oldest brother was the fastest runner in my group. He was within a few feet from where I was standing. He made a heroic dive trying his best to knock me to the ground and out of the way of the blast. As he got back to his feet, I heard him scream to my dad that the three hunters had shot me in the face but I was still breathing. Then I felt my brother drop to his knees beside me. He begged God to spare my life. He said he would gladly take my place. He felt this was somehow his fault. He started asking himself why he could not have gotten there quicker. "Could I have jumped a little quicker and taken the blast myself? Why God, why did you let this happen to him? It just does not make any sense. God please let him live."

My dad and brother and the other four hunters all arrived at the same time. I wanted to speak, but for some reason none of the words would come out, and I could not move my body. I know my mind was there, and I remember everything said by the others. I knew everything happening around me, but I just could not get anybody to respond to me. My body was completely limp. I heard Soul say in a very distressed voice that he was sorry. "Please, forgive me. I let my guard down, but God is with us."

My father immediately asked the others hunters, "Which one of you did this to my son." Three of the four told my father they had shot into the flock of birds, but they did not see me.

Once he saw blood running down my pants leg, out around my waist, and streaming from my head, his biggest fear being realized. All three were direct hits to my legs, waist, and head. My dad dropped to his knees and gave me a hug. He told me he was sorry and he loved me with all of his heart.

You could tell he was having another flashback to a time in his life he had worked so hard to forget. Apparently, during the war, he had held a dying friend in his arms, shot by a Japanese soldier. You could tell he was not sure what to do or how to respond to the pain he was feeling in his heart. He could not see in his mind how I could have possibly survived such an accident. It took him a few minutes to regain his composure, and he checked me for a pulse. The hunters from the other groups arrive at the scene and asked what had happened. When they looked down at me, all they could say was, "Oh my God." Finally, one of the men we had met at the cabin and who had been my dad's best friend for 25 years leaned over and, with a very calm and sympathetic voice, asked if I was still alive.

Dad told him yes, but that I had a feeble pulse. His friend sat down beside him and put his hand on his shoulder. Dad appeared to be in shock as he told his friend I was going to be more than a ball player. He said I had the rare gift to not only see things as they are but also how they could be. His friend motioned to the others to give Dad his space—allow him some time to deal with what appeared to be the inevitable. His son was about to die and there was nothing anyone could do about it.

Dad told him a story about when I was eight years old and we were having a terrible year with the crops. "I overheard him talking to his mother one night about the weeds in the tobacco patch near the house. The weeds were growing so fast they could have eventually overtaken the tobacco plants. We could have lost the farm back to the bank. I went out to feed the livestock the next morning at 5 AM, and I saw someone in the middle of our tobacco field chopping down weeds. I went over to see who it was. It was this boy in my arms. He was working harder than any full-grown man I have ever met. When I asked him what he was doing, he told me he felt this would be a banner production year for the tobacco crop. All I needed to do is chop down the weeds and pull some loose dirt up around each of the plants. He had finished twenty rows using an old weeding hoe we had retired years ago. The handle was full of splinters and the blade on the weeding hoe was very dull. I could see the blisters already forming on both of his small hands. I asked him what I could do to help. He told me to go on to work and he had this covered. I shouldn't worry anymore about losing the farm."

The friend asked what he did. He said, "I went to the tool shed and retrieved him a new weeding hoe. I told his mother what he was doing and to take him some water and some lunch. When I got home from work, he had finished the weeding and pulling dirt up around every single plant. I could not find one weed still standing in the entire three-acre field. My point is, he did not see a terrible year, wrong tools, too many weeds to chop down, the blistering hot sun, or a blister on his hands. He just saw a banner crop needed to help pay the farm payment."

The friend asked how it turned out. My dad responded, "It was the best crop ever grown on the farm, and we sold it at a record price."

Dad looked up at his friend and said, "My God he was eight years old. How, why, where, did he get this vision? This idea he could make such a difference? It is as if when everybody else is ready to give up, he shifts into a new gear the rest of us do not have." While dad was telling the group his story, the friend was checking my vitals, which he felt were improving by the minute. His friend said, "Wow, sounds like he has a special gift. Let's not give up on him just as he did not give up on you."

The friend could see Dad was settling down and knew it was time to take control. He told Dad the small pulse was likely resulted from the loss of so much blood. He was also a soldier and seemed to be able to give dad some hope that I might make it. "His only chance to survive is for us to get the blood stopped and to get him to a hospital as quickly as we can." Dad let me go, and his friend took over. It did not take him long to realize all three blasts from the three hunters were direct hits.

My dad knew I was physically in excellent shape because of the intense practices and his friend was right. If we did not get professional medical care soon, I would likely go into shock from the pain I must have been feeling. I was a big kid for a 12-year-old and was already 5'10" tall. At first, my dad wanted to attempt to carry me across the ridge, down the steep hill to where the car was located some five miles away.

Finally, I regained my motor skills, and I was able to move. I let my dad know I was okay. It was a turning point, and you could feel the hope return to everyone. I asked him what had happened. He explained that my two brother-in-laws and one of my dad's best friends had shot me.

I could feel his renewed strength. He had to take control of the situation. I could feel all of the shooters' pain and regret in their hearts. They were very sorry, and any of the three would have gladly taken my place. My oldest brother-in-law had been a member of our family for several years. I loved him as much as I did my oldest sister. He was on his knees crying uncontrollably, as he felt his shot was the head shot. He could see no possible way for me to survive a shot from such a short distance away.

For some unknown reason, I asked the three men to squat down where I was laying. I told them, "No matter how all of this turns out, I know in my heart it was an accident."

The hot lead shot from the shotgun shells had started to cool down, and the burning pain was quickly subsiding. Once the shot cooled down, the entry wounds seemed to clot over and the blood stopped coming out. My face had swollen to twice its normal size, and I could not see any light. This was my biggest concern. I really did not know how many of the lead balls from the shotgun shells had actually made a direct hit with my eyeball nor how many more had landed around my eyes. I told my dad to forgive those responsible for the accident and to get me to the hospital.

I also told him I had walked to the hunt and I would walk to the car. I just needed someone to stand on each side of me to help me keep my balance. Once I got to my feet, I did feel a little dizzy, but I was not in much pain. For some reason, I felt very relieved and calm. I could not feel Soul. I knew he was scared and maybe too frightened to speak. This time I could understand how he felt, but I sure wished he would talk to me. I just felt if Soul were okay, I would be too.

Before we started the long walk to the car, I asked my brother in laws if they would go back to the cabin and give Little Bear's mother a proper burial. I reminded dad I wanted to adopt the puppy and that we needed to take him home with us tonight, as I knew it would not survive in the cabin without his mother.

As we continued to walk across the ridge, I started asking my brother if he wanted to race me to the car. He was dumbfounded and did not have a clue how to answer the question from someone who looked like they should be starring in a horror movie. Once we reached the top of the hill, I was growing fatigued and needed to rest. While we sat on some large rocks, I asked my dad what was on his mind. He said he was worried about me. He could not believe I was not in severe pain. I jokingly said to him that he really did not need to worry about me; he had to burn some brain cells figuring out how to break the news to my mother. I explained the pain I was feeling would be mild compared to the pain he was going to be in once she got finished with him, especially after promising her he would bring us all home in one piece.

I guess my dad sensed I was tired from the long walk. He also knew that the longer we sat there, the less sense I was making. He said we needed get moving and his urgency to get to the car was getting more intense with every step. We finally reached within a few hundred feet of the car, and I could no longer hold my balance. I fell to the ground. My dad picked me up in his arms and ran me to the car. He put me into the back seat, fired up the old Ford, and headed to the hospital in Carrollton. The hospital was about 15 miles from where the accident happened. I remember riding across Locust Creek and passed the school. Then, apparently, I was having trouble staying conscious. My stomach felt like it was starting to bleed. My brother started to sing a thanksgiving song titled "Over the River and Through the Woods to Grandma's House We Go." I am not sure why, but I started to sing with him. He later told me he was just trying to keep me from going to sleep. He said he was afraid if I went to sleep, I might never wake up.

Locust road at the time was a one-lane road. Oncoming traffic had to move well off the road to allow other cars to pass safely. If you happened to come upon a vehicle going the same direction you were traveling and they were driving slower than normal, the expectation was for the driver to pull far enough off the road to let you pass. I am not sure why the car in front of us was driving slowly or why he decided he was not going to pull over and let my dad go by. However, he finally got on my dad's nerves. Dad blew his horn, letting the driver in front know he needed to pass. The driver in front was determined he was not going to allow my father to pass. What the fellow did not know was my dad had actually built Locust road. He knew of a wider section of road coming up, and he was going to pass the person whether he liked it or not. As he pulled out to pass, my dad did not make eye contact, but I certainly did. Just as he passed, I put my face up against the window. The look on the driver's face was priceless. He must have thought he was in the middle of a horror movie. I could see his wife yelling at him as we passed, and he did pull off the road. Later, my second oldest sister told me he came to the hospital to check on my condition. He apologized to my dad for being such a jerk. My brothers have for many years continued to laugh at the look on the man's face.

Once we turned onto Highway 36, it was a quick trip to the edge of town. When Dad drove across the last bridge the city police were in position to provide an escort to the hospital. The hospital parking lot was full of cars, and people were standing in the area around the emergency room. The emergency team met me at the car with a stretcher, and the two of the three doctors who resided in the city went to work on me immediately. I heard the doctors ask my dad what happened. He told, "All three shots hit him in the front of his body. It appears the one in the face is the most dangerous." The doctors just shook their heads in disbelief. The doctors could not believe I was still alive. Surviving the blast from three different shooters at the same time was truly a Thanksgiving miracle.

Fortunately, one of the two doctors was an old military field doctor in a MASH unit during the Korean War. He had seen these types of gunshot wounds in the past. I was a little embarrassed when the nurses started cutting my shirt and blue Jeans off me. I remember something my mother had said about never leaving the house without putting on clean underwear. I am glad I listened, but it did not really matter since they cut my underwear off with the rest of my clothes. The doctors started an IV and then ordered a series of X-rays to locate the depth of the penetration of each of the shots. I could hear the doctors talking about damage to my body. They felt I had to be suffering from shock. They instructed the nurses not to leave me alone for any reason. They said to pray that the lead buckshot did not get picked up in my blood stream. If that happened and ended up in my heart or lungs, it would result in immediate death.

Finally, they decided to remove the lead shot from my legs and chest area. Most discussion was about the swelling in my face. They felt they needed to tell my family and me that the odds of me every seeing again were very slim. The X-rays clearly indicated at least 85 shots had hit me. Twenty-nine shots landed in my face and head. Twenty-one of the twenty-nine lodged in my eyebrows, eye sockets, and eyelids on both eyes. The doctors told me they could not numb my legs or chest, but the shots were not too deep. They said it should not be too painful removing them.

I remember thinking back to the last time I had heard that speech. It was when the doctor removed a three-inch piece of barbwire from my leg without medication. I thought to myself that it was easy for him to say; he was not the one having lead shot pulled from his muscle tissue with a pair of what looked like needle-nose pliers. The six lead shot in my left arm were near the bone, four of which were in my fingers on my shooting hand. I told the doctors to remove the shot in my right hand. They had to come out because it was my shooting hand. They laughed and told me it would be a long while before I went hunting again. I told them I was a shooting guard on one of the county's best basketball teams. They both looked at each other and then realized who I was. They both had sons on my team. They did the surgery without saying a word to me or to each other. I again asked Soul if he was okay. Still there was no answer. It was the longest time in our twelve years together that we had not been able to communicate with each other, and I was starting to panic.

Once the surgery was over, the doctors went out and met my family in the waiting room. The room was full to capacity with local townspeople. The doctor starts out by answering the question on everybody's mind. He said, "At this point, we are very concerned about his eyes, but we just do not know. We placed a large wrap on his head to help control the swelling. At this point, we give his chances of seeing again at less than 10 percent. We were unable to remove any of the shot around his eyes, and we will seek expert advice before we attempt such a delicate operation. What he needs is a miracle. We did remove three different sizes buckshot from his legs, waist, and chest. We gave him something to help him relax. The best thing he has going for him at this point is that he is one of the community's top young athletes. He is strong and in excellent shape. If it were not for that combination, it is unlikely he would still be alive." Several of the women and girls who knew me from school left the waiting room sobbing, stopping to offer whatever help they could to the family. The doctors told everybody the best thing to do was to go home, pray, and wait. It was all in God's hands now.

One of the doctors was my mother's doctor. He came over to my father and asked him how she was taking the news. Dad said he felt he needed to know my condition before he went home to tell her what had happened. The doctor told my dad that upon hearing this news she would likely go into labor. The doctor said he would go to the house with Dad to break the news. Her situation would become critical since she was 15 miles from the hospital. They agreed to meet at the house to break the news, and the doctor was right. She went into labor, and the doctor told dad to get her to the hospital.

The boys met with the rest of the family to explain what was happening. My oldest sister could tell her husband was suffering the most. She told him she loved him and she felt I would be okay. All my sisters wanted to go to the hospital and be with me, but the boys convinces them to stay home. The doctor had ordered complete bed rest for me and no visitors allowed. My youngest sister asked why everyone was crying. She was too young to understand the seriousness of the situation. My oldest brother placed her on his knee and explained to her what had happened. She said, "No big deal. He is tough, and he could take it." She went back to playing with a small toy she had received earlier in the day.

When my mother arrived at the hospital, she went straight to my room. She had to see me for what some thought would be the last time. She realized I was in the best of care and her focus had to be on her unborn child. My brother was born later and was very healthy.

My mother was exhausted, but when the nurses told me about her, I told them to take me to her. I just wanted to let her know I was okay and things were going to be all right. When I arrived at her door, I ask the nurse to help me out of my wheelchair. I walked into her room and stood beside her bed. She took my hand and appeared to be in perfect control. She said, "It sure looks like you have been through a lot since I saw you last." I could hear my little brother nursing in her arms, and I said, "It sounds like we both have." I told her everything is going to be all right. I told her jokingly that I just wanted to wish her a happy Thanksgiving, and we both laughed more than we probably should have. Even the nurses taking care of the three of us had to laugh. The head nurse commented, "If this is a happy Thanksgiving for your family, I would hate to see a bad one." My mother said, "If things turn out the way we pray they will, it be our best and most memorable holiday." Nevertheless, we were going to have another Thanksgiving Day when we all returned home. I could sense she was looking at me and her heart was breaking. She said, "I knew you did not want to go hunting. I should have stood up for you, and I am sorry."

She could probably see the concern in my face and said, "Do not worry son, the Thanksgiving Day hunting trips are gone for good. Your daddy now has a clear understanding of the consequences if he ever brings it up again." I could tell from the tone of her voice the trip from my house to the hospital earlier with dad was likely not a pleasant trip for him. She gave me a hug, squeezed my hand, and told me she loved me. The nurse took my hand and helped me back to my critical-care room. I rested the rest of the night.

By Saturday afternoon, the pain was completely gone. The remaining buckshot appeared to all be in the same spots they were two days earlier. The doctors felt the danger of movement was over and took me off the critical-condition list. The swelling in my face was rapidly going away, and I was still planning to play in the opening game on Monday. I could hear the nurses talk to each other from time to time. I could tell they were very careful to say the right things when they were around me, and I heard one tell her assistant they would be bringing someone to talk to me about what it would mean to be blind. They could describe the changes necessary for me to survive and have a happy life.

Twenty-Seven

A Touch of Class

On Sunday afternoon, the head nurse brought two young girls into my room. I could not see them, but I thought they sounded nice. Their names were Joy and Sharon, and without much to go on, I could tell Sharon was a special young person. They were called candy stripers, and their roles were to help the nurses do tasks like empty the trash and make sure the patients had water and were as comfortable as possible. Sometimes they would read to the patients to take their minds off their pain. I remember the one named Sharon asked the nurse what had happened to me. The nurse explained what had happened, and for some reason I felt something I had not felt before. When she returned to my room, she asks me if I was in pain. She said she was very sorry about what had happened. I said it was an accident and I was sure it would turn out okay. She said she had no doubt. She asked me if she could read a story to me.

I could not explain it, but the second she walked into my room, I felt something happen between the two of us—an emotional bond immediately developed. She read me a story about a young girl named Wilma who was physically restricted for her entire childhood. She grew up to overcome the odds and became a world-class Olympic sprinter and won three gold medals. She said, "The doctors and nurses think you will never see again; they told Wilma she would never walk again, but she did. I say you will see again." I said, "I believe you." She said, "Good choice" and that she would see me around school someday when our schools finally merged. I told her I would score two for her in my next game. She said, "Do not bother. Just be you and I will be happy for you and for me." When she left my room, she touched my hand with her soft hands. She said she would pray for me. A few hours later, I ask the nurse if she was still around. The nurse explained that she left the hospital and that it was her last day.

For some reason I felt sad; was it love at first sight even though I could not see her or just a young boy giving into his feelings toward a girl? I asked the nurse why she was leaving the hospital. I said she was so good at what she was doing for the patients. The nurse said she was from Ghent, and it was creating a hardship on her family to make the trip to Carrollton every day. In addition, she was a farm girl. She had responsibilities on the farm, and one of the requirements to be a candy striper was to be a straight 'A' student. She was a straight 'A' student and was currently top in academics in her entire school. I remember thinking, *Wow, this girl is a straight 'A' student, farm girl, and I think she's pretty*; it could not get much better.

It does not take long for tragic news to travel throughout a small community, even on a long holiday weekend. My doctor told me he would be in to see me at 7:00 PM on Sunday night and would talk to me about when it would be safe to take the bandage off my head. He wanted to check out the damage to my eyes. By 6:30 PM, my entire family had gathered at the hospital and so had several of my friends and teammates. I had received get-well wishes and flowers from most of the local churches and well-wishes from counties as far away as Gallatin, Trimble, and Owen counties in Kentucky and Madison and Switzerland counties in Indiana. I heard the owner of the company my dad worked for tell the doctors if I needed special care or treatment, he would pay for my traveling expense. He wanted the best of the best medical care possible for me.

Finally, I heard my coach's voice ask the doctor if he could come in and offer his encouragement. The doctor told the coach, "The last thing he needs to worry about is if I is going to be in the line-up tomorrow night. I think it will only upset him to know he may never be in the line up again." The coach assured the doctor, "Playing in basketball games is the furthest thing from my mind, even though I know it is the only thing on your patient's mind. I want to share my love for him and his brave family. I want to let him know I have spoken to all of the other coaches in the entire school system, and he will always be a part of our teams in whatever capacity possible for the rest of his career." As the doctor started to restate his position, my dad stood up, and my brothers lined up behind him. He looked at the doctor and said, "I think other than his mother, I know my son better than anyone. Doc, my son loves his coach. He is going in and everyone else is going to stand down until the visit is over." My father opened the door and invited the coach to enter the room. My father stood at attention as if he were guarding the Tomb of the Unknown Soldier in our nation's capital.

The second I heard my coach's voice, it seemed as if all of the emotions I had been able to suppress since the shooting came flowing out of my body. I told my coach I was sorry and I would never forgive myself for letting him and my teammates down. I told him I was afraid and I felt lost. I did not know what to do or what to say. I could feel myself touching the massive wrap of gauze around my head for the first time. I told my coach I might never see again. I said, "Coach, I have heard the doctors talk about how the chance of me seeing again is close to zero. I have never faced those kinds of odds in my short life."

I told my coach I felt angry and cheated for the first time in my life. I had done the time and put in all of the hard work on the floor and at home. I had worked on the hottest day of summer to earn my way into the lineup. The coach did what all good coaches do. He only held me and listened until I ran out of words. I could tell he was holding back his own emotion as he moved away from me. He spoke in a soft voice and said he hoped I understood he would have taken my place in a heartbeat. "I have thought about how I would handle these new challenges in my life ever since the day I heard about the shooting. I have hugged my children a little tighter and told my wife how much I love her every time I have left the house. I prayed to God this morning in church to give me the words to give to you to help you deal with what has happened. I had a talk with my minister earlier today and ask him for advice."

"Frankly, I did not have a plan when I left the house, but something happen to me on the way to the hospital. I think I have the answers. I decided I would be the coach, and what good coaches do is make adjustments." I asked the coach what his plan was. He said, "I do not have a clue, and I was hoping you could help me with a plan." For the first time in several days, I could not help but laugh aloud along with the coach. He said, "As long as I have you boys and I am the coach I will help you any way I can, and win or lose, we will do it together as a team."

"The first thing we need to do is take the rap off your face and head and see what we are dealing with; then we will make adjustments from there." He said he would help me deal with this tragedy one day at a time. He said we would cross bridges together and find a solution to help us all achieve our goals. Then he said something by accident I was not prepared to hear. He said, as he was leaving, "Maybe your guardian angel showed up just in time. Maybe he deflected the buckshot away from the center of your eyes." I said to myself, "Or maybe he took a bullet for me as I had told him I would do for him." I could barely keep my emotion in check. I knew this was something I would need to deal with on a personal level. It would be between God and me later in the night. The coach held me for a while and then said, "May God be with you, my son." Then he left the room.

My dad asked me if I was okay and said the doctor was going to remove the wrap in a few minutes. He said the family wanted to be with me and show their love and support.

Surrounded by my family, my coach, our minister, and a hospital parking lot full of well-wishers, the doctor slowly started to remove the bandage. As he took away each wrap, he would ask me if I could see light. Each time I wanted to say yes, but I knew it would be a lie. Once he was down to the last wrap, I could feel pain as the blood soaked bandages pulled at my eyes. I could hear my sisters start to weep in the background when the doctor asks me for the last time if I saw any light. I wanted to say "Yes sir" to help the family but, honestly, I couldn't see any light. The doctor opened my eyelids one at a time and told my family all he could see was dried blood. "His retinas and pupils in both his eyes are completely coated over with blood. I have never seen anything like this." Then he said, I am sad to say, but if this young man ever sees the light of day again, it will take a miracle.

He said he would put the wrap back on and make other arrangements with a specialist.

Once the wrap was in place, the doctor gave the nurse her final instructions for the rest of the night. This was not the news we wanted to hear, but it was a fact, and we would need to deal with the information we had available to us at the time. The room was finally empting out, and only my dad and mom remained. I told Mom and Dad not to worry; God had always taken care of me, and I had a feeling he would this time. Miracles come to us in many ways, shapes, and sizes. Sometimes we just need to be patient and wait for a miracle to understand the real meaning of the gift. Maybe he actually delivered such a miracle to me on the day I was born, and I just did not appreciate it enough at the time. I would be fine except for missing my first ball game the next day. I knew that Monday, the sun would come up, and God would still be in charge of my life. I told them to go home and continue to pray for a miracle. They left the room to join the others, who were still sobbing in the waiting room. The room finally went silent and the nurses told me they were turning the lights out for the night.

Twenty-Eight

Guardian Angels. Who Knew?

"Soul, I know you are here. I felt you return earlier in the day." It seems like several hours passed before Soul finally spoke to me. He said, "You know how you said you would take a bullet for me?" "Yes, and I meant it too." "Well, I did take a bullet for you, and frankly, it hurts." He told me his injury was severe, and he was not sure if he was going to make it. I said, "Soul please be serious; I never want to hear those words from you again." I thanked Soul for what he had done to try to save my eyesight.

Soul stated in a frail voice, "What do you mean try, my friend! I did save your vision." I said to Soul, "The doctor removed the bandages earlier, and I could not see a thing." Soul said, "Sometimes you have to be patient to get what you want. Even if you do believe in miracles and guardian angels, everything has a time and a place. It was not your time, but now it is. When I realized you were blind, I made a deal with God, but I cannot tell you about it right now. He told me he would give you your eyesight back."

"Okay Soul, let me be sure I understand what you are saying to me. If I take off these bandages, I will be able to see." He said, "Yes, you will."

It just so happened, that the nurse on duty was the mother of my best friend. I turned on the nurse call light and asked her to come into my room. I asked her to please bring a pan of warm water and some new bandages.

When she came into my room, I told her the bandages covering my eyes were too tight and I was in pain. She was a take-charge nurse and told me, "The doctor gave her strict orders to not remove the bandages around your eyes. However, he did not say you could not take them off. Tell you what, I need to step out, and I will be back to check on you in a few minutes. I will just turn off this light, if you do not mind." I said, "Why I should mind? I can't see a thing." When the door closed, I immediately started unwrapping the bandages around my head. I told Soul, "This could be the happiest day of my life if I can see. Thank you Soul, you are the best. How can I ever repay you for this gift?"

I immediately told him I loved him. I told him I always thought he was faster than a speeding bullet and this just proved my theory. He just laughed between the moans and groans. I removed the rest of the bandage, and Soul was right; I could see some light, but everything was blurry. He told me to wet the cloth in the warm water and place it over my eyes to dissolve the dried blood. I could feel it start to work within a few minutes. He was right; I could see perfectly fine. The disturbing thing was, I could not see Soul. He said he could not see me but he could still hear me.

When the nurse opened the door, I asked her to bring me a mirror so I could see how bad it really was. She immediately turned on the light and ran over to my bed. She told me to tell her what color her eyes were. When I said, "Sky-blue," she said, "Tell me how many fingers I am holding up." I told her four. She bolted from the room and returned with a mirror. I asked her how I looked. She said, "About what I would expect for a person shot in the face just few days earlier." She told me it was a miracle and she was happy to see I was ok. I told her I had an awesome guardian angel and that he had covered my eyes with his body. She said, "That would be hard to imagine, but if you believe it, I will too." She asks me if she could call my mom and dad with the news. She said all she had to do was go out into the parking lot to tell my brothers, who refused to leave until I could see again.

The news traveled fast throughout the community. I was going to live, and I had regained my eyesight.

Once I realized I was going to be okay, the two things on my mind were the basketball game and Soul's condition. I saw no reason I could not check out of the hospital and suit-up. Unfortunately, my mother, father, doctors, school principal, superintendent, and my head coach had other ideas. All of them knew playing would be the only thing on my mind. I would do whatever was necessary to get the opportunity to play.

The group met at the hospital to talk about my health. They decided it would not be in my best interest to play ball. They all came into my room around noon, and my dad broke the news to me that I would not play. However, there had been a new development. He said the coach of the Saint John's Knights had called our coach and offered to postpone the game until I had fully recovered. He said the team had voted, and it was unanimous to cancel the game.

"However, I knew you would want to be a part of the final decision." My dad knew I was a team player. Canceling the game would mean the other eleven players on the team would not get to play. We all knew the school's financial limitations, and they really could not afford to reschedule this game.

I told the group, "All things happen for a reason. I do not have a clue why this happened, but I want my teammates to have the opportunity to play against the Knights." The principal told the coach to call the Knights' coach immediately and let him know the game was on.

The sadness of the moment for everyone involved had nothing to do with me playing in the game. It was about all of the hard work and sacrifices I had made to get ready for the game. Everyone knew I had been dreaming about this moment since I was five years old. I was within four days of seeing my dream come true. For some unexplainable reason at the time, it was not to be. As the adults left the room, each stopped beside my bed and offered words of encouragement. They told me they were very sorry.

My dad touched my shoulder in a way I had never felt before. It was the type of gesture you would make with an old friend to reassures them that you knew they were going through a tough time and your heart felt their pain. He said he was proud of me for putting the team needs above my own.

He said he knew I would, but he just wanted the others to hear where my heart really was.

Once all of the adults had left the room, I found myself all alone. I spent the next several hours thinking about all of the things that had gone wrong for me over the last few days. I had to put the game out of my mind and moved on. I always had the ability to move on very quickly after a loss.

I was thinking about my family and how hard all of this must have been on my brothers and sisters. I knew all four of my older sisters felt like a piece of their heart was carved out of their chest. When this is all over and I got to go home, there would be a hug-fest at the front door. There would be tears and smiles as wide as the ocean from those four girls. My younger brother told me my oldest brother-in-law had been having nightmares about the shooting. I told him to tell my brother-in-law to come and see me. I wanted to talk to him about what had happened and tell him it was not his fault.

I realized I had not properly thanked God for sparing my life—for him having faith and sending me Soul to be my guardian angel. Then for some reason I remembered the words God said to me in the speech that changed my life. I knew God was not there as he was when he delivered the speech the first time, but the words came back to me as if he were reciting them. I could feel his hand hold my hand as he said:

SOMETIMES:
"My son, sometimes terrible things will happen on earth for what appears at the time to make little or no sense at all to you. Never forget, everything that happens has a true purpose. It may not be revealed today, next week, next year, or possibly not even in your lifetime, but it has a purpose and it will come to light the second it is supposed to, and nothing will ever change that."

Twenty-Nine

It's Not Over Until the Final Horn Sounds

I heard Soul take a deep breath. His chest was rattling in a way I had never heard before. Then he took another breath. He was struggling, as if he could not breathe. I said, "Soul, speak to me. Please Soul, say something—say anything." Finally, in a frail voice, he said he would always love me. He said, "Because of you, I found my courage. God needs me in heaven. A deal is a deal, and I have to go. I am happy for you to have your eyesight back. You will achieve great things in this world. Now let me go." I said, "No! You will not leave me now or ever!" I did not know what to do, so I just put my arms around him. I said, "I will hold you tight, and I will not let you go. I will not let God take you from me; I will hold on to you, my angel. I will give you all of the strength I have left in my body to protect you. Please Soul, hold on. Please stay with me. Do not give up on us Soul! You can cry and I will cry with you, but if God wants you, he will have to take me. We are one, and I chose us for eternity. Soul, I will give my life for you. Do not give up…please, do not give up. Our boss rules the universe, and he has the power to change this." Finally, in desperation, I said to God, "If you spare Soul's life, I will give up my seat in heaven. You can take my sight, but do not take Soul. I will deal with the devil if you leave Soul with me to finish out my earthly life." I felt Soul trying to push himself out of

146

my arms. In what sounded like his last breath, he said, "No God. Do not do this; he knows not what he is saying." Then Soul stops moving, and once again silence filled the room.

I heard the door open to my room. The nurse said my game had begun and she just wanted to let me know we were doing fine, but it was a close game.

When I did not speak to her, she knew something was wrong. She moved closer to my bed. She realized my condition was critical and she needed to get me help and fast. I felt her touch my head, which was scorching hot. My heart was beating so fast she thought it was going to jump out of my chest. However, she said later the scariest thing of all was when she heard me crying and just knew I had a steady stream of tears flowing from my eyes.. She knew whatever was wrong with me touched me deeply.

She immediately called the school and asked for my doctor. The announcer called out the doctor's name on the loudspeaker and stated, "You have an urgent call from the hospital." The nurse told the doctor what was going on and asked him what to do. He told her he was at the game. His son had taken my position and he was playing his heart out for me. He said he would let the coach know he was leaving immediately and he would get a police escort back to the hospital. He was about 25 miles away. She said she would monitor my condition and her partner would let the family know something was going wrong. They needed to get back to the hospital as quickly as possible.

The nurse thought our biggest fear was happening—that one or more of the buckshot had moved and was heading for my heart or lungs. When she took my vitals, something did not add up to her. My temperature was normal, even though I was sweating profusely. My pulse rate was normal, and my blood pressure was perfect, even though my heart was pounding on the walls of my chest. She said I did not appear to be in pain, but the expression on my face was one of pure determination. She said she had never witnessed anything so scary or beautiful in her life. When she checked my eyes, she said I appeared to be so focused nothing could stop me. I would die before I let go of it, whatever it was. As I told you earlier, she was the mother of my best friend. She was a kind and spiritual person. She could only conclude this was not a medical or physical issue; it was purely spiritual.

It was time for her to do what she knew my mother would do if this were her son. She decided to sit down beside me, take my hand, and pray with all of her heart. I felt her take my hand and tell God to give me a chance. From there it would be his decision. I woke up enough to ask the nurse to help me. I told her to leave me alone and turn out the lights. I had unfinished business, and I did not want anyone in my room. I would turn on the light when it was over, if I still could. She turned out the light and closed the door behind her as she left the room.

I asked Soul if he was still there. No one answered. We sat in the dark and waited for God to make up his mind. I was begging him with everything I could think to offer him. I finally offered to give up the only thing I had left. I told God I would never take another shot or dribble a basketball for the rest of my life if he let Soul live. I folded my arms tightly and imagined Soul was in my arms. I could feel God's presence and him looking at me. He touched my forehead with his eyes closed as if he were praying for me to not give up no matter what the outcome was about to be with Soul. A verse from the Bible came to my mind. I told God, "I know this is a valley or a low point in my life and that if I believe in him enough, I will see my way past this. As long as I believe in him, things will be okay on the other side." Then I quoted the verse, just to help me keep the words in the front of my path to the other side of this dark valley.

"The Lord is my shepherd; I shall not be in want. He makes me lie down in green pastures, he leads me beside still waters, and he restores my soul. He guides me in paths of righteousness for his name's sake. Even though I walk through the valley of the shadow of death (or through the darkest valley) I will fear no evil, for thou art with me, your rod, your staff, they comfort me. You prepare a table before me in the presence of my enemies. You anoint my head with oil; my cup overflows. Surely, goodness and love will follow me all the days of my life, and I will dwell in the house of the Lord forever.

I closed my eyes and said, "Soul, I will go with you. Please let the boss know how I feel." I either lost consciousness or fell into a deep sleep, thinking I had lost Soul forever. About an hour later, I heard, "Okay, okay loosen your grip, friend, I need a little air in these lungs to breathe." Then I woke up. I felt Soul's breathing return to normal. I knew God had blessed us. He knew this journey was not over and the best was yet to come for both Soul and me together as one. I kiddingly told Soul he could thank me later. When I finally woke completely and came to my senses, I turned on the nurse's light, and 25 people came storming into my room. I asked them if they ever slept. The nurse brought me a drink of water and a towel to wipe the sweat from my face. I told them I was going to be okay. My mother said I looked exhausted and needed my rest. The head nurse said, "You heard the boy's mother, visiting hours ended hours ago. Go! Go home, I think he is back to stay." The room emptied out in a matter of a few minutes. The nurse had tears in her eyes and a heart full of joy and hope. She looked up to the heavens and said, "Thank you God for this gift. I give my heart to you forever."

When the room was empty, once again I spoke to Soul. He did most of the talking. He said in all of Gods dealings he never knew anyone so determined to keep a guardian angel. He said I could stay, but he expected nothing in return. He said, "Your front seat in heaven is still there, and I expect to see you in it when it is time. You should do everything possible to continue to be the person you are becoming. As far as I am concerned, you should continue to play the game you love. By the way, I love the way you play and cannot wait for you to lace them up for the first time."

The days went by and my condition improved daily. It was time to get back to school and start the healing process. Oh, the Saint John's Nights did defeat the Carroll County Panthers in our first game by one point. So much for the team that was to be undefeated for our entire high school career.

I did recover quickly, and with some intervention by my dad, the doctors decided I was ready to return to the court by our second game. Even though it was a long time ago and I have played in thousands of games since, I still remember what it felt like to put on my new school uniform for the first time. I spent twenty minutes in front of a mirror making sure every hair on my head was in place.

I waited until the last moment to pull my basketball shoes out of my bag. You see, many of my teammates had practice shoes and then another pair of shining new shoes to wear during the games. Money was tight and I felt fortunate to have one pair of shoes.

When I pulled my shoes out of my gym bag, my jaw must have dropped to the floor. I did a second look to make sure it was my gym bag. The bag had my name clearly marked on the label. It was my bag. You see, the shoes I pulled out of the bag were not the ones I had put in the bag when I left home. It was a pair of the best of the best basketball shoes available at the time. It was a brand new pair of Chuck Taylor Converse shoes, and they were just my size.

I looked for a note but could not find one. I scanned the locker room and I could not find anyone to thank. The locker room was business as usual.

It was all I could do to hold back the tears of appreciation as I adjusted the thick soft laces. I slipped the shoes on my feet while maintaining my composure and acting as if nothing had happened. Soul looked at the shoes. He smiled as he told me to make sure I did not hit my head on the rim. He said he was serious because my feet were not touching the floor. He said, "Keep in mind the best basketball players in the world wear that brand of shoe. Try not to let them down."

I never found out who gave me those shoes. I could not find anyone to thank, but if the person who gave me those shoes is reading this book, please accept my sincere appreciation for the gift I treasured for several years. When I thought about the events that took place over the past couple of weeks, it could have been one of several people:

Maybe the shoes were a gift from the three shooters who put me in the hospital.

Maybe it was the folks blocking off the road with their car and would not let my dad pass by.

It could have been my brothers and sisters pooling the money they were likely saving for Christmas, which was in four weeks.

Maybe it was the young girl, who stole my heart that Sunday afternoon in the hospital.

How about the head nurse that took such incredible care of me in the hospital? She witnessed my greatest victory up to this point in my life. She knew I had convinced God not to take Soul from me.

Could it have been the farmer? You know, the one who gave me a job during the summer to earn enough money just to have the opportunity to play basketball? I know I saw him in the crowd many nights throughout my career....

It could have been my Dad; he always seemed to move mountains for his children when they needed it most.

It may have been my mother. She was always willing to make personal sacrifices to help her children be the best we could be.

At the time, I could not help but think it was my little brother next to me in age. He was a salesperson and a charmer. He was so crafty he could sell chocolate ice cream at a white-glove church social on a 95-degree day.

Thirty

BATTER UP

The best example of my brothers salesmanship skills was when he decided he wanted to play little league baseball and tried to convince me to play. That way he would have someone to walk home with him after each practice and all the games. He was a little young and was likely afraid of the dark. I told him we only had one descent baseball glove between the two of us, and he could play and I would watch him play every game. I knew that hoping for new gloves was an unreasonable expectation.

We played baseball non-stop during the summers on our home field when we were not working on the farm. Our field was not really a baseball field; it was a huge pasture used to graze cattle during the day. Nevertheless, at night to it turned into our Crosby Field, and it was game on.

My older sisters and brothers had set it up to look like a baseball field, with large rocks from Conway's creek to mark the base pads and old cardboard wrapped in burlap feed sacks for home plate and the pitchers plate.

The big day came, and it was time for try-outs. My brother tried out for the team. I knew he would make it; he was a terrific baseball player.

At the end of practice, the coach told him he was an excellent player. He had made the team. My little brother said to the coach, "If you think I am a good player you should see my older brother play." The coach asked him why I did not try out for the team. My little brother explains we did not have gloves and that I could not play without a good glove. The coach told him if I tried out and was any good, he would provide us both with new gloves. My little brother told him we did not accept charity, but the coach said, "What if I hire you to mark the lines on the bases before each game in exchange for two new gloves?" My little brother said, with a huge smile, "Deal." He punched his chest out with pride and quickly sprinted away. Under his breath, he told the coach, "You had better get your checkbook ready friend because if you think I am good, your eyes will pop out of your sockets when you see my older brother play baseball."

I waited for him at the basketball court just a few hundred yards from the baseball field so we could walk home together.

My little brother ran up to me and told me he had made the team. Even though I knew he would make the team, I was proud of him. I just put my hands around his head and said, "You looked great out there little brother. You made me proud." He told me what the coach said; he wanted me to play ball with him and said it would be fun.

I decided to try out at the next practice, and 10 minutes into the practice, the coach went to his car and called out for my little brother to join him. He pulled out two new baseball gloves from the back seat of his car and told my brother, "A deal is a deal, and you are right, your brother is an incredible baseball player." The coach asked how we had learned to hit so well, and my little brother explained that when were young we would lay a bead of hay down to serve as home plate in a dry creek bed. We would collect small rocks that had washed down the creek during the rainy season, and once we had collected several hundred rocks, our oldest sisters would pitch the rocks over the plate for us to hit. We did not have a real baseball bat so we used a lathe tobacco stick as a bat. The coach just shook his head and handed the gloves to my little brother. Then he said he wanted the gloves back once the season was over. My little brother reminded the coach that we could go play for another team; they would likely give us the gloves for keeps.

I honestly think this was our best summer together. Our team won most of our games, including the game to qualify us for the league championship tournament.

We won all of our playoff games and were ready to play the championship. I still to this day remember our championship game as if we had just played yesterday. We experienced a real test of brothers going to bat for each other during the game.

I remember the coach calling time out in the top of the 7th inning with bases loaded. He went to the mound to make some player changes. I was playing shortstop at the time. He was in the process of switching pitchers, and I noticed him making a motion as if he were replacing my little brother in center field. I saw my little brother's head drop in disappointment. I went over to the coach, took off my glove, and told him to take me out and let my little brother play shortstop. To prove to him I was as serious as a heart attack, I handed the coach my glove. Without saying a word to me, the coach immediately yelled at my little brother. He asked him what he was doing, and before he could answer, the coach waved him back to his position and told him he only wanted him to move over and guard against a hit to left center field. The coach acted as if he were adjusting the rawhide strings holding my glove together. He walked over to me with a smile that filled his face and handed the glove back to me without saying a word. We got out of the inning on an incredible catch made by, you guessed it, my little brother. We were down by one run with the top of our order coming to bat. It was our last chance as the game would be over if we did not score at least one run. The opponent had the league's best pitcher on the mound, and he was on his game. Our opponents were feeling good since all they had to do was retire the side and win the championship.

I must admit it did not look good for us, as our first and second batters struck out on six pitches. You could see the parents and fans in the stands for the other team standing and ready to celebrate a championship. With bases empty and their ace on the mound, the odds were all in their favor. However, not so fast folks. A famous person once stated, "It's not over until it's really over."

My little brother was the next batter. He was standing in the on deck circle, and I could tell he was nervous. I walked over to the circle where he was standing. In a very confident voice, I asked him if he wanted to hit it out to tie the game or if he wanted me to hit it out for the win.

He smiled and said, "Once I am on base, you might as well do it so we can get started on the long walk home." He told me he had not been able to read this pitcher. His fastball was too fast for him to catch with his bat speed. He said he had been dreaming about this moment most of his life and now that it was here he was not sure he could do it.

I put my hand on his shoulder and told him, "In the bigger scheme of things, the moon will be full tonight, the sun will come up again in the morning, it will still be Friday, and your family will still love you just as much as they do at this minute." He said, "I would trade everything for a chance to be on first base and to score the tying run."

I said, "Okay kid, here what you need to look for. When the pitcher is preparing to throw a pitch, watch his wind up, and if it is a fastball, he will take the ball out of his glove twice before he starts his windup. In addition, he overthrows the ball and cannot keep his balance once he releases the ball toward home plate. If you get a fastball, bunt the ball down the third base line and run like the wind. By the time the pitcher regains his balance and retrieves the ball, you can beat the throw to first base." The last thing he asked me was if I thought the coach would be mad at him for bunting. I told him, "Not if you are safe, just make sure you do not let the dust settled under your feet while running down the first base line. One more thing little brother, we are only down one run and we are not going to lose the game; I got your back."

I remember looking down the line at the third base coach when my little brother squared up to bunt the ball. I could tell he was saying, "No, no," as his hands covered his face and he aggressively ripped off his hat and threw it in the dirt. I think if he had not been safe, the coach might have chased us both all the way home.

He laid down a perfect bunt down the third base line. He was running so fast down the first base line and kicking up so much dust, our dugout could not tell if he was safe or out. When the dust settled, the umpire gave the safe signal. The visiting crowd suddenly got very quiet. The cheering and high-fives turned into nervousness and fingernail biting.

I looked down to first base as I approached home plate to offer my little brother congratulations. He looks like his right foot was glued to first base. His head was pointing straight at second base and he was expressionless. As I stepped into the box and up to the plate, the coach for the visiting team stepped out of the dugout. He yelled, "Time-out" to the home plate umpire. I stepped out of the batter's box to rub some dirt on my bat so I could get a better grip. It was over one hundred degrees, and my hands were sweating more than normal.

The coach and the pitcher certainly did not agree on whether to intentionally walk me or go ahead and throw to me. The pitcher's father was yelling extremely loud at the coach from the stands to allow his son to throw the ball to me. He stated, "My son will strike this bum out and the championship will be ours." He reminds the coach his son was the best pitcher in the league; he needed to let him prove it. When he announced to the crowd that his son was the best player in the league and everybody knew it, I saw a smile come upon my little brother's face. I do not think he knew I was watching him, but I did see the smile. I knew what he was thinking.

The coach appeared to agree to allow him to pitch to me and avoid putting the tying run on second base. After all, parents always seem to think they are so much smarter than the coach, is especially when their children are involved.

The coach returned to the dugout, and I settled back in the box. Just before the pitcher went into his wind-up, my head coach called time out to stop the play. He met me about halfway down the third base line. He told me the pitcher might be the best pitcher and player in the league, but he had the two best brothers in the league. He said it made him feel proud to be our coach and our mom and dad should be proud of us. He said he wished he could give me some advice, but he really did not know anything to say. He said he had been coaching for 20 years and he had never won the league championship. He said this would be his last year, and he would like to go out a winner. I just smiled and said, "I will do my best coach." He turned to walk away, and I could see a tear form and run down his face as he walked back to the coaches' box.

I step back into the batter box and prepare for the first pitch. The pitcher went into his windup and delivered a fastball straight at my head. I went down to my knees. The ball would have hit me right between the eyes. I made it a point to keep my eyes focused on the pitcher's face. I was sending him a signal that it was just him and me and I would not be intimidated.

The pitcher's Dad screamed out to his son that he was proud of him. He hoped the next pitch took my head off. I could tell my little brother was about to head for the stands to settle a score when the first base coach put his arms around him and tried to settle him down. It seemed to help when I held up my hand and he saw I was okay. Soul turned into a loose cannon when the ball whistled past his head. If he could have, I think he would have done something neither one of us would have been proud of to this kid's father. The thing that confused him the most was how calm I was. He even stated I should have charged the mound and whipped up on the pitcher's head. Immediately following the wild pitch, my head coach had to be restrained by three assistant coaches and one dad in the dugout. He was a huge man and stood about 6' 7" tall. He apparently had been able to steal the other coach's signals earlier in the game. He knew the coach gave his pitcher the signal to put the ball between my eyes. He did finally calm down, but he made it clear to the opposing coach he knew what he had done. If he did it again, he would meet him out behind the dugout.

I think the next thing to come out of the dad's mouth was the most disturbing. He was obviously out of control. It really did not appear anyone was willing to step up and calm the man down. We were about to get the game started back up when he stood up and called out my name. I could not believe this grown man was calling me out. You could have suddenly heard a pin drop in the stadium. One of our team moms (as only a mom would do) stood up and told the man to sit down and leave me alone or he would be answering to her. In a very hurtful voice, he states my little brother and I did not belong on the field with the likes of his son and the rest of the civilized city boys. We were just poor country people from the backwoods and that was all we would ever be. We would always be white trash from Locust Creek right along with the rest of the trash in from the county.

I gripped the bat a little tighter as I looked up at the man making a fool out of himself. I think the umpire thought I was thinking about wrapping my 28" wooden Wilson bat up against this fellows head. Soul was certainly ready to help. The umpire said, "Let it go son, the man is an idiot." He pointed up in the stands and told the sheriff to take the man off the premises.

When my coach heard the dad call out my name and say what he said about me and my family, all he could do was lower his head in disbelief. He could not believe an adult could be so cruel to a young man facing one of his biggest athletic moments.

The thing I was most concerned about was the look on my little brother's face. When the man called us white trash, it seemed to take a little of the spirit out of his body. He had never heard anyone call anybody white trash, let alone him and his family. I saw his head drop a little, and I knew exactly what I needed to do to put a stop to this assault on him and my family.

I was fortunate to have a dad who was the exact opposite of the pitcher's dad. He had prepared me for this moment. He told me, "If you did not score a touchdown, hit the winning shot, or blast the home run over the fence to win the game, people would appear to be sympathetic. However, what they actually feel at the time is that you let them down. Even though most of them did absolutely nothing to help you get to this point in time. They somehow feel you owe it to them to get the win. The reasonable ones will eventually get over the loss. Nevertheless, when you grow old, you will remember the losses and the lessons you learned from losing. However, I caution you, when in the heat of battle, you will always have people trying to get into your head. If you allow it to happen, you will lose focus on your mission. Bottom line—they win!" My dad was a very wise man. He would have been an incredible coach.

The umpires finally got control of the players, coaches, and fans. The league president announced over the loud speaker that if there were any more outbreaks of poor sportsmanship the game would stopped without a winner. The next pitch was again a high inside fastball perfectly placed to knock me off the plate. I quickly adjusted my feet backwards but still stayed in the batter box. As the ball crossed home plate, I swung as hard as I could and lifted a high fly ball to left field. The ball landed about forty feet out in the cornfield behind the home run fence. It was down the line, and I could see my coach on his knees trying to guide the ball to fair territory. My little brother was off on the hit and had already rounded third base when the umpire yelled, "Foul ball." I felt the air leave the fans on both sides and then there was silence in the crowd. Our coach wanted to argue the call, but instead, he said the umpire was right and told my little brother to return to first base. The umpire picked up my bat and handed it back to me. He said he wanted the ball to stay fair so bad, but it did not and he had to make the right call. I thanked him, and as he looked into my eyes, he knew it did not matter. I was determined to hit the next pitch a little farther but a lot straighter.

The opposing coach had already visited the mound once. Baseball rules would not allow him go to the mound a second time without taking his best pitcher out of the game. Therefore, he just stood at the top of the dugout and yelled as loud as he could to intentionally walk me before I hit another one over the fence. The next two pitches were well outside. The next pitch appeared to be well off the plate, but the umpire called it a strike. The count was three balls and two strikes, and it appeared I would not get a pitch close enough to the plate for me to hit it. My chance to win the game I wanted to win so badly for my little brother was quickly fading away.

The pitcher checked in with catcher to get a sign and then checked the runner at first base. I think I read my little brothers lips when he called the pitcher a punk and said his sister had more guts than he did. The pitcher was actually a nice kid, and off the field, we were good friends. He looked back into the catcher, shook off the sign, and asks for another sign. The catcher started flashing signals, and the pitcher kept shaking his head no. The pitcher's coach was going crazy in the dugout. He was demanding his pitcher intentionally walk me.

We were two young athletes doing what we did best and hoping for the best. He was going to throw me his best pitch, and I was going to hit it or strike out trying. He delivered a fastball to the outside corner of the plate. When the pitcher released the ball from his hand, my little brother broke from first base to try to steal second base. When he saw the location of the ball, he was already pointing to the pond behind the outfield fence. He was screaming at the top of his lungs, "We win! We win!" He knew the pitch was in the area that he had seen me hit a country mile on our home baseball field. He knew I would not miss. I swung as hard as I could and made perfect contact with the ball on the sweet spot on the bat. When the ball cleared the fence, I had already rounded second base, so I decided to slow down to a slower pace. I wanted to give my little brother time to enjoy this moment as he stood at home plate waiting to jump into my arms once I touched the plate to win the game. The ball landed about 75 feet out in the pond behind the home run fence in right center field.

The pitcher was standing in front of home plate as I crossed. I look at him and he just said, "Nice hit. I will get you next time." I said, "Thanks, great game." He said he was sorry for what his dad said and that he really was a good person. I told him I understood and I would see him around.

Once all of the celebrations were finished and the trophies handed were over to the winning team, the only trophy left was the most valuable player award. The coach and league president walked down the line where our team was standing. They walked up to me, and our coach could read the expression on my face. I wanted him to give it to my little brother standing next to me. He just smiled, shook his head, and handed the trophy to my little brother. My little brother told the coach to give the award to me because I was his hero. The coach reminded my little brother, "The best play made this year was getting your brother in the league." My little brother told the coach we were still going to keep the gloves. The coach just broke down in tears and carried my little brother off the field.

I noticed my little brother walking toward the playing field. I ran out of the dugout and up beside him. As we walked along, I ask him where he was going. He said he was going to swim out to the middle of the lake behind the home run fence and get the ball.

I asked him what he was going to do with the ball if he could find it. He said he was going to give it to the dad with a big mouth as a reminder of whom the best player in the league really was. He hoped he had to look at it every day for the rest of his life. "I also plan to let him know my family is not and have never has been white trash, nor will we ever be, but until you change his attitude and behavior, you will always be a loser." I said, "Well said, little brother, I will join you in your search."

I think that summer was the most enjoyable summer of my life. If you could only imagine the mischief two little boys could conjure up walking twenty miles several times a week up and down the banks of the Ohio River in the heat of summer. Mark Twain could have possibly added a few more chapters to his version of Huck Finn if he had been following along in our footsteps. I will share one story only because it is likely the dumbest thing I ever let my little brother talk me into doing.

Thirty-One

SWIM BOY, SWIM FASTER

Following the championship game, it was time to make the long walk home. When we got to the end of the ballpark, my little brother asked me if we could to walk on out to Worthville. Worthville was about eight miles in the wrong direction from where we lived. We had plenty of daylight left, so I said, "Sure, let's go." As we walked along, I asked him why he wanted to go to Worthville. He said several of his friends lived in Worthville and he had never been there. When we made the final turn to walk into the city, I could hear trains running in the distance. I saw black smoke billowing out the smoke stacks on the old coal fire engines. Worthville was the location of a large railroad-switching yard for much of the Midwest region of the United States. We went into the center of town, and he met up with one of his friends running full speed toward an old railroad bridge. He waved for us to join him, as a new set of trains were scheduled to be crossing the bridge in ten minutes. Once we caught up, he explained that he and several of his friends had made the Hangman Club. My little brother asked him what he had to do to be a member of the club. His friend said, "First, you have to be from Worthville, and you are not, so you can never be in this elite club."

Once I witnessed what the boys had to do to be in this prestigious club, I was jubilant I was white trash from Locust Creek. It was initiation day, and five boys sprinted out to the center of the bridge as the train was approaching. There were no side rails, and the bridge was about forty feet above Eagle Creek.

I thought the boys were going to wait until the train was close then run back toward town and jump off the tracks as the train went by. The president of the club held up what appeared to be a starter's flag to let the boys know when the train was close enough. When the president dropped the flag, instead of running off the track, the initiation was to climb over the sides of the track, hand-walk out a wooden support beam, and hang by their arms until the caboose passed by. If they had the strength to make it back to the edge of the track and climb back up, they were officially members of the club.

Once I saw the boys were safe I told my little brother it was time to get back to Hunters Bottoms. As we walked away, I told him, "You need to stay out of Worthville because these boys have breathed in too much coal dust and it has affected their minds." Apparently, when one of their mothers told one of the boys' dads what the boys were doing, it did not take long for the club to shut its doors.

I thought our excitement for the day was over and was looking forward to getting home for supper. It was Thursday night, and that was pan-fried chicken and apple pie night at the Clifton residence. When we made the turn onto our lane, we met two neighbor boys. They claimed they were going to swim across the Ohio River to Brooksburg, Indiana and then swim back. My little brother called them idiots to attempt to swim across the river. The Ohio River is nearly a mile wide at that point in the river. Swimming in the Ohio was not a good idea. Our parents had warned us not swim in the river. It seemed many people had tried and had actually drowned in the past. Many claimed the river had developed large pools of swirling water. Once a swimmer got trapped by the swirling water, it pulled the swimmer in a downward spin to the bottom of the river with no chance for survival.

I told my little brother to let it go, but I knew he could not. We took about 20 steps when one of the older boys called my little brother a chicken. He was not a chicken, and he let the boy know he was willing to swim out just as far as the boy would.

The bully stripped down to his underwear, dove into the river, and started to swim. My little brother took off his baseball uniform shirt, shoes, and socks and jumped into the river. He started to chase the bully across the river. The boy with the bully suddenly remembered he had to get home and help his mother weed the garden. I could tell he was scared, but I really had never witnessed him run so fast to get home in the past. Meanwhile, the two boys were swimming toward the middle of the river and were rapidly getting out of visual contact. Then I heard the loud horn of an approaching barge speeding toward the boys. I knew the river was much deeper in the middle. The river was dredged to a depth of 35 feet. The Markland Dam, located about 20 miles upstream from where the boys took the plunge, was used to control the depth of the river downstream. The larger barges generally stayed as close to the deep water as possible. Finally, I saw the bully swimming back toward the shore. My little brother was nowhere in sight. I yelled out to the bully to ask him where my little brother was. He said, "He was out in front. I decided to leave him out there and swim back." I could not help but think about how irresponsible this boy was. He left my little brother in the middle of the river and did not even bother to tell him he was turning around. I am sure my little brother had no idea the barges were approaching him. He would have been killed instantly if the barge had hit him.

The river was relatively calm and clear. It had not rained for several weeks. I immediately removed my shirt, shoes, and socks and dove into the water. I was twice as good a swimmer as my brother was, so it did not take long for me to swim up beside him. I told him the first boy had bugged out—that the bully had swum back to the shore. "You are the winner, and it is time to go back." I sensed in his voice that something was wrong. I could tell he was getting tired. We were likely swimming in 25-30 feet of water. Soul whisper in my ear that I needed to give my little brother this moment. "Tell him to go for it and swim beside him." For some reason, the barge had stopped and decided to dock about 75 feet from where we were swimming. I am not sure if Soul had a plan or if the barge had stopped to allow a smaller boat to deliver food and other supplies, as they often did.

We were about 500 feet from the Indiana shore. It was unlikely anyone had ever swum across this part of the river, which is still today one of the widest points in the entire Ohio River. We were about 100 feet from the Indiana shore when he challenged me to a race. I told him I was too tired and that he should go ahead. When he reached the shoreline and stepped on Indiana soil, he jumps up and down in celebration, as if he had won the Olympics. When I reached the shoreline and stepped out of the water, he jumped on me, put his arms around me, and said, "Thanks, I needed this victory." Soul said I told you so.

He finally calmed down and finished his last victory dance. I asked him what his plan was to get back to the other side. We were both too tired to swim back. He said he did not have a plan, but he hoped I did.

We decided we had two options. One was to find a pay phone, call our mother, and tell her where we were and what we had done. This act would have been even dumber than what we had done to get in this much trouble to start with. We both knew the two bullies who got us in this trouble to start with would never tell their parents about what had happened. The second option, which is what we did, was to walk down Route 56 to Madison, Indiana. As we walked along, my brother, asked me if I knew if anything ever happened worth mentioning in Madison, Indiana. He said he knew about the rivalry between the Wildcats and Hoosiers, but that was it. I told him some of Hollywood's most famous actors made two very famous movies in Madison. He said, "Name them." I said, "I know their first names were Frank, Dean, Shirley, Marilyn, Jim, Bruce, Paul, and Mary. In fact, they lived in a hotel on the hill at the edge of town." He looked at me as if he thought I was joshing with him, but he was not sure, so he just went along. Suddenly we heard a loud thunderous roar coming up the Ohio River from Madison. Then I said, "Oh yes, I forgot to tell you about the world famous hydroplane race held under the Madison Bridge every Fourth of July weekend since as long as I can remember. Those drivers and mechanics are practicing and tuning up their boats for the race."

We made it to the famous Madison-Milton Bridge on foot, which was illegal to walk across at the time even if we had been wearing shoes. The bridge was about a half mile long. We had no choice but to sprint the full length without slowing down. We hoped we did not get knocked over the side by oncoming traffic. I had a vision of someone calling the police station in Indiana, reporting that two young boys wearing baseball pants and no shoes were sprinting across the bridge. Fortunately, we made it without incident and it was good to be back on Kentucky soil. Soul was doing his regular complaining about being thirsty. When he looked over the side of the bridge and realized we were nearly 100 feet above the water, he just closed his eyes, looked up at the boss, and said, "Why boss, why you do this to me." When we got to Milton, we decided to walk along the river shoreline to avoid any more attention than we had to. As we were walking along, my brother said, "I bet Huck did not have this much fun when he walked up and down the banks of the Mississippi River." I said, "No, he probably had a better plan than we did. He likely made it home in time to enjoy fried chicken and apple pie Thursday." Without missing a beat, Soul said, "I am hungry." It took us about an hour to get back to where we jumped into the river. Our shoes were still where we had left them, and as we walk back the lane, we both agreed we would never tell anyone about what we had done. We both knew if our parents found out, we would be invited to visit the old hickory tree and select the switch they would use to spank us both.

Sadly, this turned out to be the last year my little brother and I would ever play organized baseball together. He was involved in a horrible farm accident which caused a head injury, nearly taking his life. The glove he bartered for was the same glove I used in the Kentucky State High School Baseball finals at the end of my senior year. We lost on a pickoff move to third base. The ball got past our third baseman and allowed the winning run to score in extra innings. The pitcher who almost took my head off six years earlier took the loss.

The team we lost to went on to the state championship game. Soul cried a little, but my little brother just said, "Thanks for the ride." The father of the pitcher walked up to me and asked me if I could ever forgive him for what he had said about my family six years earlier. The mother and the pitcher both met at the mound, and we shed a few tears. The father reached into his pocket and handed me a baseball. He said, "I think this ball belongs to you. I received it in the mail a few weeks after the season was over with a hand written note saying 'Who's the Best Player in the League Now.'" My little brother just smiled and turned away. Later, the senior ball players loaded the bus and arrived back at Carroll County High school just in time to walk down the aisle and receive our high school diplomas. Sadly, our little league coach died in a farming accident a few weeks after the season ended. May he rest in peace with the great memory of the win that gave him his first and last championship.

Thirty-Two

MY FIRST BASKETBALL GAME

Oh, yes back to my first basketball game following the gunshot in the face. It was time to take the floor, and the head coach tossed me the ball and said, "Lead us out son, you have earned it." At the end of the corridor, I could see my family and classmates cheering and singing the school song. It was the first time in my life I realized dreams really could come true. I remember telling Soul, "If heaven feels this good, it is where I want to end up when my days are done." Soul told me, "This is not heaven my friend, but it is real close. By the way do not ever give up your seat in heaven again; if you do, I am out of here for good."

I do not remember how many points I scored, but it was a lot. I do not remember how badly we beat the Gallatin County Wildcats—it was a lot. But what I remember most was the happiness on the face of my teammates. Our student body packed the house, and every night we played after that night, I remember the smiles on our coaches' faces and the team prayer given by our head coach, thanking God for protecting us and giving us the opportunity to feel what winning really felt like.

Our team went on to enjoy winning the rest of the games. In fact, we did not lose another game until midway through our sophomore season.

Some of the players on the team earned promotions to JV and varsity level at the end of our freshman season.

Time went by fast, and before we knew it, we were seniors in high school. It was time to deliver the expectations of the school, parent's, community, and ourselves.

Thirty-Three

Time to Make Good on the Promise

The expectation going into our senior year was high. The pressure to be successful was unimaginable. Our coach felt it most, and our practices were long, grueling, and extremely physical. Our head coach was determined to push us to our fullest potential. He was never satisfied with our efforts. He wanted more every single day. I can remember one practice the head assistant coach got so upset with the head coach he blew his whistle extremely loud. He orders all of the players into the locker room. We could hear him screaming at the head coach about the way he was treating his players. He was ashamed of him. He needed to wake up and realize the players on the team would not quit. They would attempt to do whatever they were instructed to do even it killed them.

The second assistant coach opened the locker room door and ordered us back onto the floor. The head coach met us at the edge of the floor. He stated that he hoped we enjoyed the rest and the time we just wasted. He ordered us to hit the bleachers and not stop running until we heard the whistle blow. Hitting the bleacher meant running up the bleacher to the top of the gym at full speed, back down to the floor, and then across the floor and up the other side of the bleacher's again full speed. If any team member missed a step, we would start over and do the whole process again. Once he could see we were all about to drop from complete exhaustion, he blew his whistle. He directed us to shoot 100 free throws without talking. We would run one sprint up and back for every single missed shot. We were an excellent free throw shooting team.

At the end of practice, the head coach laced up his basketball shoes. He slammed the basketball down at midcourt and invited any player in the gym with the guts to join him in a game of one on one full contact. In other words, no fouls would be called for rough play. This was a critical mistake by the head coach. He apparently forgot 10 of the 12 players in the gym were also varsity football players. We had just completed one of the most successful seasons in school history. Several of the players were already all district and regional performers. I received the distinguished honor of being Honorable Mentioned All-State as one of the top football player in the State of Kentucky. This process had lasted about 10 minutes before the head coach realized he was not the only tough man in the gym. He ended the practice as he limped back to the coach's office.

It seemed things did settle down after that, and practices started to make more sense. The players from that the original undefeated team were back together for the first time in several years. I think the head coach finally figured out that the head assistant coach was right; it was time to stop yelling and screaming and start coaching. Even though he did continue to get upset quite often, it appeared to me that it was justified. Coach was here to lead this team to the Kentucky High School State Tournament. He was making sure the team was prepared.

Unfortunately for him and the community, he could not control the things going on in the world. The local military draft board seemed to be working overtime drafting our young men at an alarming rate. During those days, the military was forcing young men into active duty. The Vietnam War was at its highest point in causalities. Every person in America with a close relative fighting in the war watched his or her television set to see the 6:00 network news broadcast. The hope was to see one of their relatives as the reporter on the front lines provided live real-time action of the war. The news clips presented by the reporter appeared to bring the battles as they were happening to living rooms all over America. My home was one of those homes with someone near and dear to all of our hearts fighting on the front lines as an expert infantry gunner: my second oldest brother I had written about in the first part of the book. You remember the one who laughed at my dad for being so concerned about a wild bull cow on the prowl? He started his military career after basic training in Germany.

When Mom received a letter from him stating he was coming home for two weeks, we all knew what that meant. Once the two weeks were over, he would not be returning to his base in Germany; he had received orders of redeployment to the front lines in Vietnam. Just after supper, she read the letter to the family. I did not handle the news very well as I felt my heart begin to hurt. My biggest fear had come true. I knew him, and he would not back down from a fight. I had done enough research to know the enemy he was about to mess with was some of the most violent and ferocious people to have ever inhabited the earth. The rules of war meant absolutely nothing to these people. Torture seemed to be their idea of great entertainment. I had heard stories about our soldiers taking a lethal dose or a bullet to the head to avoid capture by the Vietcong military.

He wrote in the letter that he had arranged to meet up with my older brother in Hamburg, Germany. My oldest brother was in Germany where he served six years as a tank commander in the United States Army. He said when he told him the news about heading for the front line near the Cambodian border, my oldest brother just held him for a few minutes for what he feared might be the last time. Then he said, "I love you brother, keep your head low and do not be a hero."

I had two weeks to get my head on straight before my brother landed at the Greater Louisville Kentucky Airport. I could tell he was worried about his new assignment as any rational thinking person would be.

Relationships between men and women were tough to maintain during this period, and his was no exception. He and his girlfriend decided to break up during the visit. She just could not handle the thought of him possibly not surviving or even worse, being taken as a prison of war by the Vietcong. To make matters worse, while driving in Trimble County the night before his deployment, he hit a deer in the road and totaled the family's new ford station wagon. Mom and Dad tried to assure him the insurance would replace the car, which it did, but he felt terrible about the accident.

As it was with Dad 30 years earlier, he was set to leave at 4:00 AM on a Thursday morning. We had a big meal the night before. I know he wanted to leave with the memory of the smiles on our faces instead of the sad good-byes he would have received the next morning. He was already packed and intended to leave without saying goodbye to the rest of the family. I stayed up all night. I was determined to see him leave the house for the last time and give him the biggest bear hug I could muster. I knew I had to man-up. The last thing he needed was a little kid sobbing and crying. The only thing I could think to tell him was that if he became a prisoner of war by the Vietcong we would come to get him. He just looked at me before he closed the door on the car and said, "I will hold you to that."

Before closing the door on the car, he gave my mother one last hug, and she handed him a package she had carefully wrapped in a scarf. She told him to keep it with him and if things went bad to open it up; it would help protect him.

In my mind, I was already classified 1A by the military, which meant I was eligible for the draft the day I graduated from high school. My dad was trained during his deployment to fight in the jungle using hand-to-hand combat. My oldest brother was a tank commander. If my brother became a prisoner of war, I intended to quit high school and join up earlier. We would go to Vietnam to keep my promise. Between the three of us, I doubt we would have taken any prisoner in our effort to find our brother and son and bring him home.

Soul was absolutely no help. He was doing something, and I just could not figure it out. His attitude and behavior were changing right before my eyes. He appeared to be communicating with something or somebody in another dimension of the universe. I had never experienced this feeling before, and I knew something serious was going on.

Practice was finally over, and it was time to start the season. The first few games were easy wins, but the schedule was about to become more difficult. The longer we stayed undefeated, the pressure to keep winning became more intense.

In the meantime, the war had grown more violent. The number of soldiers returning home in a pine box was growing fast. The number of wounded men was growing exponentially.

I could feel the pressure building up in my mind, but I had convinced myself the weak needed help much more than I did. My fiancée (That's right, I was engaged my senior year) was the only person on earth who knew how much the pressure of school, performing my chores at home, playing basketball, and concern for my brother were affecting my health. One night after a very intense home game, which we had lost on a last second shot, she met me at the locker room door.

When I walked out, I could see she had been crying. She said she wanted to talk to me. I knew I had played a terrible game. My poor performance on the court was already explained in detail to me by the head coach in the locker room. As I walked out of the locker room, I heard him tell the assistant coach to start looking for my replacement in the starting line-up. Nevertheless, I knew in my heart that she could care less about how I had played the game. Her tears were the kind of tears you shed when someone you love with all of your heart is hurting and you cannot ease their pain.

We exited the side door near the locker room to avoid the crowd who frequently greeted the players after the game. We walked slowly to my car in the parking lot. When we reached the car, she put her arms around me and told me she just wanted to hold me and never let me go. We must have stood there for 30 minutes just holding on to each other. The parking lot was now completely empty, and the parking lot lights had shut down for the night. I convinced her to let me open the door so we could get in. When we settled in the car, she put her arms around me, placed her head on my shoulder, and said, "Please God, help me take care of my man." We drove to her house without saying another word to each other. Once we reached her house, I could tell she had something on her mind. I asked her to share her thoughts with me. I said, "Penny for your thoughts." She said she was very upset earlier in the day. She was crying in her room when her mother knocked on the door and asked her if she was all right. She told her mother about what was happening to me and she did not know what to do. Her mother loved me almost as much as she did her daughter. She said she too had noticed I was struggling. The only advice she could give her was to "be there when the tree comes crashing down. Let him know you are going to support him through the thick and the thin of everything happening."

I tried to assure her I was going to be okay and I just needed a little time to recover. Her compassion did help eases my pain for the night.

The next day was Saturday. In an ordinary world, most students were able to sleep in and not have much to do at home. This was not the case for me. We had tobacco to strip and move on to the floor at the Golden Burley warehouse to hit the first sale date. By four o'clock, I needed to meet the bus at the high school. Our team would travel to Lexington, Kentucky to take on a school that had more students in their senior class than we had in our entire school system. They had just upset the number one school in the state and the nation on Friday night. I was relieved to see my name in the starting lineup. The assistant coach gave me an encouraging wink and said, "Please do not let me down." I played as hard as I could, but I still felt like I was running through wet concrete the second half of the game. My long-range shots were off the mark for me, even though I scored 16 points. My legs were heavy and my quickness was suffering. To the untrained eye of the fans, I apparently looked good out there.

All of our high school, basketball, and football games were broadcasted live on the local radio station, 100.1 WVCM radio, located high on top of Mound Hill Road. The two announcers nicknamed Flannel Mouth Fultz and Good Game Charlie were two kind men and had between the two of them watched every single game we had ever played. I can still remember one summer night shooting jump shots at the old outside basketball goal in the high school parking lot. Good Game Charlie pulled up in his car and asked me if he could rebound for me. He said I could get up more shots if he rebounded the ball for me. About two hours later and several hundred shot, the court lights went out for the night. He told me he felt my mother was probably getting worried about me and that I should get on home. He also shared with me that he had been involved in high school basketball for nearly 40 years. He had watched all of the Carroll County High School Basketball Stars of the past. He said in his opinion I was the purest shooter of them all. Considering the fact that several of the past players were my idols, I considered his words a major compliment.

Nevertheless, those two were considered experts by most people in the state. They both made the statement during the game that I was playing okay but something was wrong. My fiancée did not attend the game but did listen along with 4,500 local fans and friends to the broadcast. She told me they said it looked like I needed a rest and looked mentally exhausted. I think most people blew off that observation when I tipped in a basket at the buzzer to force the game into overtime.

We won the game when our All-State star player hit two free throws with only a few seconds left on the clock. It was our biggest game up to that point in the schedule. No one picked us to win. By winning the game, we proved to the rest of the teams in the state we could play with and beat the big schools.

I remember getting dressed and joining the rest of the team on the bus. It was freezing cold outside, and the bus was frigid. The bus driver, who was supposed to warm up the bus, got caught up in the excitement of the game and forgot it was his responsibility to have the bus warm. He did that several times during the season. Some of the parents had prepared ham sandwiches for the team to eat on the long trip home from Lexington. I felt good about the win, but I could not believe how tired I was. In those days, it was normal for a player to lose as much as 10 pounds of body weight during an intense game. I likely lost more weight than normal because of the effort I had to exert just to look normal. Nevertheless, the ham sandwiches were delicious. The handmade meals tasted great and were always appreciated by the players and coaches. I certainly hoped the coach let the parents and school administrators know how much we enjoyed the sandwiches. The bus finally warmed up, and I fell fast asleep along with the rest of the players.

We got back to the high school about 2:00 AM due to the snow-covered roads and poor visibility. The head coach announced he was very proud of us and decided to not practice on Sunday afternoon, as usually and he was canceling practice on Monday. The next game was the following Friday night, so we still had plenty of time to prepare for our next opponent. Several of the players stated that the reason he really canceled practice was due to an ankle injury to one of our best players. The coach had a connection with the University of Kentucky Sports Medicine group. His real plan was to take the player to Lexington for treatment on Monday.

It did not matter to me what the reason was for canceling the two practices. I just felt relieved I could rest on Sunday. My family took Sunday off as a spiritual day of rest. Hey, if God decided to rest on the seventh day, so could I. When I exited the bus, I noticed my fiancée, her mother, and several other mothers waiting at the gym door. I thought it was my welcoming committee, but she told me they were there to talk to the head coach about my health. I convinced them not to speak to the coach. I told them he had canceled practice for Sunday and Monday. This would provide plenty of time to rest up. They told me they would honor my request but they would be watching me play next Friday's game. If it appeared to them that I was suffering, they would step in. It was great to spend time with my fiancée, and it was certainly unexpected. I offered to take her home, but her mother said, "Absolutely not. You get my butt home to rest, and I mean now!" Then she said, "Nice tip-in. I wish we could have been there to see it. My fiancée told her mother I was just showing off for her. The three of us hugged and the evening ended.

As I was driving home, I tried to communicate with Soul to no avail. I told him I loved him and whatever he was doing, he had my full support, but please do not take any chances. I missed him with all of my heart. I guess I finally got to him when he told me he had to leave me for a while. He had been involved in some basic hand-to-hand military type training for several weeks. He was going to join in with thousands of angels in the battle, and that was all he could share with me until he returned.

You can only imagine how lonely I felt the rest of the night. I had grown to trust Soul. We had developed a relationship of mutual respect for one another. I knew what he was doing had to be blessed by God, and I certainly trusted God, and he knew how I felt about Soul. I think I stopped worrying about things I did not have the power to change or control. I went to church on Sunday morning and spent the rest of the day with my family.

My plan for Monday was to go to class, get home as early as possible, finish my chores, do my homework, and go to bed early. The day went well up until it was time to watch the 6:00 PM news. You may remember earlier in the story my mother watched the Vietnam segment of the daily newscast. If we were home, we all watched it with her. During the six-minute report from the front lines in Vietnam, you could hear a pin drop in our living room. We all crowded around the black and white Motorola and hoped for the best. Several families had actually seen their loved ones serving in battle during the telecast and for a brief moment knew they were okay.

It is still hard to describe what we saw on our television screen. The newscaster set the story up by describing a war scene like nothing he had witnessed during all of his time covering the war. He said he filmed an actual attack on a Regiment of US soldiers by North Vietnam jungle fighters earlier in the day. The NV had crossed the DMZ and fired on our soldiers, clearly ignoring the boundaries agreed upon by the Vietnamese Government and the United States military. He reported numerous US infantry soldiers killed and hundreds more wounded by the initial barbaric attack by the VC soldiers.

He said in his expert opinion, he felt the entire regiment (3,000-5,000 men) would have been wiped out, if not for a platoon of about 50 very brave and determined infantry sharpshooters. "These men put it all on the line, dug in, and returned fire on the thousands of Vietcong fighters. The attack was such a surprise, some of the men had to engage in hand-to-hand combat to defeat the enemy. I have never witnessed the spirit demonstrated in combat today by the Americans. I saw these men become warriors today, and at times, it looked like they had super human strength. They saw things around them that ordinary people could not see. One may think they had eyes in the back of their head. I will assure you folks, the enemy found out today what fighting for freedom and having the backs of your comrades in arms actually means.

"Frankly," he said, "I am still lost for words. I know this may sound ridiculous to you, but it appears these men were led by a higher power in this battle. Within a few minutes, the VC started retreating as if though they had seen a ghost. They were tripping all over each other during their retreat. The bullets from their guns aimed directly at our troops seemed to veer off at the last second and fall harmlessly to the ground.

"The enemy soldiers were retreating so fast down the hill, they appear to be taking fifteen-foot strides. Our men, on the other hand, were fresh as a ripe tomato pulled from the vine and eaten right in the garden."

Then I heard the reporter say the commander on the ground had received orders from Washington DC to capture or kill every single Vietcong fighter who carried out the brutal attack. The order was to chase them all the way across Cambodia and try to surround them at the Mekong River. "If they escape, chase them all the way to the shores of the South China Sea and beyond. This action demands justice. God be you and the United States of America."

He let his viewing audience know that what he was about to show us may be very disturbing to many families watching the broadcast. When the tape started to roll, my family immediately saw my second to oldest brother. My mother pointed to the screen and said, "There he is; that is my son."

He was leading his men to safety toward an evacuation helicopter. At one point, he must have been not more than a few feet from the camera. We had no doubt it was my brother. He was running toward the helicopter in full stride while continuing to fire his rifle at the enemy. The soldiers on the helicopter were yelling for him to get aboard. They were ready to lift off. He was within a few feet of the helicopter when he suddenly stopped. My dad screamed out, "Do not stop son; get on the damn helicopter. Please get on the helicopter."

My brother had somehow heard a wounded soldier's call for help in the midst of the noise made by the pursuing battle. The loud sounds made by the guns could not drown out the call for help. The men yelling for him to get on board could not override the sounds from a brothers or sister's distress call. He heard, "Master Sergeant Clifton, please help me. I am hit, I have been hit, please do not leave me behind." The wounded soldier was shot in the back and could not get up on his own to make it back to safety. I had no doubt about what was about to happen, as my brother turned and looks at his brother reaching out to him. He did not hesitate for even a second as he ran back through the enemy fire. I know I saw the image of two guardian angels shielding and blocking the bullets headed straight for my brother's head. When my brother reaches his brother in arms, he puts down his hand and pulls him up on his back. He began carrying the man to safety. Once the brothers on the helicopter, realized what had happened, they provide the cover for him to return to the helicopter. They pulled both men up into the chopper as it was lifting off the ground.

"A brave soldier will always take on the risk involve in saving his fellow soldier. To civilians like me we consider this an act of heroism. To a soldier it is an act of love, and a bond that develops with each other on the battlefield. Only a soldier understands the courage and trust essential for survival for those who are in this unimaginable situation. Soldiers are willing to sacrifice their own life to never leave a wounded soldier behind."

The helicopter was taking on heavy fire, and at first, we thought he and his men were safe. Then about 100 feet above the ground, we saw the chopper start to smoke. It had, obviously been hit by ground fire from the Vietcong barrage of bullets. The chopper was struggling to land, and soon disappears from the view of the camera. It dropped out of the sky and down behind a mountain or a large hill. There was not a massive explosion or a fireball. The reporter said he did not personally witness the fate of the helicopter. He did receive confirmation it did land and everyone on board did survive the crash. He said it landed deep in the jungle, which was heavily occupy by the Vietcong militants.

The reason the men on the ground airlifted out was to get ahead of the Vietcong fighter. The idea was to force surrender or face the consequences. The helicopter was carrying the same men who fought off the original attack. The reporter on the ground said, "I know this much about the team on the helicopter. They won't be captured, and I would not want to be one of the Vietcong who shot them down."

When the newscast ended, our living room was completely silent. My mother walked over to the television and turns it off. She aggressively pointed her finger at all of us and told us not turn the set back on until she had heard from her son or the military police showed up with the news of his capture. She said she wanted us to pray as we had never prayed before: pray he escaped and was not taken prisoner of war by his captives. My dad took her to their bedroom, and I could hear her crying for the next several hours.

My oldest sister tried to calm the fears of the younger siblings. My brothers and I went to our room to talk about what to do next. I told them I had promised my brother that if he were ever took prisoner by the VC, I would quit school, join the military, and come get him.

I called my fiancée and told her what had happened. She said her family was watching the broadcast and she knew it was my brother in the scene. She said she always knew for some reason it was a high probability he could be captured. She said her dad had already led his family in prayer for my brother and his combat team to survive. They prayed he did not become a prisoner of war. She had already talked to her mom about what she would say and do. Then she said, "If he was captured, you have to go get him, but please do not die…. I will be by your side in spirit and in love. May God be with you." After a long pause, she told me she understood that a promise is a promise.

She knew this was the last thing I needed to deal with. However, suddenly none of the things bothering me before this happened seemed to be nearly as important as they once were. Then all she could do was cry as we sat and just held the phone without saying a word for almost an hour. Finally, she said, "All I can say is, I will be here for you no matter what the outcome." She said she loved me as she hung up the phone. I know it was breaking her heart as I could hear her and her mother in the background crying their eyes out as the phone went dead.

It was getting late, and I laid my head down on my pillow. My youngest brother crawled up in my arms and was sound to sleep in very few minutes. I tried to doze off, but my mind was running about a hundred thoughts per second. I missed Soul something terrible, but I knew if he could be with me, he would.

Then I started to put things into perspective. Soul had slipped up one night and said something about how difficult it was to perform hand-to-hand combat. I thought he was referring to a war movie we had been watching a few days earlier.

Bullets fired at the troops somehow missed their targets from point-blank distance and fell harmlessly into the woods. My brother's path to save the wounded soldier was cleared and protected by what appeared to me to be the image of two guardian angels.

Thirty-Four

SOUL WHERE ARE YOU?

It hit me like a ton of bricks. I sat straight up in bed and cried out to the heavens. "Oh God, please help me; please find Soul. I think he is in Vietnam."

"Soul is in Vietnam!"

At first, I thought maybe God sent him to the frontlines as a test to see if he had gained the courage, he would need for his next assignment. Then I realized God would not have sent him into battle without me because he is my guardian angel. I knew if Soul was not defending me he was on a much larger mission. The only possible answer was he was defending God and the place Soul called home in heaven. When I thought about the ugliness going on in the world at the time, it would have been easy to believe God was giving up on his creation. It was time to end it and start over again.

Between the United States and the Soviet Union, we had enough nuclear bombs to destroy the earth. The fear of war and eventual devastation was so vast, millions of people, including my family, had installed nuclear bomb shelters to help us survive the blast and fallout from a nuclear explosion. The war in Vietnam was growing out of control. The US government had somehow decided to blame the ugliness of the war on the very young men it sent over there to do the dirty work. The news media gained authorization by the federal government to film and broadcast terrible war scenes from Vietnam. Those scenes, along with a long stream of rumors and propaganda, fueled the fire, leading to protest on college campuses. For the first time and hopefully the last, American citizens turned a raft of anger on the young men coming home from the battlegrounds. There were no cheers of appreciation or celebration for our men returning home after completing their mission in Vietnam. Our soldiers were beat up and spit on by their fellow citizens when they arrived home. Airports and harbors were lined with hate signs. The instigators who produced such terrible messages on banners and signs displaying hatred should cause all Americans who participated to hang their head in shame. It got so bad, the soldiers began coming home after midnight and attempting to sneak into the country as if they were illegal aliens. We were determined that when my brother came home he would be treated like a hero. Just as we had to band together to defend one another as children, we would be there to celebrate his accomplishment.

Hard drugs, including heroin and hallucinogenic drugs like LSD were out of control and used by hundreds of thousands of Americans, young and old. Violent crimes were at an all-time high. Young men graduating from high school or over 18 years old, by order of the federal government, had to join the military for a minimum of three years. These boys had no choice but to join the military and were shipped nine thousand miles from home to fight and possibly die in a war American citizens were not supporting. The alternative was not to register with the military draft board and hide out like criminals on the run. The ones who refused the draft were label "draft dodgers." Refusing the draft was breaking the law and many left the country they loved and gave up their citizenship.

The government decided the way to break up a protest on one college campus in Indiana was to give a shoot to kill order to the armed guards. America cried when we witnessed firsthand on national television the guards shoot live fire rounds at the students participating in a non-violent protest. Several students participating in the demonstration were shot and killed while many others were left in the streets wounded and bleeding before the massacre ended.

Then protest and demonstration turned violent in the South immediately following the assassination of one of the greatest civil rights leader in the history of the world in Memphis, Tennessee. Most major cities looked like war zones: vehicles were turned over and burned, occupants pulled out of their homes and businesses, and some were severely beaten and sometimes killed. Buildings were set on fire and burned to the ground. A militant group later known as Helter Skelter ravaged the west coast led by one of the most viscous men to have ever lived. This group of certified hippies did not just kill their captives, they tortured them to death with swords and knifes and wrote terrible messages on refrigerators and entrance doors with their victims blood. Their main purpose was to survive an attack by another militant group known as the Black Panthers.

Then the second of the Kennedy brothers was assassinated following a presidential campaign speech in Los Angeles, California. The loss of one of the greatest civil rights leaders in the world and the death of a future president were two of America darkest moments in time.

Those are just a few of the things happening in this country. But in fact, the rest of the world as a whole was messed up more than the Americans were. I can only imagine the sadness God must have felt in his heart when he assessed the ugliness and violence that had laden his kingdom.

It hurt my heart so bad to know the danger Soul and my brother were in. Nevertheless, I also knew there was no limit to what Soul and my brother would do to protect heaven and our country. The action described by the reporter was only the part we could see through a television camera. Judging by what the reporter had said about the battle I had no doubt Soul had joined the other angels including the ones protecting my brother. I am now convinced it was Soul and my brother's guardian angel that cleared the path for him to recover his wounded brother.

For the American soldiers, including my brother, this was a fight for freedom and preventing the spread of Communism into the Democratic Nation of South Vietnam. I knew in my heart that if Soul was there, it was a battle he would gladly give up his very existence to win. Every angel would be willing to perish forever to protect our creator.

Just before Soul turned me off and stopped listening to me, we talked about the people who made up Cambodia and North Vietnam. These people were not only atheist, they were some of the most violent people on earth. He felt they were the biggest threat to Christianity since the beginning of the religion, when Jesus walked the earth. He had hoped the United States would virtually destroy these people before a higher power would need to step in.

It was apparent things were not going as well as our government was telling us it was. I think the angels knew if they did not join in the fight, heaven would be changed forever. If they allowed the beliefs of these people to convince others, the kingdom of heaven would cease to exist. God would no longer see the need to protect those who do believe in him.

This battle for the angels was for their very existence. They were willing to put it all on the line for God. If I was right and Soul was with my brother, I knew he was safe and he survived a helicopter crash.

I felt hurt, confused, and exhausted and drifted off to sleep. Sometime during the night, the demons came out, and Soul was not there to protect me. Suddenly I felt all alone. I begged Soul to help me, "Please help me Soul, my heart aches for my mother, and I am scared for my brother."

The image of my fiancée popped up in my head. She was talking to me about courage. I had felt such sadness when we had hung up the phone earlier. I could see her holding her pillow and see tears streaming down her face. Even though we were 30 miles apart, I could feel her heart breaking, but I could do nothing to ease her pain.

I did not know what to do or say or how to act. For the first time in my life, I was lost. I can still remember what happened next as if it happened yesterday. I found myself on my knees in front of my tree on top of Cedar Point praying to God above. For the first time in my life, my strength was gone and I felt defeat. I had no answers. I could not run faster, jump higher, or work harder to get past this time in my life. I cannot explain how I got from my bed to the praying tree on Cedar Point. I also couldn't explain how I suddenly had a front row seat to the battle going on 9,000 miles from my house. I do not know if it was God's way of reuniting Soul and me or if he had an even bigger plan, for me to someday write about another miracle.

I saw Soul and my brother first. You cannot even imagine how good it felt to see both of them, but especially my brother. I could not wait to get home to tell mom he was okay. Then I saw what appeared to be several million angels and many thousands of troops chasing the enemy toward the sea.

I heard a drum playing in the background as I watched the enemy retreat up a very steep hill. I could hear the sounds of rough seas just over the other side of the hill.

As the enemy ran to the shoreline, I could tell the angels were determined to drive them into the sea to their death. The angels felt this was the way life on earth for these people should end. They loved God and their home in heaven. No one was going to take that away without a fight to the death.

Then the sky turned very dark, and no one could see anything, not even the angels. It appeared time did not exist. The clock was still moving, but everything and everybody were not going anywhere. Then the image of God appeared above the water approximately 50 feet from the shoreline. The sky was so bright that when you looked directly into it, all your eyes could see was a thousand points of light.

The enemy could see God as he appeared at the edge of the beach. The shore was just beneath an old weathered wooden cross standing on the side of the hill overlooking the sea.

The sea was blood red, indicating that something terrible was about to happen. Without God saying a word, thousands of Vietnamese running for their life fell to their knees instead of running into the sea to a certain death. They started begging God for forgiveness. Many of the enemy soldiers lay down their weapons, confessed their sins, and asked God for forgiveness. Well over a million Vietcong chose to celebrate the Lord as their savior. The government of Vietnam does what it can even today to discourage its citizens from believing in Jesus or a God in heaven.

Before God left the shore, I could see him look up at the cross positioned at the edge of the ledge. From the expression on his face, one may assume he was thinking about what else needed to happen on this planet to convince all humankind eternal life exists in heaven. "The door is open to anyone who will accept God as his or her savior. It is that simple. I created humanity, and I purposely reward those who do believe in heaven and me and severely punished those who stand in my way. I parted the sea to save the Christians from an inevitable death. I provided guidelines on two tablets and gave them to Moses to share with all humankind. Ultimately, I sacrificed my son's life on the cross, just like the one over there on that hill.

Millions of angels crowded around our creator to share their undivided love for him. They helped him lift his head. He could now see the billions and billions of angels and people on earth who did believe in him and his word. Each individual was willing to give up their existence on earth in appreciation for what God meant to them. As God slowly turned his head to look over his flock, I could hear music playing in the background. I had learned in church and in sports that music can help us reach down and find our real sense of spirit and willingness to fight to overcome almost any confrontation. The angels lifted my spirit when they started singing a beautiful song expressing how much they loved God. The words in their song appeared to have kindled a new vision for our creator. I could feel God's emotions changing as the angels continued to sing. It was as if God discovered a new kingdom, full of love and hope he knew would last for the next several thousand years.

Then something happened right before his eyes that is almost beyond words. At the bottom of the cross, Jesus appeared. I can hardly contain my emotion to find suitable words to describe what happened next. Jesus was smiling and seemed to be at peace. He was happier than in any painting or portrait I have witnessed of him.

Jesus told his father he did what was necessary at the time to begin the healing process the world needed so badly. Jesus described his time on earth and his pilgrimage across the holy land to remind his father it was never easy and likely never would be. Jesus said, "I found a world rapidly turning into the place you destroyed with a great flood, my father. On the other hand, I also found thousands of people everywhere I went searching and reaching out for something growing in their hearts. They could not define it because it was new. They knew if they kept moving they would eventually find it, and it would be worth all the sacrifices made along the journey. Before my pilgrimage, these very people were shamed and beaten, but not even when faced with such brutality could the spirit they carried in their bodies be killed.

"When I walked across the holy land, I met millions of these same people whom secretly believed in you and the message I was sharing about a better life. These saints were willing to put their lives on the line to make a path for me to preach your message. Father, they sacrificed their life for something they could not see. They could only feel the joy that filled their hearts when we talked about heaven's gates and what waited for them on the other side. When my followers found out about my crucifixion, they rallied together to create a world through their own sacrifices, fulfilling your great promise. You promised these people, father, that if they believed in you and heaven they would find eternal life. Father, look around you; these are your angels. They are my people. Father, I beg of you, please do not let my life and my ultimate sacrifice of death on earth end this way."

To be honest I felt frozen in time, but Soul felt right at home with everything happening. Then I learned something about Soul that brought me tears of joy and pride. I was so proud of him and the fact he is my guardian angel.

Jesus did something next that surprised me, along with the other billions in attendance. He certainly caught his father off his guard. Some of the most beautiful music ever composed now filled the earth. The music sounded like the best from Bach, Beethoven, Mozart, Wagner, Schubert, and Tchaikovsky combined. Then I heard a melody being sung in the background by the greatest singers to have ever lived. The group consisted of Horne, Pavarotti, Sutherland, Domingo, Callas, Houston, and you guessed it, Soul. His voice and words filled my heart, and the power in his words delivered such a strong message.

I think what happened next was the biggest surprise. Jesus looked up at his father from the base of the old wooden cross, and he starts to sing the most beautiful song ever sang. In his song, he sang about faith, love, joy, happiness, hope, and a future that seems so far away if you look at the world today. When the song ended, the world rejoiced.

Jesus was encouraged by the millions working hard to follow the words written on those stones. He applauded the people who teach the young the real meaning of life, love, and the true meaning of God's word and promise.

When a tear formed in his father's eye and ran down his face, I knew he was suddenly having one of his best days. When Jesus finished his song, he turned and looks up at the cross. He smiled and said a prayer only the angels could hear. Jesus turned and looks at his father and said, "My father, I will let my people know, 'The best is yet to come. Keep spreading the word my people. The best is yet to come, and I will show you the way.'"

His father placed his hand on his face and decided to meet with Jesus, father to son and face to face. He said, "I believed you my son. I believe in you. You sacrificed your life on the cross, and the pain was more than I could watch. I can look around and see the fruits of your labor and sacrifice. However, today I realized it was not only your death that brought them here; it was the incredible amount of love you shared with them on your journey. The heavenly spirit you carried across the land during your pilgrimage has lasted for thousands of years. People still fight for the very love and spirit you gave to the earth. We now have the Christians, Jews, Muslims, Buddhists, Hindus, and others finding their way to the kingdom of heaven in record numbers." Then he said, with what I think was humor, "We will need to build a much larger gate to let them all in. Thank you my son."

Once they finished, the sky was once again bright. The surrounding was full of peace as the birds sang "Heaven Song," sung by the angels earlier. As I witnessed earlier in my life, God said, "Let us pray." He thanked the angels for their sacrifice and once again assured them the kingdom of heaven would always be their home. Amen!

The troops finally reached the shoreline. At first, they could not figure out what the enemy was doing. They had never witnessed these people on their knees. They certainly did not understand why they lay down their weapons. Finally, my brother told his troops they were praying. The men decided to take the entire group as prisoners of war instead of sending them into the sea to die.

I knew it was time for me to go home. I had the answers I was looking for and just needed a few days to recover. My little brother got up early to go downstairs to tell mom I was sick. He was worried about me and she needed to check me out. I spent the next three days in a local hospital in complete isolation recovering from what the doctor called "Total exhaustion." The no visitors sign posted on my door at the hospital provided me the time I needed with Soul and God. The only people I saw the entire stay in the hospital wee my future wife, her mother, and my parents. Finally, on the fourth day, I was able to convince the doctor I was fine and ready to leave the hospital.

Thirty-Five

PARENTS TO COACH TIMEOUT

My mother, my wife to be, and future mother-in-law made it very clear to the coach that I would be sitting out for at least one game. My mother told the coach that if sitting out cost me my starting position, he would be answering to her. The coach agreed and assured my mother my health and wellness was more important than a basketball game. I and the other injured starter with the sprained ankle watched the next game from the stands with our girlfriends. We watched our teammates play the game we love. They were incredible to watch. For me, it was the first time I saw our team through the eyes of our fans. We won the game as we watched our teammates put up over 100 points again against the Gallatin County Wildcats.

Our next game was against one of the top teams in the nation. We had to have our game face on for the game or we knew it would end in a blowout. Even though I was able to convince my family and coach I was ready to play in the game, something was still missing.

The game started, and I was still sluggish. I was off the mark and missing my long-range jumpers. The first assistant coach just kept yelling for me to keep shooting they will eventually go through the basket. The head coach was not so sure, and he called my substitute to sit beside him for additional instruction. I knew I was one missed shot away from spending the rest of the half on the bench. A few minutes later three players, including me, dove into the bleachers after a loose ball. As we were returning to the floor, one of the opposing players intentionally placed his large shoe on my head and neck, pushing my face into the hardwood seat. Then he called me a loser. Both radio announcers were directly in front of where we had entered the bleachers. They saw the whole thing and needed restraining by the fans from coming onto the floor to my defense. My future wife and mother-in-law both wanted a piece of the player. Once the referees got control of the game, they signaled the scoring table that a technical foul would be assessed on the player who stepped on my neck. We learned by the time the quarter ended that because of what the announcers had said over the radio, people came from their homes to show up at the gym and defend the team and players they had adopted as family members. The police asked Good Game Charlie to make an announcement I was okay and the players were safe. He asked everyone surrounding the school to go back home and enjoy the rest of the broadcast from there.

The official signaled the score table that I would shoot two technical free throws because of the aggression from the opposing player. My head coach called time out so the trainer could stop the blood from pouring out of my mouth. As I was returning to the floor, the head coach for the other team told me he was sorry and that he would take his player out. I told him to let him play. I said we would take care of his aggressiveness on the floor. The referee asked me if I was okay and then handed me the ball for the first of two free throws. I still felt weak, and to add to it, I was in pain. I was going through my regular routine used every time I shot free throws. I pointed my toes toward the rim, dribbled twice, took one look at the rim, dribbled a third time, and I was relaxed and ready to shoot the ball. Just after the second dribble, Soul popped in my mind. Just before I shot the ball, I closed my eyes and said this prayer: "God, thank you for giving me a front row seat to watch Soul do what he had to do in Vietnam. His acts of courage will never be forgotten in heaven and on earth. Soul, I saw you on the front lines, and I know what you did to save my brother's life. Please come back to me as soon as you can."

As I put the ball in my normal shooting position, something happened. A flash of light hit me, and apparently the rest of the fans in the building, like a bolt of lightning. My mother told me later the two radio announcers made the statement that something had happened, but they could not explain it. As I took my final look at the rim, I heard, "Swisheroo Clifton has two. I am home." I tried not to smile, as I knew 4,500 fans were watching me. Soul said, "Do not smile, they will think you have lost your mind. Your brother is fine. He had a wound to his hand, but he is going to be okay." With my eyes closed shut, I released the ball as I had done millions of times on the old court next to my house. I could tell by the cheers from the fans it went through the hoop. I felt something that was missing since the day Soul had gone to defend heaven and protect my brother return to my life.

The two announcers knew immediately I was back and said, "I think we are about to see something special here tonight folks. Just sit back and enjoy the moment as we bring it to you play by fantastic play right here on WVCM radio high atop Mound Hill."

When we returned down the floor to play defense, I asked our best player to switch with me and let me guard the player who had called me a loser. He agreed, and by the time the game had ended, I had outscored him 25-0. Our team won the game by thirty points. Winning the game was important but not nearly as important to me as having Soul back in my life.

I think Soul and I both knew our relationship had changed, and we both had reasons to celebrate. Soul needed time to recover from what he had been through during the war. He told me he was very sad and he and some of his friends had to spend some time with the families of the soldiers who had died during the battle. I told him I understood and to come back when he was ready.

Thirty-Six

The Pearl Makes it Home

Once I got dressed, I walked back out into the gym. My wife to be met me at half-court for our usual embrace and kiss following every game, win or lose. I could tell she had been crying, but this time it was happy tears. She had what she had prayed to God to give her, and she did not intend to let me get away again. She held me in her arms, and I told her my brother was okay and so was I. She said, with the biggest smile I had seen on her face in months, that she knew the second she saw me smile just before the first free throw things were going to be okay. She said, "I could not believe you hit the free throw with your eyes closed." I said, "I guess it was a miracle shot; I must have had help from my guardian angel." Soul just smiled until she told me the ball touched the corner of the rim. I said, "Well, he must have been a little tired tonight, I know I was…."

As we left the floor, we walked past the two radio announcers; they shouted out to her to take good care of me. They also said to me, "Welcome back son, welcome back!" Good game Charlie just winked as if he knew the story of my life.

The next day, my family received word my brother was okay and he would be coming home soon. It was the first time in several weeks we could watch the evening news, and I am glad we did.

The announcer asked the station to run some footage from a previous war scene. He said the footage was a battle he had covered a few weeks earlier. My family had our eyes glued to the set as we recognized it was the footage from when we last saw my second oldest brother. The announcer said, "This footage is about the evacuation. This young soldier returned in the line of fire to help a wounded soldier to the helicopter. As the soldier was jumping onto the rail of the chopper, a bag fell out of his backpack and landed on the ground. I saw this happen, and after the bullets stopped flying, I went over and picked it up. I knew it must have been important to the soldier. I decided I would track him down no matter where he lived in the world and do two things: First, I would thank him for saving his friend's life and for his bravery, which was one of my proudest moments while covering the front lines. Second, I would personally return the package to him."

He said late at night he could not sleep until he knew what was in the package. His curiosity got the best of him and he had to open the package to see what was inside. When he unfolded the silk scarf, the first thing he found was a letter from the young man's mother.

The letter described how much she loved her seven sons and seven daughters. She went on to explain that this item had been saving the lives of young men from all over the world for several hundred years and it had even saved her life. She prayed every night it would save her son's life and he could return home to his family in Locust Creek, Kentucky. She wrote in the letter that the item in the package was a gift to her husband while he served in World War II. She explained that her husband was on duty one night while serving in the Philippines when he noticed a Japanese soldier was obviously starving to death, and her husband slipped him some MREs that apparently saved his life. "The Japanese soldier placed the gift into my husband's sleeping bag one night while my husband was sleeping. My husband tried to find the Japanese soldier to return the gift but was unsuccessful before he deployed back home to the United States.

"My husband has stated many times he wishes he could find the man and return the gift. He understood why he did what he did, but this item was a part of this man's ancestry and it belonged to him and his family."

The announcer had to take a deep breath and appeared to choke up when the camera moved for a close up of the war-beaten reporter. He said, "As I finished unwrapping the scarf, I noticed three holes in the outer layers. As I removed the final layer, I found three bullets that undoubtedly would have killed her son. The beautiful pearl handled pistol inside had done its deed one more time. It stopped the bullets fired from an enemy rifle that would have hit her son in the back.

"A few days after I found the gun, I was transferred to Tokyo, Japan for a few days of rest and relaxation. I was telling a Japanese colleague about finding the pearl-handled pistol on the battlefield. Then I shared the story about how it had saved this young soldier's life. I could tell the Japanese reporter was very interested and asked me if he could see the gun.

He took one look and started to cry uncontrollably. Once he regained his composure, he told me the pistol belonged to his father. His father had told him the story about how this American soldier had given him some of his food one night, which saved his life. He said he left the gun in his sleeping bag as a token of his good deed. He said he knew the officer would immediately know the value of the gift and would have never accepted it, but he said he knew this man was a good man true to his country and true to his faith and his family.

"The young reporter's story matched the one my mother had described in the letter. The young reporter took me to his father's house to show him the gun, and the tears immediately started to pour down his face as he pulled the gun to his heart.

"I told him the story about how the gun had saved the life of the son of the man he gave the pistol to. I told him about how the young man had returned to the battlefield to save the life of a fellow soldier. I read him the letter from the boy's mother, which explained that the gift had served its purpose. It needed to be where it belonged.

"The man invited me to his home for the night meal, which I accepted. I took the gun along, and once the meal was over, I handed him the pistol. He invited me to join his entire family into a special worship room in his house. I felt very welcome and privileged to be in the room.

"The room was full of special keepsakes passed-down from generation to generation. Cases full of military medals honoring his family for bravery lined most of the solid mahogany shelves, which seemed to encase the entire room. Mounted over the fireplace was a big samurai sword, surrounded by large portraits of his great grandfathers and father all holding an individual case. The man used his key to open a beautiful glass case and removed a box matching the one in the pictures. The man unlocked the box and handed it to his son. His son opened the box and, to my surprise, inside was a twin pearl-handled pistol. Next to the pistol was an empty case designed to hold the other pistol. The Japanese soldier placed the pistol in the box next to its twin." As I listened to the reporter tell his story, I could feel Soul reliving every moment of what he had just endured over the past several weeks. My mother's eyes were full of tears, and my dad seemed to want to stand and salute the bravery of his second oldest son.

"The Japanese man led his family in a special prayer that had been passed down for thousands of years. He asked his son to take a picture of him holding the case. Once his son took the photo, he handed the case to his oldest son. The gun has been returned, and legend stated that as long as the guns remained in the sealed case, their country would remain a peaceful country and they would grow as the world grows." To this date, the Japanese have not engaged in another battle. They seem to have learned a lesson shortly after those two bombs exploded some seventy years or so ago. The rest of the world should understand that war is hell but easy to start, and peace is easy but hell to keep.

The reporter said, "To the family and especially the mother who wrote the note and the father who gave the man some food from Hunter Bottom right near Locust Creek, Kentucky. I would like to tell you the gun has returned to its rightful owners. The owners will be forever grateful it made yet another journey and found its way back to where it belongs. I think this is one of my most important stories about this war to date, God Bless America and good night."

I knew my brother and the men he led to victory understood this battle was not just for freedom. The men he lost under his command would always have a special place in his heart and would remain on his mind for the rest of his life. Shortly after the battle, the war was over for my brother and he did come home a hero in the minds and hearts of all the people who counted. He did return during the light day. His family met him at the airport. As he walked past the flag that we hung in his honor and the men he served with, he stopped and saluted. He was our hero and he did everything his country asked him to do. If there is anybody out there that would like to dispute his contribution and the contribution of all of the men and women that served this country during the Vietnam War, his thirteen brothers and sisters would like to meet you down in Hunters Bottom right near Locust Creek. Watch out for fastballs between the eyes, and this time we will use a real baseball. By the way, in this part of America, we celebrate all of our men and women who serve our country. So if you happen to show up, do not be surprised to find 5,000 of our best friends ready to defend and fight to protect our soldiers who willingly protected us.

My brother returned to a loving family, and he found his true love in our hometown. The two of them have been married for over forty years now. They have two fantastic children. Both of his children have graduated from the University of Louisville and have enjoyed successful careers. Both are loving parents and have given my brother and our family five amazing grandchildren. If you ask my second oldest brother about what he treasures most in the world, I do not think it would have anything to do with the war or his personal accomplishments in his life; it would be all about his wife, children, and grandchildren. His family has remained faithful to the Lord, our savior.

I am sure he still remembers those men who died during the war. He remembers his men every time he visits the Vietnam Memorial in Washington. Many of the names on the wall are people he personally knew and truly died defending freedom for his family and all Americans. Even though it was a terrible time in his life, I do not think he would have changed a thing. All of those experiences made him the incredible person he is today.

Thirty-Seven

Time to Get Our Game Face On

In basketball, we went on to win most of our remaining games. It was time for the team and the student body to prepare for the post season. The post season included the district, regional, and state tournaments. If you lost, your season was over. Soul was back, and he loved basketball. He especially enjoyed the Carroll County Panthers. I think if he were allowed to make bets with his angel friends and peers, heaven would have been broke by the time our senior season ended.

My routine at school was to spend the first hour of the day in the library reading the newspapers and finishing the previous day's homework. My favorite publications were the local newspapers, including the Carrollton News Democrat, Madison Courier, and the Trimble County Banner. The two state papers were the Lexington Herald and the Louisville Courier-Journal, which was the largest publication in the state. I could tell by the kind words of the columnist in the Louisville Courier journal that he really wanted to declare our school the favorite to win the district tournament and possibly even win the regional.

However, he knew it would not sell papers, and he needed to praise the larger schools located in Lexington, Louisville, Western Kentucky, and Northern Kentucky. His editorial did point out other teams in the tournament had better not look past the little school located where the Big Kentucky River met up with the mighty Ohio River in Carroll County. "This team is well coached and has a potential all-state center and a supporting cast of players who can shoot the eyes out of the basket from anywhere on the floor. The coaches give their two outside sharp-shooters the green light to let it fly from anywhere in the frontcourt."

I remembered the mood of the student body at school the day the tournaments started.

As I walked from class to class, I could hear laughing and students having a good time, wishing the coaches and ball players good luck in that night's district game against the Trimble County Raiders. I felt a sense of confidence from my classmates, but our coaches had done an excellent job of keeping things in perspective for all of the players.

We were on a mission, and we certainly did not want to feel the same pain and disappointment we had felt in the previous year. We lost in the regional final game by the closest of margins. We also had our first wake-up call in the district tournament when we barely squeaked past teams; we had beaten handily in the regular season match-ups.

Once the regular season is over for a high school senior ball player, every tournament game could be the last time he ever has the privilege to put on his school uniform. Therefore, every game is a great game for your team and for you personally.

I think the uncertainty is what makes the end of the season high school tournaments so exciting and pressure packed for the players and the fans in attendance. We all understand you can forget about past results, and any team with a few breaks can upset even the best teams in the tournament.

Our team won its first two games of the district tournament, and each day, I could see the expressions on the student body's faces become more serious. The chatter in the halls lessened each day. Both games were much closer than expected, and some doubt may have been entering the minds of the students. It did not take long to figure out why the students seemed so concerned.

We traveled to district rival Oldham County to play the district finals on Saturday night. The gym was pack with people to the rafters. The fire marshal must have made an exception for the attendance for this game. I remember there were so many people in the gym it was hard to warm up due to fans standing under the basket directly on the end lines.

Oldham County was the favorite to win the game, according to the Courier-Journal, even though we had already beaten them three times during the regular season. The game was very close and was stopped by the referees several times to move fans away from the end lines. With one minute to go in the game, our teams traded baskets, with Oldham County taking a one-point lead. The game turned into a good-old Kentucky high school shoot out. With only six seconds to play, I stole the in-bound pass and hit our all-state player, cutting to the basket for an apparent layup to win the game for Carroll County by one point.

The referee blew his whistle and stepped in with one second left on the clock and waved the basket off. He went to the official scores table and reported that our player was fouled prior to making the layup. The filmed game later clearly showed he made the layup untouched except for a fan who punched him in the ribs as he got close to the baseline after making the layup. The referee announced that the basket was no good and we would need to shoot a one and one at the free throw line. Our all-state player had to hit the first free throw to tie the game and hit the second to win the game.

When the official waved the basket off, our fans got a little angry but stayed in their seats. It was just one of those games where you knew the team who had the ball last was going to win the game. The Oldham County crowd was yelling some ugly stuff at our fans and our team. When they witness the scoreboard keeper take the points our All-State player had scored to win the game for Carroll County off the scoreboard, this put their team up by one point. The police did a splendid job of stopping a fight and protecting the player. Once things settled, down the referees got the players lined up in the lane to shoot the first free throw.

The official under the basket held the ball until the fans standing on the baseline directly under the basket were moved by security. The official handed our all-state player the ball, and he shot the first free throw. The ball went through the net without touching the rim. The referee who had waved off the original layup was standing near the half-court line. When the ball went through the basket to tie the score, the Carroll County crowd got very excited. The referee standing under the basket motioned to the official scorer that the basket was good. He was preparing to hand the ball to our all-state player for the second free throw to win the game for Carroll County if he made a basket.

Just as he started to hand him the ball, the second referee ran into the lane and said that the fans were still too close to the end line and that he was going to disallow the first free throw. Our coaches could not believe what was happening, and our head coach was very close to picking up a technical foul for arguing with the referee. After several minutes, the school officials and the security team got control of the crowd. The Oldham County Superintendent announced the free throw was not going to count due to concern for player safety with the crowd being too close to the end line.

Once the crowd moved back and management agreed to resume the game, the players lined up for the repeat of the first free throw. The referee handed the ball to the Carroll County All-State player, and he hit the free throw to tie the game. The crowd never moved, and the referee handed the ball to the player for the second free throw. As the ball was going through the basket to win the game for Carroll County, the other referee stepped in and waved the shot off. He told the referee under the basket that the fans were interfering with the concentration of the shooter. By this time, it was hard to figure out if the referee was determined not to let Carroll County win the game or if he refused to allow Oldham County to lose the game. For us, it did not matter how many times the referee disallowed the free throws; we were confident our all-state player was going to continue to hit the free throws if it took all night. We had practiced this situation numerous times over the years, and several of us had hit over 100 consecutive free throws many times. On the fourth free throw, he decided to count the basket, and Carroll County won the game.

Once the game ended, it was time to win the fight that actually happened. The fans from Carroll County came on the floor to congratulate our players. Many of the Oldham County fans entered the floor to fight.

Players on both teams were, caught in the middle of the fight while attempting to run off the floor. Several were hit in the face and ribs by flying fists. Some received injuries by hard objects being launched from the top row of bleacher on the Oldham side of the floor.

One fan clearly went over the line and broke a beer bottle across the bleacher. He came after our all-state player with the intention of putting him out of the regional game the following week. One of our cheerleaders, who just happen to be the girlfriend of our all-state player, saw what is about to happen and attacked the drunk fan. She grabbed the assailant by the hair, pulled him to the floor, and held him until the police arrested the man.

Winning the game put Carroll County in the winner's bracket for the regionals, scheduled to start the following week.

When we return to school on Monday, I could tell the students were tired and not really focused on schoolwork. In the first period, a fellow student (president of the national honors society) who had never spoken to me in the four years we had known each other stated she had never been a sports fan. She believed athletes (especially basketball players) received special recognition and privileges that should be reserved for top academic performers. "After all, that is why we actually go to school." Her classmates immediately booed her. The teacher told the students to calm down and let her finish her thoughts. She said she attended the game Saturday night and that she had so much fun and became emotional when the referee waved off the winning baskets. She said it touched her in a way she never knew existed. "I saw my classmates and thousands of members in the community in attendance come together as a team. It felt so good to know we had a winning team on the floor and in the stands. I had never felt such pride in our school and our community."

She said she observed the players on the floor for both teams, and they were as calm and cool as the other side of her pillow. She asked me what was going through my mind when the referee waved off the winning basket and then two more made free throws that would have won the game. I told her our team had been through many games like that one over the past six years. Frankly, the referee was well within his rights. The fans were too close to the playing surface of the court.

She was amazed to hear this from a player's perspective compared to how mad it made fans for the home team and the away team. We had spent thousands of hours over the years dreaming of being in this situation and doing what we needed to do as a team and as individuals to win the game. She said the noise was so loud she could scream in the ear of her best friend sitting right beside her and she could not understand a word she was saying.

I told her, "When we are playing the game, we generally do not hear anything but the commands our teammates are sending to each other and the signals sent to us by our coaches." She said she would be attending all of the regional games and she had spent the weekend actually learning the words to our school song.

One of her classmates challenges her to stand up and sing the school song. She stood up and starting singing the school song, and the next thing I knew, my classmates started to stand one by one and join her. Then students in the hall started showing up at the door to join in. The next five minutes turned into an unscheduled pep rally for the entire school. The moment seemed to help the students forget about what happened Saturday night and start focusing on the next challenge starting in three days.

Immediately following the rally, the principal announced on the school intercom that he wanted to congratulate the school on winning the district tournament. He also found out quickly who started the unplanned pep rally and asked her to report to his office.

He told her he was surprised, considering her position on academics and her constant criticism about how he and the other school officials treated ballplayers better than they did academic excellence. She informed the principal she had attended the game and her perspective had changed.

The principal told her the punishment for her and the rest of the academic team would be to teach the entire school and community the words to the school song before the planned pep rally on Wednesday. He expected her and the academic team, when called upon, to lead the pep rally in singing the school song. Good Game Charlie would be there along with Flannel Mouth Fultz to broadcast the song over the radio. He could tell by the smile on her face that his theory about winning and school pride was contagious.

He had found some common ground to help all of the clubs and teams feel they were are of equal importance to him and the rest of the schoolteachers and administrators.

I must admit the teachers and school administrators seemed a little more forgiving and understanding when students did not perform as expected in the classrooms during the week.

It seemed every student realized we were up against the wall and the players alone could not win the games. They were, maybe for the first time, starting to understand what it feels like when a school goes from almost winning to actually having what it takes to cross the line and enjoy the thrill of an important victory.

The victory would be something they could share with their grandchildren about what they did to help, how proud they were to be a part of the final win, or even to say, "I was there when we won the championship game." I could tell some of the students had more on their minds than just a basketball game.

Finally, something important was about to happen at the school and in the community, they loved. The students, players, school leaders, coaches and every person living in Carroll County were ready to fight for a victory with every ounce of strength we had left. Most people in a small community followed the lives of every player. They knew where the players lived in the county and who their girlfriends were. They knew our favorite food and restaurant, our favorite colors, and what each player had done during their careers to prepare themselves for this tournament.

I remember being picked up by a family while I was walking home from basketball practice one night. When I got in the car, the dad told me he was listening to Flannel Mouth Fultz on the car radio. He said Mr. Fultz announced on the radio that basketball practice was over and if anyone was traveling on 36 toward Milton, Kentucky to stop and give me a ride. I do not think Mr. Fultz realized how many trips home he got for me over the years by making that simple announcement. I also know many of those rides were from people who heard the announcement at home and decided to drive down and pick me up and drop me off at the road to my house. I observed those kind folks turn the car around at the next lane down the road and head back to their homes in Carrollton.

This car had several children in the back seat, and the mom was holding a young child in the front seat with her husband. I thanked the man for stopping and expressed how much I appreciated the ride.

We drove for a few minutes, and finally one of the younger children broke the silence. She asks me if I was really the shooting guard the radio announcer talked about on the radio. I told her yes. She appeared to be very excited as she asks me if a player from Ashland I had gotten the tip on the other night really was 6'6" tall. Before I could answer her question, one of the other young girls asked me if I were open when I spotted our all-state player under the basket with a bullet pass who hit the winning shot. I confirmed the player was 6'6" tall and yes I was open for a shot, but our all-state player had a better shot. Considering the age of these two children, the questions caught me a little off guard. The game they asked me about was played in Ashland, Kentucky, and Ashland is located 200 miles from where these folks lived. I could not imagine they were there to watch the game in person.

The father told the children to stop asking me so many questions. A few minutes later, the mother turned and looked at me. She apologized for her children's behavior. She said her family had never been this close to a person as important as I was. I was not sure how to handle such a statement. I certainly did not feel any more special than normal.

She explained that her children had never attended a game, but the radio announcers always made them feel like they were there. "They hang on to every word the announcers use to describe how you players are doing in the game. To be honest, they feel you are the best shooter to have ever played in Carroll County. They felt you should have taken the shot the other night against Ashland. They were all prepared to follow along with Good Game Charlie as they always do when he says 'Swisheroo-Clifton-Has-Two.' One of my sons has those words on a poster in his bedroom hanging above the table holding his bible. All of my children have basketballs, and when the game is on the radio, you can hear a pin drop. However, when they go to commercials, those balls are flying all over my house. I do not think I have a lamp or wall hanging that has not been broken or knocked off the wall during basketball season."

She said, "You can probably tell from our attire that we are not a wealthy family." She quickly assured me they loved each other very much. "We barely have enough money to shop for groceries tonight. By the grace of God, we were able to get a good price for one of our beef cows today, which makes this a very special day for us.

"Our entire family gathers around the radio, and we listen to every game. Many times, we find ourselves praying for our team and for your safety. Another night against Ashland, when you went into the stands with the 6' 6" tall player to force a jump ball, our hearts stopped. You could have heard a pin drop in our house when we learned you were hurt. When Good Game Charlie said he could see blood coming through your jersey, my family dropped to their knees and prayed for your health.

"Good Game Charlie, in the opening ceremonies, said security had installed a ships anchor rope all the way around the gym for crowd control. When we heard your side actually slid across the 2.5" round ship anchor rope, we could feel your pain. My husband was in the navy and told us the rope has small strands of wire in the core as sharp as a razor blade. When Flannel Mouth announced you were up and on your feet, you could have heard my family cheering for five miles. Then when Good Game Charlie announced you refused to come out of the game, we were bursting with pride. It was as if you became a member of our family. When you got the tip and we won the game on the last shot, you made my family so happy we all cried with joy. I hope you know what you mean to us and the thousands of people who live in this community. Every player on our team is a hero to my family.

"My husband told our oldest boy that if you could come back from such a serious injury and finish the game you are someone he would want to know better someday."

One of the older, boys asked me if I was hurt as bad as the announcer claimed I was. "Were you actually bleeding through your shirt?" I told him I was hurt and I was still on the mend. I could tell he was older and had some doubt about how bad the injury was. I could tell he really wanted to see for himself how bad I was hurt. I raised my shirt, and he saw the size of the bandage covering my entire rib cage. Then when he saw and the part that had started to heal and was not covered by the bandage, all he could say was, "Oh my God."

The father asks me if the coach made me practice with such a wound. I told him I had to practice or take a chance on losing my spot on the starting five to another player. I told the father the only thing on my mind was winning the regional championship for our school and community before I graduated from high school. Our coach told us from the time we were sophomores that every practice was a new beginning and the best of the best would be the ones on the floor at game time. The father looked me in the eye and said he felt I was going to have a great life. He hoped he was there to help me along the way. It was a strange statement, but I did not reply.

The mother told me that following the success of our team was the best time of their life. Nothing had ever provided her family so much pleasure and such a sense of pride. She and her entire family would continue to listen to our games. They would pray for our health and victories for the Carroll County Panthers.

The father pulled into my lane, and before I opened the car door to get out, one of the smaller boys asked me if I would sign his basketball. This was the first time anyone had asked me for my autograph, and I felt obliged. He said he wanted to grow-up and play ball someday as good as his daddy and me. I signed his ball and started to step out of the car. Then I heard his older brother tell the little boy to get those stupid ideas out of his head. He said, "Only privileged kids like him have a chance to play ball at the level he plays."

I asked the father and mother if I could sit back down in the car and say something about what the older brother had said to his little brother.

They agreed, and I spent the next several minutes telling them about my family: how we had to struggle sometimes to make ends meet and how our family was just like their family only much larger. Most of my family had never actually watched me play a game in person. The only times my mother had seen me play ball was during family games we played on Sunday afternoons.

I told the little boy about how hard I had to work to play at the level I was playing. "Basketball is a passion. When properly nurtured, it cannot be harnessed to prevent it from growing. From the time I was four years old, my mother made sure she opened as many doors as she could to keep me on the court.

"However, it was totally my responsibility to improve my game every day. Many times, I would shoot a thousand shots a day in all weather conditions and sometimes so late at night I could barely see the rim. I had to dribble up and down roads made of gravel and dirt to fine-tune my ball-handling skills. I had to do my homework and perform my chores at home just as the rest of my brother and sisters were expected to do. During the summer, I worked long hours in the hot sun on some of the hottest days for the neighbors putting up hay, cutting tobacco, and picking corn by hand to make enough money to cover my expenses to play ball during the season."

I focused on the little boy with the dreams of playing for the Carroll County Panthers when he grew up. I told him our team goal was to win the regional tournaments from the time we were in the seventh grade. This was an enormous target. It had never been accomplished by a school as small as Carroll County in modern history. "We will accomplish our goal, so maybe your goal should be to win the state tournament when you get in high school."

Until this night, I had not spent much time thinking about what our team meant to the community. It fueled me to work even harder toward reaching our goal to be the first team to win the region and represent the folks like the ones who gave me a ride home.

Many of the students in the school had faced bad times, lost parents due to accidents and illnesses, and lost grandparents and other loved ones, which left them sad and sometimes depressed.

Students have always struggled with the changes in their life, especially when they reach high school. They have to learn to deal with bullying by students in the upper classes, the heartbreak of losing a boyfriend or girlfriend, rejection from social groups, and friends betraying them.

Sometimes students do things they do not want to do just to fit in with a particular crowd. Some struggle with passing a class they need to pass to graduate. Some blame themselves or their family members for not having what it takes to join a popular social club or make a sports team.

However, as I walked the hallways to my next class, I could tell they were ready to take a stand and say, "Not this time. I will join my fellow classmates and do what it takes to support my team and my school."

Our school teams had been close to winning the regional tournament in the past. The school spirit was incredible: students were putting up signs, wearing school colors to school every day, and decorating everything that didn't move in black and gold. In the classroom, they stayed as focused as they could on what the teachers were trying to teach them.

Every storefront in the community displayed signs supporting the team. Former students or their parents owned most of the stores in the community.

The students in our school finally understood they were an important part of the plan.

Traditionally small schools are supposed to play in the first round of the regionals, take our loss in stride, and go home. The big schools are left to finish the tournament and move on and represent the eighth region in the Sweet Sixteen State Tournament held, at the time, in Louisville Freedom Hall, home of the Louisville Cardinals.

The tournament was full of teams with excellent records for the regular season. Four of the eight teams rated number one in the region at some point during the regular season. Anderson County was the reigning regional champion and played in the final game in the state tournament the previous year.

The drawing for brackets seating was on Sunday. Carroll County received the absolute worst draw possible. We were in the lower bracket with Anderson County and powerhouse Scott County from the Lexington area, which is also home of the Kentucky Wildcats. More importantly, we would have to play the late game Thursday, Friday, and Saturday nights to win the tournament.

The games were all scheduled to be played in the Henry County High School gymnasium, which held about 5,000 fans.

Thirty-Seven

Worst Tournament Drawing Ever

The first game was against Scott County, which was one of the teams favored to win the tournament. I remember the loud roar from the fans when we entered the floor to warm up for the game. It appeared Scott County had about 500 fans and the rest of the stadium was filled with our Carroll County family. The game was very physical, but we came out hitting on all cylinders. We were scoring from the outside, and that opened up the inside game for our 6' 6" tall all-state player. We won the game by 12 points.

The game finished late, but our fans refused to leave the stadium until we were dressed and ready to leave the floor and get on the bus. When we walked out of the dressing room, there was no loud cheering or band playing; in fact, nobody said a word. My fiancée gave me her normal hug and kiss and said she would see me tomorrow. Soul joined in with the crowd and never said a word to me. The message I felt from our fans was, "Excellent job, now go home and we will see you back here tomorrow night same time, same place, same result." The fans helped escorts us to the bus and said, "Good night, we got your backs."

The second game was against Andersons County the reigning regional champion. The newspaper reported they were a little upset about the 30-point beating we had put on them earlier in the year. It was payback for beating us in the finals the previous year. We knew Anderson was going to play a sagging zone defense to prevent the ball from being passed to our best player. Our coach decided we would run our pressure defense and run our fast break offense, which would lead to quick shots for our guards. The strategy worked to perfection, and we won the game by 9 points. Even with three defenders on him most of the night, our all-state player still scored 27 points. Our fans repeated the same post-game routine they had done the night before.

The two games on consecutive nights took their toll on us physically. The game on Friday night did not end until midnight due to the first game running late. We spent all our energy on the floor by having to play a full-court press most of the night. I remember falling sound asleep on the bus trip back to Carroll County. Once we arrived back to the gym, the coaches told us to go straight to our vehicle and go straight home to bed. "In one hour, the coaches will be calling your parents to make sure you have met the curfew. If you miss the curfew deadline, you will not play in tomorrow's finals."

The coaches would spend the rest of the night reviewing the game films for the team we would play in the championship game, the mighty Bullitt Central Cougars. The coach told the team he wanted to see us back at the gym at 3:00 on Saturday afternoon to review the game plan. The Cougars had won the upper bracket, easily beating some of the teams we had struggled to beat during the regular season. I think the coaches knew a lot about this team and knew it would take a super effort from every member of our team to beat them.

I did exactly what the coaches ask me to do, and when I arrived at home, the house was dark and my entire family appeared to be in bed. When I walked through the door, my mother had a congratulatory hug and a big meal ready for me to eat as she had done many of the nights I had gotten home late from an away game. Did I tell you earlier in the story she was an incredible cook? I do not think it was possible for a human being to walk past a plate of food this woman prepared without sitting down and eating every bite on the plate and wishing they could have more.

She sat down beside me and talked to me while I ate. She said she had just got off the phone with the head coach. He told her what we had done to win the game. She said he was worried you were utterly exhausted and would have nothing left for the championship game, which by now was less than 18 hours away. She said she told the coach not to worry, that I would be ready and that I would never give up on my team and never give up on the dream.

He told her about a situation that happened near the end of the game. It was the turning point of the game. "He said Anderson's big man stole the ball at half court and headed straight to the basket for an easy shot. He said he watched the twins of Worthville (Identical twins, not even their mother could tell them apart) and you sprint the length of the floor and catch the player just as he shot the ball, which would have cut our lead to three points. He said you had both hands above the rim to block the shot." Soul said, "I told you before to watch your head around the rim when you were wearing those new Chuck Taylor Converse." "The twin who was our point guard caught the ball while falling out of bounds; threw a perfect behind-the-back bounce pass to our all-state player for a layup 94 feet away. It was the most incredible play he had ever seen. He said all three of you landed on the floor extremely hard and slid into the wall some twenty-five feet from the court. The officials immediately waved the coaches and the training staffs onto the floor. The PA announcer called out, 'If there is a doctor in the house, please report to the floor area.' He said you could have heard a pin drop in the gymnasium. The coaching staff for both teams sprinted the length of the floor to get to the four players as none of you were getting up. The head coach for Anderson was the first to arrive. Your head coach said, 'When he looked up at me at half court and shook his head, all I could do was pray.' He said your uniforms were completely soaked with perspiration and each of your chests was pounding so hard he thought your hearts were going to pop out of your chests.

"He said the doctor checked each one of you out and told him you were exhausted and should be out of the game. 'As a father, I wanted to take them out of the game, hold them, and tell them it is not worth it. As a coach, I knew as long as they were breathing they were not going to come out of the game even if I sent substitutes to the score table. I told each of my assistant coaches to forget about coaching and spend all their time finding ways to give our players a chance to rest without coming out of the game. I used all of my timeouts to give them a chance to rest. It would be difficult to prove, but I think one of our clever radio announcers even tossed a full glass of ice on the floor during a close play in front of the area they were announcing the game. It took five minutes to clean up the water and ice from the playing surface on the court.'"

My mom said she told the coach she knew all about the play. All she wanted to know was if I had really hit my head on the rim when I blocked the shot as Good Game Charlie had declared on the radio. The coach said I did, but the doctor felt I would be okay in the morning.

I told her I was fine and that my head did not hurt. All she said was, "Right," and she did her own examination. She told me to eat and go straight to bed. I finished the meal and went to my room, which I shared with my next youngest brother.

I knew he was awake, and I asked him what was up. He told me, "The coaches called Mom and told her you played so hard you lost 12 pounds by the time the game ended. He told Mom and Dad to get you to bed as soon as possible." He told me all of my brothers and sisters were still awake, but Mom told them not to bother me. He said, "According to the announcers, you played an incredible game." He put his hand on the side of my head and said, "Looks like the rim did not do too much damage to your skull. All I see is a little cut and a bruise. Did your head dent the rim?"

I told him I was fine and to go get my family. We always have time to celebrate our wins. I had learned a long time ago the importance of living in the moment. We should always celebrate the joy of winning with the ones we love the most. He immediately summoned the rest of my brothers and sisters to our room, and the questions started to roll. They knew more about every single play in the game than I did. Some sounded much more dramatic to hear them tell me about it than it appeared at the time it was happening in the game.

Finally, the questions stopped and we all knew it was time to forget about that game. It was time to get ready for the championship game. My youngest sister was the last to leave. She said the announcer said the team we were going to play was from Louisville. Louisville was a big city and we were just a little town. I told her not to worry; we had played teams from all over the state and we were not afraid of anyone. I picked her up and carried her to bed. When I tucked her into her bed, it seemed to take all of the worries from her face. When I turned out the light, she said she loved me and she prayed we could win the game.

It was the last thing I remember hearing until the next day. I was apparently so tired I did not wake up until one o'clock. I went downstairs expecting to see my family before I had to leave for the pregame walk-through at the high school. Much to my surprise, the house was empty and the only vehicle in the driveway was mine. My brother left me a note stating he had done all of my chores for the day and wished me luck in tonight's game.

When I reached the high school, I wondered why the parking lot was completely full of vehicles on a Saturday afternoon. When I entered the gym, I was welcomed by loud applause from what appeared to come from all 4,200 people living in our community.

Our gym was only three years old at the time and held about 3,500 fans. The population of our town was 4,200. Our gym completely sold out for every game starting in the middle of our junior year until our last game. I went past the crowd with the rest of our players to the locker room to get dressed for the walk-through.

When I opened the locker room door to enter the floor, my entire family greeted me. It was a photo moment. If I actually had a camera, I would have taken a picture. I will always remember the smiles on the my younger brother and sister's faces and the concerned looks from my mother when she saw how thin I was. I told her it was just because of how hard I played in the games the previous two nights and that I would be fine once the season was over.

The players entered the playing surface of the court to more loud applause and cheering. The head coach thanked the fans for coming out and greeting the players.

It was an unusual move, but the coach asked the fans if they had any questions about the championship game. Not one fan or family member had a question for the coach. You could have heard a pin drop in the gym.

It seemed that no one wanted to talk about the game, thinking it could be bad luck and somehow jinx the team's chance of winning. Most of the fans had already read the newspapers. Just as the reporters had written the two previous nights, our team showed a lot of promise but would not be physically capable of taking on the big boys from Louisville. The reporter went on to write that we had put out too much effort to win the night before, and no rationally thinking person could possibly expect us to have enough energy left to win the game against such a dominant team. The reporter wrote about how the Louisville team had breezed through the tournament and had rested their starters most of the second half of every game. The reporter interviewed the head coach of Bullitt Central, and the coach stated he would give his players a chance in the championship game to display their talents. He could not wait to attend the drawing for the Sweet Sixteen State Tournament on Sunday afternoon to see who his team's next opponent would be in Louisville Freedom Hall Arena. He said the head coach for the Louisville Cardinals was looking at one of his players and would get a chance to see him live in tonight's game.

Our head coach told the fans he knew what was on their minds when they read the paper. He said they should not pay attention to the words written by the press. This was just one reporter's opinion, and the one thing he could never write about was the size of the hearts of the players standing before them. He said he had been coaching a long time and he had never coached a team like this one in his life and would likely never again. He talked to the fans and parents about the journey this team had traveled to get to this point.

The coach told the fans he had some important stuff to go over for the game. It was top secret, and he would appreciate it if everyone left the gym as quickly as possible. He said he could not guarantee a victory, but he could ensure we would never give up. Our players would go to a hospital for exhaustion to avoid losing this game.

It was obvious our fans were focused, and now it was time for us to get ready for the finals. The crowd quickly filed out of the gym as if they had attended a funeral. I think the fans were beat down as bad the players were. My dad motioned me over to where he was standing. He told me money was a little tight and the family would not be able to attend the game. He said they would be listening to the radio and that was almost as good as being there. I could tell he was disappointed, but I assured him it was okay and I understood.

Soul had just been through the worst time of his life, but even he felt sad when my dad told me the family could not attend the game. I knew they would all be there in spirit and that was all I could hope for. I hugged my mom and my brothers and sisters as they exited the gym. My oldest brother put out his hand to shake mine; I pulled him into my arms and thanked him for making me the player I was. I told him I still remembered the games I had watched him play at Locust Creek. He was still the best I ever saw play the game and he would always be my hero. He said he knew I was tired but to not ever show it on the floor. "You may fall behind tonight, as I think they will try to open the game with a full-court press and attempt to blow the game open early. Just remember, a basketball game is a marathon, not a sprint. Once you have taken their best punch in the mouth, you get up and pour it on. Do not stop until the final horn blows."

Once the gym was empty, the coach locked the door and we went through our pre-game walk through. The coaches seemed to be convinced this team was our worst draw. It sounded like our goal to win the region was not possible. The coach told us this was the best team we would ever play. It would be almost impossible for us to stay with them. They could very well win the state tournament and had in fact beaten several of the top teams during the regular season.

We went through the things our coaches expected us to do during the game. We all realized he was asking us to do things different from anything we had done the entire season. It was a little confusing since we had also played and beat some of the top teams in the state. I think we knew something our coaches did not know about us. We were a whole lot better than they thought we were.

Once we understood what the coaches wanted us to do, we left the floor, got dressed in our formal team attire, which included black pants, black shoes, white shirts, black or gold ties, and gold blazers. We went to the school cafeteria and ate our pre-game meal. We could feel the pressure getting to our head coach. He was back to yelling and screaming at us during the walk through.

The bus ride over to the game was quiet with an occasional whisper between the players coming from the back of the bus. They were talking about the game plan just to make sure they understood what to do in each situation that came up during the game.

I sat beside one of my best friends, who was also a Locust Squirrel transfer. We talked about our journey to get to this point in our life. We started first grade together and were both tall and very muscular for our age. Many of the older boys in the school felt intimidated by our size and wanted nothing to do with us.

One day, I had noticed my friend was bullying some of my other friends. He had intentionally picked a fight and beat up the boys. His aggressiveness had bothered me, so during recess one sunny day, I had decided to ask him to stop hitting some of the other kids I enjoyed playing ball with in the schoolyard. The fight was on, and as best I can remember, it was a tie. He said it was a tie, but he felt the school principal gave me more hits on the behind with the paddle than she did him. We just laughed and continued to talk about our journey as friends. The conversation moved on to a discussion about our plans. I told him I planned to marry my fiancée later in the summer, and then it was off to college. He said he was tired of school and wanted to be a carpenter.

When we exited the bus, we walked past our fans, who had ridden the pep-buses to the game. The gymnasium was already starting to fill up, and we still had two hours before the tip-off. The school official had already announced on the local radio stations that the game was a sellout. If you did not already have a ticket, you would not be able to attend the game. This information may have resulted in the very first tailgate party in sports history. Apparently, one of the upstanding citizens from Carroll County convinced the head football coach from Henry County to allow him to bring his camper and set it up on the football field. The football field was located just behind the school gym. The plan was to let those folks without a ticket have a place to hang out as close to the team as possible. They listened to the game with Good Game Charlie and Flannel Mouth Fultz on WVCM radio. The football stadium was completely filled with Carroll County Panther Fans.

The moment was finally here, and you could have heard a pin drop in our locker room when the coach called the team together and went through the game plan one last time. He asked the minister to say a final prayer, and then it was time to take the floor. Before taking the floor, the senior players shook hands and stated our will to fight to the end. Our motto was 'We are one. Give all, leave nothing. The underclassmen knew it was a privilege to be in the locker room and have a chance to receive the torch to keep burning once the seniors were gone.

When we entered the floor, the award-winning Carroll County band started playing the school song. My wife to be was sitting with her friends and gave me a look that said, "No matter how this turns out, I will be here for you."

The game started and they jumped up on us just as the reporters and my brother had anticipated. I felt good but was having the same issues the rest of the team was having with the head coach's game plan. The whole first quarter was a complete disaster but ended with us cutting their lead from 14-3 to 18-17.

Our fans were feeling the pressure. I saw one little girl sitting close to the front row of bleacher's turn and go down to her knees to pray. It reminded me of what my little sister told me the night before. The end of the second quarter did go a little better than the first. Our all-state player hit a jumper from the top of the circle, and I made a shot falling out of bounds deep in the corner as time ran out to end the half. Those two shots put our team ahead by a score of 34-30 at halftime.

When we entered the locker room, the head coach was upset and screamed at us for not following the game plan. He said, "What is wrong with you people out there on the floor? We told you in a walkthrough about everything they were going to do to you on the floor tonight. You men are just going through the motions and are a step slow in doing what we told you to do." He told us if we were too tired to play, he had a place for us at the end of the bench. I remember thinking that if he took us out of the game and we lost, the school principal would have likely made him walk back to Carroll County. He said we were going to lose the game and that we would be a disgrace to our community and turn our school into a big joke in the state of Kentucky. He asked the seniors to stand and pointed us out one at a time by name. He said we were not getting the job done, and if things did not change quickly, we could sit on the end of the bench and watch our team lose the game. He could just see the headlines in the Carrier Journal the next morning describing how the big school showed us the door just as the reporter said they would.

When we return to the floor, Soul could no longer keep his mouth shut. He started talking to me when the locker room door opened for us to report to our benches to start the second half. One thing he said was, "We are spending a lot of time trying to keep them from doing what they do best. The question you need to answer is, 'When you are going to do what you do best?' When you do you guys can beat this team by 30-points. You are allowing them to stay in the game because you are too worried about what they are doing. It is time to shine. You are the best team in this region and maybe even the state, and it's time for you to show the other team who's boss."

It was good advice, but how could we do our thing without upsetting the coach even more than he was already? The second half started the same way the game started, with the other team jumping all over us from the opening tip. Two minutes into the third quarter, our coach called his first time out. He asked us what was wrong. "Why aren't you doing what we ask you to do?" When we broke the huddle, I looked up at my wife to be and I could read her lips. She said, "What are you doing? It's now or never. Do it!"

Just before the official handed me the ball to inbound, I looked over to the official and signaled time out. The official said okay but then asked me if I was sure. He said, "Your coach looks very upset." I said, "A man's got to do what a man's got to do," and he said, "It's your funeral." When our team went back to the bench, my head coach was running up and down the bench area looking for my substitute. He asked me what I was thinking out there. Before I could answer, my best friend, the other Locust Squirrel on the team, stood up. He walked up to the coach and got about two feet away. He told the coach in a very loud and angry voice, "He is thinking your game plan was not working."

The coach told him to sit down and shut up, but he was a big man and had the entire bench and all of the assistant coaches on his side. He said, "What we needed to do is stop playing to lose and start playing to win coach." He calmed down, dropped his head, and looked down at the floor. Then he raised his head up, looked at the coach, and said, "I guess coach what I am trying to tell you is you need to have as much faith in these guys as we do. We have 5,000 fans that traveled over here to support us. We have several thousand out there on the football field in the cold hanging on every moment. We have done everything you have asked us to do for you all year. We have done it all to get the opportunity to play in this game tonight. Four hours before the game, you decided it was not good enough and we are not good enough."

Finally, the coach settled down, folded his arms, and turned his back on the players and our fans. It was just for a few seconds, but it seem like an hour to me. He turned back around and asked us to sit down so he could see us. He said he was sorry and thanked our big boy from Locust for helping him realize he needed to believe in us. Our coach was back, as he said, "What I want is for you to go back out there and play our game. Forget about everything we talked about up to this point as it relates to the game plan. The score is nothing to nothing, and now I am turning it over to you seniors. The only thing I will tell you is if you want to win, you have got to shut down their best scorer." I looked at the coach and said, "No problem coach, we got it covered." The coach said he would love us forever, win or lose. He was truly sorry. I said, "It is a game coach, not a war. I've seen a war, and this isn't it."

When we walked past our fans back to our positions, we could see they certainly had not given up on us. I winked at my wife to be and gave Soul the thumbs up. He liked to watch the games with some of his angel friends he had met in Vietnam from the top of the scoreboard. I saw him telling one of his friends, "Watch this, big boy, you haven't seen anything yet." Those words brought a smile to my face. Ten seconds from the time the clock started, one of the twins stole the ball and passed it to me. I heard our all-state player yell out to me, "Time to fly son. Let it go; I got your back." I dribbled over the half court line about three steps and pulled up for my longest shot of the season. For that split second, I felt the air suddenly leave the gym as our fans, coaches, and players for both teams stood and took in a deep breath in disbelief that I actually shot the ball from that far out on the floor. As their eyes followed the ball to the basket, they suddenly realized they were about to be a part of something incredible when the ball went through the rim and swished the net. While the ball was traveling to the rim, I had time to look up at Soul and then over to Good Game Charlie and Flannel Mouth Fultz and pointed, symbolizing, "This one's for you," to my wife to be as she said "Swisheroo Clifton has two." As the ball went through the net, I watched the head coach for Bullitt Central sit back in his chair. He told his assistant coach, "This is going to get ugly. Make sure we play all of the seniors. Maybe we will get them next year." For the next play, one of the Worthville twins stole the inbound pass and hit our all-state player for a jump shot at the top of the key. I called nets from the backcourt (A confident shooter will some-times call 'nets' which means the ball will touch nothing but the bottom of the net from the time it leaves the shooters hand.) as it swished through the basket. When I spotted the head coach of the University of Louisville, he was frantically checking his program to find names and watch the boys dressed in Black and Gold from little old Carroll County, Kentucky about to put a beat down on his home town school. Then I made eye contact with the legendary coach of the University of Kentucky, Coach Adolph Rupp. He pointed his finger at me, winked, and shook his head in appreciation for what he knew he was about to witness. Our fans could tell from the smile on my face that this game was over and it was time to sit back and enjoy the ride. The only thing left to do was let our opponents on the floor know it was time for them to start preparing for next year's regional final.

By now, you probably figured it out, but just in case you haven't I did shut down their best scorer, and our all-state player took over the scoring. We outscored our opponents 17-0, and by the time the third quarter ended, we had taken a 58-44 lead. Our fans sensed we were about to achieve our dream but were still a little apprehensive to declare victory. Halfway through the fourth quarter, the victory was no longer in doubt and the celebration had started. We had opened up a 25-point lead, and the place was going crazy. It was the first time I had actually heard the band play during a game. For the next four minutes, the world was an incredible place to be.

Our players were having fun doing what we loved to do. The court was our stage, and it was our time to show case our talents and give the fans the show they so rightfully deserved. I think from the time I hit that long shot until the game's ends our fans never sat down. Our fans were enjoying every second ticking off the clock. I actually stopped playing at one point just to make eye contact with Soul. The tears streaming down his face shadowed by the huge smile was priceless. I think all of the emotions and horrible scenes of the war he had bottled up came pouring out. He had been through nine months of hell on earth and in heaven. It finally hit him hard, and his angel friends were trying to console him. When the clock reached 10 seconds, the entire crowd, including Soul and all of his friends, started counting it down. When the final horn sounded, it looked like a New Year's Eve celebration in Times Square, New York.

The problems and concerns for every person who lived in our small community were set aside for one night. When the final horn blew to end the game, I looked up at the scoreboard and saw tears in Soul's eyes. The final score was Carroll County Panthers 80, Bullitt Central Cougars 55. Once the fans returned to their seats, it was time to present the trophies for the most valuable player and the all-tournament team. I am not sure if Soul had anything to do with it or not, but my name was called out by the announcer first. The place went wild and a chant broke out from our fans: "MVP-MVP- MVP." I shook hands with the commissioner and held my trophy over my head in appreciation as expected. I took a particular look at Soul. He had both hands open and his arms pointing to the heavens thanking God for this moment. His friends were gently touching his back and screaming congratulations to him. Once we made eye contact, I just said, "Thanks, this belongs to you." He pointed his finger at me and said, "No, this is our moment, and we are a great team." Moments later, the second player from our team received his all-tournament team trophy. Seconds later the announcer asks the fans to quiet down so the most valuable player award winner could be announced. The trophy was, deservingly so, presented to our all-state player. I felt he was actually the most valuable player and still do to this day.

We celebrated the victory for hours, and neither our team nor our fans wanted to leave the gymnasium. I can remember getting dressed in the locker room and hearing the cheering and the band playing. The students section, was packed to the rafters and was still singing the school song at the top of their lungs, undoubtedly learned by many fans just a few days before the big game thanks to the National Honor Society. When we left the locker room, the fans had formed a human chain around the stadium. I met my future wife at half court for our usual congratulatory hug and a small kiss.

The principal of the school asked the players to take a walk around the gym and shake hands with the fans. We all walked with our girlfriends around the gym and received handshakes and hugs from the fans. Once we walked outside to get on the bus, it looked like we were getting ready for a football game, as the football stadium behind the school was lit up with the thousands of fans that did not have a ticket to get into the gym to see it live.

We celebrated well into the night along with the other 4,200 people from our hometown. The caravan back to Carroll County consisted of fire engines, police sirens, and 20 buses carrying the pep club for the school. The caravan of vehicles was seven miles long and traveling about fifteen miles per hour. In those days, it was against school policy for players and their girlfriends to ride on the same bus to away games, but on this night, the school principle approved the change. To my knowledge, it was the first and only time a player's girlfriends and cheerleaders rode the team bus home.

We made several trips through town and finally ended at the high school. The rally lasted well into the night at the high school. Mission accomplished!

We did lose our first game in the state finals. It was the second straight year we lost to a team who went on to play in the final game of the state tournament. We knew we had achieved the impossible, but we had no idea how impossible it was. No small school has represented the Eighth Region in the state tournament since our team accomplished that feat in 1972. It is a record still standing the test of time as of the writing of this book, 43 years later.

Thirty-Eight

Time to Reflect

I must admit I felt like a thousand-pound boulder was lifted from my shoulders once the season ended. It was also good to know the entire team was excused from joining all spring sports teams for at least two weeks. The time off gave me time to catch up on some homework that had slipped a little and to regain my strength.

It also provided me more time to spend with my wife to be. We spent the time planning for our next life at a university somewhere in America. I had numerous letters of interest from universities from Maryland to California to play basketball, football, and track, and I even had a few baseball offers. Our plan was coming into fruition, and the only thing left was to make a decision of which school to apply to.

We wanted a school that could offer her the best opportunity to meet her future desires. She had put her plans to go to school on hold and waited for me to graduate before moving on. She had graduated the year before with highest academic honors. She was a top-level recruit by many respectable academic schools for her brilliant mind. She wanted to get a liberal arts degree and teach high school advanced math or chemistry. Mostly she wanted to be my wife and spend the rest of her life holding me anytime she wanted to.

My plan was to continue my education and develop my skills to a level that would allow me to play professional basketball in the ABA or NBA. My dream was to play for the professional basketball team that represented the state of Kentucky named the Kentucky Colonels. Many coaches in the state rated me as one of the top shooting guards, and I would likely make it if I continued to improve.

My rest time was up and it was time for me to join up with the track team and the baseball team. We were a small school, and playing multiple sports was important to the school. Sports had been magnificent to me and were the root of all of my success. Strangely enough, the love of my life was not a big sports fan. A better description for her was closer to an academic geek. She was a member of every brain club in the school. The day she graduated from high school, she won an academic award from the governor of Kentucky recognizing her as one of the top graduating students in the state of Kentucky. A few days after graduating, she received the who's who award in academics from the college board. This honor is for students with the greatest potential in the United States to carry on in academics and make a difference in our nation.

OFFICE OF THE GOVERNOR
FRANKFORT, KENTUCKY 40601

LOUIE B. NUNN
GOVERNOR

July 26, 1971

Miss Sharon Lynn Owen
R. R. #1
Ghent, Kentucky 41045

Dear Miss Owen:

My sincerest congratulations on being an honor graduate at your high school. Your outstanding scholastic achievement is a credit to both you and your family.

In recognition of your exceptional academic record, I am pleased to present to you the Governor's Merit Award. The enclosed certificate attests to your achievement, to our pride in you, and to our faith that you will enjoy continued success in whatever you decide to do.

Since you have recently emerged from commencement addresses and admonitions, I hesitate to add to the mass of advice you have already received. I need not remind you that youth is the season of hope, enterprise and energy.

What I trust you will remember is that the way you channel your hope, enterprise and energy will in large part determine the destiny of our state and nation.

With warmest regards and best wishes to you and your family, I remain,

Sincerely yours,

LOUIE B. NUNN
Governor

Thirty-Nine

REUNITING WAS NOT BY CHANCE

The next question you may have is why she would want to stick with me. I was an okay student, but certainly not in her league. I thought it was an important question, and to tell you the truth, I needed to find the answer.

This time I knew exactly how I ended up on top of Cedar Point and to the top of my favorite tree. The sun was shining and a cool breeze caused the tree to, gently sway from side to side. I wanted to take my time and revisit our relationship and how our feeling had matured over the years into what can only be described as an incredible modern-day love story. I went back to the first time I laid my eyes on her in high school, and I relived all of the events that took place in our life up to this point.

She told me she actually fell in love with me in the hospital when I was fighting for my eyesight to return. She said ever since then she had kept a copy of every single newspaper clipping and photo of me receiving awards for my sports accomplishments. She had kept copies of the speeches I had given in the community supporting Future Farmers of America Association. I think she liked that accomplishment more than the rest since we both were born and raised on a farm. I still have those photo albums with thousands of pictures and articles.

She said the day my friend (Tooter) and I showed up in biology class and we were trying to decide where to sit, she and her friend already had a plan. Each one of them would sit at separate tables directly across from each other. Only two people could sit at each table. Hence, we would have to sit with the two of them in the only two seats left.

When we looked into the classroom, I asked Tooter who the two girls were sitting at separate tables directly across from each other. He told me the redhead's was name Sharon and the other was named Joy. When I took a second look, I could not believe my eyes. I had never actually seen the girl, since at the time we were together I was blind. I asked Tooter if she was the girl who held my hand and read the story to me in the hospital four years earlier.

I felt my heart pounding, and I told him I was going to marry her someday. Tooter just laughed and said, "Right, she is a straight 'A' student and will likely ace this class with very little effort. The only reason those two girls are in this class is because the redhead wanted to meet you. Both of them will probably walk down the hall after this class to advanced geometry or college chemistry. You are out of your league son, leave her alone."

"After all," Tooter said, "the only reason you and me are in this class is Mr. Franklin is our favorite teacher and coach in the world. We will pray for a 'B' and be happy with a 'C'." Tooter knew he was wasting his time talking to me, and I could not wait to sit down beside her. I sat down beside her and introduced myself. She introduced herself, and we just sat and stared at the chalkboard at the front of the room without speaking.

Finally, she broke the ice. She asked me if I thought we would beat Bellevue High School in our football game that Friday night. I told her I thought we had a good chance, but that it would be a great game. I asked her if she liked football, and she told me, "No, but I do have a favorite player, so I do come to the games just to watch him play." I could feel my heart drop into my lap when she said she already had someone she liked.

Then she asked me if I remembered her and I told her yes. She fessed up and told me I was her favorite football player and that she loved to watch me play. I asked her why she had not tried to find me and tell me how she felt. She said she felt she would not have a chance with a man like me. I was popular and a major athlete in all school sports and everybody knew my name. She said, "People see your picture and write columns in every newspaper in the state about your accomplishments in football, basketball, track, and baseball. Do you know the state sports writers picked you to be our schools first all-state football player? Many feel you could get that award by the end of your junior year. By the end of your senior season you will definitely receive the votes to be all state." I told her, "No, I did not know that, but it is two years away and a lot could happen in two years." She said, "I told my mother how I felt about you, and even she said you were out of my league. She wants me to date some of the boys from Ghent I grew up with, but I did not want to. I am just a country girl and the only people who know my name are my geek friends. I have a cousin who goes to Gallatin County High school, and she told me she would go for it. It was time to make my move or lose you forever."

She said she worked in the office as an assistant to the principal, and she had access to my schedule. She and her friend had decided to test out of biology, but when she saw my name on the schedule, she talked her friend into actually taking the class.

I told her I could not help what others thought or wrote about me and that I was proud of my accomplishments. I had worked extremely hard to be an athlete and had no apologies. I told her she had stolen my heart in the hospital and I had not dated or went steady with another girl since. "So tell your friend in Gallatin County thanks, even if she cheers for one of our archrivals, the Gallatin County Wildcats."

Then she asked me why I did not try to find her. I told her, "The only thing I knew about you was your first name. The nurse at the hospital told me you went to a different school district."

Soul chipped in his two-cents worth. "Tell her you have prayed to the boss many times since the time you spent in the hospital. You promised him if you ever found her again, you would not let her slip away." I thought about what Soul said and decided it sounded good, so I did use it. I think Soul loved her as much as I did. I could tell by the gorgeous smile on her face she believed me.

From that moment in Mr. Franklin's biology class, two hearts started beating as one. We never were apart for more than a few days during the entire school year. I will never forget the first time she invited me to dinner at her house. I was a little nervous to meet her parents. After dinner, she told me, she had a surprise for me. She left the room and went into one of the back rooms in her house. She invited me to join her on the front porch swing. When I sat down, she pulled several thick photo albums out from under the swing. At first, I thought she was going to show me pictures of her family and tell me about their interests and whereabouts. When she opened the front cover, I could see that ever pictures in the albums were of me. She said that since the day she left the hospital she had been collecting my pictures and stories from every newspaper in the area. She had the score and the story line for every game and track meet I participated in from the time we met. She said she was not sure why she did it, but one night she had a vision that this was what she was supposed to do. She said she wanted to continue the project and expected to fill up several more before my playing days were over. I told her, "That could be another twenty years or so because I plan to play college ball and eventually play in the National Basketball Association as a professional." She said, "And you will, I have no doubts."

The summer between my sophomore and junior year was a long hot lonely summer. One of the top songs played on the radio went, "I will see you in September or lose you to a summer love.' We did not intend to let that happen. I had taken on extra work at a cattle ranch in English, Kentucky to earn enough money to cover my expense for the next school year.

The summer was about over and it was time for the two-a-day football practices to begin. Our team was the favorite to win the district and possibly even the regional in football, which would have been the first time in school history. I could not wait for the season to start so I could spend more time with my girlfriend. I had received my driver license and was very fortunate to have a good car, thanks to my next to oldest sister.

We were two weeks away from starting the regular season, and the football coach had invited the alumni to play a Friday night practice game. I called her to tell her about the game and ask her to meet me after the football game at the local Taste Freeze. This was an after the game hangout for the students at the time in Carroll County.

It was supposed to be a practice game, but it became a sellout, and the alumni even had several of their cheerleaders come out of retirement to cheer on their team. Things got out of hand, and before the coach could get control of the game, disaster struck. The alumni decided this was not a practice game and showed up in full pads and ready to play tackle football. Some of the players were already playing for major colleges and were twice the size we were. The rest were grown men and felt this was their chance to play real Friday night high school football one more time.

Our best senior player and potential all-state linebacker was taken out on the first play of the game with a possible season-ending knee injury. Three plays later, I ran the ball up the middle for a good gain. On my way back to the huddle, one of the alumni players warned me that if I did it again, he would put an end to my night. Those are kind words compared to what he actually said. I know it was by accident, but the coach called another running play right through the hole where he was standing. I took the handoff and did a quick short forward jab step, then two steps backward and did a spin move that made him look like he had never played football. I went right past him for a 25-yard gain. I heard the referee's whistle blow to stop the play. I took a deep breath and relaxed my left arm, which was carrying the ball, and I was preparing to get up to return to the huddle.

The alumni player I had beaten on the play got up after missing the tackle. He loaded up and took a cheap shot hitting me while I was still on the ground with the ball still wedged under my left arm. The hit was so hard the ball drove my left shoulder completely out of the joint and it ended up next to my collarbone. When the coach got to me, he knew right away I was hurt bad, and that his decision to play this game was quickly going south. The next person I saw was my girlfriend and then the rest of my family. When my girlfriend saw my shoulder, I could tell she felt my pain. When I was finally able to get to my feet, I could not lift my arm no matter how hard I tried. I started back to the huddle, but the trainer said I was done for the night. He pointed at the ambulance sitting at the fifty-yard line and said it was taking you to the hospital. My girlfriend rode with me in the ambulance and held my one good hand all the way. She called her mother to let her know what had happened and to tell her she was very scared. The doctor met me at the hospital examination room and immediately ordered up a full set of X-Rays. The doctor informed me that I had two choices. He could send me to University of Louisville Medical Center to have my shoulder surgically reset to its proper location, or he could do it the old fashion way.

I told him to do whatever would get me back on the field the quickest. He put his right hand under my arm and his left hand on my elbow. He slid my arm away from my collarbone back to where it belonged. Then he removed his right hand from underneath my arm and took the palm of his hand to drive my arm back in the joint. I heard a loud pop and felt my shoulder go back in the joint and the pain was instantly was gone. He placed a bandage around my shoulder and told me to leave it there for four weeks. "With a little luck, it will heal itself if you keep it completely still." My girlfriend was by my side while the doctor spoke to my mother outside in the hall. The doctor told my mother this type of injury may never heal and that my playing days might be over for good.

I know my girlfriend's heart was breaking, and I felt I had somehow let her down along with the rest of the family. She told me no matter what she would always love me.

Four weeks later, I took off the wrap and played in the game against Beachwood High School from Northern Kentucky. I scored three touchdowns and intercepted two passes in the end zone. I was feeling good about my return and my team's first victory of the season. My girlfriend told me if I scored a touchdown I should give her a look. I did check her out in the stands after all three scores, and she was the most beautiful girl in the world.

The shoulder never healed properly after the doctor reset it in the hospital. It was knocked out of the joint during the next game against Owen County. The doctor told me the only solution was to have surgery, which would end my football season. Also it would likely prevent me from playing any sports until my senior year. I asked the doctor if it would do any more damage if I delayed the operation until the end of the school year. That would give me all summer to heal and strengthen my shoulder after the surgery. He said no but he could not imagine someone going through that much pain repeatedly. I told him my future college career depended on me playing ball and I was willing to take a chance. The only person I could think of who supported my decision to continue to play was my girlfriend.

The doctor trained my girlfriend, the team trainers, and me in how to reset my shoulder if it got dislocated. It was dislocated thirty-eight times during the football and basketball seasons. I wore a special strap support brace around my chest and then around my arm to restrict its movement. To get a doctor's release to play sports, I had to agree to wear a brace during all sporting activities.

At the end of the school year, I checked into the Jewish hospital in Lexington, Kentucky and had the surgery to repair my shoulder. My head coaches in all four sports agreed they would not allow me to play my senior year if I refused to have the surgery.

The surgery was experimental and offered no guarantees. The doctor was the chief of surgery at the University of Kentucky had developed the procedure for another professional player. The typical hospital stay for the surgery was two weeks. I had never been away from home, and the thought of being that far away was very scary. It also would have been the longest I had been away from my girlfriend in nearly a year. I know this does not sound very romantic, but I told my girlfriend I would be asking her to marry me once the surgery was over. She said not to unless I meant it because she would accept. I had the surgery and it was a complete success. I convinced the doctor to let me go home after the second day. I knew the cost of traveling to Lexington would be an expense my mom and dad did not need. Shortly after returning home. I asked my fiancée to marry me and she said yes.

I spent much of the summer strengthening my shoulder, and after completing my training each night, I would spend several hours meticulously answering her letters. In my mind, I could see her doing the same for me.

On the days when the mail did not arrive at my house, I felt alone and disappointed. Our parents allowed us to talk to each other on the phone on Wednesday nights for 10 minutes. You can bet we spent several hours during the day preparing the dialogue for those 10 minutes. Most of the time we would talk about our families and what was happening to them.

We never had to spend time talking about our plans for our Fridays and Saturday nights. One of the two nights we would go to Madison, Indiana and watch a movie at the Ohio Theater and then get something to eat. By then it was time to make the 40-mile trip back to her house. We would spend the time we had left talking and describing how much we were going to miss each other the rest of the week. At 11:58 PM, her mother would flash the front porch light telling us our date was about to finish. We jokingly called it the two-minute warning, like you have at the end of a football game

I remember one Saturday night in particular. We joined up with her best friend Joy and her date and watched the movie *Love Story*. It was a sad movie about this couple that had gotten married without the consent of his family. However, it was a good example of how love will always defeat money when it comes to true love and life in general.

The woman in this movie, out of nowhere, came down with a terminal disease that took her life at the end of the story.

I normally do not get too emotional during sad movies. Joy's date was a tough-nosed lineman on the football team, and I looked over at him during one of the scenes when her husband was talking to her about the future and saw crocodile tears flowing down his face. By the time the movie ended, you could have heard a pin drop in the theater. It was the most emotional movie of its time and certainly changed the lives of those who read the book and watched the movie.

Once we left the movie, we turned to walk down Main Street to a place we called the hamburger joint. I will never forget the restaurant sign advertising Hinkle's Hamburgers: four burgers, a side of fries, and a coke for a buck-fifteen.

Both girls walked without speaking, which was different for the two of them. Most of the time we could not get them to stop talking about some experiment they completed in advanced chemistry or some other homework assignment they could not wait to get into.

My football friend and I really enjoyed those conversations. They may have been even more interesting if we had a clue what they were really talking about to each other.

But this night, my fiancée stopped walking and asked me if we could skip the meal and start the journey back to Carrollton. She said we could get something to eat at the local Saturday night hangouts named Churchill Manor and Taste Freeze (Now known as Cooper's Restaurant 'Best Fried Chicken receipt in America.') with the rest of our friends. We agreed and went back to the car.

Just as we drove over the Madison–Milton Bridge, I could feel my fiancée move over to my side closer than usual. She put her head on my shoulder, wrapped her arms around me, and started to cry. I tried to comfort her by gently touching her face and telling her I understood and it was just a movie. It did help, but I finally pulled the car off the road and held her for 30-minutes. It was the first time I had felt that level of emotion with her. Her friend Joy in the back seat made the statement "Wow. So this is what true love looks like."

Keep in mind, my fiancée was a brilliant, physically tough, and incredibly beautiful country girl. She made me promise right there and then that I would never leave her. She said she knew we would face hard times but felt in her heart that our love would handle the test of time. She promised me with all of her heart and soul that she would love me until the day she died. She would never stop loving me. If anybody or anything tried to pull us apart, we would work our way through it. She said she prayed that if she died before I did, the last words from me to her would be "I love you." She said that would do her for eternity. Every person in that car just sat and stared at each other, realizing we had just witnessed the most loving and beautiful testimonial of love we would likely never hear again in our lifetime.

We got back on the road, and I dropped her friend off at their car. Before we made it to her house, I pulled off the road and asked her to tell me what was wrong. She said more than one person had told her she was dreaming if she thought she could keep me for her own.

She said her mother had doubts about our long-term relationship and that she struggled with how we could stay together. "You will be starting your senior year in high school, and relationships like ours never seem to make it. I guess the theme of the movie hit too close to home for me. I am a smart girl with all the right answers just like the female character in the movie. You are a star athletic with an incredible future ahead of you, again just like the male character in the story. I feel I may be standing in your way toward playing ball in college and getting your degree. Do you realize you would be the first in your family to attend college?" Once she finished talking, there was complete silence.

I learned a long time ago in life changing moments like this one you better think about the next words coming out of your month. The wrong words could change your life forever. All Soul could say was that he sure was glad he was not in my shoes and to be careful.

We sat for a few minutes without saying a word. I broke the silence by referencing something she had said to me on the side of the road. I said, "Many things are possible, and we will face many challenges over the next few years." I turned my body toward hers. I placed my hand on her heart and said, "Please, understand this my love: I cannot imagine my world without you in my life sharing the good times and the hard times. Your love makes me feel whole inside my heart. Touching your hand or caressing your face makes my life complete. I love you with every ounce of love in my body, and I never want to be without you. It is time for us to show the rest of the world that our ambitions to be successful will never stand in our way to be together. Whatever changes I need to make or you need to make to secure our love for eternity will happen. I have a magnificent friend that told me to get the most out of every minute with the one you love. Life is short and we never know when it will end. When two people love each other the way we love each other, not even one second in time should escape us without knowing how much we love each other." I felt Soul take a deep breath and say, "Praise God, I think he has it." Then Soul said, "You two had better practice what you just said because you really do not know how much time you have left together."

It must have been the right words because from that moment, she never had any doubts about our life together or what destiny had to offer for the two of us.

Forty

CHANGE OF PLANS

The day we lost in the state basketball tournament I could tell my dad was upset on the trip back to Carrollton. We never talked about it, so I just assumed he was upset we had lost the game. Several days went by, and I could tell this was much more serious than losing a basketball game. For the next couple of months, I could feel his sadness, but I could not figure out what was wrong. During the spring of my senior year, I received numerous letters from colleges all over the country expressing an interest in me playing for their school once I graduated. I had talked to my coaches about the letters and all seemed to be encouraged by the interest.

I graduated on a Friday night. On Saturday afternoon, my dad said he needed to speak to me about something paramount. He started the conversation by telling me how proud he was of me and that I should be jubilant with what I had accomplished up to this point in my life. I told him I was and I appreciated all the sacrifices made by my family over the years to help me become the person and player I was.

He dropped his head, and I saw tears form in his eyes. He knew he was the father and it was his place to tell me what was about to happen to me. He said, "This is the worst day for your mother and I. We have some bad news, and we both have been searching for several months to find the right words. The head basketball coach scheduled a private meeting with us because he just could not handle giving you the news he had to deliver. With a sad face and streaming tears, the coach informed us you would not receive a college scholarship to play sports, especially not for football or basketball. The coach said he could not convince any schools that your surgically repaired shoulder could handle the physical pounding it would take playing those sports. You will have to face it; your dreams of playing college basketball are over, as no school is willing to take the chance of you permanently injuring your shoulder."

He said he was sorry and if he could change this, he would. He said it was about the most unfair thing he had every witness in his life. "You did it all the right way, and the result was supposed to be the happiest time of your life. I never saw this coming, and I cannot believe your road has to stop. I told your older brothers and sisters this morning what was about to happen. They are very upset, especially your brothers. They understood the sacrifices and hard work it took for you to play basketball at the level you are capable of playing. Your sisters wanted you to be the first in our family to continue your education and eventually graduate from college. The whole group is at the house now trying to figure out how to come up with the money to pay your tuition so you and your fiancée can keep your plans to attend college.

The news was devastating to me, but you should have seen what it did to Soul. I do not think anything could have hurt his heart more than hearing this type of news. You see, he was there all the time and he knew firsthand what it had actually taken for this kid from Hunter Bottom Kentucky to make the mark I made on the community and the state. He said he loved his boss, but he could not understand where this path was supposed to take us. It is as if you are running full speed ahead doing everything right, you are at the top of your game, and out of nowhere, this wall jumps up in front of you and you hit it head on without any warning.

I told my dad to tell my brothers and sisters not to worry about the money. I would find a way to accomplish my goals. My dreams would still somehow come true with or without a scholarship. "This is a serious setback, but as you have always told me, when one door closes another will open if you stay the course. I plan to stay the course." He said he had spoken to the owner of the company he worked for and that I had a job waiting for me in a couple of weeks. I thanked my father for sharing this news with me and assured him I was going to be okay.

I knew I had to spend some time with Soul and help him deal with this news. He had already learned the University of Kentucky fight song and was ready to enjoy college life. I think he had already told his friends he was going to be rubbing elbows with some very famous people and he could not wait to have that pleasure back in his life. After all, he was one of Gods best angels and he deserved only the best of the best. I said to Soul, "I am going to give you several words, and I want him to think about each one and for you to tell me your thoughts.

The pearl handle pistol that saved my mother and I
   The two bull attacks by the same bull
   The flood that nearly drowned us
   The white wolf attack
   The gunshot to my face, chest, and legs on Thanksgiving Day
   Regaining my eyesight
   The miracle God granted me by letting you survive a gunshot to the back of your head
   Finding my fiancée
   The battle to save heaven
   The pearl-handled pistol that saved my brother's life
   The reporter who gave the pearl handle pistol back to the Japanese's Soldier
   The doctor who performed the surgery allowing me to play my senior year
   Winning the regional championship game
   I could feel Soul changing his thoughts and regaining control of his emotion. He asked me what I felt was the most significant thing on the list. I told him for me it was getting him back in my life. He

said the most important thing to him was the battle to save heaven. Then he said not getting a scholarship to play basketball would not even make the list compared to the rest of the things we had been through together. I said I felt the same way, but I was not sure how my fiancée was going to feel about the news. He said she would love us no matter what direction our life took. I think God gave us both an attaboy that day.

My fiancée had found a job and had the money saved to pay her tuition. I told her what had happened and that our plan needed one more detour. I told her she should choose a school and I would join her later once I could arrange to find the funding.

She said, "No way," and told me what she really wanted to do was become my wife. She did not want to spend one more day than necessary not being able to hold and kiss me anytime she wanted to. I agreed, and we decided to use her savings to pay for the wedding.

Her uncle had spent 40 years in the military as a civil servant in Washington DC. When he heard about our plans, he met with us and laid out a plan to help us with the wedding.

Ghent, Kentucky was my wife's hometown. The family had been a member of a small church for more than a hundred years. About ten years prior to our wedding, the church could no longer afford to hold family services and was shut down.

When the uncle arrived home from Washington, he visited the church and had the vision to bring the old church back to life once again. He had attended the church with his family for the first 18 years of his life before joining the military. He instantly became one of Soul's favorite people in the family. He wanted us to delay the wedding long enough for him to make the repairs needed to re-open the church. However, once he understood our plans, he decided to hire a contractor to replace the roof and some of the windows and siding on the exterior.

He, along with several other family members, spent many long days and nights sanding and refinishing the pews, alter, and the staging area. His motives to re-vitalize the church were soon noticed by the community leaders. One by one the folks who had attended the old church for most of their lives started showing up to help with the refurbishing project.

Many of the volunteers shared stories about what the church meant to the community and to the parishioners decades ago. Besides the regular service on Wednesdays and Sundays, the church was a sanctuary during the depressions. Some of the community's most prominent citizens at the time were married in the church. As with many churches in those days, it also served as a school for young children. But the children were eventually moved to the elementary school located on the edge of town heading for Carrollton.

Once all of the modifications were complete, the family, friends, and members in the community spent several days decorating the church for the wedding. The big day was June 24, 1972. We did all the traditional things required to have a wonderful marriage. I remember watching her walk down the aisle with her father standing at her side. She was so beautiful but a little nervous. She could not help but look at me halfway down the runway and smile. Soul was at peace and we both knew this was our best day.

Forty-One

THE CALL

Married life was great, and each day I could not wait to get off work at the ladder factory and head home to my wife. My first surprise was that she really struggled in the kitchen. When she cooked at home, she was cooking for 8-10 people every meal. The first few weeks I did everything I could to eat most of what she fixed. The last thing I wanted to do was give her the impression I did not like the taste or the types of meals she was fixing. After a month, I started gaining weight and was having trouble fitting into my clothes. I thought I was clever when I asked her to cut back on the amount of food she was preparing for each meal. That was a dumb move, as I ate TV dinners for the next two weeks. Newlyweds know I was cutting off the hands that fed me.

When I got home from work one day, she said I had received a very strange phone call. The message from the caller was, "If you want it, you have to go get." I told her it was likely a prank call from someone who knows we are new to the Madison area. She said it was a man's voice and she was concerned and a little scared. The next day about the same time, she received another call from the same man with a different message. The man told her to tell me if I wanted to beat the system and play major college basketball to give him a call. When I got home, I immediately called the number just to put my wife at ease. The voice sounds familiar on the phone, but I could not quite figure out who he was. He told me we had met one time a couple years ago. He said I gave his son some great advice that also inspired him to make changes in his life. He just wanted to give something back to me. I ask him if he was a college recruiter offering me a scholarship to play basketball. He said, "No, I am a coach and the owner of a summer basketball association." I asked how playing in a summer basketball would get me a college scholarship.

He said his team consisted of players just like me caught up in the politics of major college athletics. He said, "The system is not designed for people like you to succeed. It is set up for the most popular kids with prominent fathers and wealthy ancestry. You never had a chance son. When you have finished playing for me, you will not need scholarship money. Just show up at any university and walk on. I guarantee you they will play you. You are a better shooter than 90 percent of the players currently playing professional basketball. You were screwed over by the system, and all I want to do for you is make a wrong a right.

He congratulated me on my recent marriage and said she was a great girl and I needed to give her a real life.

The next obvious question was if this was legal. Then I asked how much money I would make for pay-to-play services. He said I would need to sign a contract. I told him signing a contract would end my amateur status and make me a professional. To play college ball, I would need to maintain my amateur status. I told him I would discuss it with my wife, but if I decided to play the terms would be cash only, and I would expect my pay before I played the game.

He gave me a landmark close to our apartment and a time for our first meeting. He said that if I did not show up, I would not get a second opportunity.

My wife thought this was crazy and I should call the police. I convinced her that it was my last chance to achieve my dream. If I were successful, I could give her a life most women would love to have. She said she already had the life she wanted, but if it meant so much to me, she would agree and support my mission. If she only knew what was coming next, she would have never agreed to let this happen in a million years.

As you know, it was not my first trip down the lane of uncertainty. I knew it was never a good idea to take a knife to a possible gunfight. If this was a set-up, I needed a plan for a quick getaway. Then I thought about inviting a few of my brother's military friends who had guns and were not afraid to use them to have my back. I called my second oldest brother and talked to him about the opportunity. He felt it was risky, but he knew how badly I want to play ball. He told me to go to the meeting and he would be in the background with a few of his friends. If I needed him I should just send a signal and a few of his boys would be there to help me out.

I got to the meeting place a few minutes early and made sure my brother and his friends were in position. A white car pulled up beside me. It looked like it was 40 feet long with fully tinted windows. I could not see anyone in the car, including the driver. A few seconds passed by before anyone exited the car. I think my brother was ready to move in until a man stepped out with a huge smile on his face and shook my hand. It took a few seconds for me to recognize the man, but as soon as I heard his voice, I knew who he was. He was the man who offered me a ride home after ball practice a few years prior with all the kids in the back seat. I shook his hand and said, "Wow, something must have gone very right for you. I did not know we had any gold mines in Hunters Bottom. The last time I saw you, your wife said you barely had enough money to buy groceries." Before he could speak, I asked him if he would not mind meeting my second oldest brother and some of his friends. He said, "Yes, it would be an honor. Is he the brother who saved the soldier's life and capture the VC at the edge of the sea?" I said, "Yes, but he does not want to talk about it; he feels he was just doing his job." He said, "Okay, but the soldier he saved was my brother's only son and my youngest nephew." I waved my brother over and introduced him to the man. They talked about the military and the man respected my brother's wishes by not discussing the event. The only thing he did say was his family was very grateful and he thanked him for his service and bravery.

He told my brother about how the two of us had met. It was my speech in the car that inspired him to take a chance. "He told my son no one was going to hand you anything. If you want it bad enough, you have to go get it."

"When I saw the injury and the condition of your brothers side and how he was willing to play past the pain, I decided to go after my dreams. You see, I was a superstar player just as your brother is. I think that is where my son got his desire to be a star someday. When I got out of high school, I was a top player in the area. Nevertheless, the system got me and I lost my chance to play college ball. Instead of fighting it, I decided to join the navy and see the world. At the time, I had no idea how many players like me and like your brother there is out there in the country.

Shortly after joining the navy, I met some other men with a similar story to mine. We convinced our commanding officers to let us put up a goal and play ball right there on the ship. It did not take us long to build a team and start to make money playing the game I loved. Soon those Saturday night games became the main entertainment for the men, and the games became some of the best basketball played in the world. Each naval ship in the South Pacific created a team who traveled from ship to ship, and our main job was to play basketball. I am not sure what my official title was in the navy. I really did not care as long as I played ball and entertained the sailors.

As he turned to me, he said, "My time was up, and I wanted to marry the woman you met in the car with the children. One thing led to another, and before I knew it, I was farming from daylight to dark. We all know it is a great life, but it would never help my children see their dreams come true."

I told him, "I understand that, but what does all of this have to do with me playing ball and making enough money to go college?" He said he had played ball all over the world and he kept in touch with his former team-mates. "During a reunion, we talked about the old days and how much we missed the game. All of us were behind a plow and not going anywhere with our lives. We were talking, and I told them about what you had said to my son. We decided this was our time, and within a few weeks, we decided to go out and get it. We decided to form a company named B-Ball Plus. We had contacts with some of the best outdoor court managers in the world.

Therefore, we formed a league featuring some of the best street ball players in the world. We got money from the GI bill and set up a schedule for the players to travel all over the world to challenge each other in real games. The group who formed the company receives paid sponsorship from some of the largest sporting goods and sports supply companies in the world. In other words, my friend, I made more money in the first month doing something I love than I had made in five hard years plowing fields and milking dairy cows. And I might add, farming was not something I loved to do.

"I already know you can play. I have reserved a spot on my team for you to play if you want it." I told him when the world came crashing down on us I had taken a job in a local ladder factory in Carrollton. I needed to work to pay our living expenses. He said, "All of the players work jobs during the day, and the games are on Friday nights and all day Saturdays and Sundays. I would be home by Sunday night each week in plenty of time to go to work the following Monday morning.

He said the deal included all my travel and meal expenses and a little spending money. He said, "I understand the situation with keeping your amateur status, and the money will be paid in cash to your wife for helping at the apartment complex you will live in while you are playing. Many of the fans in the stands are high rollers and do make thousands of dollars each night betting on their favorite teams and players. If one slips you a few hundred-dollar bills, just say thanks and keep on moving. They donate money during the regular season to the league owners. The money is split up evenly with the players who win the tournament championship at the end of the season.

"By the way, I own the building you live in. You do know the building housed some of the most famous Hollywood actors of its time? They stayed there while making two films nominated for Oscars." I told him I did know that but that I was very young when they made those movies.

He said, "You will receive instructions every Thursday night on which airport you will fly out from and where you will land. Once you land, a chauffeur will take you to the hotel and then to the court. You will play three games to 35 points. Each basket scored will count as 1 point. You will play two games with the best two home court teams. The third game will be a league game between our team and another team in our association. The league team with the best record at the end of the season will have preferred games in the tournament. They will stay on center court until you win the tournament or get beat by another league team.

"The games will start in about two weeks, and the first time you will meet your teammates will be about an hour before your first game. In the meantime, you had better get in the best shape of your life because the local boys play for turf supremacies. The bad boys (especially the boys in the hood in New York City) do not enjoy losing and at times can get a little rough. You should get used to something they call trash talking, which will include a series of insults about your momma, your intelligence, and other slang that I do not have a clue what it means. We do not use referees; there's too much of a chance of them being shot by the locals for making even an excellent call. We do have a side judge, and if the judge calls out your name, it will be your first and only warning. So expect at least one cheap shot a game. I will be your coach. We only have seven players, so do not be tossed out of the game, and no one fouls out because no one calls any fouls."

He said I needed to spend the next two weeks down on the river road next to the Madison Regatta Arena. "The Long Boys and Crosby's play ball down there at night and make 5-dollar bets with any takers. Do not be fooled or sucked into their style of play. They are Hoosiers, and they play slow, fundamental basketball just the way the Indiana University coach has been teaching his players to play for twenty years. They are not in your league, and you should be able to pick up a couple of hundred bucks a week. They do not give up easy and have brought in a ringer or two from all over the country just to keep their pride intact by not letting a Kentucky boy get the last laugh."

I was a little nervous, and so was my brother, when we heard the games were not against the local team. My brother asked him where the games were going to be played. He said they would be in several major cities in the United States, South America, Europe, and in Asia.

He told us not to worry; the host country's military provided security. None of the league players had been injured that he knew of. He said he needed my answer immediately before he drove away. "The deal will be a handshake deal. I am a man of my word, and I know enough about you to know you will keep your word." I had a side meeting with my brother, and we talked about what a life-changing opportunity this could be for my wife and me. He felt good about the offer and he said he knew I could play with anyone, anywhere, anytime. I shook the man's hand. It sounded to me that I was on the up and up. After all, our favorite Uncle Sam was financing his company with the GI bill passed in Congress.

I talked it over with my wife, and we decided it was an excellent opportunity that we could not turn down. We decided she would tell her family I was playing ball out of town every weekend. Our goal was for me to be noticed by a team willing to sign me to play ball.

I received my first scheduled game on Thursday just as he had told me I would. I was to meet my escort at the Greater Louisville Kentucky airport. Once I arrive at the airport, he handed me a packet that included some spending cash, two round trip airplane tickets, and a special visa signed by a government official from Spain. One ticket was from Louisville, Kentucky to Madrid, Spain, and the other was from Madrid to San Francisco, with a return ticket to Louisville, Kentucky. For a man that had not been more than fifty miles from home in his lifetime, this was a nerve-wracking experience. Most of the teams we played included players that were much bigger and older than we were.

By the time we made it halfway through the season, we were undefeated. I could tell our fans were getting more aggressive with the bets, and the money being made on the side had nothing to do with basketball. At the three-quarter mark in the season, we were still undefeated and had started playing in larger cities. Most of our victories were the result of our shooting ability and the fact that we were trained players. Our competition seemed to stay with us until it got down late in the games. They would usually try to pull off some street ball move that did not work and would lose the game. Sometimes one of their players would decide he could go one-on-one or take an ill-advised shot just to bring attention to him. Their failures substantiated that basketball is a team sport; it always has been and always will be.

I knew we had made our success well known when I received tickets from Louisville to New York City. There was only one round trip ticket, so I knew we were headed for the most famous street ball courts in the world. Some of the most storied professional basketball players in the world had spent most of their childhood playing on those courts. One of the players on our team was from New York and had played much of his life on the court rightfully named "The Cage" in Greenwich Village.

Our limousine went through Manhattan and right past the most famous pastrami delicatessen in New York—and many claim in the world. The deli's name is Katz and has been in business for over 105 years. I told my New York friend that that was where I wanted to eat later that night. When we arrived at the court, I saw him take a deep breath as if he was thinking, "Okay, I am home." What I was thinking was, "Why does the court feature a 25' tall fence around the perimeter? And where are the exits?"

Our uniforms were silver and black. The coach said the colors each team wore were symbols of their characters. The silver meant we were there to shine and the black stressed our mental toughness. I jokingly told the coach the silver would glow in the dark and make us a good target as we ran off the courts back to our limousine after beating their favorite local team. He said, "Well, that too!"

We beat the two local teams rather easily, and it was time for the two visiting traveling teams to match up. Most of our match-ups were scheduled at midnight everywhere we went. The crowds were a mix of young adults who just loved to watch great basketball. Occasionally I would notice a young couple sitting hand in hand in the homemade stands.

Those times made me think about my wife back home and what must be going through her mind. At first, she spent most of her weekends with her family, but later in the season, she decided she wanted to stay at home. She had made friends with a lady about her age down at the hamburger joint and would go down and help her clean-up after closing time. I think it took her back to a time when we were dating when life was simple and our love was incredible.

For some reason, about halfway through the game, the crowd started chanting, "Ringer, ringer!" At first, I could not understand whom they were directing their displeasure towards. Then I realized the player on our team from New York was nicknamed Ringer in the past. It took the crowd until then to figure out who he was. They were calling him Ringer because of a rumor one of the street gangs started when he disappeared just before the All Cage City Championships a few years earlier. They said he had gone pro and was playing ball in another country. Apparently, a number of fans in the stands had lost a considerable amount of money when he failed to show up for the game and his team lost.

We could not wait to get to 35 points and get out of town. It was a thrill to play on the Cage, such famous and notorious court, but I was not sure if I would want to play there at midnight again.

The next night we moved on over to Rucker Park. As we drove through the city to the park, it was apparent the city was a culture in shambles. The newspapers were covered with page after page of stories describing the racism, drugs, violence, and poverty that symbolized this community. The trip was very upsetting to Soul, as he witnessed firsthand how people were struggling to survive. He spent his time talking to God about how he could reach out to these people and offer even a little bit of hope. He closed with the statement "We sure have a lot of work left to do God."

The park had room for several thousand fans to sit and enjoy great basketball. The local teams we played were well coached and played team ball. Both games were great games, with our team coming out on top by two points each game. The traveling team we played was from Los Angeles and came out in warm-ups displaying their ability to slam-dunk the basketball. This made them a crowd favorite and turned a team 3,500 miles from their hometown into a home crowd.

We decided to turn up our game with some incredible long-range passes for dunks, and a few 35-foot jump shots barely touched the bottom of the net for scores. We went into a full court press and denied them the opportunity to get the ball down the floor for the first half of the ball game. It did not take long for the home crowd to show their appreciation for the style of play we delivered. We won the game rather easily, and as usual, every player on both teams walked around the court and acted as if we were the best of friends, even though it was the first time most of us had ever met our opponents. We would sign autographs, make marketing comments about how much we liked our latest style of shoes, our jerseys, and even the sports drinks we liked the best. We went from playing to being walking, talking billboards for our sponsors.

Every player had a nickname, and when we signed autographs we were required to sign the number on our jersey and our nickname. Just in case you are wondering, I kept my nickname from high school, which was "Shooter." Our all-state player originally gave it to me during an interview one night. He always said I never met a shot I did not like or was afraid to take.

Once we were finished, another team walked out on the floor, and then a number of young adults escorted the mayor of New York and an elderly black man to the mid-court circle. It was an award ceremony. I could not help but be impressed by what he was being honored for. He had apparently organized several street ball tournaments that netted enough money to send over 300 high school seniors to college. It appears all 300 were there to show their appreciation for what this man had done to improve the quality of their lives. Each person personally walked up to him and shook his hand or gave him a big hug and then showed him and the mayor their degrees.

What I really thought was, "I am happy for the ones that got the money to go to school." But this problem did not limit itself to the streets of Harlem. I personally knew 50 young adults with high school diplomas deserving to go to college who did not have the money. I was very thankful for what my coach and his navy friends were doing to help every person in the league continue their education by doing something we loved.

Our next two games would be the last regular season games. When I received my packet, it contained the typical contents, but the tickets were a bit unnerving. The first stop would be in East Berlin, which was the communist block of Germany. The second stop would be In Moscow Russia's Red Square.

Every American living during this period of history thought about the hideous crimes carried out by Adolph Hitler and the East Germans anytime someone mentioned the Berlin Wall.

The Americans were engaged in a cold nuclear war with the Russians. We were only three years removed from the Cuban Missile Crisis, in which the Russian planted nuclear warheads in Cuba and aimed them at the United States. It was one of the scariest time in my childhood. When our plane landed in West Germany, we were escorted to the Berlin Wall gate crossing named Checkpoint Charlie. This was the most famous of all wall crossings. A few short years later, the president of the United States challenged the ruler of East Germany to tear down the wall, which he did.

We went straight to the courts and played our three games, in which were determined not to allow the East Germany teams to score any points. The two German teams scored three points in both games. The traveling teams played a great game. The minute our team scored the winning basket, we were ordered to return to our cars and leave East Germany. I'm not sure if they were still mad about the outcome of the war or just sore losers. We did not stick around to figure out which was correct.

The trip to the Soviet Union was uneventful. When we stepped off the plane, the temperature felt like we were in the middle of winter. The Russian people's kindness and generosity were in direct contrast to the German people. The Russians were extremely polite and let us know we were there as guests of the dictator. They provided the finest of accommodations and the best of fine dining.

The next night, the Russians escorted us to the courts and, much to our surprise, it was not the usual outdoor court but a private invitation-only event in the palace.

It was a good thing because even if it was the middle of summer, the temperatures late at night dropped into the mid-thirties. We easily won all three games. Our contingency was directed by the league owners to be polite and show our gratitude for the generosity of the host nation. To tell you the truth, I could not wait to get out of Russian air space. I think it had a lot to do with being required to humble down to a country led by a dictator. I will take freedom and democracy for the people, by the people, with the people, any day over any other form of government.

The coach sat down beside me on the plane and said it had been a pleasure to watch me play. He said we would host the playoffs in our neck of the woods. I thought about what he said and thought he may have consumed too much Russian liquor. I could not think of even one outside court large enough in our community to host such a large event.

I was glad the season was winding down. I know my wife was sad with me being gone every weekend for the past ten weeks. My job at the ladder company was a good one, and the people there were great people. Most had advised me to get out of there as quick as I could. They all felt I could do a lot with my life, but the opportunities would never be at the factory.

I got my schedule to report to the old Locust School gymnasium at midnight on Friday night. I thought it was a mistake, since the school had been shut down for more than 12 years. The last time I drove by the school, it appeared to be in terrible shape. I knew the county had sold the school to a small company to use as a parts assembly plant. As it turned out, my coach and B-Ball Plus owned the building. He later told me it was his first purchase after starting up his company. The second move was to hire a professional coach to lay out the floor and provide private coaching for each of his sons wanting to play basketball.

I started thinking about all of the incredible places I had played ball over the past ten weeks and wondering how the other teams would deal with traveling to Kentucky. If Soul had a hard time finding Locust Creek, Kentucky just imagine the difficulty people from New York, Los Angeles, Russia, Germany, and Madrid would have. The invitation was address Locust Creek, Kentucky stay left where the East Prong road meets the West Prong road and drive slowly for one half-mile. I drove by the old school on my way home from work one afternoon. It still looked the same as it did when I attended the first and second grade there. My wife reminded me it was my job to play the game and the rest was up to the company. The week passed by slowly, and I could not wait to play in the gym my older brothers made famous.

When I turned right on Locust Road, I could see automobile lights for miles away. It must have looked like one of those movie scenes where people are trying to avoid the aliens from outer space by getting out of town quick. When we finally passed thorough security, I could see the school. The school and the field we used to play baseball on were transformed into a field of lights, ball courts, and portable bathrooms.

I stepped out of our car and did everything I could to keep a hold of my wife's hand as we were ushered through the fans to the reception area and to the dressing rooms. I never realized until then how famous our team and coach were. Many of the fans were yelling out my nickname, "Shooter!" My wife said she thought my nickname went away after high school. "I guess it did not take them long to realize you never met a shot you would not take." I just smiled and introduced my wife to the rest of the players on my team and to the coach. She thanked the coach for giving me the opportunity to play on the team. She told the coach we had been paid enough money to put both of us through school with or without a scholarship. I could tell he was excited about what we had accomplished, and he had one more surprise for me. He asked me how I liked the look of my old gym and playground. I told him someone spent an awful lot of money to get this place ready for such an incredible event. I jokingly said, "Wow, I guess your ship actually did come in."

He said, "In the car that night, you said your mother was your number one fan, but she had never watched you in person play a single game. She is here tonight so it your chance to show her what she paid for." He notices me start to tear up and placed his hand on my shoulder. He said, "It is time to put on your game face. We still have some unfinished business on the courts and it is not going to be easy to win this tournament. Every team you beat this season is here and can't wait for another shot at knocking you out of the tournament."

He had my wife escorted to a special area set aside for player's families and his special guests. While we were warming up for our first game, I made eye contact with my wife. She smiled and said, "Good luck." I could tell she was a little nervous about the surroundings and the people she was sitting with. She told me later it all became clear when she noticed the man sitting directly in front of her holstering a 357 magnum. This was not a high school regional final; these people were serious about their basketball and their gambling skills.

The woman sitting beside her was waving and yelling my name. It took a second, but I finally recognized the woman. It was the woman in the car, and all six of her children were sitting beside her. She was wearing an outfit worth several thousand dollars. The children were all decked out in the latest sports fashions attire and designer sports shoes. The crowd around her included a couple of dictators from major countries we were not supposed to like very much at the time. A handful of local politicians and public officials and their wives sat alongside her. The front row was reserved for high rollers consisting of Vegas-style gamblers from every civilized country in the world. These folks were well protected by their own security personnel. We notice the same security team in every country we had played in during the tour. They were very peaceful people who loved two things: winning bets and watching teams and individual players play great basketball. From looking at their posh appearance and the smiles on their faces, I would say they did not lose many bets.

As I was warming up, I could not help but survey the school and the classrooms I had attended. I was wondering where the people who taught us had ended up. Educators like Thomas, Broberg, Eason, Mattes, Yocum, and Bradley and her best friend Cotton were incredible teachers, cooks, and mentors. I often wondered if they realize at the time how much the students loved them.

I could not help but have flashbacks to when my brothers played in this same gym. This night was real, but it felt like it belonged in a fairy tale similar to the one where the prince finally found the lady who's foot fit the glass slipper and everybody lived happy ever afterwards.

Since we were a team with the best record for the season, we would have the honor to play on an indoor court until we lost. After all, this tournament was not a cheap tournament to host. The high rollers wanted to see the best on center court. I must admit I likely hit a few shots from far away distances player are not supposed to shoot. I was determined to continue to win to stay on center court. Winning gave my mother an opportunity to see in person what she missed for the first ten years of my basketball career. Up to this point, all she had was a vision described by Good Game Charlie and Flannel Mouth Fultz on the radio.

We went on to win the tournament, and I never saw the coach again or any of the players. Just as they had appeared in my life, so unexpectedly, they disappeared the same way. I drove by the school a couple of weeks later and it was all gone.

By the time the season ended, it is too late for us to enroll at any of the major universities. We decided to continue to work and save our money and enroll during the winter semester. My wife and I had planned to enroll at the University of Kentucky in the winter semester and I would go through spring basketball practice as a walk on to make the basketball team the next year. The University of Kentucky had become one of the most prestigious academic colleges in the world and had everything my wife needed to fulfill her dreams of teaching others someday.

This unexpected journey just happened. Maybe it was fate or the work of a higher power. Nevertheless, it just goes to show that if you work hard and stay patient, goods thing can happen. In my mind, I could not wait to join a college team and do the thing I enjoyed the most: play ball and look at my wife sitting up in the stands sharing her incredible smile just before tipoff.

A few weeks after the season ended, I was offered a job to join one of the local chemical manufacturing companies. At first, I was very reluctant to leave the ladder factory. However, once the chemical plant superintendent offered to double my salary, I really had no choice but to resign from the ladder company.

Things were going very well for my wife and me at the time. We moved from Madison to Carrollton and lived a month with her aunt and uncle until our apartment was available.

Once we moved into the apartment, it felt good, and it was actually the first time we felt at peace for several years. I spent much of my free time helping my wife's family work their farm. Farming was my first love, and I enjoyed working with animals and at the end of the harvest season for all of the cash crops. Her parents owned one of the best farms in Carroll and Gallatin County, and helping to improve the operation of the farm was a lot of work but worth it.

The farm had been in my wife's family for over 200 years, and most of her family lived on the adjoining farms. Working on the farm reminded me of home when I was growing up. Her brother and three sisters had chores to perform, but her parents were very strict when it came to getting a good education.

I will never forget what happened one Sunday afternoon while walking through one of the fields holding hands with my wife. We spent many of our Sundays hiking on the farm, mostly following paths made by the livestock during their travel to find water and to the feeding lots at feeding time. I noticed the line fence separating my wife's parents farm from the corporate farm was down and appeared to have fresh cattle tracks pointing in the direction of her parents' farm. The corporate farm owners were in the National Cattleman's Association. They used the farm to raise a variety of livestock to help meet the world's meat production.

There was no such thing as the Department of Health or any other federal department to help manage the activities of the corporate farms. In other words, they could bring livestock from all over the world to live on the farm without treatment for any of the deadly viruses livestock can carry from farm to farm.

I asked my wife if her father had purchased some new cattle. I told her I knew his herd and these were not his cows. Several of the cattle started displaying a strange behavior and became very aggressive with the other livestock in the lot.

They knew we were close to them, but they did not attack us. I told my wife we needed to split up and I would distract the cattle while she ran to the house to get her father. By the time her father arrived, the cattle had settled down, and he thought we had done something to disturbed them. I explained to him I had been around thousands of head of cattle and their behavior was not normal. I also mentioned that I did not recognize several of the cattle in the herd.

I think he had an idea of what was going on with the herd but did not want to face it. Once I got back to the house, I called my dad and told him what the cows were doing and how they were acting.

He asked me to put my wife's father on the phone, and I could tell what my dad was sharing with her father was not good news. He told my father he would call the vet in the morning and the local officials. He handed me the phone, and I thanked my dad for the help. He told me he had no doubt it was a virus. He said it was a long shot, but he was going to check in with his friends at the University of Kentucky to see if the vaccine that was in development was ready for commercial use. He told me if it were not available, the herd needed to be put to death and buried to stop the virus from spreading.

He said he could tell my wife's father was devastated, and if he wanted help taking care of destroying the herd, he would bring in a team to take care of the process.

Her father went back to the main gate used to connect all of the lots. I heard him call for his cattle, and they quickly came to the gate they had entered thousands of times in the past several years. I saw him put his hand through the gate to touch the heads of two of his favorite mother cows. Then he just dropped his head, and I could tell he was crying and emotionally overwhelmed by the idea that in a few days he may have to put his entire herd to death.

Back in those days, many farmers killed their herds to prevent the spread of viruses. He knew if his cattle tested positive, he would have to join in with the rest of the local farmers and kill off every cow in his herd.

The next morning, he called the vet, and the vet took samples from several of the cattle. The vet sent the test samples to a special laboratory for testing. In a matter of a couple of hours, the sheriff delivered my father-in-law an order from a local judge; it was a quarantine order. This meant the owner had to keep the cattle isolated and he could not sell any of the livestock. This was routine procedure if the test lab officials suspected the virus was present, and he felt it was.

I know my wife loved me with all of her heart, but I could never take the place of the bond that connects a daughter to her father. I knew she was hurting just as bad as her father was. Some of the older cows in the pen were raised on the farm from the time she was a baby. Most had sentimental names and personalities she understood and loved. These were her pets, and she could not imagine hurting even one of them. The idea of killing them was more than she could deal with.

Several days went by before the tests were known by the local authorities. Finally, the local authorities delivered the news. The tests were positive, and my wife's dad was ordered to destroy the entire herd in two weeks. Up to this point, my wife had always been by my side. She helped me get through many bad breaks and hard times. I decided it was my turn to take care of her. I remembered my dad telling me about a possible vaccine being develop at the University of Kentucky.

It just so happened, the best man in my wedding was at the University of Kentucky majoring in agriculture. He and I had been friends for many years. We were trained to judge the health and wellness of cattle as members of the Future Farmers of America. We competed together and won numerous competitions in cattle judging and public speaking across the state during our high school days.

I called him and made him aware of what was happening with the herd. He had a particular interest in the problem because his family farm was within five miles of my wife's family farm. Moreover, the corporate farm was also connected to his farm.

It did not take him long to work his way into the college laboratories and review the issue with one of his professors. The professor told him the vaccine was available and the federal government had tested it and approved it for production. The problem was that sufficient quantities of the vaccine were not available and the cost of producing the vaccine was expensive. The only way the company could make the vaccine in the period required was to have the money up front.

When I found out about the vaccine and the fact the only thing between survival and death was money, the decision became very simple for me. I called my friend and arranged a meeting with the professor and the company that would manufacture the vaccine. The day before the meeting, I met with the bank president and told him why I needed to close my account. I needed a check for twenty-five thousand dollars. The president handed me a check and shook my hand. He said this was one of the most incredible acts of love he had ever witnessed.

In the meantime, my wife's father was making plans to follow the order to destroy the cattle. He set a date, and within a few days, a number of bulldozers arrived at the farm, and the process of digging graves was underway.

I met with the local vet and told him he would receive a shipment of vaccine to vaccinate the entire herd. The newly formulated vaccine would kill the virus and not harm the cattle. He told me he knew about the anecdote, but he also said he doubted any farmer in the valley had the money to purchase enough vaccine to cure the herd. I told him I paid for the vaccine. Then I showed him the order and the shipping instructions.

I think everybody in the county, including the vet, knew about our college plans. The vet just smiled at me. Then he said, "For you to give up what you are giving up, you must truly love your wife." I said, "With all of my heart, and it is about time for me to show her."

I knew the date was rapidly approaching for slaughtering the herd. I was checking with the VET every day to see if he had received the shipment. Many of the local farmers were getting very nervous. Some were pressuring my wife's dad into getting it over with in fear that it would spread to their herds.

The night before the scheduled slaughter, my wife told me she was going to the farm the next morning. She wanted to say goodbye to her friends. I asked her if she wanted me to go with her. She said that this was something she needed to do with her dad and the rest of the family.

My dad had followed-through with his commitment the day we found out the herd was sick and was prepared to manage the process. The day arrived, and the process was scheduled to begin at 1:00 in the afternoon. I skipped work and went to the vets office. We could not wait for the mail to come to see if the anecdote were in the shipment. When the mail carrier arrived, he came inside and told the vet he sure had a large shipment of something. He wanted to know if we could help him bring it into the office. I could not wait to get to the mail carrier van and see the name on the packages. The vet could tell by the smile on my face that the package was from the company I had hired to manufacture the vaccine.

I jumped in my car and broke the land speed record getting out to the farm to stop my dad. I do remember that when I jumped out of the car, it started to roll backwards and then I heard a single gunshot. I left the car and hoped it would stop on its own, which it did. The single shot was the signal for the shooters to load their weapon and get ready for the signal from the sheriff to start the slaughter. I ran as fast as possible to the feed-lots, which were about a mile from where I had to park my car. When I got close, I started screaming at the top of my lungs to get the shooters' attention. I think Soul was screaming louder than I was. My father finally heard me screaming, "Stop Dad! Please do not shoot!" He yelled at the sheriff to hold up so he could settle me down. My father and his best friend jumped off the coral fence and ran up the hill. They grabbed a hold of me just as I approached the edge of the large trenches dug as a final resting place for the herd. I did not know the ditches were there. Once I got my breath back, one of the men offered me a drink of water out of his canteen. I finally got my heart to slow down and made it back to my feet. I asked my dad if I could speak to him. The other men gave us our privacy. I told him not to slaughter the cows because the veterinarian was bringing out the vaccine needed to kill the virus.

After a long pause, he said, "You know son, I spoke to the man who owns the patent rights. He told me he would not make a vaccine without the money paid in full before he started." I said, "I know Dad, he told me the same thing." He said, "I know what you did Son. The bank president also called me. The president said the old expression that love is blind went right out the window when you told him how much your wife meant to you. I also know, Son, that it took every cent you had in the world." I told him I did it for her and I would do it again if I had to. "I love her Dad." I just could not stand by and let her entire past and all of her memories be gone if I could prevent it from happening.

All he could say was that he was proud of me. He said something deep down in his soul just told him something incredible was going to happen today. He was proud his son made it happen. He asked me if my wife knew about what I had done, and I told him no. "I will tell her someday, but just not today."

I knew my wife and her family had already completed their goodbyes and had left the farm for the rest of the day. They would not return until after the slaughter had ended.

The veterinarian finally arrived with the anecdote. My dad told me he and his men would stay on to help the vet perform the vaccinations.

The vet told me he had plenty of help to perform the vaccinations and that I should take the day off.

I decided to spend the rest of my day down at General Butler Park just shooting baskets and relaxing. When I arrived at the court, I started putting up shots between 35 and 40 feet from the basket. By then that was my normal range. Out of nowhere, this little boy walked up to me and said, "You sure are good, you must be a professional ballplayer." I told him, "Not yet, but it does not hurt to dream." He asked me if I could help him with his game, which I was delighted to do.

Before I knew it, I was playing full court basketball the rest of the day with a group of kids between the ages of 11 and 17 years old. Just before the sun went down, I told the boys and girls it was time for them to go home. I was sure their mothers would be getting worried about them. They asked me if I would be back the next day to help them with their game. I said maybe, and one of the boys said, "Okay, see you tomorrow coach."

I left the court and went to our apartment just long enough to call my dad and find out if the process was over and how the cattle were doing. He said it was over, but some of the cows seemed more friendly than normal. I explain that those cows were part of the original herd and several of them had babies out in the herd.

"I meant to tell you, all you need to do to get the mother cows to come to you is to call them by their first names." He just laughs. I said I was not kidding and that many of the names were the same names we used to name our newborns when I was a child. He said, "Okay, you got me. What are their names?" "Well, there is old Betsy; she is the oldest and has delivered 13 babies over the years. In addition, there is Mable and Sally, and they like to use their heads to gently butt up against your back to influence you to move in the direction of the feeding lots. They're both overweight but are great mothers. Mary is the largest mother in the lot and she produces enough milk to help nurse 2-3 orphan calves at a time. I think my wife's favorite is Molly. Molly thinks she really is a member of the family and actually has her own stall in the barn. My wife painted Molly's name on the stall door when she was seven years old.

My dad said, "Okay Son, I get it. This was not all about protecting the herd; it was about keeping the family." I just said, "Yes sir," and thanked him for his support.

Dad said that just as they were finishing the vaccination process my wife's family came home. He said when the family got out of the car and heard the cows singing a familiar tune, "It's Feeding Time," they became quite confused. He said my wife's dad walked up to him and asked him what was going on. "Well, as you can see sir, your prayers have been answered. When I told him about the vaccine, the father put his arms around my waist and starting swinging me from side to side in jubilation.

"The look on your wife's face was precious, and none of the girls could stop crying. Her mother was in shock and wondered what they had done to deserve such a miracle from God. Her little brother went straight to the barn and started dropping down bales of hay to feed the cattle."

Then Dad said my wife's father asked the vet, "How much did all of this cost?"

"The VET asked the two of us to take a walk with him. He told us the vaccine cost about $25,000 dollars and that the total amount of the invoice required full payment up front before the company who owns the patient would produce the vaccine. Your wife's father told the vet he could not afford the money and would likely need to sell the cattle to pay for the vaccine. The vet asks him to let him finish and to please relax and enjoy the moment.

"Within a few minutes, your wife's mother joined the three of us. Your wife and three sisters could tell this was a serious conversation and stayed away.

"The vet said a member of their family walked into his office a week after the test results showed up positive. 'He asked me for a favor. He told me a delivery of vaccine would arrive at my office in a few days. The vaccine was to be used to save the herd. He said the company required two weeks to produce the volume needed to treat the herd, and he gave me the name of the company where the vaccine would come from and the purchase details. He asked me if I would vaccinate the cattle.

"'At first, I thought he had lost his mind. I knew this stuff was very expensive and could not dream someone his age had enough money in the bank to cover the cost. However, judging from the determination in this young man's eyes, I realized he was as serious as a heart attack.

"'The only thing he asked me to do was not tell anyone, just in case the vaccine did not arrive on time. Well, I got the shipment this morning exactly two hours before your herd was to be slaughtered. The young man was sitting in his car this morning when I arrived at the clinic before 6:00 AM. He looked beat down and anxious about the shipment.

"'I must say, we were both very nervous and could not wait for the post office to make today's delivery. When we opened the door on the mail bus and saw the vaccine inside, the young man just drops to his knees and said, "Thanks boss."

"'By the time, I got out here with the vaccine, you and your family were gone for the day. We assumed you would want us to save your herd, so we did.' The father thanked the vet for saving his herd and invited him out for Sunday dinner.

"He put his arm around his wife and then asked me why my son would do what he did. 'Everybody knows what the money was for and how hard he worked to earn it.'"

My father saw it as an opportunity to do what dad's do: brag on their sons and daughters. He told him, "My seven sons are all very mature for their ages. I think they get their feelings of 'family first' from their mother. You see sir, playing ball is important to him, and he saw it as his future. He knew if he made it to the top of his dream, your daughter would never have to worry about money like the rest of us do. He knew she was also very special. Who knows, maybe she will go on to find a cure for cancer or become the first female president of the United States?

"However, when you have a chance to ask him why for yourself, he will likely tell you playing ball is something that *might* happen. The sure thing is that little girl over there; he fell in love with when he was twelve. I can assure you sir, he did this for her, and he may never get a chance to play ball on a college team and certainly not as a professional. Nevertheless, he will always have her by his side and her love forever. In his mind, life just could not be better."

The father asked the three men to excuse him; he needed to talk to his daughter. He went over to her, took her by the hand, and asked her to walk with him. They walked down to the pin where the cows were finishing the hay, and he yelled out the mother cows' names one at a time.

They immediately ran straight to my wife. She stuck her hands through the openings between the gates and rubbed each of the mother's heads. Through the tears, she asked her father if he remembered how she had come up with the names for each of the cows.

Then she said, "Dad, I need to know how this day took such an incredible turn for the best." He told her he did not know about it, but there was a new vaccine. Because of the vaccine, they would not need to destroy the cattle. She told him, "We are so blessed to have the opportunity to be with the herd, and these cows are like members of our family."

She asked her father how he came up with the money to pay for the vaccine, and her father put his arms around her and told her the truth about how the herd was saved. He told her he did not know the vaccine existed, nor did he have the money to purchase the vaccine to save the herd. He said a member of the family financed the full amount. He said, "It was someone who loves you more than I even thought it was possible for one person to love another." She looked very confused but stayed very much in control.

After a long pause, her father told her, "Your husband did it for you." He explained to her that it was not for the herd. "He did it purely for the incredible amount of love he has for you in his heart. He felt you were the one always making sacrifices to support him. This was his chance to give back and help you the way he has always wanted to support you."

He said, "I know it was the money he had saved for you and him to attend college in the winter. If the crops are good and the herd continues to do well, I will give you the money to pursue your college dreams.

Dad told me later that she told her father she was not surprised but that she needed to find her man. As she was walking back to the house, he told her I was likely still at the ball court. My dad offered to drive her to the courts. When they drove up to the court, I could tell from the redness in her eyes that she had been crying. Her tears were tears of love. I knew from the start she could care less about the money. She stepped out of the truck, walked over to the center circle at the mid-court line, and just sat down on the court. Over the years, she had sat in the exact same spot for hours and watched me play a game we both prayed would be our ticket to achieving all of our goals. My father stopped his truck next to the court. From his window, he gave me a stop sign, indicating he did not want me to come over to the truck. I could tell from the happy look on his face that he just wanted to watch me play one more time. Within a few minutes, I hear him start up the truck. I busted a forty footer from well past the top of the circle. He pointed to me, and I could read his lips as he said, "I am so proud of you son. Today is my best day." He pointed to me as he drove out of sight.

After about ten minutes of her maintaining the most beautiful smile imaginable, she could no longer hold back her tears. The tears flowing down her face symbolized the love she had in her heart. She kept motioning for me to continue to play, but I knew it was time to lay down my ball and go hold her. I went over to the side of the court to retrieve my ball, which had rolled off the court, when I heard her say, "Hit one more for us."

Of the millions of shots I had taken over the years, I still remember everything about the shot. I remember watching the rotation of the ball as it approached the rim. I glanced away from the ball and saw the look on my wife's face. She looked like she was somehow guiding the ball to the basket. When I looked back to the ball, the manufacturer's label was in perfect alignment, as if it were spinning on a pedestal. I intentionally shot the ball higher than normal so it would touch nothing but the bottom of the net. As the ball was traveling to the rim, I knew it was time to move on to the next phase of my life. I had two loves in my life: the one headed toward the rim and the one standing at half court. I know Soul was cheering for the girl, even though he loved basketball. It was no competition for either one of us. I knew my choice would end my dream of running out on a college court and even an NBA court to play the game I loved.

When the ball went through the bottom of the net, she came running down the court, yelling to the top of her lungs, "I love you with all my heart. Thank you for believing in me." I remember thinking about what a lucky man I was and I thanked God and Soul for allowing our two hearts to beat as one.

In the material world, all of our assets were gone and it would appear we had nothing. Nevertheless, through our eyes we were the wealthiest people on earth. Over the years, we had both learned that money and material things have nothing to do with real love. The only thing you need to keep true love alive is two hearts beating as one.

Once the celebration on the court was over, she said, "Let's go home. You will not believe what an incredible day this has been." I smiled and told her to tell me everything and not to leave out anything. On the way to the car, I told her some little kid called me Coach today. She said, "Smart kid."

Forty-Two

Moving On

My job at a chemical plant was very exciting and challenging. I did not know much about chemistry, but for what I was assigned to do there it was not necessary. We were working a rotating shift schedule, which turned out to be the most difficult thing I had to convince my body to accept. For nineteen years, my body was used to sleeping at night, working during the day, and playing ball until it was time to go to bed. This shift required me to work a dayshift one week. The next week I would work second shift, from 3:30 PM until midnight, and the following week I worked from midnight until 8 AM the next morning.

I liked the people I was working with in my department. They all seemed to want to help me learn how to operate the chemical reactors as quickly as I could. The more reactors and processes you learned to operate, the more money you made. I soon learned a lot about the people working on my shift. Some of the people were intimidating. My supervisor's name was Buck, and the man training me was Shift Leader Bill. Shift Leader Bill put major emphases on making the product meet the quality spec. He would not allow the other six members on the team to rush through things just to meet the production schedule. Both Buck and Bill were great people, and we spent a lot of time during lunch and breaks talking about the success of Carroll County High School basketball and football teams.

I did notice we would spend the last 90 minutes of each shift cleaning the floors and preparing the batches for the next shift turnover. The team coming on duty always seemed to be nervous about the turnover. It did not take me long to figure out why: a little person in stature they all called General Frank.

It turns out General Frank was not really a general in the military; he was the nice little old man who hired me. During the interview, he was a very soft-spoken person and appeared to me to be very personable. It did not take me long to figure out his demeanor inside the operating plant was much different than it was outside the plant.

When our team schedule rolled to day shift, he would meet Buck in the central foremen's office and review the control sheets from the night before. The control sheets described the systematic procedures to produce the 100 products produced in our area of the plant. Each step required an operator's signature by the operator completing the step. At the bottom of each sheet was the shift-turnover that described any process issues we may have had during the previous shift. Fortunately for me, I was required to complete my training before I could sign-off a control sheet.

General Frank had a photographic memory. He could remember each step of every process and where it was at the time of the shift turnover. However, more impressive was where it should have been by the time he reviewed the control sheets the next morning. No one would come near the office while he was reviewing the control sheets. I think the plant could have been burning down around him and no one would tell him to run. It usually sounded like World War III in the office, and General Frank was the commander in chief. I often thought about my high school coach when he got angry with the players and how he appeared to be a bad-boy, and he was 6' 5" tall. He was a preacher compared to General Frank. General Frank was the best in the business at taking your emotions to an all-time low and then making you feel like a hero ten minutes later. Once he finished the formal review of the control sheets, it was time for the morning walk through. During the walk through, he would seek out the associates operating the chemical reactors not meeting the quality specifications. He frequently started each conversation with the words: "Do you like your job?" He expected to hear a "Yes Sir" from the associate. Then he would ask, "Does your family like you working for the company?" Again, he waited to hear "Yes Sir." Then he would ask, "How are you going to explain to your family that you no longer have your job because you screwed up a batch?" Hopefully, Buck would step in and defend you as best he could.

General Frank cared about the company and understood the business from top to bottom. He could perform every process and knew the hazards associated with each. He also knew what could happen if the processes were not operated as the chemical engineers had designed them to be operated.

Within six months, I had learned to operate each of the processes in my assigned area. It was a fast track, and some of the operators were a little upset with me for making so much progress so quickly.

I learned the hard way how sometimes people can be cruel and will do what they can to make you look bad. Other operators had cautioned me about one such person, but I just did not have the maturity to think a person may not be a team player.

I reported to my department and Shift Leader Bill on the night shift. He told me my process was not running properly and the laboratory was trying to figure out how to make an adjustment to bring it back into spec. He said the reactor was in a holding pattern until he got word from the lab. Bill was a hard worker and expected all of the people reporting to him also to work hard.

He told me he needed someone to go inside and hand scrub a large chemical drying machine in an adjacent department. Bill walked me over to the department where the dryer was located, and introduced me to a man named Joe. Joe was the department lead. Bill told Joe he needed me back in his department as soon as the lab was finished with the adjustments. Joe agreed and told me about the dryer.

Joe led me over to the dryer, which was located in the middle of the concrete floor. To me it looked like something from outer space. It was a conical-shaped machine with high-pressure steam connected to the side. The machine was 20 feet off the ground. It had support pedestals, which were made of solid steel. The base of the machine was about 40 feet wide. Joe told me the machine weighed about two-hundred thousand pounds and cost well over a million dollars to install. When operating, it would turn in both directions on the pillar block bearing located on each end. The steam heated up the dryer to 300 degrees Fahrenheit to dry the product inside the dryer. Note: this was the first time I had to take the man-way off a piece of equipment and climb down a rope ladder to get down to the bottom of the unit.

Joe introduced me to the operator, and the name immediately ran caution up the flagpole. He was the person the other operators had cautioned me to keep an eye on. I smiled and shook his hand and introduced myself. He said he knew who I was and to not expect any special treatment from him. He said, "This is not a basketball game, and you had better watch your back." I told him I was there to help him and I would do what he needed me to do.

The operator explains the cleaning procedure. He told me he had already cleaned the machine and it was safe to go inside. I was a little apprehensive, so I checked to make sure the high-pressure nitrogen lines were remove from the dryer. Pure nitrogen is a deadly gas for human beings. I checked the line and found it was still connected to the drier. He said "Oops, I guess I missed one." I had some doubt about it being an honest mistake. He said he had completed the final wash and the dryer was ready for me to go inside and hand scrub.

He climbed up on the department forklift and told me to step on the forks so he could lift me up to where the man way was located. The man way was about thirty feet off the floor. I asked him if it was safe, and he assured me all of the operators in his department did it the same way. I thought it felt very awkward to step on the forks, but I was strong and my balance was exceptional. He lifted me up to the man way, and I disconnected the fasteners and opened up the door to the dryer. I looked inside the dryer, but it was pitch black, and I could not see a thing. He lowered me back down and handed me a bucket, some cleaning rags, detergent, and a flashlight. Then he lifted me back up to the opening and told me to climb inside the unit. He dropped a water hose into the dryer from the top and turned on the valve, which allowed maximum flow. By the time the joke was over, I was wet from head to toe. He just said that my clothes would eventually dry and that I needed to keep working. He told me he was scheduled to go to lunch and he would be back to check on my progress later. I said okay, but in the back of my mind, I was frightened to think that if this machine started turning I would be trapped inside and no one would even know I was there until it was be too late.

I wanted to do a good job, but I also wanted to get out of dryer as quickly as I could, so I started working as fast as possible to hand scrub the inside of the dryer. Within a few minutes, I knew something was wrong, and the skin on my back and legs felt like it was on fire.

I climbed up the walls of the dryer to where I had entered the unit. I yell for help, but no one answers, as the background noise created by the rest of the equipment in the department was very loud. Then, in a panic, I slid out of the dryer onto the forks of the fork truck and again yelled for help. No one came to let me down to the floor, so I climbed down the mast of the fork truck and reported to Shift Leader Bill back in my department. He must have seen the panic and the pain on my face when I walked through the door. He immediately shut down his machine and ran down the catwalk to where I was standing. I pointed to my back, and he and operator Danny ripped my shirt off to examine it. Shift Leader Bill took one look at my back and told me in a bit of a panicked tone of voice that I had a chemical burn and blisters were already beginning to form. He said, "Follow me," as he led me to the department safety shower and said, "Get under the shower and stay there until I come to get you." The gushing water pouring from the drier was cold, but it did help cool the chemicals that were continuing to burn my skin. He ran down the catwalk to alert operator Danny of what had happened and told him to run to the chemical lab to retrieve the antidote. Danny sprinted out of the building and down the street to the lab. He returned in a few minutes with a chemical neutralizing agent, and Bill rubbed the agent on my back. The burning was starting to let up, and

I told Bill I was doing better. He informed me it was a caustic burn and he did not understand how I was exposed to caustic chemicals while cleaning the dryer. He said I would be okay, but my back would be very sore for the next couple of weeks.

The remaining workers had gathered around and started asking questions. I went through the process we had used to prepare an entry. When I said the department operator told me he had actually completed the cleaning process before I arrived in his department, they became infuriated. The second I made the statement, I could feel the tension growing. These people were smart and knew exactly what the department engineer had done. Bill sensed his team was ready to declare war on the other department, so he told me it was his fault. He should have told me to do a final wash before entering the dryer. My teammates were not buying Bill's story and told him I could not go back in the dryer, but they knew who was going in. They went to the department and told the other operators in the area what had happened to me. Between the operators in the two departments, they decided to inform the operator that I had got hurt while he was at lunch. He would need to finish cleaning the dryer.

It was now 2:00 AM, and for those of us who have worked in a chemical plant at that hour, we know to the untrained eye and ear it can be the scariest and spookiest place on earth. Inside the buildings, chemicals are flowing through pipelines made of clear thick glass, large mixers are stirring the chemicals inside the reactors, and the mechanical equipment used to pump and transfer liquids is very loud and has a very distinctive pitch that lets the operator know things are okay. Someone once described the sounds as a night at the symphony: when the orchestra gets it right, you appreciate it, and when they do not, it sends chills up your spine. Shift Leader Bill knew this was one of those nights that things were about to go wrong, and it had nothing to do with the operation of the chemicals, but of his crew.

The 10 operators on duty emphatically approached the operator that night and asked him why he allowed me to enter the drier without doing the final rinse. They showed him the burns on my back, and he just laughed. He lied and said he did the final rinse, but it must have not worked the way it was supposed to work. He said it was not his job to hold my hand and that he was certainly not my trainer. He said I should have been trained by my shift leader before I was sent to help him perform such a dangerous task. The operators just shook their heads in disgust and told Shift Leader Bill he had better keep an eye on him because they would be out to get him and when they did it would be ugly. My team told me to come back to the department with them to finish out my shift.

It did take a couple of weeks for my burns to heal up enough for me to sleep on my back at night. My wife felt I should have stayed at the ladder factory. I told her it was not the company's fault and I had learned a good lesson about trusting everyone in my path.

A few days later, the same operator caused another associate to be sprayed in the face by a strong acid chemical. If the operator had not been wearing his goggles and a face shield, he would have been blinded from the chemicals. The operator did not get off so easy this time. He was suspended and assigned to another position that did not involve making chemicals.

During my six-month performance review, my manager told me I had learned how to operate all of the processes in my department. He was giving me a raise and promoting me to a certified operator's position. This meant more responsibility, and my name would start showing up on the control sheets General Frank would be reviewing each morning. I certainly was not exempt from my share of butt chewing from General Frank.

My goal was to make enough money to start school during the 2nd semester. The word got back to Buck that I was planning to quit the company and enroll in school in January.

Buck called me into his office and told me he understood why I was going to leave. He said under normal circumstances he would never tell a young man not to follow his dreams. "However, in your case, I think you will have a lot to think about when I share with you what our company has in mind for you. You know our business is growing and we need to keep good people like yourself if we are going to continue to grow.

"You learned in six months what it took others an average of two years to learn. I have recommended a transfer for you to another department working a straight day shift Monday-Friday. In addition, the promotion, should you accept, will add two dollars an hour to your current pay. If you are interested, report to the plant engineering manager's office Monday morning. He will interview you and provide the rest of the details about our expectations." I felt stupid, but I had to ask him where the plant engineer's office was located. The rest of the workers had told me to stay out of that department because it was full of professional engineers and degreed technicians who did not want to be bothered with the operators. The associates in the department are like the cavalry in the military; they come in riding to the rescue when processes are not running properly. They were responsible for all process controls and the electrical operation of the entire plant. When they made a mistake, it usually resulted in a large explosion, fires, and the release of hazardous chemicals into the atmosphere. I knew it was an exaggeration, but it was something to think about before making a final decision.

I went home at the end of my shift and told my wife about the opportunity. She was trying to be supportive, but she was still worried about my safety. She said her dad was willing to sell some of his livestock to help us out on our expenses.

She said she was no longer interested in going to college. She was very happy being my wife and supporting my needs. In other words, it was up to me. I went to the court the next day to think about what she had said. I spent a lot of time talking to Soul. I told him we had a good run, and in reality, I had already played pro ball during my trips overseas and had been to some of the most incredible street courts in the world. I told him it was a dream that had already come true. I knew in my heart I could do it and he agreed. On the other hand, the most important thing in the world to me was my wife and supporting my family. Soul was disappointed, because he loved to sing out "Swisheroo Clifton has two." He said he would miss it, but maybe it was time to get on with the next chapter in my life. "After all, life is short, and you need to take good care of your wife. I think she feels responsible for you not having the opportunity to get your degree. She is a smart girl and knows that for you to be as successful as you have the potential to become in the business world, you will need proper education.

When I returned home, I told my wife I was going to report to the plant engineer's office on Monday morning and at least hear what he was going to propose.

On Monday morning, I reported to the plant engineer's office. He was a remarkable man and very soft-spoken. He started out by telling me he knew I wanted to go to school and play ball in the pros someday. He said playing in the NBA was a big dream, especially for a young man from the town as small as Carrollton. However, if I was as good as he thought I was, I might just make it come true.

He said he had done his homework on me and he knew I was trying to make enough money to attend college. He said, "I can help you with one dream, but if you are going to pursue the NBA route, you are on your own."

He said, "Here is the deal. Up until last Friday, we were going to offer you the opportunity to transfer to the utility production unit, but after learning a little more about your background, I'm taking it off the table. I am going to offer you the opportunity to join our electrical engineering and process control department. It is the highest paid team in the entire company."

I was clueless about what all this meant, but it sounded good. He said I would have to start at the bottom and work my way up. After about a year of training, I would be required to work second shift with one of the electricians one week out of a 10-week cycle.

There was a silence in the room as if he were waiting my decision. I said, "Thank you, this is an excellent opportunity, and I am indeed grateful. However, how does this get me the education I need to be successful and promotable?" He just smiled. Then he opened the top draw on his executive desk and pulled out his organization chart. He pointed to where my name would be on the organization chart. He was right when he said I was starting at the bottom.

Then he said, "Before I answer your question, where do you see your name in 10 years on this chart?" I thought about it and knew it was probably not a good idea to pick his position, which was at the very top of the chart. Then I thought, "I have always been a big dreamer and have been willing to do what I need to live the dream." Soul immediately said, "No, no. Do not do it!" I put my finger on his name. Soul said, "The meeting over you dummy…" but the plant engineer said, "You learn quickly, and that was the perfect choice." Nevertheless, he also shared many of the people on the chart who had the same dream.

"Here is the rest of the deal. I will buy your books and pay your tuition for you to attend the University of Cincinnati. We expect you to maintain a passing grade, and you will attend classes on your own time. If you fail or drop out, you must pay us back every penny we invested in your education.

"The trip is 138 miles, with a minimum of three round trips from this site each week. You can commute with the other three engineers attending classes with the same understanding. Along the way, you will attend specialized training in numerous other cities and universities across the country.

"Once you finish with the University of Cincinnati, you will have graduated from one of the toughest engineering programs in the country. This program is a special engineering program, and you will not be taking physical education classes or theology; it will be purely technology and design, as it relates to the chemical industry, including chemistry, physics, and advanced math. The other specialized training will prepare you to become one of the most sought after people in the chemical industry. You can take some time to think about what we have said here today. Here is the list of classes you will be required to take, and you must pass them all. It will likely take you 10 years to complete. I know you need to talk to your family about this, so take some time. I expect to see you in my staff meeting in the morning at 8:00. If you do not show up, I will assume your answer was 'no' and we will offer the opportunity to someone else."

I thanked him again for his time and anticipated he was about to stand up and excuse me from his office.

Instead, he leaned back in his chair, put his arms behind his head, and shared his personal feelings about our business and the challenges it was about to be confronted with. He said, "Up to this point in time, our business has always been about getting the production out. Our attitude is about to change, young man. We are a small company compared to the giants in the chemical industry. Most of the small companies will be purchased by the giants or will be a forced out of business due to the cost of complying with new safety and environmental regulations."

Just to act as if I were interested or had a clue what he was talking about, I said, "What new regulations?" He said, "President Nixon is about to send new proposals to the hill in Washington DC, introducing new legislation directly targeting our industry and the way we operate. He will be creating a new department in Washington named the Environmental Protection Agency. This agency will become the watchdog for the American people." He went on to say the safety performance of the chemical industry as a whole was not very good. Most people looked at our company and the industry in general as an evil force continuously sending employees to the hospital with major chemical burns.

"Many people think we intentionally emit pollutants in the air and water that is harming communities and families living near the manufacturing sites." In the late sixties and early seventies, most people were convinced chemicals were wrong and that we need to stop making them altogether.

The Vietnam War was winding down and what people wanted most was to sit back and take a deep breath. The media needed something else bad to talk about since the war was no longer the headlines of the day. They started reporting on every single emission and speculating everything leaving a vent inside a chemical plant was terrible and likely destroying the quality of the air.

One musical artist even made a popular song about how he would rather see worms in his apples than have them sprayed by some of the chemicals we were manufacturing. He got a lot of attention from millions of people who agreed with him and purchased his records. However, what he failed to put in his song was that if it were not for our industry meeting the challenge, there would not be any apples left to eat. Bugs, mites, and other insects were literally destroying the food crops in the United States. It was so bad, we would not have been able to produce enough food to feed America, let alone the other 85 countries we were feeding. The population was growing at an all-time rate, which meant we needed to find better ways to increase yields from the same farmlands.

He continued, "Many of the environmental accusations against us are untrue. Activists are paid by special interest groups to convince the local, state, and federal government officials we are dangerous and should not be allowed to continue to operate.

"Sorry for rattling on about the chemical industry. For almost 20 years, we have focused our efforts and money on increasing our production rates. All of our pay grades and bonuses are based on the amount of product we produce each year. We created landfills where we buried our waste, which we thought was the right thing to do. Turns out it was a bad idea, as the chemical has leaked and cause some major environmental issues.

"Over the next five years, the team you may be joining will have the authority to stop production in its tracks. Your department will find ways to reduce emissions, control inventory losses, and automate processes. You will find root causes for the incredible number of incidents and safety-related accidents we have in our company. Moreover, you will have the power to make the necessary changes even if it means shutting down production. You will lead the maintenance team, which will evolve from where it is today into a world-class organization that will reset our industry standards forever.

"We will be starting up new departments, including environmental, safety, emergency response, and health and wellness. We will be hiring and training associates like you to carry the torch into the future. You will see some of the people in charge today moved to other positions. This will allow your team and a couple of others to lead the plant in a new direction. It will change the chemical industry for good and forever." He sat up in his chair, looked at me across the desk, and said he hoped I would decide to join his team. He had a good feeling about me and he said, "Who knows, I may be calling you boss someday." He stood up, stepped from around his desk, shook my hand, and wished me luck.

My wife and I were still living in our apartment and were having a great time. I made enough money to pay our bills and had enough left over to go out on the weekends. We had started to save some money and, in general, we were very happy. I joined the basketball church league and the local industrial league. The defense was not very good, but I enjoyed my 65 points per game average. It was a good way to keep in shape, and my wife went to all my games. Our lease was be up in November, and we planned to move in with her mom and dad until we went off to college. This was a lot to think about and too good of an opportunity to not consider. I would receive my education and specialized training to make a good living for my wife and our future children. Oh yes, we planned to have a girl first, and four years later, a boy I would nickname Shooter II. Nevertheless, for the next three-four years, we would continue the plans with those two little people on the back burner.

I showed my wife the curriculum, which included a number of technology classes. The classes she agreed to help me with were physics, calculus, and other advanced math and chemistry.

She did not pay much attention to the technical list but spent most of her time going through the advanced math classes. I think she was more excited about the opportunity than I was. Soul said he knew why and that we should take the opportunity to share in this venture. "She can help you with the advanced classes, and God knows you will need help. It will remove the burden she carries each time she looks at you." I was shocked to hear him say what he said. Soul said, "She still feels responsible for you not being in school or having the chance to play ball. If she had not entered into your life, it would be so much different than it is today."

We talked to our parents about the opportunity, and at first, her mom was against it. She felt the chemical industry was too dangerous and would never change. In her opinion, I would have been safer in a war zone like Vietnam. Soul cringed with the thought and said, "Not there again." I quickly said I had already been working for the company for six months and that it was not dangerous.

Her dad was excited for us, but he mostly was excited he would keep his family close together. My parents were okay with the decision. My dad said, "You do realize this will be the start of a new journey for you and the past will become the past. It does not mean you cannot play ball; it just means it will not be at the level you dreamed about since you were five years old." I told him I loved the game, but I loved my wife more.

My wife and I signed a new one-year lease on Saturday. I joined the team on Monday morning and was introduce to the department heads. Then a mentor was assigned to me who immediately took a keen interest in my work ethic. I took breaks and ate lunch when time allowed, but I spend all of my free time asking questions, studying procedures, and reading control manuals. By the time my training was to be completed, I needed to know how every single process in the facility was supposed to operate. I spend countless hours working with the operators and chemical engineers learning everything I could about specialty chemicals. I was primarily interested in tin-based chemicals. I wanted to thoroughly understand chemical reactions and reactors. I quickly learned how to take control of an chemical reaction going out of control. I took product manuals and drawings home and studied them on my off days.

The associates in my department represented one of the best industrial-league slow-pitch softball teams in the tri-state area. When they found out I was a baseball player in high school, they invited me to join the team. I went four for four at the plate and made three run-saving catches in the outfield my first game. Being on the team gave my wife the opportunity to meet the wives of the men I spent most of my time with at work. Over a 40-game season, she made several friends who would last a lifetime.

Slow-pitch softball was at one time in the United States more popular in small towns than major league baseball. In the late seventies, several cities began professional slow pitch teams and filled stadiums everywhere they went. Several organizations invited me to play on their teams during the summer. By the end of the season, we were playing in tournaments nearly every weekend. The tournament would draw teams from all over the country and have thousands of fans lined up around the outfield fence area with tents and lounge chairs. I think what made the sport so popular was that teams were paid to play in the tournaments but fans did not pay a penny to enter the fields and watch their favorite players play the game they loved. The game was fast paced and there was lots of action on every play. Most of the tournaments started on Friday night and would not end until a champion was crowned on Sunday afternoon.

Our team was one of the best teams in the area, and between games, my entire family would join the families of the rest of the players on the team for a picnic lunch. My wife and the other wives would prepare the meals while the younger children played a much smaller scale softball game with a plastic ball behind the tents. It was not abnormal for a team to lose early in the tournament and then go on to win eight to ten games in the remaining two days to win the tournament.

The fans and players were some of the kindest and most generous people on earth. I must have played in 50 tournaments during the years to make a little money to help support a family having tough financial times. The wives from the visiting teams would bring baked goods to sell to the fans and setup raffles to pick up extra money during the tournaments. All of the proceeds were turned over to the family at the end of the championship game.

One time, I was playing left field in a game at Trimble County Kentucky, and I made a critical misjudgment, earning me a nickname to follow me the rest of the time I played softball. The field had no home run fence, which meant if an outfielder were fast enough, they could run down just about any high and long fly ball to the outfield. Most of the outfielders could run as fast as a deer when chasing down a long fly ball. We had also learned to take a quick look at a high fly ball and make a judgment on where we thought the ball would land. Instead of continuing to watch the ball, we would sprint to the spot and at the last second look up into the sky and extend our glove to catch the ball. I am not sure what happened, but a long fly ball was hit to me, and I started to run back to catch the ball. I knew the ball was well over my head, so I picked a place where I thought the ball would land. I was right on the correct spot, but just as I looked up to catch the ball, a reporter for the Trimble County Banner took a picture with a very bright flash bulb. It blinded me just long enough for the ball to land in the middle of my forehead instead of my glove. The ball hit me so hard in the head it bounced up high enough for our center fielder to catch the ball before it hit the ground for the out.

It was the third out, so I started to run back to our bench. When I made it to the shortstop, he said I needed to stop running. The ball apparently cut my head, and my face was soon covered in blood. Apparently, the ball hit my head so hard the stitching on the ball busted the skin on my forehead and caused the bleeding. The hit did not hurt badly and I must admit I was a bit embarrassed to let the ball hit me in the head. Once I reached the bench, my wife cleaned off the blood from my forehead with a wet cloth. That is when I got my career-long nickname: Dudley. Dudley was the manufacture of the ball, and back in the earlier years, they would stitch their name on the ball with thick raised thread. The name 'Dudley' was perfectly but temporally tattooed into my forehead. The tattoo stayed very visible for about three weeks. Finally, the wound healed and the name disappeared. Unfortunately, the reporter took a picture and printed it in the sports section of the paper.

The last tournament I would play in was for a young girl diagnosed with cancer. Aside from her family, her next two loves in the world were men's slow pitch softball and the local fire department and emergency medical technicians. Her family did not have the money to take her for treatments in Louisville, so the men and women who made up the fire department held fundraisers to help the family. Some of the best teams in a 100-mile radius of Gallatin County Kentucky played in the tournament. The little girl attended the Saturday morning session, and her father carried her from the car to the pitcher's mound. She was too weak to stand, so a chair was placed near the pitcher plate on the mound for her to sit in. When her father lowered her to the chair, a smile appeared on the child's face that lit up the crowd.

This little girl was not there for people to feel sorry for; she was out there to pull strength from all of us in attendance. It became evident she did not intend to let cancer kill her without one hell of a fight.

The local radio station carried the game live. The announcer went out to the mound to do a live interview with a little girl. This girl was a super fan and knew the names and the nicknames of all of the top players playing in the tournament. Most of the top players were skilled enough to have played in the baseball major leagues. Many of these men were capable of playing in the majors before an injury or a girlfriend they just were not willing to leave behind cut their dreams short. They all had full-time jobs, and softball filled the empty void in their heart for the game they left behind.

It was incredible when she started talking about her favorite players and the joy they gave her when they would make a great play or hit one over the fence.

Before we knew it, the players she called out came walking out of the crowd in full uniform carrying their glove and a ball. They all lined up down the third base line.

The radio station had received a list of player's names from the little girl's mother several weeks before the tournament was scheduled. The station had contacted each of the players and told them about the little girl's situation. The little girl tugged at her father to help her stand. He leaned down to his daughter and said, "No, the doctor advised against it." The little girl looked up at her father and said, "Yes." When she started to get up on her own, the father could no longer handle tough love, and he bent down to help her. She moved his hand away and said, "No, I want to do this myself." When she started to stand, the entire crowd was on their feet, but you could have heard a pin drop in the stadium. All you saw was people with their hands out as if they were right there beside her to help stabilize her as she attempted to stand. Many of the fans and players were begging God to give her the strength she needed. This was her time. The players in the dugouts waiting for the next game to start were leaning on the fence. They went down on all fours with their fist clenched tightly together, mumbling to themselves, "Come on baby, come on you can do this." I know what they were saying because I had the privilege of being one of those players. Soul was sitting there as if it was no big deal. I think he already knew she was going to stand, but I also think he knew it would be the last time the little girl would be upright.

The superstars lined up down the third base line where no longer carrying their gloves. They had put them on the ground and were down in softball stance as if they were waiting for a hard smash off the bat to come to them. At one point, the little girl leaned to the left and, in unison, the superstars moved their hands to the right as if they were helping the little girl regain her balance. When the little girl made it to her feet, she received a standing ovation for her display of courage and determination not to give up.

When things settled down, the players walked past the little girl one at a time. These people were generous men; some weighed 350 pounds and stood 6' 8". The dad looked like a little boy compared to these men. Each of the men gave her a ball with an autograph and a handwritten message of encouragement. Each had something to say to her that made her smile. Once the field was clear, the little girl returned to her seat on the mound and threw out the first pitch. The superstars returned to the mound, picked up the little girl in the chair, and paraded her around the bases to a standing ovation. When they rounded third and headed for home plate, the little girl was ecstatic. When they reach home plate, they let her down low enough so she could touch the plate with her left foot. The second she touched the plate, the umpire, dressed in full attire including his facemask, bent down and put his hands up. He delayed for just a couple of seconds and then motioned safe. The little girl looked at him as if he had better call her safe or he would have to deal with her.

The little girl, along with her family sat in a special air-conditioned box seat behind home plate. The announcer went back to the mound and thanked everyone on behalf of the family. Then he said, "Play ball." My team was ready to take the field, and were getting our last-second instructions and batting order from the head coach. While the coach was talking, we noticed something going on out on the field.

The announcer went back to the field with the head coach for the superstars. He motioned to my coach and the umpire to join them on the mound. The announcer told my coach the superstars wanted to play. My coach said no, and one of the largest players for the superstars walks up behind the coach on the mound. He had on his game face, including a chaw of tobacco. He spit on the mound, which was very common thing for players to do in those days. After all, we were the tobacco belt of America and proud of it. He asked our coach if we were chicken. I could not help but keep an eye on the little girl. When she heard what the superstar said about being a chicken, I could read her lips. She started a chant, "Chicken, chicken," and then she led a chant with the thousands of people who had now joined in the crowd.

It became a show, and the superstars were great showmen. They walked out on the field in front of the little girl and waved large towels in the air, supporting the little girl's chant. Several of the players walked over in front of our dugout and flapped their arms, indicating we were chickens. Just at the right moment, our head coach threw his hands in the air as if he were disgusted but willing to give in.

The crowd went wild, and the little girl was waving and screaming her satisfaction at the top of her lungs. She could not believe she was about to watch her favorite players all play on the same field at the same time. This was truly a game come true for her. The umpire said, "Play ball." The superstars decided they would let us bat first. I led off the game with a long drive off the top of the fence. The player in center field picked up the ball off the ground at the base of the fence and nearly threw me out before I could reach second base. The second basemen put the tag down and waited for the umpire to make a call. I know the umpire was reluctant to call me safe, but the second basemen whispered to the umpire to call me safe. The umpire motioned safe, and the crowd went wild. A chant broke out, "Bad call he was out.' The umpire shook his head and infuriated the crowd even more. I saw the little girl raise her hand in disgust as if she could not believe the umpire called me safe.

I thanked the second basemen for his generosity. He said in a very deep voice with a slight New York accent, "It does not matter, you will not score anyway, Dudley." The next hitter hit a hard ground ball to the shortstop, and instead of throwing the ball to first base, as most people would do. He looked at me and motions me to attempt to move to third base. I shook my head no, and he threw a fastball to the first baseman for the force out. The pitcher waived the next hitter to first base for an intentional walk. I thought he was setting up his team for a double play to end the inning. Then he waived our next hitter to first base for another intentional walk. Bases were now loaded with one out. We had no clue what the pitcher was up to. The little girl looked at her little brother and said with confidence, "They will not score. Watch this." He gave her a look as if she had lost her mind. Her little brother knew as well as the rest of the crowd that we were one of the top teams in the area. We had never failed to score in this situation. We had our best fly ball hitter at the plate and one of the fastest players in the area on third base. All our next hitter would need to do is lift a high fly ball to the outfield and I could tag up on third base and quickly score. It meant we would have scored on possibly the greatest softball team ever to take the field.

Just before the next pitch, the umpire screamed, "Time out!" He turns and looks down the driveway leading up to the ball field. A fire engine came up, blowing its horn and sirens blasting as it approaches the area. It caught all of the players and the crowd off guard, but before we knew it, the radio announcer had moved back on the field near the pitcher's plate. The players on our team lined up on the field from second base to third base in a straight line. The Superstars lined up between first base and second base. The fire-fighters march out onto the field and form a half moon semicircle around the pitcher's mound, facing home plate. The umpire ripped his facemask off his head and yelled out to the fire chief, "What do you think you are doing chief? Don't you see we have a softball game in progress?" The fire chief was one of the coolest fire chiefs of all time. He casually walked up to the umpire who had moved directly in front of the little girl's booth. The fire chief went nose to nose with the umpire and said, "You know the play at second base a few minutes ago? You called safe." The umpire said, "Yes I did, and he was safe." The fire chief said, "Would you like to see the video replay? I have it on the truck. He was out, and you are as blind as a bat in the daytime. Where did you get your license to umpire? I bet it was from the ten-cent store down in Carrollton." The little girl looked at her father with one of the most sincere faces possible and said, "Dad, I told you it was a bad call." The fire chief motioned to the local sheriff to join him in the discussion. The sheriff pulled a pair of seeing glasses out of his vest. He told the umpire he needed to wear them or consider quitting the umpiring profession.

Once the crowd and the little girl stopped laughing at the umpire, fire chief, and sheriff, things got a little more serious. The fire chief walked back toward the other firefighters and the radio announcer. The announcer told the crowd and his listening audience the fire chief would like to read a proclamation of honor. The fire chief ordered his commanders to approach the pitching mound. They were dressed in full celebration attire as they marched out on the field in perfect time. They stop in unison and saluted the fire chief. Then the highest-ranking commander announced to the fire chief that his team was fully accounted for and ready for duty. The fire chief ordered his lieutenants to approach the area. They lined up between third base and home plate. The highest-ranking lieutenant announced his team was fully accounted for and ready for duty. The players on the field in unison went down to one knee, removed their hats, and pointed to the fire fighters. It was the Superstars' way of telling the crowd and the world the real superstars had just entered the arena.

The little girl received the individual medal of courage honoring non-firefighters who have shown incredible courage when confronted and battling a life-treating situation. The Warsaw Fire Department was one of the top fire-fighting teams of their time. Several members of my family were firefighters, but none could compare to my brother-in-law. He became one of the most respected and honored firefighters of his time before his sudden death just before his fiftieth birthday. My second book, titled, *I Took Soul to Church Book II* will have several stories about his life and the thousands of others who have stood the test of time and lived and died in the face of danger.

As the fire fighters were marching off the field, the umpire, as usual, got the last word. He yelled out to the fire chief to get his fire engine off the field before he tossed him and his team out of the stadium. Then he yelled, "Play ball."

Our next hitter received the signal to hit a fly ball to left field so I could tag and score. I saw the third baseman laugh and he told me to forget about trying to tag and score. "Our left fielder will make you look as slow as a toddler taking your first steps." The pitcher threw three straight balls, and the crowd could not believe what they were seeing. Then he tossed two incredible pitches for strikes. With three balls and two strikes on the hitter, the pitcher had no choice but to throw a strike or walk the hitter and force in the first run of the game. The hitter knew if the ball were a strike, he would need to swing.

The ball was a strike, and the hitter sent the ball flying to left field. I returned to third base and waited for the left fielder to catch the ball so I could run home and score the first run. The left fielder was a member of all world softball team and had the strongest arm in the game. I saw him take off running back toward the outfield fence. The ball hit deep was clearly going over the fence for a home run. The left fielder placed his left foot on the chain link fence, and then his right foot until he had climbed to the top of a ten-foot high fence. He leaned over the fence and caught the ball to prevent the grand slam home run. When he came down, he landed on his back. I could not help but look at the little girl, and the expression of approval on her face was priceless. Nevertheless, my job was to tag and score as expected.

Under normal circumstances, I could have tagged and jogged home before the ball was returned to the infield. Soul chimed in and told me I had better rush home or this man would through me out by ten feet. I said to Soul, "You do not know much about softball do you?" I knew this player was good, and I decided to sprint home for the score. I made it about halfway down the line and I noticed the crowd was coming to their feet. I knew it was not for me. About five feet from home plate, I heard something coming at the back of my head, making a sound similar to a heat-seeking missile. Within a nanosecond, it went past my left ear and landed in the catcher's glove. The catcher motioned as if he were yawning while waiting for me to make it to home plate. I heard the crowd break out into a laugh of approval and amazement for the strength and accuracy of the throw from the left fielder. I slid into home plate and the catcher put down the tag. This time the umpire became very popular when he put his hand up and emphatically motioned that I was out.

The game featured amazing plays, as each of the superstars had an opportunity to display their incredible talent at least once during the game. I know some of the greatest players (names like Joe, Lou, The Babe, and Mickey) to chase a little white ball around a diamond stood and cheered for the players and the little girl. The game ended, and we had lost twenty to zero. The little girl had stolen our hearts. When tears formed in her eyes and rolled down her face, the fans in attendance cried and cheered for her courage.

The little girl lived longer than any child had ever lived with that particular type of cancer. Since then, the cure rates for childhood cancers have increased beyond imagination thanks to state of the art treatments and monetary support by folks just like the ones who supported this little girl and the thousands since.

Forty-Three

READY FOR SCHOOL

It was finally time for me to travel to Cincinnati to school. My first classes were in process control technology and advanced geometry. One trip to the advanced math class helped me figure out why I married my wife. I told her the professor told us from the start he did not care if we learned anything or not. His job was to teach, and ours was to make a high enough score to pass the course. If we did not, he would see us next semester. The problem with failing a course or withdrawing from a course was the no pass-no pay policy with my company.

The classroom was an auditorium style design, and the professor spent all of his time writing on the board. He never took attendance, and he told us his assistant would teach most of the classes. He would require photo identification prior to taking the final examination. I decided this class was right for her, so I talked my wife into going to class with me and helping me understanding the formulas.

This would happen several times over the next few years. I remember convincing my physics professor I was from the back hills of Kentucky and she was my interpreter. I wish the family could have seen the look on old miss goodie-two shoes' face. I thought she was going to slide under the desk, but then the teacher said she understood and that she could take a class with me. It took a few days for the bruise to go away on my arm from the hit she put on me once we left the class. The good news was, I passed the class; the bad news was she refused to take any more classes with me.

Our lease was about up, and we intended to sign up again. Our plan was to save a down payment and purchase a starter home as soon as we could. Her mom and dad invited us out to Sunday dinner. Once the dinner was over, her dad asked us to take a walk with him. We walked out to the eastern edge of his farm, and he said, "It's yours." It took me by surprise, and my wife was astonished. He said she told him when she was a little girl she would like to build a house on this land. He said he would give us the land, and when we were ready, we could build our dream home. He told me he knew how much I loved to farm and he would help me buy the adjoining farm. He had heard through the grapevine that the owners were about to sell and move back to Cincinnati. He said it would be his chance to return the money I invested to keep his herds a couple of years ago.

I kept staring at my wife to see how I should be reacting. I know he did not have a clue I was already making more money a month than he made in a year on the farm.

I had made the decision several years prior that farming was not for me. I did work on his farm during harvest season and enjoyed every minute of it; nevertheless, I knew I could not make the kind of living I wanted for my family by staying on the farm. Our plan was to purchase a plot of land located about three miles from where my company was located. This move would have placed us on Blackrock Road 20 miles from the plant. This road was so hilly, winding, and dangerous, it got shutdown for days after a small snowstorm. Once I finished my training, I would be required to take my turn on-call, twenty-four-seven, three-sixty-five days a year.

I did not want him to feel like we did not appreciate his offer, so we decided to buy a mobile home and set it up on the property. We decided it would get us by until we could afford to build the house we wanted to build. Our plan was to live there for two years, which would give us the time we needed to save the down payment we needed to buy the land we wanted to build our home on.

It was working out okay. I had enough land to plant a small garden and provide an opportunity for my wife to harvest and store fresh organic vegetables and fruit for the winter. We loved to ride our bicycles on the country roads and down to the flowing creeks just off the main highway. One day I saw my wife looking at my bicycle, and I asked her what was wrong with it. She said she was trying figure out if a child seat would fit on the back. I said I thought I could make one fit. She said, "Good, it is in the house, and I think you will need to install it about this time next year." I was good in math by now, and I figured out what she was telling me quick. We spent the rest of the day planning for our first child and picking out baby names.

When I got home from work the next day, she said she had signed us up for Lamaze classes and that they would start in a few months. Soul asked several times in the next minutes, "What are Lamaze classes?" I responded, "I will do whatever you want me to do. I will be there for you; I want to be a great father."

She laughed and could tell by the look on my face that I did not have a clue what Lamaze classes were. She told me we would be a part of the first classes ever in the community and she wanted to try to have a natural childbirth. She was already the great mom I knew she would be when she said she did not want to expose her baby to any drugs if she could avoid it.

She decided to explain the process, and Soul started to complain. Within twenty seconds, Soul said, "You have to be where and do what? I think your wife has developed an oxygen deficiency issue. She knows God let a doctor invent the epidural and other childbirth interventions. You do know I was there when you were born using the Lamaze method. I heard screaming, yelling, and "Push" then "Do not push," and finally you popped out. She took one look at you, and then I heard your mother say things to your father I just cannot repeat. Believe me—you need to find some way to get out of this. The last place we—you—want to be is in the delivery room."

I told her the decision was final and I would be thrilled to be her Lamaze coach. Soul just said, "Oh brother, here we go again." It turns out several of our friends were pregnant and due within a month of each other. Therefore, our class became a social event and gave husbands an opportunity to take a more active role in the childbirth process.

The time finally arrived, and my wife was miserable. We went to the doctor for a final checkup. The nurse told her that things were going well and she could deliver at any time. The doctor said she could do whatever she felt like doing until the baby was born. The doctor's office was in the middle of town and required one right turn to head back to our house. It was July 30th, and the temperature was already 96 degrees. When we reached the intersection, she instructed me to turn right at the light. I knew better by then to ask why, so I put on my turn signal and headed toward interstate 71. As we approached the entrance to General Butler State Park, she said, "Turn right." I thought, *Well, she must feel like driving through the park.* It is a great park, and we had spent time there in the past picnicking and hiking. We traveled up the hill and headed toward the pavilion. When we got to the golf course entrance, she said, "Turn in here." I must have displayed a strange look on my face, but then she said, "Do not say a word." She said, "The doctor said I could do anything I wanted to do, *right?* I just shook my head up and down in the affirmative, but I am not sure he meant she should play golf. She said, "Physical activity should put me into labor, *right?*" Again, I shook my head up and down. She said, "I am tired of being pregnant, and I want to see my baby."

She said, "I know you have your golf clubs in the back, and I want to play golf." Come on men, what would you have said? I said, "Okay, I will get us a cart, and we will play a round of golf." She said, "No carts, we are going to walk." I wanted to say something, but still I knew better than to even attempt to change the mind of a pregnant woman. I pitched my clubs over my shoulder and off we went to the first hole. She did have an incredible drive off the tee that made her smile. Then I thought, *This must be the right thing to do.* The golf course is very hilly and walking the course was a challenge for a person not carrying a 9- pound baby in their belly. We made it to the fourth hole, which was coming back toward the clubhouse, when she announced it was time to go back to the hospital. Her water had broken, and she felt if I did not hurry, she would deliver on the fourth green. I ran up the hill to the clubhouse, jumped in my car and drove it to the number four green. She stepped in, and I rushed her to the hospital. Our daughter was born a few hours later. Moreover, we did follow through with the Lamaze method from start to finish.

We lived on the farm for another year. Then one Sunday night about 6:00 PM, an act of Mother Nature made the decision to buy the original land we had picked out a very simple decision for my wife and me. It was just before dark, and we had finish putting the entire tobacco crop into the barns for curing. The baby was in her crib, and my wife and I were preparing to settle down for the night and watch a movie titled *The Towering Inferno*. It looked a little like rain, so I told my wife I was going outside to the ball court to shoot a few baskets before dark. Just as I leaned over to pick up my basketball, I heard a rumbling from the southwest side of our house trailer. The ground was vibrating. It took me a few seconds to figure out what was happening. Then I remembered what the sound was, and I knew I had a matter of a few seconds to get my wife and child out of the house trailer. I knew our only hope was to attempt to make it to her parent's house to the basement. I ran in the house and said, "Let's go! I will take the baby and you hold my hand." I told her a tornado was coming and we had to run as fast as we could to her parent's house.

When we made it outside, it was still light enough to see off in the distance. As we were running, I was trying to find the path of the storm. We had already seen the amount of destruction a tornado could cause during the tornados of 1973 that hit our local communities.

My wife was scared to death, and all she could say was, "Whatever happens to us is okay, but please God, do not take our baby." I told her to keep running as I looked down to check on our baby. She was sleeping as if nothing was going on. I spotted the tornado, and we were about halfway to her parent's house. At the time, I felt we could make it based on the direction the tornado was traveling. Then suddenly, I saw the tornado hit the first tobacco barn, and it exploded as if a bomb had been dropped from a warplane. The entire sky filled with debris, and it was hard to tell which way the tornado was traveling. Within a few seconds, it became apparent we were not going to make it to the house. The tornado was heading straight at us, along with about two hundred head of cattle stampeding to get out of the way. The only place to seek shelter from the tornado was in a sinkhole located along the road to her parent's house. The sinkhole had just formed a few years earlier. I felt the line fence would cause the animals to turn and take a route away from the sinkhole, but I was wrong; they went right over the fence and ran past us without touching us.

I had grabbed a quilt off the sofa before leaving the house, and I placed our baby at the bottom of the sinkhole and moved several large stones around her. My wife lay down on the stones and held our baby in a fetal position. I lay the quilt down over the two of them, and then I laid down on top of the quilt to shield the two of them the best I could.

Within a few seconds, I felt the wind try to lift me off the ground. I was able to grasp a huge boulder and overcome the pull from the tornado. The center of the storm was now directly over the top of our shelter. The noise was extremely loud, and I could feel my wife shaking underneath me. My arms were weakening, and my grip on the stones was starting to loosen. I asked Soul to help me and to give me the strength to hold on. For some unexplainable reason, the storm took a sudden turn to the east. We were in the middle of the debris field, and everything the storm had picked up for miles started falling from the sky. I kept an eye open to try to divert any falling debris away from our shelter. I saw trees, building materials, and the entire tobacco crop we had just finished hanging in the barn, which exploded earlier, fly over our heads. I watched the tornado attempt to pick up our mobile home and turn our cars sideway in the driveway. We were okay, and I had only a few cuts and bruises while acting as a human shield for my family. When the tornado turned to the east, it headed right at my wife's parent's house.

The house was about a half-mile from the sinkhole. I told my wife I would run back to our house and attempt to call her parents to warn them to get into the basement. I did make it to the house and made the call. My wife's sister answered the call, but before I could tell her to take the family to the basement, the phone went dead. I knew I was too late and felt their fate was now in God's hands.

When I returned to my wife and baby, my wife told me the tornado hit her parent's house directly. I told her I was sure they would be okay. The house was only a few years old and built by Wilson's, and he was one of the finest builders in the area.

I assured her the tornado was gone. I saw it hit the barn behind the house, and then it lifted back up into the sky and disappeared. I ask her to stay in the sinkhole until I came back to get her and the baby. She was holding the baby in her arms, and she said, "Look, this child is still sound to sleep." I was not surprised. From the time she was born, when night arrived, she went to sleep. It did not matter where or what was going on around her. I often read her bedtime stories, and I do not think I ever made it past page five before she was out like a light.

My wife agreed to stay with the baby. I told her I would be back as soon as I could. I wrapped the quilt around her and the baby. As I climbed up out of the sinkhole and onto the main road, all I could see was debris lying all over the place. I then realized I needed to slow down and apply the training I had received from my employer. I was trained to perform rescue and fire-fighting, and if necessary recovery. I made my way to the house and checked for downed power lines, structural damage, and God forbid, fire and smoke. I found downed power lines that were arcing, and the arcing had caused a small fire close to the house, so I stopped and put the fire out.

The house was dark, and I did not see any smoke or fire. I approached the house and assessed the damage to determine if the house was structurally unstable. From the look of the damage to the front of the house from the outside, I was expecting the worst.

The family room is where the family spent most of their Sunday nights, watching television. My wife's brother and sisters would line up around the coffee table in the middle of the living room floor, finishing their homework for school the next morning. Her mother would be sitting on the sofa to answer the frequent questions asked by the older children about their homework.

The living room walls were laying out in the front yard, and the front door from the outside was missing. The living room picture window was shattered into thousands of small pieces. I could see the sofa flipped upside down on the coffee table, and I could not find the children or the mother.

Her dad's recliner was normally located about three feet from the entry door. It was missing, and my fear was that the tornado had sucked my father-in-law out of the house and carried him away.

I decided it was too unsafe to enter the front of the house, so I went around back and made my way through the back door leading to the kitchen. I started calling out the names of the family, but there was no response. I kept telling myself not to panic.

Out of nowhere, my future brother-in-law came busting through the back door and screaming his future wife's name. I will never forget the look on his face as he ran up to me and said, "Where is she." He was a bit of an excitable person, and I told him to calm down. I had not located any of the family members.

We searched the entire first level of the ranch style and found no one. We were both screaming at the top of our lungs and then would go completely silent to see if there was any response. After about fifteen minutes of searching, I began to have some terrible thoughts. *Maybe my wife's whole family was carried away by a tornado.*

We checked the basement door and thought it was locked. I told my future brother-in-law, we needed to move our search outside the house. He worked in the coating division at the same plant I worked at and had attended the same rescue and recovery classes I had attended at the plant. We both knew if the they were outside the house, their chances of surviving were close to zero.

Just as we started to exit the house through the back door, I heard sounds coming from the basement. I motioned for my brother-in-law to freeze and to listen for a few seconds. He heard similar sounds and went into panic mode. He said, "Oh my God; the basement has fallen in on top of them." It took a few seconds to convince him we needed to calm down and do what we knew we had to do to save the lives of those still breathing. We were still not sure if one of the survivors was making the noise or if the house was ready to cave in. He dropped his head and said, "It is no use. We might as well give up; I know they are all dead." As he dropped to his knees, he looked up at me and said, "Why does all of the bad stuff have to happen to us?" We both had been through a hard stretch and had dealt with several disasters over the past few months.

One of our best friends, whom I had played high school football with, was working on the late shift at one of the I-71 service stations just off the Sparta exit. A man had filled up his car and walked into the station to pay for the gasoline, and the video camera caught the tragedy in its entirety. The thief pulled a knife from his large jacket, and, with the quickness and speed of a trained ninja warrior, he stabbed our friend through his heart. Our friend instantly fell to the floor behind the counter. The robber assumed he was dead. As the robber was empting the cash register he heard a baby crying in the office connected to the left side of the bar. When he opened the door to the office, he found our friend's new wife and baby hiding under the desk. He pulled his knife from his jacket to kill the two of them, but somehow our friend was able to lift himself from the floor and retrieve his gun from under the counter. He yelled something to the effect that the robber would never harm his child or wife as he pointed the loaded gun toward the robber. The thief turned and faced him and drew back his knife again in a ninja style and attempted to fling the knife toward our friend. Our friend discharged the gun, and the thief fell to the floor dead as the knife fell at the feet of our friend.

His wife climbed from under the desk and attempted to catch our friend while he was falling to the floor. She was able to slow down his fall. She softly touched his face, and he asked her to let him hold his baby. He struggled with the last ounce of life he had left to kiss his baby and wife goodbye for the last time and then he closed his eyes and died in their arms. The baby was only three months old.

Three days prior to the tornado, we had both been involved in fighting a serious fire at the plant. The south wall of the structure collapsed trapping our entire team with no escape route. The fire was so hot and explosive that to this day we don't know how we survived until we were rescued by the A-Team. Many of the firefighters and support team members later reported waking up at night in a cold sweat and shaking while reliving the events of the fire. We never determined the cause of the fire or why we received the miracle we received.

I was able to make contact with my wife's dad in the basement. He told me where they were and that the cistern connected to the south wall of the basement had started to leak water into the space. I knew the location he was describing, and I knew that the cistern had had several thousand gallons of fresh water pumped into it the day before. We had to work quickly to get them out or they would all drown. My brother-in-law started to make a hole in the floor directly above where the family was trapped. He was using a sturdy lamppost with a very sharp point on the bottom to make the hole, but I told him it would take too long and that our best shot at recovery was to find something to pry the basement door open. The door was jammed when the entire structure had shifted and twisted the doorframe to the point that we could not open the door. My brother-in-law told me he would be right back. Did I tell you my brother-in-law was a large person and was strong as a horse? He suddenly walked back into the house carrying this large stone landscape boulder. He said, "Stand back," as he rocketed the boulder with all of his might toward the door. As the boulder struck the center of the door, it shattered into several pieces. The first one out of the space was his future wife. I think he became a hero to her that day for good.

The entire family had made their way into the basement. I asked my mother-in-law how they knew the storm was approaching the house, and she said it was a miracle. She said she got a chill up her back out of nowhere. Then she said she heard two knocks at the front door. She went to the door and then opened the storm door but could not find anyone outside. She stepped out on the front porch and saw the barn explode across from the house. She then ran back inside and got her entire family in the basement just as the front door flew off the house.

Once we had everyone out of the house and in a safe location, I started to leave, and my mother-in-law followed me around the corner of the house. She wanted to know immediately where my wife and her first grandchild were. I told her we tried to make it to the house but the tornado cut us off and that we had to jump into the sinkhole. Even though I assured her they were okay, she had to see for herself. She followed me back to the sinkhole and quickly sat down beside my wife and took our baby in her arms. My wife looked up at me and asked if our entire family was okay. She appeared to be in shock as I told her we were all fine.

Within a few minutes, the whole family had congregated at the sinkhole. It was as if it had become sacred ground and we just felt safe there. I knew I had deflected some of the debris falling all around us. My father-in-law and my wife's only brother started picking up hammers, saws, and four pitchforks that had stuck in the ground inside the sinkhole boundaries. Those items were hanging in the barn, which I witnessed get blown to pieces just few minutes earlier. The barn was nearly two miles from the sinkhole. Three large trees, over a hundred years old, had fallen within five feet of our shelter. The entire area around where we had taken shelter was, in fact, the debris field.

My wife's youngest sister kept staring at the minor cuts on my arms. They had stopped bleeding, but the severe bruise on the side of my face was very painful. She climbed up in my arms and wanted to know if I was going to die. I reassured her I was okay and we would all be all right.

I guess the thought of me dying was more than my wife could handle. She jumped up off the ground and put her shivering body in my arms. I held her for a few minutes and tried to calm her fears. She put her left hand over the bruise on my face and said she would take my pain if she could. She whispered in my ear, "You have always been my hero, but tonight you are bigger than life to me. You just saved me, our daughter, and," she placed my hand on her stomach, "the life of your unborn son." I think deep down she wanted me to know about my child before I had to leave.

We were about 12 miles from the nearest town, and many of our neighbors were in the path of the storm. I told her we would celebrate when I got back. The men all loaded up the chainsaws and shovels in the back of my father-in-law's truck, and we started backtracking our way back through the path the tornado. This was very dangerous work, and the path of a tornado leaves numerous hazardous that can kill you in a New York minute if you are not very careful. We had to cut up a number of trees that had toppled and landed onto the main road. We cleared some debris and a high voltage power line from Blackrock Road and made our way over to Sharon Road. We could clean up the rest of the trash later, but our first mission was to make sure no one was hurt.

We made it to our first neighbor's house and found they were okay with minimal damage. As we made our way from the farm to farm, the neighbors joined our search and rescue team. We had made it through to the last house and we were feeling good that everyone was okay even through every neighbor had suffered some property damage. We could see the last house from a distance and it looked like it was still intact.

The tornado had apparently formed about 300 feet from the last neighbor's house. The house was an older home built at the top of a hillside overlooking Ghent-Sanders Road. The woman who lived there was elderly, and we knew she would have a hard time getting out of harm's way. As we approached the house, the elderly woman's son and grandson's met us at the yard gate leading to the house. The son asked one of the men in our rescue party to go call the coroner and the sheriff.

He explain that his mother had made it to the basement, but the chimney had fallen in on top of her. He said they were able to get the brick from the chimney off of her and she said that she was not in any pain. When they started to move her out of the basement, she fell into his arms. He said the shock of the event was too much for her heart to handle. Before she passed, she told him she loved him. She just wanted him to hold her as she died in his arms. Several of the women in the rescue party went to the basement where the woman had passed. They told the son they would not leave her alone and would wait for the sheriff and the coroner to arrive.

We finally made our way back to the house and shared the tragic news of her death with the family.

We all decided we would stay together and spend the night in the remaining safe section of her parent's house. We needed time to settle our nerves and reflect on what we had experienced during the past four hours. It was just another example of why when you love someone, you had better let him or her know.

I offered to let the family sleep at my house, but no one felt safe sleeping in a mobile home. I think my mother-in-law sensed I was not going to allow my family to sleep there much longer either. My wife made us a temporary bed on the kitchen floor with some quilts her mother gave her. She placed my daughter in my left arm and then lay down beside me and put her arms around the both of us. She said she felt safe there and that she did not plan to move until the morning light.

After the house was silent and everyone was sleeping, I told Soul I knew he protected us in our hour of need. I knew who the real hero was during the storm; he saved my family with his courage and his love for my family. I told him I knew tornados do not just change direction as fast as this one did. He deflected the pitchforks away from my family just as he had done in the field when he took the buckshot in his back that was heading toward my eyes.

Soul just sighed and took a deep breath and said, in a very calming voice, for me to go on to sleep; tomorrow was going to be an exhausting day.

It took me several hours to calm down. In the silence of the night, I could hear my heart still pounding from the anxiety caused by the tornado. My wife woke up and told me she felt safe and more in love than she had ever been in her life. She pulled me closer to her body and placed my hand on her heart. She closed her eyes and drifted off to sleep. Just before I went to sleep, a prayer slipped into my mind. It was the Lord's Prayer, which I had recited hundreds of times in the locker room before every game with my teammates. As I silently recited the prayer with Soul, the words suddenly took on a significantly different meaning as I looked at my wife and my child—excuse me—children lying beside me.

The next day we spent several hours on horseback herding cattle and repairing fences destroyed by the tornado and the stampedes. Soul loved to ride horses, and he sounded like a cowpoke, making gestures and crazy sounds to get the cows to go where we wanted them to go. It took several weeks to recover from the damage caused by the storm. The entire front half of the house had to be torn down and rebuilt.

The following week, I met with my banker and told him I intended to build a house on the land my wife and I had purchased. I used the value of the property to cover the deposit needed to build the house. By this time in my life, I was trained in construction and project management and had worked with contractors for several years. I decided I would save some cost by doing some of the construction myself and managing the project. The original plan did not include a basement, but I changed the design and swore I would never own another home without a basement after experiencing what my family went through out on the farm.

Forty-Four

Time for a House Rising

By the end of summer, I had finished the second story of our new bi-level home. It was time to say our goodbyes to the rest of the family, as my brothers loaded the last of our procession into the moving truck. It was an awkward departure, and we spent several hours reminiscing with my wife's family. The move meant a new beginning for my family. My wife was very proud of her new home and settled right in by unpacking our belongings. The best part was, she finally had the space to put things we had not seen in years due to the lack of space.

Our family was growing, and we enjoyed spending time with our neighbors and watching their families grow right along with ours. My daughter had won several 4H competitions at the county fairs, including the prettiest baby contest two years in a row for her age group. My son was growing and had already learned to dribble and shoot a basketball by the time he was three years old. My wife finally agreed to let us hang a basketball goal and backboard up in the unfinished section of the lower level of our house for rainy days.

I came home from work one day, and my son met me at the door all excited about a new move he had learned. I went down to the basement with him to watch his new move. He told me to stand where the coach is supposed to stand on the sidelines and watch. He took a couple of dribbles at the top of the circle picked, up the ball in both hands, and sprinted toward the rim mounted not more than three inches from a solid concrete wall. Before I could stop him from crashing into the wall, he took three steps up the wall, turned his back to the rim, and slams the ball through the hoop. To this day, some 57 years later, I have witnessed thousands of dunks, but none were better than his dunk and likely never will.

Once I got my heart to slow down from the fear of him hitting the wall and hurting himself, I told him he was only to do the move one more time so I could get a picture of him slamming the ball through the net. I got my photo and explained that if his mother saw him do the dunk again, she would make me take down the backboard and rim for good. I think I sent him the wrong message about not letting his mother catch him doing dangerous things that could get him hurt. No—I am sure I did, as you will read about the incident later in the story.

Forty-Five

DIAGNOSIS: SPINAL MENINGITIS

When our son turned three, we decided, he needed more interaction with children his own age. We had a close friend who owned a babysitting company at her house, so we decided to leave him at her house two afternoons a week to interact and play with children his age. When my wife went to pick him up one day, the owner told her she had heard about several cases of spinal meningitis affecting young children in the area. None of her children had the virus, but she needed to be cautious because the virus is deadly. We made the decision to keep him home for the rest of the week and avoid contact with children until the virus was out of the area.

Ever since the day he learned to walk, he would get out of his bed at 3:10 AM and come into our bedroom. He would place his face about two inches from my eyes and just stand there until I moved over and let him into our bed. In less than a minute, he would be sound asleep. By the morning alarm, he would somehow end up with his head on my wife's stomach and both feet in the small of my back. I guess my body knew the routine so well, I woke up at that time every single night.

I woke up and waited for him to come into our bedroom. Five minutes went by, and I realized he was not coming. I got out of bed, and as soon as my feet hit the floor, my wife awakened and asked what was wrong. I told her that he did not come in as usual and I was going to check on him. When I walked into his room, I quickly found him motionless. I leaned over to pick him up, and as soon as I touched him, he cried out in pain. He was soaking wet from a high fever. I knew the symptoms of spinal meningitis, and he had them all.

My wife called the Carroll County Hospital and told them his symptoms. They told her to rush him to Audubon Hospital in Louisville. The only ambulance available was about halfway to Louisville, carrying another child with the same symptoms. When we got to the hospital, we went straight to the emergency room. Three other children from the area, all his age, had already passed away from contracting the virus. The hospital was alerted that we were coming, and they ran a test to verify what was wrong with him. One of us had to be in the room with him during the procedure, so I told my wife I would go with them and witness the test. The test was a spinal tap, and the expert told me that if the fluid was clear, he would be okay, but if it was cloudy, he was in a lot of trouble and most children his age could not handle the treatment.

The second I walked out of the emergency room, my wife knew the test results were positive. She said she knew he would survive and she was never going to leave his side. I told her the doctor said he was strong for a three year old and his body was in excellent shape. The incredible amount of love she carried in her heart for her children would be a great strength to him to win the fight. The days in the intensive care unit turned to weeks. He was on every prayer list in every church within three hundred miles of our house. All of the children from the area diagnosed with the virus were deceased except for our son. His mother visited the chapel every day to thank god for answering her prayer for her son. His temperature reached 105 degrees and there was very little at the time that could be done to bring it down. The doctors said his body was stressed, but he continued to struggle.

Finally, good news came from a test result, indicating his body was winning the battle, but he was not out of danger and would need to stay in the intensive care room for another week. This would take us through the Thanksgiving holiday.

My wife asked me to stay with her in the hospital the night before Thanksgiving after I got off from work. Our son had not opened his eyes or even moved on his own for six weeks. I was hoping when I got there that she would have some good news. Instead, I found a mother emotionally spent and beaten down, and her strength was gone. She said his temperature had returned and she didn't know what to do. I held her for the next several hours and finally convinced her to get some sleep and that I would stay awake and keep an eye on him. This was another one of those times Soul just disappeared or went silent. He could offer nothing, but I knew he loved our son and was dreaming of the days when he could watch him play high school basketball just as he had done with me.

Earlier in the day, my second oldest brother and his wife had visited the hospital and had brought our son a small basketball, backboard, and rim. He put the backboard and rim on the end of his bed and laid the sponge ball beside his hand.

I was very tired and realized that if I did not stand up, I was going to fall asleep. I stood at the end of the bed and just lay my head on the end board and watched him sleep. I closed my eyes to rest them, and out of nowhere, I felt something hit me right between the eyes. I noticed my son was still lying in the same position, but I notice the ball was lying on the floor beside his bed. I picked up the ball and put it back near my son's hand. I was praying he had thrown the ball at the rim but then said, "Impossible. He has not moved a muscle in weeks." I put another blanket on my wife, tucked my son in, kissed his forehead, and said, "I love you." I placed my head in the same position as before at the end of his crib, and I cautioned Soul that if he was responsible for the ball on the floor, it was not funny and he should be ashamed of himself. He assured me had had nothing to do with it. He reminded me miracles happen every day and to not count one out tonight.

This time I was wide-awake, and if the ball left his side, I was going to know how it did. Twenty minutes later, I noticed my son was moving around more than he had moved in six weeks. Then he stopped moving. I went over and tucked him back in and returned to the end of the bed. I stood there perfectly still with my eyes closed for the next hour.

Suddenly I felt my son's eyes looking straight into mine as he had done every day since he had learned to walk. I just lay there with my eyes closed as I felt him coming closer and closer to my face. I did not want to open my eyes. I feared this was a sign the meningitis had finally won and he was saying goodbye before going to heaven. I wanted so bad to have him back in my life. Then he got so close I could feel his breath on my face. I had to open my eyes. I knew if it was actually happening, I had to react as I had done every time in the past when he was there beside our bed. I could not cry, nor could I shout to the gods, I just had to act normal. I opened my eyes and it was real. There he was, looking into my eyes. I felt him gently put his hands on both sides of my face. He gave me a hug and asked where his mommy was. I told him I loved him, and I asked him if he hurt anywhere. He said he was thirsty and needed a drink of juice. The doctor had told us earlier that if he ever woke up, he would return to normal almost instantly.

He asked me if I wanted to play ball, and I told him yes but that I had someone else he needed to see before we played ball. I picked him up and very gently placed him in the arms of his sleeping mother. She awoke and asked me what I was doing. I told her she might want to hold her son before we went to go play ball. She looked at me as if I had lost my mind, but then she realized he was awake and acting as if he had never been sick. I never saw a bigger smile on her face; she kept kissing him and hugging him. Between the tears, she repeatedly told him she loved him and that God had answered her prayers.

While she was holding him, I fumbled to find the call button to let the nurse know what was going on. I found the button and told her my son needed some juice. The nurse did not believe me until she walked into the room and found him standing up playing ball with me in his bed. She quickly turned on the light to see for herself. She immediately told the rest of the nurses on the floor what was going on and that she needed some juice.

One of the nurses asked me if this were the best Thanksgiving ever. My wife just looked at me and busted out laughing and crying at the same time. She told the nurse she was sorry and explained what some of our past Thanksgivings were like. However, she said for her this was the best and she could not imagine any future Thanksgivings topping this one.

The doctor came in about 8:00 AM to observe our son. He said that as best as he could tell, he was healthy, but he needed to run some tests to make sure. I asked the doctor if we could take him home for the day and bring him back at night or in the morning. I felt the best thing for him and the rest of our family, especially our daughter, was to have a celebration at home. The doctor said he had never heard of giving a pass to the patient, but he did not see any harm for just one day.

It seemed my dad was the one affected the most when our son got sick. He loved him so much and he just could not deal with the fact that someone that young was so sick. He even told my mother to cancel all Thanksgiving Day celebrations at his house. I called my mother when we got home and told her my wife and our daughter and I would be there for the traditional Thanksgiving Day meal. I could tell she wanted to ask who was with our son in the hospital, but by this time, she was just happy to have us there.

I was the last of the children to arrive, and my mother met us at the door with hugs and kisses. I asked my brothers and sister to meet me outside on the front porch. I had a big surprise and I wanted them to help me surprise my mom and especially my dad. They pointed to his chair in the living room. I went over gave him a hug and wished him happy Thanksgiving Day. He looked at me with the saddest eyes ever and told me he felt my pain. "The only thing that would make this a happy day would be to see your son walk through the door. I know it is not possible, but it is my wish."

My two oldest brothers walked into the living room. They interrupted my dad's train of thought, telling me they had no idea what was wrong with my car. My sister came in and told me that if I got a call, I might need to leave very quickly. What are you going to do if your car will not start? My dad looked at me, and said, "Those two boys could not fix a bicycle. I will put my shoes on and go immediately and check it out." He put on his shoes and went through the kitchen to let my mom know she may need to delay dinner until he got my car running. She knew almost as much about vehicles as my dad did. She said, "Wait for me. We need to take care of this now in case he has to go back to Louisville." When they went out the door, the other 56 people in my family followed them to my car in the driveway.

When my dad opened the door, he saw my wife and his grandson sitting in her lap. My son yelled out, "Grandpa- Grandpa, I love you!" My father reached down and asked my wife if he could hold him. He took him in his arms, and after we all stopped crying, my mother told us it was time for dinner. This actually became my family's best Thanksgiving Day ever.

Forty-Six

My Children are Growing Up, Who Knew

I knew our children would grow up to be athletic and would need some place to play sports. The sports programs back in those days were limited for young children in our community. If our children were going to get an early start, I needed to get involved and remove those barriers for our children. My son enjoyed basketball and playing in the oversized sandbox we had built for him and his sister the summer following our move to a new house. Therefore, during the winter, I was one of the directors and coaches for the youth basketball association. Kids were not supposed to be eligible to play in the league until they were six years old. My son was already one of the best ball handlers in the league, so we decided to amend the rules a little by allowing the coach's sons to play. One of the other coaches had a son named Ross, who was also an excellent ball handler. My best memory of Ross as a young boy was when he recited the titles of every single book in the bible in order during a bible school ceremony at the Whites Run Baptist Church. Soul was excited and cheered him on to the end.

After a few years, I was able to convince the league organizer to allow girls to play in the league. The thought was to get my daughter to play basketball, but she said she did not want to play basketball and her mother ended my thought very quickly in supporting her decision.

The process of selecting your team players was a draft procedure following the sign-up. All of the coaches met on Wednesday night following the sign up deadline and took turns choosing their player for the upcoming season. We had nine girls sign up. I was unable to attend the meeting, so the other coaches decided that since it was my idea to let girls play for the first time, I should be willing to take my share. By the time the draft ended, I had twelve players on my team, which consisted of four boys and eight girls. The only reason I did not get the last girl in the draft was she was the daughter of one of the other coaches. It was a surprise, but I must say it was one of my best coaching experiences in the thirty plus years I coached youth sports. Nearly every one of those girls went on to play high school basketball, and five were the starters on the high school varsity team their senior year.

Youth baseball was nonexistent for children under the age of nine for boys, and baseball for girls did not exist at any age. Several of the fathers decided it was time for the community to support youth baseball. I did some research and found some information about tee-ball for young children. There were no rules or information about how to lay out the field, for the game did not exist. One baseball equipment manufacture did make a device called a tee stand. The bat was very short and made of lightweight aluminum. My friend Tooter and I pooled our money to purchase one of these funny-looking devices. Once it arrived, we met with several of the parents with young boys and girls and explained how to use the equipment and how to play the game.

The parents were supportive and were willing to let their children play. All we needed was a field to play on, enough equipment and supplies to support the teams, and a few coaches. The field and the coaches were easy to get, as the company I worked for had built a softball field just across the road from the plant. We were allowed to use the field for practices and games. Many of the employees at the plant and the other large manufacturers in the area were more than willing to supply the coaches.

The biggest hurdle, which is normally the case, was finding the money to buy the equipment and pay the umpires. Our league development group decided it was time to visit our local elected officials for help with this barrier. It was an election year, and two of the long-time officials were being challenged in the fall elections. We met with Sheriff Bobby and Judge Bill and explained how the league would operate. At first, they were reluctant and claimed the county did not have the money. Then I told them they could throw out the first pitch to start the season and that we would name the league after the both of them. They called me at work a few days later and told me they had found a surplus in the county budget. They would be willing to support the league for one year, but after that, we would need to find new funding.

We started the season on the softball field across from the plant, but halfway through the season, we moved the games to a new park named Point Park. The park was a beautiful facility located at the mouth of Big Kentucky River where it emptied into the mighty Ohio River. After the third season and several drafts of the rules and field layouts, the league went through several changes and continued to improve each year.

Forty-Seven

Season Over. What is Next?

At the end of the third year, the seven-year-old children turning eight including my daughter, were no longer eligible to play tee ball. The boys were not old enough to play little league, so there was nothing left for about 150 children who loved to play baseball. To make a long story short, the same group who started up the tee ball program created another league called the G-ball league. The main difference in this league was that the coach of each team pitched to the hitter on his or her team. The game was played like real baseball, using the official baseball rules. By the 4th year, the two leagues merged into one organization, and a group named the American Legion sponsored the leagues for the next several years. The president, who we just called President John, was one of the original founders and the anchor who kept the league going for years. His goal was to offer the opportunity for all children in the county and surrounding communities to play the game free of charge to the parents.

Five volunteers had a vision to start the leagues, and over the years, hundreds of volunteers since must have done it right. The league has now been in existence for more than thirty-five years. The tee ball original rules and field layout are used by thousands of leagues across the United States and in at least thirty other countries. Recently, I was reviewing the official rules for little league baseball and ran across the identical rules we created in the early years. I think tee ball will be around for many years to come.

The biggest break came when County Judge Executive named Bobby, had the vision to create a country park using federal grant money. The park was rightfully named after him. To this day, I can remember him pulling up in his old pickup truck and watching the kids of summer having the time of their lives playing America's game out his window.

My involvement in the association lasted for seven years. I served as president several years and held other positions as well. I got the most pleasure coaching my daughter and son's teams. Soul kept telling me I needed to stay involved. I never thought to ask him why, and I am glad now I did not ask him.

Halfway through my next to last season, one of my players called me one night around 9:00 PM. After a few minutes, my wife asked me who it was. I told her it was one of my players and it sounds like he was in trouble. I switched the phone to speaker and asked her to listen to the conversation.

The little boy was one of the top players in the league at the halfway point of the season. We had practiced a couple of days before the call, and his mother told me he was unusually tired after practice. She asked me to keep an eye on him and, if possible, limit his time on the field during the next practice. I agreed and felt things went okay during the practice.

I remember the conversation with his mother and asked the little boy what was wrong. He told me he had some medical test the day before and his mom told him he was very sick. He said, "But that is not the bad news coach; she told me I will have to quit playing baseball." I could tell by the tone of his voice he was about to cry and I likely was not far behind. I tried to reassure him he would be okay and he needed to listen to his parents. "I am sure you will be able to take treatment. I promise you a spot on the team as my assistant coach the rest of this year, and you will be back playing on our team next year."

After a short pause, he said, "Coach, you are my only hope, and I have to play this year." I felt I was no longer talking to a seven-year-old child. I was having a conversation with a person who knew his fate. He knew he needed to get all out of life he had left before it was too late. He told me his parents respected me and that I had to come to his house and convince them to let him play out the season. He said, "Could you come over tonight coach? I really need your help." When he said, "Please coach," my wife broke down in tears and had to leave the room. She went to give her two babies a second hug for the night. I had nothing left to say to the young man that would offer hope for a long life. I told him I would talk to both of his parents and that between the three of us we would do what was best for him.

As we continued the conversation, I learned a lesson that has helped me get through many similar situations during the thirty-plus years I coached youth sport in my community.

He elegantly described to me how it felt to be a young athlete. He said when he put on his uniform, laced up his baseball cleats, and pulled his glove on his hand, it becomes his best day. "When we arrive at the ballpark and I look out on that field, I cannot wait to get between the lines and take ground balls from my dad. When the umpire yells, "Play ball," something good inside of me starts to flow and I want the hitter to hit me with his or her best shot." He could not quite explain what it was, but it made him special in the eyes of those who he loves most. "My family just fuels my desire to improve, grow, and get better every minute I have the privilege to be on the field."

He said, "The first time I ran out of the dugout and on our field, I looked up in the stands and saw the expression on my family members' faces. I became more than just my mother's son. I became a hero to my mom and dad just as the rest of my teammates did for their parents. We were playing baseball on a team for the first time, and every decision was up to us. All our parents could do was sit in the stands, cheer, watch, and pray we did not do something stupid to embarrass the family."

We both had a good laugh, and I shared with him the number of times I had to calm down a parent and politely tell them to get off the field and back up in the stands. I told him about one time when a mother got so out of control one day while I was umpiring a baseball game that she climbed over the backstop behind home plate and dropped ten feet to the ground.

I stopped the game and she stepped up in my face like Yogi Berra auguring a call and told me I had made a bad call and that her son was safe. The little boy asked me, "What did you do coach?" "I told her she was mistaken because I had called her son safe on the play. She asked me if I was sure I called him safe because from where she sat, it looked like I called him out. I pointed down to third base and asked her if that was her son standing on the base. She took a hard look down the line and looked back at me and said, 'Well okay, you finally got one right.' Then I raised my right arm over my head, pointed my finger to the gate, and said, 'But you are not safe. Momma you are out of here, and next time, use the gate.'" The little boy just laughed and said, "I hope my mom never acts that way, but she loves me and she probably will."

He said his teammates always seem to have much more fun than their parents do. "All we have to do is the best we can, just as the coach tells us to do each time before we leave the dugout. Our family members have to worry we are going to run to the wrong base or drop an easy pop-up that loses the game. Even worse, we could get tired or bored, and just decide to take an inning off and sit down on the infield and make funny designs in the infield dirt with our fingers."

He said when his team lost a game, his entire family felt his pain of defeat for days. "However coach, when we win it, they feel the thrill of victory and it is the talk at the supper table until the next game." Finally, he ran out of words and said, "Please coach, convince them to let me play; let me do this my way." I told him to go on to bed and if his mom was near the phone to put her on the line. "You go to bed and have faith in your family, God, your teammates, and your coach."

When the mother took the phone, I could tell she had been listening to the entire conversation between her son and me. If I were in a similar situation, I likely would have done the same. She had shifted to her special mother mode that I wrote about earlier in the book. She was preparing to do whatever it took to try to save her son's life. She told me right away I was only his coach and she appreciated me talking to her son but she would never allow him to play another baseball game.

What she needed most was to get all of her feelings on the table, so I just sat and listened to her for about ten minutes without saying a word. When she paused, I told her, "Until about an hour ago, we had no idea your son was sick and his family was suffering so severely. I just want to assure you my family will be there for you. We will do anything we can to help your son and his family any way we can. The compassion and sadness my family feels in our hearts tonight has nothing to do with baseball. When a children playing on our team or any other team in the league is suffering, we want to extend a helping hand."

My wife returns to the room, turned off the lights, and laid her head on my shoulder. We sat in the dark listening to this mother pour out the rest of her heart and soul as she talked about her son and family members for the next hour.

Finally, there was silence, except for the sound of breathing and sobbing as the mother continues to weep. My wife felt her pain and began to cry. I looked to Soul for help, but he had his eyes closed, and not even his closed eyes could stop the stream of tears flowing down his face.

The mother asked me what I would do if my young son had stage IV cancer and the chances of survival were less than 10 percent. I heard the husband immediately tell her in the background that it was not fair to ask me such a horrible question. I heard her tell her husband that I was the coach and I was supposed to have an answer. She told her husband, "Our son loves this coach with all of his heart. Our son reached out to him for help; why can't I? Right now, I need help. So I too love him and need his help. Before we hang up this phone, I need to know his thoughts, and mostly, I need to hear his words of encouragement. That is what coaches do best you know? They help us find the strength we did not know we had to stay in the game and compete." My wife turned on the light and wrote on my coach's white board, "You can do this coach; just do the best you can and that will be good enough."

I told the mom and her husband, "I do not have an answer to save your son's life. As a coach, I can share with you my experiences. After that, we will need to deal with whatever the next day brings. This is a one day at a time situation, and if it is a good day, we will all rejoice. If it is not, we will help each other up with prayer so we can get to the next day." I felt a calmness I had never felt before. I think Soul was ready to help me chose the right words. I heard the phone change position on her end, and I heard her embrace her husband. She had finally reached out and was asking her husband to help her carry her burdens. This is how God intended it to be in a marriage, when the minister says, "And from this point on you will be one."

I told her I was going to share something with her and her family that had nothing to do with baseball. I did not realize it at the time it happened, but it had everything to do with being a coach. This was coaching that had nothing to do with athletics and everything to do with real life. I said, "I know this may sound strange to you, but two years ago, I had a calling to be a volunteer counselor at the local Easter Seals Camp out on 227 in Carroll County. I do not know if it was God or my guardian angel but I knew I had to answer the calling.

"I read in the local newspaper about a summer camp for children in need of coaches and councilors for their summer sessions. I knew the camp was there but had no idea what its real function was. I talked to my wife about it, and she said 'Go for it.' My initial thought was that I would help children learn to paddle a boat or catch a fish—maybe even share my farming experience on how to grow food or take care of a baby calves abandoned by their mothers.

"I reported to councilor training a couple of weeks before the children were scheduled to attend. The team leader welcomed us to the training and then shared something with us that caused several volunteers to get out of their seats and leave the class. He said, 'The children are between eight and twelve, and the one thing they have in common is they all have terminal diseases. In other words, barring a breakthrough in medical science or a miracle, they know it is just a manner of time. Each of you will be assigned three children and will deal with a wide range of emotions. Your job is not to cry with them but to lead them past what is causing them to be sad by encouraging them to continue to live on and get everything out of life they have left. Believe me councilors, these children and their families have already shared millions of tears together when they learned their fate. Our first mission is to make sure they have fun and to help raise their spirits. What we know is, when people of all ages have a good spirit, it makes more difference in their survival and happiness than all the current medicines combined.'

"The first little boy I met was named Roy. He had cancer but had a great attitude and was ready to face whatever life brought his way. Late at night, Roy would say, 'Coach, are you awake?' When I told him I was, he would say he did well until the nighttime when the lights went out. One night he was very upset. I could tell the demons had come out and the only thing I could think of was to ask him if he wanted to go for a walk. He said, 'Coach, you know that is against the rules. We are not supposed to leave our cabins once the alarm sounds. We could get into trouble.' I said, 'Get your baseball glove and I will take all of the responsibility.' We went out to the field, which was lit up by the common area security lighting. While playing catch, Roy spent the majority of his time talking to me about how much he was going to miss his family.

"The second child's name was Henry, and he too had cancer but had given up on life and wanted to spend most of his time talking about death. Henry was about to meet two incredible peers and a loving mother that were going to make my job easy.

"The third was a little girl named Mary, and she was likely the sickest of the three, but you would have never known it from the smile she had on her face most of the time.

"Within the first few minutes following the introductions, Mary heard all of the negative words she could stand from Henry. She told him she knew he could play the guitar and sing. She asked him to play her a lovely song during the talent show at the end of the week. He angrily said that he would never play the guitar again and would never perform in a talent show. The little girl just smiled as if she knew something he did not know.

"Each day, Roy started out the day telling Henry what he planned to do during the day, and he prayed Henry would join him. On the third day, Henry decided to take a walk and see if Roy was actually doing what he said he was going to do. Henry found Roy at the top of the rock-climbing mountain and invited Henry to join him. He told Henry he could see the entire camp from the top and it was incredible. Roy sensed Henry really wants to join him at the top of the mountain, so he climbed down and put his hand on Henry's shoulder. Then he said, 'Come on man, I will climb with you. You cannot imagine how different things look up there; it is *fan-tas-ti-cal!*

"Henry did climb to the top, and for the first time in months, he smiled and allowed life to reenter his body. Before climbing down the mountain for lunch, Henry stood up straight, pointed his finger toward the sky, and smiled. During his time at the camp, he played baseball, went fishing, learned to paddle a canoe across the lake and back, and raced and beat his friend Roy in the swimming competition.

"Traditionally, on the last day of the camp, we would build a giant bonfire and hold a talent competition for all of the councilors and campers. Mary did a magic trick and returned to her seat without taking her eyes off Henry. Near the end of the show, a young oncologist stood up and made an incredible motivational speech, which seemed to lift the spirits of the children and their parents. Then he said he would like to introduce the next act. When the curtain opened, a young woman was standing in the middle of the stage. She was holding a guitar, but she was not playing it. She was holding it out away from her body as an offering to someone in the audience. She said, 'This is my testimonial to my son. Please, please forgive me; I was wrong. The way he plays this guitar was physically stressful for his body. When my son got sick, I decided I would do everything I could to protect him. This week in this camp, I realized I had taken something away he loves to do. As she lowered her head in shame, she said, I broke his spirit, and he just gave up.' When she witnessed him receiving the awards he had earned during the camp, she knew what she had to do. She looked out in the audience and located her son. She said, 'Henry, I love you more than you could ever imagine. Please forgive me and play me our special song on the guitar.' She held out the guitar well away from her trembling body as the audience was in complete silence.

"Henry placed his elbows on his knees and put his hands over his face. I think Henry knew this was a turning point and he had two choices. He could refuse his mother's apology and continue to be sad, or he could let his anger go and enjoy what time he had left. Roy puts his left hand on Henry's shoulder. Mary did the same on his left shoulder. They looked at each other, and Roy said, 'You can do this my friend. We believe in you, and your family needs you. Go ahead Henry; give it a shot.' Henry rose up from his seat, walked up to the stairs leading to the stage, and looked up at his mother. He leaned over and asked me if I could put a chair up on the stage. I thought I was putting the chair up on the stage for him to sit on. I knew he was growing physically weaker every day and might need it. A smile appeared on his face as he slowly made his way onto the stage. He reached out and took the offering from his mother. He looked at the guitar, and a smile came to his face as if he had found an old friend that had been missing from his life.

"Henry asked his mother to sit in the chair. Henry was giving a gift of healing and acceptance to his mother just as Roy and Mary had given to him.

"As it turned out, Henry was a musical prodigy. His mother, without shedding a tear, just sat there with her eyes closed, enjoying the sound of every chord delivered as Henry plays their song. When Henry finished the song, his mother stood, walked over to Henry, and whispered something into his ear. He gave her a hug and a smile to indicate he was going to be okay.

"He played notes on the guitar I had never heard before, and I had attended concerts with some of the most recognized pickers in the world. When he finished the classical piece of music, he said that he had another special song he would like to play and sing to his new friends Mary and Roy. Mary's eyes lit up and the smile on her face was as vast as the ocean. He played a fast-beat, spiritually uplifting song about life, courage, hope, faith and an untraveled path to destiny. Then when the audience sat down, he spoke words he had not spoken or used in years, and we knew it was a mission accomplished. He said, 'Until a few days ago, I was ready to accept my fate, but not anymore. I'm going to be more like Roy and Mary. I may not live long enough to do it all, but I sure am going to try.'

"After that night, I never saw Roy, Henry, or Mary again, but during the next two years, I met over a hundred children at the camp, and our team of volunteer counselors and child experts were undefeated in meeting our mission by the end of the camp sessions. I learned more about coaching from that experience and just how precious life really is than I will ever learn on the court or playing field."

I stopped talking, and we just sat in the night: me holding my wife and her husband holding her. The mother said, "Thanks coach, for sharing such a beautiful and personal message with me and my husband. I am going to hang up now. We have a lot to talk about, and I have some decisions to make. Goodnight coach. I love you." My wife asked if I would continue to hold her for a while. She said, "I do not know how you found the right words at the right time. It is a gift from god that only particular people seem to have, and I am glad I have you." Soul said, "Nice job coach; your best victories will come from the heart not the score on the scoreboard."

The little boy was the first child in the dugout for our next game. He told me he was sorry for missing practice and if I did not play him, he understood. He said his mother and father were standing outside the dugout and wanted to talk to me. I stepped outside the dugout and was greeted when I rounded the corner by the little boy's entire family with cheers and applause (well over seventy-five people). They were all wearing hats and shirts with the inscription, "Mom says he is going to do it his way." When they took off their hats, they were all wearing black war paint under their eyes with his name in the center. As it should be, the eldest grandfather was the spokesperson for the family. He said, "Coach, our boy and his family need a win tonight." I said, "Well, we are playing the best team in the league tonight, but even if we do not win on the scoreboard, we will win in our efforts and in our hearts." The grandfather removed his hat, and I saw a tear drop from his eye and roll down his face. He extended his hand to mine and said this was the toughest thing his family had ever had to deal with. "Until you spoke to my daughter and her husband a few nights ago, we were heading down the wrong path. Thank you coach, for helping us back on the right track." The mother put her arms around me and said this was the most difficult decision she had ever had to make. She said she just thanked God she had people in her life to help her make the right choice. As they turned to take their seats in the stands, she looked back and said, Thanks coach; I love you." The family came to every single remaining game dressed with the same attire, including the war paint.

Our team won the championship game 19 to 18. The little boy made an incredible game-winning catch down the right field line. He landed in the middle of his family, and when the umpire checked the ball in his glove, he called the third out, ending the game. His family celebrated as if they had watched their son win the World Series. As president of the league, I had the honor of presenting the little boy with the most valuable player award. He took the trophy and ran to his mother. He presented her with the trophy, which is the way it is supposed to be. I closed the ceremony with the statement, 'TEE-BALL Strong Forever.'

I looked at Soul and thanked him for encouraging me to continue my involvement in the league. "Now I know why you were so persistent that I continue to manage and coach." Soul just looked away without saying a word. Finally, he looked at me with sad eyes and said, "It is not over; you have to keep coaching. It is a part of your destiny." From the tone of his voice and the look in his eyes, I knew he felt very strongly about this, and I just said, "Okay."

Forty-Eight

SCHOOL'S OUT THIS TIME FOR GOOD

The ball season ended and it was time to take a family vacation before school started back up. We had a family meeting with just the four of us on Sunday afternoon after church. My family thought the only item on the meeting agenda was to figure out where we wanted to spend our family vacation. We decided to travel by car to Washington DC and visit the historical sites we had read about in our history books.

Once the meeting was over, I began going over our schedule for the next month, and we found an opening and selected the day we would leave for Washington. When we had decided, I said, "Okay, that is it. Now lets us go down to the Taste Freeze and get some ice cream." My wife said, "Wait, you forget to review something on the list." I scanned down the list and said, "No, I think I covered it all." She said, "We have had the same item on the list for nearly ten years." I think my daughter had figured it out before my wife did, but from the look on her face, she decided to keep quiet and let her mother set me straight. I looked at the list again and said, "No, I think it is all covered." I could tell this redhead was starting to get a little excited.

She said, "You forgot to list your classes at the University of Cincinnati." She pointed her finger at me and said, "If you think you are not going to

330

finish after all of this time, you are wrong. If I have to, I will drive you to the door of the school and drop you off just as I do our daughter and our son at their schools." My daughter was about to blow a gasket with laughter just watching her mother scold me.

I had opened up a book I had placed on the table next to her before the meeting started. I ask her to remove and read the letter inside the book aloud if she did not mind. She opened the letter that informed me I had passed the engineer's test for the State of Ohio and that my studies and commitment at the University of Cincinnati had concluded. The next line read that I could graduate with my class at the end of the winter quarter or wait for the spring graduation the following year. I had gotten up from the table to get a glass of water from the refrigerator across the room as she was reading the letter. The next thing I knew she had tackled me, and I ended up flat on my back on the kitchen floor. She was on top of me kissing and hugging me, and the kids were not too far behind.

Later that night, we talked about where we were and what was next for our family. She said she would arrange a party for me when I graduated in the spring. To be honest with you, I think she was more excited about my graduation than I was.

We had done quite well during the first twelve years of our marriage. We had two new vehicles, a new home, and two beautiful children. Our finances were in excellent shape as she was an incredible money manager. Four of our friends we had attended high school with had purchased the rest of the land around us and had built new homes. They had children about the same age as ours; we had grown into a splendid neighborhood. I had several promotions over the years, and I was in training to take the last step toward making my goal when I started with the company. My wife said that in her opinion I had sold myself short and I needed to take a little break, but she wanted me to set new goals. She felt I should shoot for president of the company and that she would be right by my side all the way. She said, "I have watched you from a distance convince people to achieve things they never thought was possible. It is a gift you need to share, and it can never be bottled up." I told her, "I have been thinking about my career and what is next, but first I want to spend more time with you and my children. We have spent fourteen years getting to this point in our life. I want you to know I could have never done it without you by my side. We have been through a lot, and now it is time to take a year off and just enjoy the fruits of our labor."

Fourty-Nine

THE FALL

Our vacation was over, and it was time to get on with our lives. For many years, my wife and I had spent Sunday nights talking about our schedules and the children's schedule for the coming week. Her list included spending several hours canning vegetables from our organic garden and cleaning the house from top to bottom. She said if she had time, she was going to wax the kitchen floor. I told her if she wanted to wait for me to get home, I would wax the floor since I no longer had to go straight to school.

I went to work the following Monday morning. It was a sunny day, and things at work were going very good. The plant was setting production records and the safety and environmental programs were at full strength. We had gone several years without any injuries and we were 100 percent in compliance with all environmental regulations.

I attended the daily production/maintenance communication meeting in the afternoon. Everything seemed to be fine, and I picked up no additional action items from the meeting. When I arrived back in my office, my phone rang. It was my wife on the other end, and she sounded like she was crying. I asked her what was wrong. She said she was waxing the kitchen floor and she had fallen. She fell on her left leg and it was hurting. She did not know what to do. I told her to put an ice pack on her leg and that I would be home in five minutes.

When she said okay and hung up the phone, I knew this was not just a hurt leg. This woman was a tough country girl who had delivered two babies without the use of any anesthesia. For her to cry, she must have been in an incredible amount of pain. I left the office immediately and rushed home. When I arrived, she was still lying on the floor and was unable to get up. I put the phone back on the wall. She had apparently used the mop handle to knock it down to where she had fallen.

I lifted her off the floor and put her on the sofa in the family room. I checked her leg and could not see any indications of a broken bone or torn muscles. I put some ice on her leg to prevent any more swelling. Once she was able to move without severe pain, I took her to see the family doctor in Carrollton. He ordered up some x-rays at the hospital and said nothing was broken or dislocated. The doctor prescribed some pain medication and told us to continue to apply ice to keep the swelling down. He said he felt she had damaged a tendon and had possibly dislocated her left hip but it had popped right back into place and the injury would not show up on an X-ray. He felt a few days of bed rest would allow time for the injury to heal.

The only thing she was worried about was finishing the floor waxing, which I did when I got her on the sofa at home.

Within a few days, the pain was gone, and even though she still had a slight limp, she said she felt fine. By the end of the week, she was back to playing softball with me during the family reunion at Butler Park. All of the pain was gone. The follow-up visit to the doctor the following Monday went great. He even commented that she was as healthy as she had ever been. If we wanted to expand the family, the timing was right for it.

A week later, we scheduled a complete physical, including blood work and other preventive health examinations and exams. The next week, we went back for a final consultation to review the results of the test. The doctor confirmed what he had told us the previous week. He said she was as healthy as a horse. The doctor told me he had been her grandmother and mother's doctor. "You can stop worrying; she is healthier than both of them had ever been. You are thirty-one, she is thirty-two, your daughter is ten, and your son is six. If you two are going to expand your family, this is the best time to do it. We left the doctor's office on top of the world with the news she was healthy and had completely recovered.

We had talked about having at least two more children, but I had some additional specialized training at work I still needed to finish up. One of the training classes was in Colorado Springs, and the plan was to take her with me. She could spend the days shopping while I went to class. Soul was excited about going to Colorado but then informed me he had something else to do. If I needed him, he would be there, but he had to go meet with God and some of the other angels. I could tell something was wrong; I just could not figure out what. We had decided to wait one more year before expanding our family.

Late one Saturday night, for some reason neither one of us could go to sleep. When this had happened before, we would usually reminisce about the past. She loved her life and she would open our bedroom window and just look out at the stars and tell me what she was thinking.

This night she told me she had opened this window many of the nights when I was going to school and got home well after midnight. She said she had talked to God and tried to look past the stars and see heaven. When she heard me turn up in our driveway, she would meet me at the door and say, "Thank you God for bringing him home safe." She would always have my supper waiting for me when I got home. She would move her chair up close to mine and put her hand on my shoulder. She said, "Those were hard times for us, but they were also some of my best times." She would tell me about her day, which mostly was spent taking care of the children.

The conversation usually started, "You will not believe what your son did today." He was six at the time and was not afraid on anything. His balance and strength were exceptional for a child his age. He rewrote the book on what six-year-old boys could get into. What he could not think of on his own, his two cousins, which were seven and eight, did.

I asked her if she remembered the day she franticly called me at work and said he had climbed up the antenna pole and was on top of the house.

She said, "I sure do. You told me not to panic with my son 35 feet in the air leaning over the side of the roof with a concrete pad to catch his fall directly below him. I thought you had lost your mind, and if this were not panic material, nothing else would ever be." I said, "I do not think I ever told you the rest of the story." She lay down beside me and said, "Tell me the whole story. Tell me how you got here so quick."

"I ran out into the maintenance shop and told one of my supervisors to get the flatbed truck and meet me out front.

"My oldest brother was a mechanic in the shop, and I told him what my son had done. He shut down his machine and grabbed an extension ladder from the tool room. On our way out of the shop, a couple of the mechanics asks my oldest brother were he was going. He told them and they said, 'Wait for us; we have to see this.' By the time the flatbed truck made its way through the plant to the front security gate, six more mechanics has had climbed on the flat bed of the truck.

"The supervisor turned the truck onto the main highway to our house. He was not letting any dust settle under his wheels. We arrived at my house in less than five minutes, which was normally a fifteen-minute trip. As we drove up the drive, it did not take long to find my son's location. He had walked across the eve of the house and was waving at us as we drove by. I could not begin to understand how he could have walked across the steep roof without falling. It became a little clearer when I saw you-know-who sitting beside him. Soul was complaining to me about spending all of this time getting me out of trouble, and now he had to babysit my son. He said, 'It is hot up here, and I have done my job. He all yours.'

"My brother placed the extension ladder against the house and I ran up the ladder to where my son was sitting. The ground team got a thick rescue rope out of the maintenance truck and tossed it up to me to use as a tie-off rope. I tied the rope around my waist and threw it over the opposite side of the house. The ground team grabbed the rope, tied it around their waists, and yelled up to me to start down when ready. I put pressure on the rope and placed my feet on the steep incline of the roof. I told our son to wrap his arms around my neck and to wrap his feet around my waist. Once he was in position, I could feel his trembling body next to mine. I knew I could not show too much emotion to avoid scaring him more than he already was. I just stood there for a few minutes, holding him as tight as I could. I told him he was safe now and we were going to be okay.

"My brother quickly realized that the thought of him falling off the roof finally hit me hard and that I needed a little time to regain my emotions. There was complete silence on the ground among the men. All of us were about the same age, and we all had sons and daughters about the age of my children. I think while I was holding our son, all of those guys were thinking about their children and how much their life would be changed forever if they lost one of them.

"My brother climbed to the top of the ladder and said, 'It is time to get the boy off this hot roof.' I slowly backed down the roof to where the ladder was position just above the roofline. My brother took him out of my arms and carried him down the ladder to safety. When they reached the ground, my son took a deep breath, looked up at his uncle, and said, "Thank you Uncle Russell. You sure are tall." We all laughed and shook each other's hands just as we had done many times after a rescue at the plant.

"He ran to you, and you picked him up in your arms and could not help but cry. You told him he scared you and if he had fallen off the roof, he would likely have been killed. You would have been sad for the rest of your life without him. He said he was sorry and he would never do it again. You took him into the house and gave him some water then carried him to his bedroom.

"You later returned to where the men were drinking cold glasses of lemonade. You thanked them all for helping us get our son down. You said the two of you were playing in the sandbox and he told you he was thirsty. You said you went into the house, got a glass of water for him, and came straight back out. At the most, you were gone for 45 seconds. When you returned, he was gone. You started screaming for him and ran around the house and then back into the house, thinking maybe he had followed you in to get a glass of water. You started screaming for him from inside the house and could faintly hear him responding. You said you went back outside and you heard him as plain as day answering, but could not find him. Then you realized that he was saying, 'I'm up here!' You walked up on the bank behind the house and there he was as bright as day. He was calm, and you realized you needed to go easy before you scared him. You told him to stay put and that you were going to call his father to help him down from the roof. He looked down at you and said, 'No problem; I can climb back down the antenna pole.' You told him no and that I would be home soon to rescue him.

"One of the rescuers asked you if he was okay, and you said he was fine. You had put him into a time-out and he was in his room playing. He asked you how long you planned to keep him in time-out and you said, without hesitation, "Ten years." I followed you into the house to make sure you were okay. You seemed to be handling things okay, so I opened our son's bedroom door and he was lying in bed sound asleep. You said, 'Just look at that little angel.' From that statement, I knew the crisis was over and things were fine at the Clifton house.

"I went back outside to let the men know it was time to load up and head back to work. I saw the truck, but I could not find the men. I heard a conversation coming from the end of the house where the antenna pole was located. My brother was up on the ladder spraying the antennae pole with a very slick Teflon spray-on material. He looked down at me and said, 'There is no way your son will get a good enough grip to climb the pole anytime in the future.'

"We arrived back at the plant and I thanked the men for helping me out. I asked them if they did not mind keeping the little incident between us boys.

"The next morning, during the staff meeting, the plant engineering manager started out by telling us about a conversation he had with the district manager. The manager was describing this wild story about a young boy who had climbed up an antennae pole onto the roof of a house. Then he said some of our people sitting at this table had left the plant and rescued the boy. I stopped him right there and told him I had a young boy and I had an antenna pole just like most of the people who lived in the area. I told him my son could not climb the pole and his story sounded ridiculous. I told him he was wasting my time and that I did not have time to listen to such a wild story. I told him I was sure he had better ways of spending his time and if he were smart, he certainly would not repeat such a wild story to any other managers.

"He looked straight at me sitting at the end of the conference table and asked me if I had ever heard such a ridiculous story. I said, "No sir," not one exactly like that one. I said, "The manager should have gotten all of his facts before he wasted your time on such a trivial issue." Most of the people sitting at the table knew about the incident. We were expecting the plant engineer to call each of us out one at a time to tell him what we had done.

"Instead, the plant engineering manager said that that was the last he wanted to hear about the situation and finished the meeting. I was the last to leave the room, and as I walked by the manager, he asked me how my son was doing. I told him he was fine. He said, 'I heard he likes to be a little, shall we say, adventurous.' I said, 'Well sir, he is a boy.' He said, 'Well, boys will be boys.' I replied, 'Yes sir, thank you sir.'

My wife said, "What an excellent manager."

I was still a very young manager compared to the rest of the managers on the staff, and I learned a valuable lesson from that incident. Good managers learn how to manage and apply the rules, but great managers figure out how to manage the gray areas between the rules. My goal was to be a great manager. My plant engineering manager was a great manager.

My wife climbed back out of bed and looked out the window at the bright universe above. We talked for a couple of hours, and then I ask her if she had found heaven. She said no, but she was sure it was out there. Soul said, "I know it is. Tell her I said it is and she can relax and stop looking."

Fifty

Bad Times to Come

Exactly two weeks later, she was very restless in bed, and I could tell something was wrong. She woke up about 3:00 AM with severe pain in the exact same spot on her left leg. She said it felt like something was trying to separate her leg from her hip. This time I could feel the swelling in her leg. At the time, we felt maybe she was trying to do too much too quickly, even though the doctor had given her a clean bill of health. We put ice on the swelling, and she took a pain pill left over from the previous injury. The pain went away, and the swelling was completely gone by the next morning. She got out of bed pain free and made me my breakfast as she had done several thousand mornings since we were married. I told her to take it easy all day and not press our luck. She did, and for the next two weeks, she was pain free.

In the third week, the swelling returned and was not going down—if anything, it was getting bigger. She said she was not in any pain. We went back to the local doctor and ran additional tests but could not determine what was causing the swelling. He arranged for us to meet with a doctor in Louisville. When we set up the appointment, the doctor told us to come prepared to spend a couple of days in the hospital if it turned out he needed a biopsy.

We met the doctor at the hospital, and he ordered up some x-rays and ran several other tests. He told us the test results would be available in a couple of hours. We returned to the office, and he told us the test did not indicate any issues. He said the only way to find out what the mass was was to do a biopsy. He said once the surgery was over it would take at least a week to get the results. He felt if she felt okay he would let her go home and they would notify us when to come back for the results.

The nurse told me to stay in the waiting room just outside the operating room. She said the doctor would let me know when the surgery was over and how she was doing. I waited in the room along with her mother and father. After a couple of hours, I called the nurse and asked her how the surgery was going.

She paused for what seemed like five minutes. She said the surgery was over an hour ago and she was already in a room and would need to spend the night. She said she was sorry, but the doctor was supposed to come out and let me know how it went. I asked the nurse if she was okay, and she said I would need to talk to the doctor. From the tone of her voice, I knew something was wrong. I asked the nurse what room she was in, and I ran to her room. Just as I reached for the door, a man inside the room introduced himself as a doctor. I had not met him before, and I ask him why he was in my wife's room. He said he had told my wife what was wrong and was there to offer her some spiritual guidance.

Before I could say that her spiritual belief was none of his business. He asked me if I had made any arrangements. I asked him, "What arrangements?" He said she would never leave the hospital alive. He felt she might have a few days left at the most. She had a very aggressive form of cancer and the chance of survival was zero.

The news sent me to my knees. My father-in-law was completely devastated. My mother in law convinced me to find the strength to hold my wife. I finally realized that as bad as my heart was hurting it could not compare to the pain she was suffering.

I was shocked to find my wife was not crying. She looked at me and said, "What changed?" I said I did not know what she meant. She went through the process we had been through since we reported to the hospital. She said, "Our doctor told us we would not know the results for a week and he would share the results." I asked her if she knew the doctor that was in her room, and she said no. I told her I would be right back. She knew exactly what I was about to do.

My father-in-law and I went back to the operating room, and I told the nurse I wanted to see the doctor who had just finished meeting with my wife. The nurse told me the doctor left the hospital several hours ago and that he never went up to my wife's room. While she was checking her records, I happened to see the man who introduced himself as a doctor.

The nurse told us the man was a lab technician and would never have permission to consult with a patient. He had only been with the hospital for two weeks and was a guest in the area from the Middle East to learn how American hospitals worked. She said he was a real pain in the butt and she was getting sick of him continuously shoving his religious belief on the rest of the staff. When I told the nurse what he had done and what he said to my wife, she clicked into emergency response mode and pulled out the hospital emergency procedures manual. She said she would contact my wife's doctor, the hospital security officer, and the head nurse immediately.

I had no intention of waiting for a supervisor to try to smooth this over. I told my father-in-law to stay with the nurse. I hopped over the counter and chased the man into his office. I shoved him against the wall, placed my forearm against his chest and told him not to move. I asked him what in the world he was doing and why he would treat someone the way he treated my wife. I wanted him to take a swing at me so I could really do some damage to him. Instead, he closed his eyes and started a spiritual chant I could not understand. I told him if he did not start speaking English, I was going to shove the test sample on his desk down his throat. When he opened his eyes, all he could see was my fist moving toward his bearded face. I think at that point he realized whatever God he was praying to was not at home. In addition, he also knew if he did not stop chanting, he was about to take a severe beating and he was right.

He said he was just preparing us for the worst. He was guessing my wife had a specific type of cancer that was fatal. When he said he was guessing, I wanted to kill the man with my bare hands and probably would have if the nurse had not begged me to take my hands from around his neck.

The shift supervisor and a security officer entered the room. The security officer told me to stand down and that he would take it from there. He pulled his gun and told the man to get up against the wall or he would shoot him. The nurse whispered in my ear that my wife needed me and led me out of the room. Within a few minutes, I saw the man with an escort. He was in handcuffed, and I never saw him again. The supervisor must have apologized fifteen times to my father-in-law and me.

The supervisor immediately placed an urgent announcement for a councilor to report to my wife's room over the hospital intercom. She told the nurse to call my wife's doctor and find out what to do next. The situation was over, and I knew I had to regain my composure and my train of thought before I could enter my wife's room.

The doctor called my wife and reiterated what he had said a few hours earlier. He said he could not tell us without the results of the biopsy. "I can tell you this. If it is cancer, it is not the type of cancer the imposter told you it was. If it were, she would have never made it to the hospital in the first place."

The hospital did an excellent job of calming my wife down and increasing security on her floor. I told her I would never leave her side and she would be safe. The doctor was in early the next morning and released her to go home. We spent the next week worrying about what would turn up on the biopsy. The pain was under control and the swelling had gone down some but was still there.

The doctor called the following Tuesday and said he would like to see her in his office the next day. We both prayed every day that it was not cancer. The doctor requested we both meet him in the examining room. He tried to break it to us as best he could: it was cancer. He gave us a few minutes alone to regain our composure.

She handled the diagnosis much better than I did. I had just attended the funeral of one of my friends who passed with cancer the previous week. In those days, the chance of living more than a year with any type of cancer was slim. She asked the doctor what type of cancer she had and what her chance of survival was. Then she used a phrase she had heard me use many time in my professional life as a coach and a motivational speaker. She said to the doctor, "Do not look down. I need to see some eyeballs looking straight at me because you need to understand what I'm about to say...."

The doctor told her the truth about the type of cancer she had, and it is was a very rare type of cancer called a small cell muscle tissue Ewing sarcoma. "This type of cancer is mostly found in very young children. Most do not survive because by the time we find the cancer it has metastasized and the survival rates are very low." Then she said to the doctor, "What about my cancer? Has it metastasized?" He said, "As best I can tell it is local and we can treat it with chemotherapy and radiation. If the tumor responds the way it should, you might be able to beat this thing." The next question was how the disease lived in her body undetected for thirty-two years. He said, "One common activity for adults attacked by this type of cancer relates to an injury." We both knew the injury in the kitchen was probably what started the process. I shared all of the dates and times of the incident and the ups and down she had been through since the fall. The doctor felt it was the event that triggered the cancer cells to start growth and had caused all of the damage. He said he was sorry and he knew this was terrible news and that she needed to take some time to think about what she wanted to do next.

My wife asked the doctor to give us a few minutes alone. He excused himself and said, "Take as long as you need."

When the doctor stepped out of the room, she looked at me and said, "I know he was being kind. This is serious," and she put on a game face like nothing I had ever witnessed before. She said, "I want to live, and I am going to fight with every ounce of strength I have in my body to survive. God put us together for a reason, and now I think I know why. I have to do this for my children, you, and me."

She said, "I have watched you over the years do things that are impossible. I have witnessed you go to a special place inside your heart that only real champions get to visit. I have watched you reach for things no one else could see, and before we knew it, right before our eyes, it happened. Watching you do things on a ball court, in school, in business, and in life has at time left me speechless. You have given me, and the thousands that have watched you, hope and a spirit that nothing is impossible if you just keep going."

She took my hand and placed it over her heart. She covered my hand with her hand as if to form a seal. She said, "I need something from you that we will talk about in a few minutes. The thing I need most right now is for you to show me how to go to that place I have never been. I have to get to your special place where your courage lives and where you have *no fear*, or I may not survive this battle. Please help me."

All I wanted to do was place my head on her chest and cry. I could feel Soul on his knees praying. He prayed, "Please God, please give me the strength to help her find the strength to fight. God, I think I know now why you sent me to him. You sent me to him so I could find her. I can see clearly now. She is about to take cancer treatment to a new level to help the millions of people to come after her. I can see her path and the plight of her journey, but I cannot see the end. I know what he needs to give to her and what I need to give to him and what you need to give to us all."

She needed that look and expression on my face she had seen many times when I was in the heat of battle and refused to quit. I told her I would help her keep hope and the spirit to walk through hell and back to survive. "I will give you all of my strength to find the courage to keep reaching for the next level. We will never give up on us. I thought our love was at its all-time highest point, but now I know I was wrong. The highest point of our love is still to come. We will climb to the top of Love Mountain together hand in hand, heart-to-heart, and soul-to-soul."

Since the day we met in the hospital, she had collected clippings from the local paper containing a verse and a cartoon that just read "Love Is." As she pressed my hand deeper into her chest, she said, "Now I know what love really is." She closed her eyes and said she could feel my strength entering her heart every time my heart beat. She asked me to close my eyes, and I did. Again, it was one of those moments for me where time stood still. I could feel Soul giving her every ounce of compassion and spiritual love he could pull from heaven. Then she opened her eyes and said, "It is time for us to fight the monster that lives inside me. As long as I have you by my side, I will have no fear—I will not quit, and I will fulfill my destiny."

Fifty-One

When I looked into her eyes, I knew she had prepared herself for this moment. She said, "I need you to promise me four things:

Her Needs

"First, you can never leave me alone while I am in treatment.

"Second, I want you to find all possible treatments for this type of cancer. I will go where they exist in the world if they cannot come to me. Always keep options to turn to if the current treatments are not working.

"Third, I need the heart of a lion I know you have inside of you to help me through this. If you have tears, get them out of your system now because after this day I never want to see you cry until this is over.

"Fourth, I am sick not dead; continue to treat me as your wife. Who knows, maybe in a couple of years we can travel to New York City on New Year's Eve to Time Square. I always wanted to watch the ball drop in person."

My Promise to Her

I placed her hands into my hands and promised:

"First, I will be there for you at all times.

"Second, I will take on the devil if necessary to find you a cure. If it is out there in the universe, I will go get it and bring it back to you.

"Third will be my biggest challenge because you know I love you so much and I feel your pain. I will be strong for you. I will be your anchor when you need the motivation to go on.

"Fourth, I promised you many years ago, 'From this point on we are one.' You really want New York in January? Consider it a date, and put it on the calendar."

She just put her arms around me and said she could not even imagine going through this with any other person on the face of the earth.

She pressed the button and requested the doctor to come back into the examining room. She told him she did not want to die. She told the doctor about our children and me. Then she said, "I think you can now see why I want to live." She told the doctor I would be her strength and he could share everything about her condition with me at all times. Then she said to set up the treatment schedule and that she wanted to get started right away. She did not want to take the chance the cancer would spread.

The doctor left the room and returns a few minutes later with his partner. He introduced her and told us they would both follow the case and would be available at all times. I could tell my wife's determination and strength touched them deeply and she was instantly a high priority.

I told the doctors what I had promised my wife about becoming an understudy and staying on top of the latest treatments available anywhere in the world. The partner referenced me to the medical library at the University of Louisville and the University of Kentucky. She provided contacts at M.D. Anderson, Mayo Clinic, and the Cleveland Clinic. I thanked her for her help. Then I asked if she had any medical contacts in Asia, Europe, Africa, or South America. I said, "This cancer does not limit itself to any boundaries." She said she did not have any of that information. I told her, "The world is our stage, and I plan to find it all. I will sell everything we own to save her life or even give up my life to save hers. My dad has over one-thousand acres of rich farmland, and he has assured me he will sell it all to save this girl's life." I think from the look on the doctor's faces, they clearly understood my wife was not in this alone. Her family would do and provide anything they needed to save her life.

My employer had manufacturing sites by this time on every continent on earth and offered to take us anywhere we needed to go for life-saving treatments. The team I work with told me to take off work as much as I needed and that they would cover for me. They knew I would do the same for them at the drop of a hat. My plant engineering manager called me into his office and told me I had his full support, along with the rest of the staff.

By the time the community heard the news, we were well into the treatments. The amount of cards and letters sent to my wife and our family was incredible. Her name was entered on prayer lists in most major city throughout the world.

We started the radiation treatment the first week of July and were finished in three weeks. She wanted to be okay for our daughter's birthday, which is July 30.

The tumor started to shrink after the second week of treatment. It was responding exactly the way the doctor thought it would respond. Every trip produced better results, and by the time this round of treatments ended, we were flying high with excitement. She was in no pain and felt good. The radiation treatments did not affect her physically, and she suffered none of the side effects. She was excited to celebrate our daughter's eleventh birthday. It was an awesome day. I can still remember the smile on her face every time she looked at her children.

When we were with the children we did everything we could to be positive and upbeat. We were confident things were going to turn out great. This was the first time in our family's long medical history any member of the family was diagnosed with cancer.

Fifty-Two

Time for the Next Treatments

The week following the birthday party, it was time to change gears and get mentally prepared for a new round of chemotherapy. We both knew this time it would have side effects we could not hide from the children or the family.

I called the whole family together and told them what was about to happen. I explained any temporary change in appearance they would witness once the treatment started.

I told them about my promises to my wife and that I would need help with my children to keep them safe. My next to oldest brother's wife stood up and said they would go to the ends of the earth to help my wife survive this battle. She would make sure my children had a loving supportive home. She said, "Go do what you do best and give her all the love and support you can find; we will do the rest."

My wife called her friend, who was also her beautician. She asks her to cut her hair a little shorter than normal. My wife had had long, brownish-red hair ever since she was a child. Once the children got used to that length, she decided she wanted it shorter before she started the treatment. There was a 95 percent chance it would come out once the treatments started.

Our next goal was to have the treatment completed before our son's birthday, which is October 12.

The chemotherapy was difficult to handle and could not be administered as an outpatient. We spent four days a week over the next two months in the hospital. By the time it ended, she was doing okay and could not wait for her hair to grow back.

By then, all of the nurses at the hospital knew who she was and stopped by her room to visit her while I was at work each day. The nurses and hospital staff who worked on the cancer floor had one of the most difficult jobs on earth. Most of them never wanted to get too emotionally involved with their patients. In those days, over ninety percent of the patients they treated never made it. When someone like my wife came along that was doing incredibly well, it renewed the nurses' faith. It encouraged them to continue the mission and to continue to do what they loved most in the world.

I will never forget the last night we spent in the hospital. All of my wife's treatments were scheduled for when I returned from work each day to the hospital. I held her hand during every treatment. I talked to her about what was going on at home and assured her the children were doing fine. It seemed to make the treatment bearable. We had finished the last treatment, and she was ready to rest for a while. Just before she went to sleep, one of the nurses she had grown very close to came to visit her. She talked to her about things that were personal between my wife and me, so I knew my wife must have trusted her.

The nurse was sad, and we could tell she had been crying before she came to visit. My wife took her hand and asked what was wrong. She said she was caring for a patient who was giving up on her treatments and wanted to go home to die. She said the reason she wanted to quit was her family had given up and had stopped supporting her in her quest to survive. "I had the chaplain and her minister visit her and offer some encouragement. Both did and were unable to convince her to continue. It is difficult for me to handle because she had an excellent chance of surviving if she finished her treatments. She has no chance if she quits now."

I could tell from the look on my wife's face that she would love to trade places with this woman. All she had to do was finish her treatment, go home, and spend the rest of her life with our children and me. My wife started to dose off. Then, unexpectedly, she opens her eyes looked at me, smiled and said, "This woman needs a great halftime speech, and you are the best. Go talk to her while I rest." She closed her eyes and went sound to sleep before I could respond.

The room was silent. I looked at the nurse and she looked back at me. I said, "Nurse, I have no experience talking to people who have decided to die. I have spent all of my time and prayers on the woman laying here beside me who wants to live more than anyone I know." The nurse said she understood and that most people could not even think of a word to tell someone who has made such a choice.

Then, again, the room was silent as the nurse gently took my wife's hand. She said, you sure do have a special way about you with people who want to live. She lifted my wife's blanket and covered up her shivering body. This often happened immediately following the treatments. The nurse said she did not even know my name. "But your wife has told me a lot about you. You have a God-given ability to help people who have lost hope find hope again. You are exactly what this woman needs, and your wife knew it."

I told the nurse the only reason I would talk to the woman was because my wife asked me to. The nurse just smiled and said, "Let's go. I will show you her room." The nurse took me to the women's room and introduced us. She excused herself, and I found myself eyeball to eyeball with a woman willing to throw in the towel and die. On the other hand, she could live if she finished the cancer treatment. It was very difficult for me to look at the woman. Soul tried to convince me she needed help and I needed to quit feeling sorry for myself and help this woman. I told Soul I would be happy to help if he would help my wife. Soul never said another word. At first I felt angry with the woman, and then the more I thought about her situation, my emotions changed to pity.

I spent the next hour listening to the woman explain how her family had given up on her. She just wanted to go home and die. She talked about her home, her last vacation, and her financial situation, which was in very good shape. When she thought about how hard she had worked in her life to obtain her assets, she seem to be getting mad. Then she said she had obtained a million-dollar life insurance policy just before she got sick. She said her husband was the sole benefactor once she was gone. Once she had run out of words and blamed God for all of her misery, the room grew silent. The woman just stared at me as I stared back at her.

I think she was waiting for me to say something inspirational so she could argue with me on or invite me to leave her room.

I just said, "Wow; you sure know what you want in life. I sure wish I could be as sure about my life as you are yours. You get to go home tomorrow from the hospital with only a little pain to deal with until it's time. You can tell your loved ones goodbye and make sure your life insurance is up to date so your husband will have a little nest egg to keep the family going once you are gone. Why, you even get to plan your own funeral, and then you get to die. Sounds to me you got it all covered. Good luck to you."

As I reached for the door handle, I heard the woman start to cry. She said, with the tone of voice of a desperate person, "Please sir, please do not leave me now. Please help me!" I pulled my hand from the door and walked back over to the woman's bed. She put out her left hand and took my right hand. Through the tears, she said she did not really want to die; she wanted to live. I told her, "I am good about talking to people who want to live but had nothing for you when you said you wanted to give up and die." She let go of my hand, pressed her hands together, and closed her eyes as if she were trying to pray. She said, "Tell me about living. What makes life so special for you?" I spent the next forty-five minutes telling the woman about my family. We talked about my wife and children and how precious life is to all of us. I talked about God's plan for all of us if we do everything we can on earth not to ever give up. I said, "God said to me: sometimes you will face danger and find yourself in harm's way."

I could tell my words had touched her heart. From that point, her life decisions were in her hands and she needed to spend a little time in reflection.

I finished up by telling the woman I needed to get back to my wife's room. I hoped she would make the best decision for her and her alone. She said, "I just did," and she reached for the call button, which I noticed, was already lit up. She asked me if she could hug me, and I said sure. I wished her good luck and left her room. As I walked out into the hallway, which was near the floor nurse's station, I notice a large number of nurses standing near the call station intercom. Some appeared to be drying some tears, which happened often on the third floor of the hospital. As I walked by the station, they all acted as if they were having a meeting, but I knew they had listened to the entire conversation.

We had a great team taking care of my wife. Many had grown emotionally close. I returned to my wife's room as she was recovering from her treatment. She told me she was thirsty, and I poured her a glass of water. Before she took a drink, she looked at me and said, "Well?" I told her I did talk to the woman and I thought it went well but I did not know what she was going to decide.

A couple of hours later, the head nurse asked my wife if we could go visit the woman I had spoken to earlier. My wife was out of the bed in a flash and was ready to go. This was normal for her—to be ready to roam the halls following her treatments. The nurses called it the chemotherapy victory dance. They often joined in when a patient had finished a round of treatment and was ready to go home and hope for the best.

The nurse told us the woman had called her husband right after I left her room. She told him she was about to have a treatment. If he or the rest of her family did not like it, they could all get out of her life and out of her house. She planned to outlive them all and "Oh, by the way, I just canceled my life insurance policy." When she hung up the phone, the nurses on the floor let out a scream of joy.

She wanted to personally thank me for my encouragement and for giving her hope. The woman was taking the treatments when we entered the room. She was sporting a big smile on her face. She said the treatment was not hurting, and my wife said, "She is not hopeless; she is crazy." We all laughed, and I could tell it was the first time both patients had laughed in a long time. She said she could not believe it took a perfect stranger to get her to do what she had wanted to do for several months. She said she would complete her treatments and she would be forever grateful for my visit. She said she would like to speak to my wife alone if I did not care. I said sure. I wished her good luck and left the room. Soul said, "Nice job." I said, Thanks Soul; it feels good, and now why don't you do your job and help my wife." Soul never responded.

My wife came out about ten minutes later, said, "Nice job coach," and gave me a long hug. Then, on cue, she said, "I am hungry. Let us go wake up the cook."

When we got back to the room, the nurse had laid me out a pillow and a blanket. She told me I needed to get to sleep and that she would wake me in a couple of hours so I would be able to make it to work on time. She turned out the light and said, "Goodnight coach." The last thing I remember seeing was the smile on my wife's face.

The birthday party for our son could not have come at a better time. It turns out to be a big party for him and a wonderful celebration for the entire family.

It was on a Saturday, and we had spent the day before at the doctor's office doing tests to determine the next round of treatments. The doctor came into the examination room and sat down beside us. I could not tell at first if he had good news or bad news. When going through cancer treatment it is always day to day, and you never know what to expect; you just spend all of your time hoping for good news.

He started out by saying he believed in miracles and knew for a fact they do exist. In his line of work, he had seen things happen for the best that made absolutely no medical sense at all but they did happen. He did not fully understand the results of the test, but at that time, he could not find one sign of cancer in her system. He sent us home and said he would see us back in one month. On the way home, my wife told me to continue my mission to learn everything I could about her cancer. Then she changed gears and said she wanted to enjoy the moment.

The month went by fast, and we were back in the office going through the same regiment of testing. The news was the same, and now we were two months cancer free. We both understood we would need to go through this same test every month for the next ten months. If the test stayed negative of cancer cells, she would have made it to her first milestone. Then she would be tested yearly for the next five years.

She had grown back all of her hair and was physically in better shape than I had seen her in many years. Our perspective on life and the things important to the both of us prior to the cancer had completely changed. Before cancer, we focused on material things like how much money was in our savings account and taking care of our social responsibilities. After cancer, we cared more about the little things and spending more time with our family. For ten consecutive negative tests, we would trade our new home, new vehicles, and all of the promotions I had ever received at work.

She had an incredible smile and a happy outlook on life. She did everything she could to stay active. I had missed her smile most during this entire ordeal. Folks, the smile was back and we were ready to move on with life one month at a time until we were sure the cancer had been defeated.

We celebrated her birthday on November 8th with a cake and thirty-three candles. The cake was signed by about one hundred fifty of her family members and closest friends. They all brought a covered dish and spent several hours just talking about past birthdays and funny stories about the family. I think it was her best birthday. When everyone had left and we were all alone, she talked to the children about past birthdays and events that led up to that point. Later that night, I went outside after everyone was sound to sleep. My thoughts drifted to what she had talked about earlier, and I begin to pray. I prayed for that moment we had that day at the General Butler basketball court, right after she had learned I had spent all of our money to save the herd. I asked God to take every material possession we had in the world in exchange for her life—to please return us to that moment to let us share the emotions we felt and the love we shared with one another. In all of the love stories he had created since he created heaven and earth, none could have equaled the love we felt between the two of us. I went in the house, lay down beside my wife, and held her next to my heart the rest of the night.

Thanksgiving took on an entirely new meaning for her family and it brought back a memory, my family would never forget. Traditionally, my dad would bless the meal with a special prayer he had recited for as long as I could remember. When it was time, the house grew silent and you could hear a pin drop anywhere in the house. He would place his left elbow on the corner of the table and his hand on his forehead. He would lean his head forward and give the blessing. This Thanksgiving, he surprised us all when he stood up. We all started to stand out of respect, but he said we should continue to sit. My dad was very close to my wife and loved her as much as he did his daughters. He looked out across the table without saying a word. He took off his eyeglasses, folded them up, and placed them in front of him on the table. Each time he started to speak, he would stop and take a deep breath. He was trying to speak, but the words would not come out. After a long pause, I said, "Amen." I looked around the room and said I was thankful to have this family by my side. Then I turned to my brother and asked him, "What are you most thankful for, and you cannot repeat what I said." My family spent the next several minutes, one at a time, opening their hearts and talking about what they were thankful for on this special day. It was my best Thanksgiving.

The December trip to Louisville provided the same positive test results. It was time to rejoice. It was time to get ready for Christmas. My wife loved Christmas more than anybody I had ever met.

I notice she and my daughter were making more candy than normal. I ask her about it and could tell from the smile on my daughter's face it was a surprise and I needed to stop asking questions. I just said to her, "Too many cooks in the kitchen is not a good thing, and I need to leave." They both pushed me away from the stove and out of the kitchen. I heard the two of them laughing and talking for the next several hours.

On Christmas morning, she was up earlier than normal. I started a fire in the fireplace to warm up the house. I went into the living room and sat down on my recliner next to the Christmas tree. I just sat back, enjoyed the time watching her work, and thanked God for the moment. She was hurrying around and wanted everything perfect for when our children would enter the room in about two hours. Once she was finished, she pulled a quilt from the rack that had been a gift from her grandmother the year before.

The quilt was a wedding ring designed quilt, and it had sections of cloth from six generations, including all of our family. She knew the names and the relationships by heart for each section. She snuggled up in my arms, pulled the quilt up around us, and went sound to sleep.

We all have memories of what we consider to be our best Christmas. When I was growing up, on Christmas morning, I can remember my parents telling us to go back to bed numerous times. You can only imagine the celebrations around our house with fourteen children stampeding to the living room and gathering around the Christmas tree in anticipation of what Santa had brought for us. I am not sure how my parents did it year after year, but we always seem to get what we wanted on Christmas day.

I heard our children coming down the hall at exactly five-thirty on the nose. It was always hard to tell from the sleepiness in their eyes how long they had actually been awake.

When their mother heard the pitter-patter of little running feet coming down the hall, she was up on her feet and down on all fours ready to greet the children. She would always take the two of them in her arms and say, "Look, Santa came while you were sleeping. Look at what he brought for my favorite two people in the world."

We would all sit down on the closest piece of furniture, and she would pass out the presents. We would all open our presents at the same time from Santa, and once we finished, it was time for the one special gift not under the tree.

Our budget had been stretched about as far as it could go due to the medical expenses. I had told my wife she could skip me this year—she was the gift I wanted. She knew full well I would not skip her, as I had taken on some extra work to make sure this was the best Christmas ever for my family. This was the point where I would take over and hand each person their present from me and they would open it one at a time. When I finished, I sat back down in my recliner and enjoyed the smiles on my family's faces.

This Christmas something was a little different, as all three suddenly disappeared to one of the back bedrooms. I heard them moving something around and then my wife telling the children to climb under the bed and scoot it out from underneath. The three of them came back into the living room caring two gifts. My children handed me the first gift, and my daughter could not hold the secret back any longer. She said, "You remember the candy Mom and I were making?" I said, "Yes I do. I think I gained ten pounds just from the sweet smells coming from the kitchen for days." She said they had sold the candy to the neighbors and bought me a special gift because they loved me so much. I wanted to cry and just take all three of them into my arms and never let them go, but instead I just maintained a look of complete surprise on my face. The gift was a beautiful, soft, leather-lined briefcase that I had looked at numerous times down at the Hodge's Jewelry store in Carrollton. I knew the price, and it had been something I had wanted for several years but could never afford. The briefcase cost well over a hundred dollars. It was then I realized how hard they worked to earn the money to buy me a gift. I thanked my children for the gift and gave a special hug for my daughter for her extra effort.

It is sometimes difficult to figure out where some people get that special gift that just makes you feel good all over to just be in their presence. When you are a parent and it is your children who have the unique gift, it's impossible to describe your feelings for them in words. From the time my children were very young, they took much more pleasure in giving someone a gift they really wanted than they did receiving a gift for themselves. It was not difficult at all for me to figure out where they found that unique trait. All I had to do was look at the woman standing beside me dancing from one foot to the other; she could not wait another second to hand me the gift she had picked out for me.

My wife handed me the second gift. I could tell it was the most precious gift she had ever given me. She could not wait for me to open it, so she and the children joined in unwrapping it for me. I could see right away it was something in a big frame. When I turned it over, it was my degree from the University of Cincinnati, which I had earned earlier in the year. I missed the graduation ceremony to do something much more important.

Before I could say thank you, she started telling me the story about how she got the document. I do not remember the title of the song playing in the background, but it described the birth of a child and a new beginning for all of us with a little faith and a big dream. I know she had picked out the song, but I do not think she had any idea it was going to be playing at that moment.

With astonishing pride, she went on with her story. She said she had called the dean. "I explained to him that during the graduation ceremony in the spring you were holding my hand while I was taking chemotherapy. I told the dean I was sorry you missed the ceremony and that I had tried to get me to leave me and attend graduation. I told him you said nothing was more important to you and that leaving me was out of the question. I told the dean how much this would mean to me to give you this gift for Christmas." At that second, I knew even if my heart had turned to stone I still could not have controlled the stream of tears flowing down my face. I quickly use my shirt to wipe away the tears before she could tell I was getting so emotional. She sat straight up and got even closer to the huddle we formed around the gift. She said, "The dean asked me for our address and then for directions to our house. He brought the degree down to me a few weeks ago and gave it to me personally, along with a receipt that said, 'Paid in full.' The kids and I took it down to my friend in Carrollton, and her and her husband did the framing. Your daughter picked the matting material colors and your son picked the frame. I did the rest."

My wife was a very intelligent woman and she knew everything could change with one bad test. Nevertheless, today, none of that existed in our world. She just wanted to see me smile and her children happy. She wanted to feel the love and appreciation for what this day means to all Christians throughout the world. Her excitement did not end there. She placed our son in one of my arms, and she climbed up in the other. She motioned for our daughter to lay her head in her lap. I was hoping my old recliner would hold us all without collapsing to the floor. She handed me the framed document and asked me to read the writing on the certificate. I told her it was her gift to me and that she should read it to all of us. She cleared her throat and began to read each word aloud. As she read the words, I noticed her gently stroking our daughter's face and neck. My daughter closed her eyes, and I could tell she was thanking God for this moment and prayed the certificate would never run out of words.

Some of the words she said in a voice and with an expression that made us all laugh. Some of the words hit home and brought back memories that made her a little emotional. She paused for a few minutes to tell the children about the blizzard of 1978. She said, "The storm seemed to come out of nowhere. When your father left the house to travel to the University of Cincinnati for a five-hour class, the wind was blowing and it was freezing cold, but the skies were clear. The class was an accelerated five-hour class and would not end until midnight.

"Just before dark, a weather bulletin flashed across the television screen, warning people to stay where they were and not get out on the highways. Within a few hours, the area would experience record snowfall. The high winds would cause the snow to drift in low-lying areas up to fifteen feet deep." She said she knew I only had enough money in my pocket to cover the parking fee at school and enough gas in the car to make it to school and back home. My only choice was to come home. She said all she could do was look out the living room window and watch the snow pile up on the highway in front of our house. Within a few hours, the snow in front of the house was at least six feet deep and she knew I would never make it in a car. She said she never felt so alone in her life. All she could do was continue praying, watching the weather on the television, and praying the power stayed on.

She said she was looking out the window at about 10 PM and she could hear the wind blowing. "I could not help but think about what your father must be going through. I cannot logically explain what happened next, but I heard a voice say, 'Turn on the lights, light up the night.'" I did not say a word because this was her story and I did not want to interfere, but I knew it was Soul who woke her up. He was doing what he had done for me so many times in the past.

She said she started running through the house, and within a few minutes she had turned on every single light in the house. As she turned on the switch in our bedroom, she happens to notice the container that stored our Christmas decorations from year to year. She opened the container and removed the set of multicolored lights designed to blink and flash. She said she placed the string of lights across the railing on the front porch. When she plugged them into the outlet, they seemed to flash a sequence she had never seen before and they were so bright she had to look away to keep from hurting her eyes. By the time she finished securing the lights to the rails, her hand and face felt like they were frozen. She paused for a few seconds and then continued with her story.

She pointed to a string the lights on our tree and told the children, "It was those lights that lit up the night and helped your father find his way home." My daughter asked her what happened to the car. She said I had hit a big snowdrift on Sharon Road about five miles from the house and the car overheated and stopped running and would not restart. My son interrupted and said, "Hey Mom, that is your name." She just looked at him, smiled, and said he was right. "Your father had to make a choice to stay in the car and freeze to death or attempt to walk the rest of the way. The wind was still blowing and visibility was bad, but as he reached the top of each of the five hills between the car and our house, he could see the lights, and he knew he was going the right direction.

"At exactly midnight, I heard a knock at the door. When I opened the door, it was your father, and I immediately jumped up into his arms.

"Until he knocked on the door, it was her lowest moment, and words could never describe how scared I was. Even though Christmas had already passed and it was late January, it was my best Christmas ever."

She finally got back to reading the document. She told the children she should be the one receiving the degree because she went to over half of the classes and did over half of my homework. My daughter gave me a look out of the corner of her eye and said, "Dad, you cheated? I cannot believe it." Then I cleared the air when I told the children the professors knew who she was and why she was there.

Once she finished reading the document, I just sat and held her as long and as tenderly as I could. I topped all my compassion and love off with about a hundred I love yous.

I know my children had no idea what this gift really meant to my wife. They were more excited about her special gift to me than the gifts they had waiting for them under the Christmas tree. When my wife handed me the framed diploma, it brought closure for her. It lifted a burden she had carried around with her from the time we were married. She could stop blaming herself for falling in love with a man ready to move on to college and get my degree the traditional way. I had told her numerous times over the years that this was our journey, and what an incredible one it was. I would not have changed a thing. The rest of our day was filled with special moments as we traveled from family home to family home. I guess by now you have figured out this was the best Christmas ever.

Fifty-Three

Time to Refocus

The holidays were over and it was time to refocus our attention on my wife's health. She was still doing well and was in splendid shape. One of the things we learned from the previous experience was the importance of proper nutrition. We continued to follow our diet during the holiday as we felt it might be contributing to her incredible test results. The January test results were encouraging and had the best numbers yet. The doctors were using the best technology available to perform the test and she was cancer free.

On our way home from the hospital, she asked me what I was thinking. I told her I was very excited about her progress and I thought we had done everything the right way. She said she was also excited but still very worried. I told her the struggle was not a sprint; it was a marathon that would take us five years to win. We needed to continue to thank God for the progress we had made so far. For now, we would continue to enjoy excellent test results, but we knew what the next steps were if the numbers turned up something. I told her in the meantime she needed to focus on our son, who had started in kindergarten and our daughter who was picking up where my wife left off in the academic world.

We had great results so far and I never took those moments for granted. The day she learned she had cancer, we started living our life one day at a time. We never looked back and we never looked past the next day. My wife was an incredible person, but until she faced cancer, I did not know how much courage she had.

It was time to celebrate the results, and I knew exactly what she would like to do.

She loved the Ice Capades. We had seen every show within one-hundred miles of Ghent, Kentucky. When each show started, she went to a place in her mind that put her in the center of the action on the ice. It was easy to read what she thought when I watched the expressions on her face and the movement of her body as the skaters floated across the ice. She was out there floating along with the skaters with just as much grace as the skaters on the ice were displaying. When they danced to her favorite love song, it was obvious she was dancing with me.

She had told me many times when the children were old enough she wanted them to see the show in person and enjoy the moment with them.

I had held back one of her Christmas gifts, and I could not think of a better time to share it with her. I told her I had a surprise for her. "Please open the glove compartment and remove the envelope." She was excited as I told her to open it up. When she opened the card and saw four front row tickets to the upcoming Ice Capades inside, she was ecstatic. She said I should not have and she knew we could not afford such an expensive trip. I told her I had purchased the tickets for her before Christmas and was waiting for the right time to give them to her. By the time we made it home from Louisville, she already had the entire trip planned.

The big day came, and when we arrived at the stadium, I noticed we had some people sitting in front of us. I notified the usher and told him I had purchased front-row seats and that was what I expected to have. He told me the seats in front of us were for special guests of the skaters. I told him I wanted to speak to the event manager. He told me it would be impossible. I said okay and started to move my chair out onto the ice. My wife deserved a front row seat and she was going to get one. He called for security, and when I explained to the security officer why I had purchased the seats for my wife, he looked at my tickets and told the usher to move the folks in front of us to the side.

The show started with a bang. The first skater jumped out of the stands and started skating as fast as he could around the outside perimeter of the ice. The music was loud and speeded up as the skater gained more speed. Then a second male skater jumps out of the stands and started chasing the first skater. At first, we thought it was a chase, and then we realized it was a race. The music was perfectly choreographed as the drama was about to unfold. The chase was a comedy skit designed to make us laugh and duck when they made turns directly in front of us, and they cut ice from the surface with their skates. On the fourth trip around, a piece of ice about the size of a hockey puck landed in my wife's lap. I do not think that part was supposed to happen, but it was still funny. The looks on my wife and children's faces were priceless, and I will never forget it as long as I live. Our son told her they needed to duck down beside the chair the next time they raced in his direction.

The first two skaters were incredible athletes and did skating moves and maneuvers across the ice causing the sold out crowd to stand and applaud. Our daughter told her mother she wanted to skate like those two guys someday. Her mother responded, "So do I," as they both laugh.

The show was incredible, and at one point, my wife looked over at me with a huge smile from ear to ear and said "Thank you." At the end of the show, the skater who caused the ice to end up in my wife's lap skated over to her. He went down on one knee, handed her a rose, and said he was sorry. She said, "Don't worry this is my best day!" The skater gave her a hug, pointed to the crowd that it was okay, and they applauded him for his kind jester. My son, as you know by now, is usually a bit restless, but five minutes into the show, he was mesmerized with what he was watching on the ice. I do not think he moved a muscle or said a word during the entire show. When it was over, he looked up at his mother and said, "Wow Mom, this was fun-fun-fun. Can we come back tomorrow?" She picked him up, gave him a big hug, and said, "Thank your father. He is the one who made my dream come true."

The show ended late, and I could tell my family was tired. I made them a temporary bed in the back seat of the car. My wife bundled up with the children in the back seat. By the time I made it to the interstate from the arena, they were all three sound asleep. Soul made it a point to tell me, "These are the good times, and this was a great day. You need to remember this day because you will not get it back." I told Soul he did not know what he was talking about and that I had already planned the next big entertainment event for my family. The night was silent as we made the long trip home; apparently, Soul got the message.

I carried my children into the house one at a time and safely tucked them into bed. I went back out to the car to wake up my wife. I touched her face as I had done many times in the past. She opened her eyes and asked me to get in the back seat with her. I climbed in and put the cover over us both. She sat for a long time just looking at the stars above without saying a word. After about an hour, she snuggled up close to me. She asked me if I remembered all of those nights we had spent in the car when we were dating. She told me our most special moments together were those nights we just snuggled up in each other's arms. Many nights she fell sound asleep and they were the most peaceful times of her life.

I held her the rest of the night, and in the early morning, we went into the house just in time for me to get ready for work.

A couple of weeks later, it was time for our monthly trip to the doctor in Louisville. The doctor asked her how she was feeling, and she told him she had felt a little more tired than normal for the past week or so. He told her it was normal to feel this way and he was sure she was okay. He said, "All of you tests look good, and your progress is right on schedule." He asked her about her trip to the Ice Capades and said he heard she got a rose from the star skater. I promised her I did not say a word and asked the doctor how he knew about us being there.

Her young oncologist opened the door and walked in the room. She said, "Your husband did not blab a word. I told the doctor about you being there and accepting a rose from my husband. I will have you know, I am a little jealous."

My wife was confused. She told the doctor her husband was very talented and she felt he was the best skater on the ice. The doctor said, "He should be good for the amount of money we have spent on his training." We all laughed and spent the next few minutes talking about the performance. She told her oncologist how much it meant to her for my family to be there. The young doctor said, "I knew you had a great time, as I was sitting two rows behind you." The doctor and my wife spent the next few minutes talking about how gorgeous our daughter is and how well behaved our son was during the show.

Before leaving the room, the doctor asked my wife what she was going to see next. She told him *The King and I* with Yul Brenner at the Taft Theater in Cincinnati, Ohio. "This time it will be a date with me and my man, and I cannot wait."

It was difficult to read what she was thinking about as we made our way back to Ghent. I asked her about being a little more fatigued than normal, and she said the doctor did some extra tests but that he was sure it was normal. She asked me for the first time in several months if I had continued to look for information and was staying up on the latest treatments available for her if the cancer was to return. I said yes, and then she looked at me for an answer for her fatigue. She wanted to know if it was a normal symptom for cancer patients. I told her it was but that we should listen to her doctor and wait for the test results. She continued to ask questions about my research. She wanted to know what I had found and how many options she had left.

I asked her why she was so inquisitive; she knew I would never stop doing my research. She said she had thought that if she had the cancer, her children could get the same thing and would have to go through the same thing she was going through. I reminded her about the marathon and taking one day at a time. She said, "You are right, and I cannot wait for our date night."

The play in Cincinnati was on a Saturday night, and her dad had taken her to the fanciest dress shop in the city the day before. He purchased her a new dress, new shoes, and a very eloquent, stylish purse. She was bubbling with excitement when I got home from work, but she did not want me to see the dress or shoes until she was ready for the night out. She had spent several hours at the salon with her mother getting a perm and her nails done the day of the play. She had arranged with her sister to babysit the children for the night, so he decided to take the children out to her sister's house on Easter Day Road. She would get dressed there, and I should pick her up there.

When I walked into the house, I could not take my eyes off her. She was more beautiful than I had ever seen her. I felt like we were going to the high school prom, and that, as I did then, I had the prettiest date at the dance. We walk to the car, and as I opened her door. I told her she was going to be the most eloquent princess at the ball. Before she stepped inside the car, I showed her the corsage I would place on her wrist when we arrived at the theater.

As I walked back around the car to get in, I felt like a teenager picking her up for the first time.

Fifty-Four

A Majestic Performance

It took about 90 minutes for us to make the trip up I-71 to Cincinnati. When we drove down the stretch of highway labeled "the cut of the hill" in Kentucky, we could see downtown Cincinnati, Ohio. The city is beautiful, with a wonderful history of people with great leadership and pride. This night the lights seemed to shine even brighter than I remembered in the past. We crossed the Brent Spence Bridge, which spans the Ohio River. Riverfront Stadium, home of the Cincinnati Reds baseball team and the Cincinnati Bengals professional football team, was lit up. The route to the theater was lined with amazing structures that seemed to tell the history of its people and the hope for a bright future. The facades of each building displayed amazing architecture, which symbolized the creations of the city's finest designers.

When I pulled my car up to the entrance to the theater, a man stepped up to the car, opened my wife's door first, and offered her his hand, which she took and stepped out of the car. The man on my side of the car handed me a ticket and told me he would park my car. Once the performance was over, he would return my car. The inside of the theater was constructed of the highest quality wood finishes, magnificent columns and chandeliers made of crystal. The Brazilian Cherry trim around the entire theater was hand carved. The lighting in the balcony was dim, so it was difficult to see the "who's who" crowd gracing our presence. It seemed every two minutes a couple would arrive in a very fancy car or private limousine with drivers at their command. The orchestra was playing soft music and setting the mood for the audience. A host met us at the door, checked our tickets, and escorted us to our seats. This was the next big surprise for my wife. I had again purchased front-row seats. When we arrived at our seats, the host asked my wife about her dress. She said it was the most beautiful dress she had seen all night. My wife smiled and thanked the host. My wife said she could not believe the fantastic location of our seats. She couldn't imagine being this close to the star of the play, Yul Brenner, on the stage. Once we sat down, I began reading the biography of the main actor. He was a great example of a person with a big idea who made it come true. He followed his passion and paid his dues over time to achieve his dream. As I looked around the theater, I felt a little out of place. I guess after reading his biography, I started thinking about where I had come from and questioning if I really belonged in this crowd. I was a long way from Locust Creek, Kentucky. When I looked at my date and thought of her struggles, I made my mind up right there that I would never allow those feeling of not being good enough to cross my mind ever again, and I never have. I feel just as comfortable talking to the CEO of a major company as I would the President of the United States.

A rumor started circulating through the crowd that the first curtain call was delayed due to the late arrival of the royal couple. Most people in the crowd had the same thought: could the royal couple be Princesses Diana and Prince Charles of Wales? We knew they were traveling the world celebrating their five-year wedding anniversary. They finally announced the opening act would be delayed for about twenty minutes. If it was the royal couple attending the performance, we never saw them. I can tell you this: the four security guards stationed at the steps of the balcony were armed and dangerous. Our host finally told us it was the royal couple and the main actor was the princess's best friend.

The principal actor put on the show of his life. The most thrilling moment for my wife was when he leaned down on one knee directly in front of her and delivered his lines as if he were speaking them directly to her. He could tell that he had touched her deeply, as a tear drops from her eye. When he touched her face to gently dry her eyes, the audience rose to their feet in appreciation with a five-minute ovation. I will promise you this; she knew every single line of the entire play and could have taken the place of any actor on the set at any time. He received five curtain calls and one major hug from me, now, his biggest fan. Soul told me to let the man go, as I was embarrassing him. The fifth ovation was for the royal couple sitting directly above our heads in the center of the balcony. When they stood up, the cameras started flashing from every angle. Everything about the night was incredible, from my glamorous date to the spectacular pageantry surrounding us everywhere we went.

On the way home from Cincinnati, my wife took my hand and told me she felt like a princess and that I was her prince. She soon fell sound to sleep on my shoulder as she often did. As I drove down Interstate 71 and just before exit 44 to Carrollton, Soul woke up. He warned me to remember this night; I would never get it back. I told him, "Thank you very much, but I have already planned our next date night."

Fifty-Five

The Call

The weekend was over, and it was time to come back down to earth and get back to work. The plant manager called a meeting with the rest of the Managers in his office. He announced, "As of this morning at 9:00 AM Paris, France time, our company is now owned by the French, and things would be changing." He said he would pray for the best for all of us and that our company would likely never be the same. Overnight, we went from being a small American company to a company twenty times the size.

Weeks later, the plant manager accepted a position with another company for a five times his current salary. He would immediately relocate to Western Kentucky and assume his new role. It was a sad day for those who had grown to know and love this fine man. He was a great leader and had that special skill to balance priorities between business and family.

The company promoted one of the production managers to the position of plant manager, and a few months after she took over, several of the managers decided to leave the company. She had nothing to do with the mass exit; it was mostly people who felt they should have received the promotion.

Over the years, the two of us had our disagreements about how my group should be supportive of her group. I knew if I did not adapt to her way of thinking very quickly, I would face termination. Within a few weeks, she told me she did not feel I was qualified to lead the maintenance and engineering team in the direction she wanted the company to go. She did offer me an opportunity to interview and make a recommendation on the selection of the next plant engineering manager. Once the selection was over, I knew my dream was also over. What I realized was that I cared more about my associates, the plant, and our company than I did about the position. It did not take the new person long to realize I was his number one supporter and I had the skills to help him achieve his dreams. He made sure our upper management knew my capabilities to organize, coach, and achieve our goals. He provided me opportunities to reach out and help many of our other thirty-three sites across the country.

Fifty-Six

LONGEST DAY

It started just like most of our trips to the doctor's office in Louisville. She grew silent, and I could tell something was weighing on her mind. Before we got out of the car at the doctor's office, she said she needed to tell me something. My heart dropped to the bottom of my chest. She said when she got out of the bathtub she felt a small pain in her leg. While she was getting dressed for the trip, she felt the same pain again. I asked her if the pain was in the same area as before. I checked her leg and could not see a bump or any sign of a tumor. She was relieved to hear that, but it was the first time she had felt any pain in over five months. She explains to the doctor what had happened, and he did a very thorough examination. He felt nothing and had no answer for what she had felt. He orders additional tests including an ultrasound and X-rays. He said it would take a couple of days to have the results of the test.

The doctor called me on Thursday and told me the test was negative but the blood count was a little low. He asked me to bring her back down the next day for a retake on the blood test. The test showed the same result and the doctor decided she needed to check into the hospital and have a blood transfusion on Saturday.

Following the transfusion, she felt good and had all of her energy back. However, the open question was what caused the blood issues in the first place. Within a few days, her energy was gone and she was even more anemic than before. Even though they could not find the cancer, all of the signs were there that it was back.

The decision was to take another round of chemotherapy. This time around, things would be much different from the last time. The last time we knew where the tumor was and we could see an improvement. This time they were treating the entire body, and all we could do was wait and pray the treatment would put the cancer back into remission. We spent a month in the hospital and took the treatments every single day.

The blood test continued to show a low blood count, and the transfusions continued. It was as if the cancer were hiding and moving all the time. It seemed to know that if we could find it, we would be ready to send it back into remission. By now, it was August 1st and we were down to our last treatment option. The other treatments worked for a few months at a time, but the cancer was back and had metastasized. She told me she was tired and she wanted to do this experimental treatment for her children and all of the children with this type of cancer that up to this time had no hope. She said it might help her survive a little while longer, but most of all it would provide the doctors and researchers enough information to use it in the future for others facing this type of cancer.

It was time to travel to the hospital. She hugged and kissed her children and told them she loved them and that that would never change. She somehow found the strength through the pain to smile and said what she needed to say to help them smile with her.

I have written many stories about the incredible power a mother has for her children. At times, she can display the courage of a warrior in battle when her children are in danger. In an instant, she can cure their pain with her gentle touch or calm then with just the right words. I think what I watched this mother do at that moment was the most incredible and loving thing I will likely ever see. She brought them into her world and she shared with them not only her love and beautiful words, but also her vision for their future. She helped them understand it is okay to be sad and happy and to move through life without any blame or guilt.

She asked me to invite her aunt to the hospital, who lived down the street from the hospital in downtown Louisville. She wanted to confess her sins and clear her path to heaven.

She told me the past year was the worst year of her life and the absolute best. She felt the two of us had forced 20 years of marriage into the past year. She said if the treatment worked, we would slow down and take our time the next twenty. She said it was okay for me to cry now because she wanted to take the moment with her wherever she ended up. She said, "My body hurts, but my heart is so full of love and peace. You have kept all of your promises, and I know I would have never made it this far without your courage and the strength you gave to me. Most of all, it was your love that got me through the days and nights. My children gave me strength to fight one more day, and my family was there to support my mission."

I wanted so bad to tell her to remove any negative thoughts of this treatment not working from her head. I knew what she needed was a miracle, and I offered everything I had to Soul and God to grant her a miracle. It was no longer up to the doctors or me or the nurses who had given her everything they had.

It was time for the treatment to start, and she asked her head nurse to clear out the room. She whispered to the head nurse who had become her best friend that she wanted one more moment with her husband. They had grown very close, and I think the nurse knew what was about to happen. Once the room cleared, she asked me to stand at the end of the bed and said, "Coach, let me see your eyeballs." I stood at the end of the bed. She removed the eye patch from her eyes and told me to put up some of my fingers on each hand. The fourth treatment had caused her to lose her eyesight, and we were praying this treatment would help restore her vision. I put up three fingers on one hand and two on the other. She smiled when she saw the combination 32 (32 was my number in all the sports I played in high school). She told me how many fingers I had up on each hand. She said she prayed to God to grant her one wish. It was to be able to see her husband and children from heaven if it were his will and her time on earth would soon end. She said, "I did not clear the room for that wish. I know

God will come through for me. I did it for us." She was smiling, and I saw a glow about her that had been missing for a year. She said, "Come closer. I need you to show me your smile, which I have missed for the past several months. If this treatment does not work out, I want you to find your smile as quick as you can. I want you to go on with your life, and for God's sake, take care of my children."

Then she said, "Hold my hands and touch my heart, so I can feel our love pumping through my veins. Tell me those three words you know I want to hear." Maybe it was Soul—but that likely it was a bigger mission than he was capable of at the time—God gave me the strength to honor her last request. "I love you!"

Fifty-Seven

WE NEVER GAVE UP

I had lots of trouble dealing with the pain of losing my wife. Things just happened too fast. It was difficult for me to handle all of the emotions pouring out day and night. So many little things we had taken for granted for such a long time were suddenly very significant. At home, everywhere I turned and everything I touched and smelled brought back memories of my wife. Every room in our house brought back memories I never wanted to forget.

For the first month after the funeral, the only real peace of mind was during the day at work. Everything seemed normal there, and the co-workers did not talk about my life outside the plant.

I spent most of my time at home trying to understand why God had allowed this to happen. I talked to Soul every night until well after midnight about how unfair this was and how he did nothing to help me stop it. I started reading the Bible every night and every day. I went to church every Sunday morning and sometimes at night. I listened and did my best to analyze every word the minister said during every sermon. I remember thinking, "I am an engineer, and there is always an answer to everything if we dig deep enough and think about it long enough." I took notes, went home, and tried to build a better understanding of every verse in the Bible in an effort to find the answer.

I fixed my children supper every night and made sure they had their homework finished. They would watch TV until bedtime while I spent the entire time on my porch swing or in my bedroom with the door closed reading the Bible. In the six weeks following the funeral, I read every word in the text three times. I just could not let it go; I had to know why my wife was gone, and the answer was supposed to be in this book. Each time I finished, I asked Soul to explain it to me because I could not find the answer. Soul would just say, "Keep reading, you will finally get it."

I asked my dad to share his wisdom and guidance. He told me he had never seen anything this bad happen to a person. He told me I had to stay the course and continue calling on my undying faith in God. "Let us face it son, without your faith you have nothing left. I know emotionally you are at rock bottom. Who wouldn't be at this point? If you can just hang on a little while longer, I know God will show you a new path and will open new doors for you to enter."

Every night I would take a break around 8:00 to check on my children and remind them it was about bedtime. One night I went to my son's room and he was not there. He was now seven years old. I went on down the hall to my daughter's room and found him cuddled up in her arms. He was crying and I could tell he was shaking in her arms. My daughter was trying to calm his fears, and instead of being a sister, she was trying to play the role of a mother. When my daughter saw me at the door, she started to cry.

I went in the room, stood by the bed, and told them I was so sorry, but I could not change what happened. "I am doing everything I can to find the answer so at least I can explain it to you. However, I cannot stop it and I cannot reset time to change it."

After a few minutes, my daughter opened her big brown eyes and, with tears flowing down her face, she asked me if I loved her and her brother. Those few words melted every emotion I had left in my body. I realized right there and then I had hurt and neglected the last two people on the face of the earth who deserved to be treated that way. I would have taken a bullet right through my heart for them both.

My strength was gone; I just fell to my knees and pulled them both closer than I had since the night I had to tell them their mother had gone to live in heaven.

My daughter had all of her mother's wisdom and said that was not the reason her brother was crying. I asked her why he was crying. She said, "He was afraid you will go to heaven too and we will be left all alone." Through those big brown eyes, the crocodile tears started to fall again. What she said next was the lowest point of my life.

She said, "Up to now you have been my only hero in the eleven years I have been on the earth. Dad, we understand mom is gone and she is not coming back. But we need you back. Do you realize we are hungry? You forgot to make our dinner tonight. When we heard you crying in your room, we were afraid to tell you. I could have fixed our dinner, but I was afraid.

"Daddy, we know you are sad, but we are too. We lost our mommy and now we are scared to death we are losing our dad."

It was then something inside of me kicked in that had been missing since the first day I learned about my wife's cancer. I could no longer be a husband grieving for my wife; I needed to be a father to my children. Maybe this was the path my dad had spoken to me about just a few days earlier when he said, "When God opens the door for you to step through, you needed to be ready."

I could feel my heart start the healing process. My tears were gone, my strength was back, and it was time for me to raise up my head and take care of my children and myself.

I looked at my daughter in a way she had not seen me look at her in over a year. I saw a smile appear that had been hiding behind the pain she was afraid to let out. She looked at both sides of my face and saw my face. Then she said, "Okay Dad, my hero is back in town. If you help us, I know we can help you." I dried their tears, said, "Dad's home, and this is where we belong. This is where I plan to stay. You children are the most important people in my life, and I love you both with all of my heart. I will work every day to show you both how much I love you starting right now." Soul whispered in my ear, "Now you got it."

I told my son and daughter to get dressed and that we were going out to supper. While driving to the restaurant, the car was silent. Then, out of nowhere, my son said, "Hey Dad, I love you, my sister, and my mom in heaven." He said it was all he could think of right now. I said it was plenty for such a little boy to have on his mind all at once. I told him, "I will love you, your sister, and your mommy in heaven forever. I am planning for that to be a very long, long, long, time." I looked through the rearview mirror and I think it was the first smile I saw seen on his face for a long, long, time.

We went to their favorite restaurant and ordered dinner to go. It was an early fall day, and it was still daylight outside. I drove them to General Butler State Park, and on my way to our favorite picnic table up on top of Park Hill, I pulled into the parking lot at the golf course.

I intentionally parked my car in the exact same parking space we parked in the day my daughter was born. My son wanted to know if we were going golfing.

I told them the story about their mother playing golf to speed up our daughter being born. It was not because she was tired of being pregnant; it was because she could not wait any longer to see how beautiful her daughter was. There was a short pause and my son said, "Well that was probably her first disappointment." A moment of laughter broke out between the three of us that seemed too last for ten minutes. When things died down, I had to put on the parent hat and told him to tell her he was sorry.

"You do know your sister won the prettiest baby in the county during the fall festival two consecutive years." Then I said that it was another story for another day.

It was the first time we had talked about her since her death. The message I was sending to my children was that it was okay to talk about her. I never wanted them to forget even one of the special moments they had with their mother.

While we were eating dinner, I told them about all of the things that had happened over the past year. I wanted them to understand that their mother did it all for us and she was willing to go to the ends of the earth to find a cure for her cancer. Now it is time for the three of us to show the world we were going to be okay—to show their mother in heaven who I know would keep an eye on us from heaven. We have to show her every day that we got this and we are going to be okay. It was starting to get, dark and I knew it would be well past the children's bedtime by the time we got home. I think they were too excited to show any signs of slowing down. They wanted this night to last forever, and so did I.

On our way out of the park, we had to drive past the lookout. The lookout, located at the highest point on top of General Butler State Park, is not only a historic site, it is also a place of great natural beauty. The Civilian Conservation Corps constructed the Butler Park pavilion in 1859. The men gathered the large rocks needed to complete the pavilion from every small community in the county. The stones were layered one on top of the other to form a stair design that seems to lead you straight into heaven. The climb to the top was about fifty feet. The entire formation was approximately 75 feet wide and formed a circle to match the crown of the hill overlooking Carrollton and the Ohio River valley.

Following her passing, I had spent many nights alone sitting at the top of the pavilion looking out over the town I love so much. For many of us in the community, is a place we go to be next to God—the place where we go to mourn our losses, cry when life just gets too complicated, and rejoice when life's light returns and the lights shine back on our path leading us to our next journey. In the valley below, I could trace the path of our journey together. To the left was the cemetery where she was laid to rest; the inscription on the marker simply read "When two hearts beat as one." Across the street was the hospital where it all started. Across town was our high school, where our love for one another was nurtured and strengthened each day. Just a few weeks before this visit with my children, I remember asking God for forgiveness for whatever I had done for him to construct this never-ending wall around my life. I told him I could not see over the top. "I cannot run around it to the other side, and I have not the strength left to climb over it. God please, help carry me to the place I need to be so I can see even a glimpse of my next journey."

This particular night the moon was full and the stars were shining brighter than normal. My daughter asked me if we could stop for a few minutes and enjoy the sights. I told her we could. In the back of my mind, I knew from the top of the lookout they could clearly see the I.O.O.F. cemetery below, where their mother was laid to rest just a short time ago. When we left the car, I wanted to protect them, so I told them it was getting late and we would climb to the top another day.

I noticed a young couple sitting on the top holding hands and enjoying the peace and quiet on such a beautiful night. When we made it up to the first layer of stones, the couple got up and moved as if something was telling them this was our moment. I apologized for disturbing them and said we would just be there for a few minutes. They quickly got in their car and left us all alone on the pavilion.

A woman appeared from behind a large rock at the base of the pavilion. She walked up to me. In a very soft, nurturing tone of voice, she said, "Enjoy the moment. God bless you and your children." I took a closer look to see if I recognized her, but as quickly as she appeared she was gone. I think it was the same woman or possibly an angel, who sat beside me in church when God came to visit Soul and me the first time when we were young.

My children had made it up to the next level, and I told them to stop and wait for me. It became very quiet, and all I could hear was the laughter and the discussion between my children about where the North Star was located. My son asked his sister how big the big dipper was, how little the little dipper was, and where the North Star was located up there, as he pointed to the sky. The darkness of the night and the twinkling of the stars made it very easy for her to find all three answers to his questions.

Soul spoke to me in a very low voice. He told me God was with us tonight. He said, "He is not here to visit me. He is here to hold your hand this night and give you the glimpse you ask for." I wanted to believe Soul, I really did. However, I was furious at Soul, and I felt he had done nothing to convince God to help my wife beat the cancer. I did everything I could to convince Soul to help me find a cure for her. I told him I would walk to the ends of the earth if he would show me where to look. I would walk through the deserts barefoot on the hottest days, climb the tallest mountains in a blizzard, and swim to the deepest parts of the sea to save her life. At one very low point when she was in pain, I asked him to persuade God to take my life and leave my wife with my son and daughter. I could not believe he would not help me after everything we had been through together for over thirty years. Soul would not listen to me, and at one very low point, I asked him to leave me and said I never wanted to hear from him again.

I knew we could not go on this way without breaking our original promise to God. I just could not figure out in my mind how to stop the merry-go-round of emotions filling my heart and mind twenty-four seven. Finally, I realized the time had come and this was the night for the healing and forgiveness to begin. I told Soul I was sorry and that I never meant all of the bad things I said to him. I asked him to forgive me. Soul said he never left my side and neither did God. "We were both here to catch you every time you fell down, my friend. You earned it. A couple of hours ago you asked God to help you heal your broken heart. You could not do it alone. He helped you lay down the Bible and go check on your children. You have done all you can do alone, and from this point on, we will help you get through this part of your life. I think you have fought as hard as any person could to protect the one you loved most in your life. Your time with her was one of the most incredible love affairs ever created in heaven. Your life together on earth was a glimpse for other people to see how special true love can be when you share your love with that one special person. In the history of the world, I could count the couples on one hand who shared the amount of love you two had together. You two were able to step past every obstacle in your path, through good times and bad times to fulfill your promise to God on the day you wed. My friend, because of her faith and conviction, there are thousands of couples who hold each other's hands late at night and confess their love for one another and pray their journey together never ends."

He flashed our entire life together in front of my eyes to help me realize it was destiny. He said, "I told me often to tell her you love her because you never knew when she would be gone. From the beginning, I told you to enjoy and celebrate the good times and the people you have in your life.

"Unfortunately, for the millions of couple in love tonight, there are also millions of husbands and wives out there in the world who take their love for granted. Sometimes the angels in heaven would like to push them together and help them realize how precious and fragile love really is." He asked me if I remembered what God said to me in the church about how sometimes you will lose your love ones and it will seem so unfair. I said yes, but I did not know he meant my wife. "He also said those who believe in him would be rewarded with a place in heaven." I said, "Yes, I remember." He said, "It may not help you right now, but your wife is in heaven and she is okay."

"God made this night for your family. If you believe in God and heaven above, as I know you do, take your children's hands and walk with them to the top of this pavilion. God is waiting for you there." I trusted Soul and knew he would never do anything to hurt me and certainly not my children. I walked up to where my son and daughter were standing and told them to take my hands. "I will walk beside you to the top so we can get a better look at the stars and the scenery below."

The area around us was pitch black, but the stars and moon lit up our path as if it were a spotlight on a stage. The three of us walked together hand in hand and stood at the top of the lookout. I never felt so at peace as I did at that moment. It felt like we were the only three people awake in the world. It was hard to tell if our feet were still touching the rock ledge at the edge of the stone structure. The clear sky and the stars seemed to go on to infinity. My son kept pointing at the sky and changed the expression on his face a hundred times as he watched the stars twinkle in sequence. My daughter said it looked like they were telling us a story straight from heaven's gates. I said I thought they were happy tonight and maybe everything is okay in the universe. My son said, "I know I am happy," and my daughter squeezed my hand a little firmer. They both moved very close to me, as if they were holding on to something they had been missing for a long time. I was not sure who was trying to protect whom the most.

All three of in unison raised our heads to the sky above as if guided by Soul's eyes to look past the stars, and down the path straight into heaven. My mom and dad had often spoken of the magic of the night sky; maybe they had seen what we are about to witness.

I am not sure what my children saw. I felt it was between them and their mother. I knew she is in heaven and that if it had to end when it did, I could not think of a better place to end up. What I saw was peaceful and tranquil, and I too will never share with humankind what I felt and saw. It is not because I do not want to but because I lack the words to describe the beauty of what sits on the other side of heaven's gates leading to paradise. I saw her face and an image of her that brought back so many happy memories; she was smiling, and all of her pain was gone. I sensed I could not touch her, but I wanted to hold her so much. In her own way, she was releasing me to move forward and continue my life, as she intended to go on with hers in heaven. She was letting me know her heart was at peace and even though things did not turn out the way we wanted, we fought together to the end. "You kept your promise to me that read, 'Until death do we part.'" I wanted to hold her so bad just one more time, but I knew I could never cross the line. I knew this moment was from God to confirm in my mind she was in heaven and she was just as beautiful as she was the day we met at the altar and said "I do."

After a few minutes, the sky started to turn darker and the images started to fade. I just said aloud, "Thank you God and Soul for this moment," and to my wife in heaven I said, one last time, "I love you."

I told my children to sit down on the top step so I could regain my balance. I picked the two of them up and just sat there holding them and allowing them to hold me. Finally, when it was getting too dark to safely exit the pavilion, I said to them, let's go home; it has been an incredible night.

When we got home, I told them to get dressed for bed and that I would be in to tuck each of them into bed in a few minutes. I went into my son's room first, and for the first time in over a year, I rocked my son to sleep and carried him to his bed. He rolled over and said, "I love you Dad. Please do not every leave me." I said, "You got it Son. I am here to stay." I could see the worry and the fear of losing me drain from his little body.

When I entered my daughter's room, she gave me a big hug and said, "Thanks for this night." I told her I would fix what was broken. From that point on, things were going to be different around there without her mother here to help us. I shared with her what her mother said about all of us before she went on to heaven. "She said we would all be sad: the three of us on earth and her in heaven. She said she was going to do what every God took her up there to do. Nevertheless, she would keep one eye on her mission and the other on us. She said you were better at making homemade candy than she was. She wanted you to be the little girl you are and do the things beautiful little girls do. She said your brother would be lost for a while because she had been with him since the day he was born." She was a stay at home mom and they spent every day for the past six years together doing what moms and sons do.

My daughter asks a question I knew she had wanted to ask for several months. She was just waiting for the right time. I could tell she was searching deep for just the right words, but they never came. She lowered her head as if she were asking the lord to help her say what she needed to say. Finally, she said, "What about you Dad? What are you going to do?" It was a great question, and if she had asked me earlier, I would have fallen apart. This time I was determined to show strength and be a father and the hero I had been to her from the time she was born. I took her hand and said with a very soft voice, "I am going to be okay." I think I felt the burdens lift from her shoulders that she had been carrying around for some time.

My babies' lives turned upside down in the flash of an eye when their mom got sick. They had been left full of uncertainties no child should have to worry about. For the first time in a long time, I saw those beautiful big brown eyes shine, and a smile on her face warmed my heart. I said I was going to take better care of her and her brother. I told her we were going to stay in our home and we were going to be a family. It would always be different without their mother, but we were going to, from that night on, live our lives one day at a time.

Together we would deal with whatever came our way. I had spent every waking moment over the past fourteen months helping my wife fight off cancer. It was fourteen months I missed with my son and daughter that we would never get back. I knew I could never bring her back. I had no answers as to why this happened to her. I had spent months looking for the answers and I finally realized that there are no earthly answers to the question.

My family could go on for the rest of our lives with our heads hung low and angry at the world; no one would blame us, and in fact some may have encouraged us to feel this way.

"I do believe with all of my heart that there is a God and there is a heaven. I know God needed your mother to handle something important. It will take me some time to sort out all the stuff we have been through over the past months. I may have a few setbacks from time to time. Nevertheless, I promise you, the three of us will together to make things better for each other every day from this point on. This is the first step, and we still will have many sad times to deal with." I told her this was enough for one night and she needed to get a good night's sleep. She said she would and she would do her part to help. She asked me to sit beside her just the way I had done when she was a little girl. She took her favorite book from the shelf and asked me to read it to her just the way I had read to her when she was young. When she made her request for me to read to her, it reminded me of something she would say to me when she thought she might be in a little trouble. When she did something wrong, which was rare, she would say, "Now Dad, when you were little and I was big, this is how I would handle the situation." I tucked her in, and within five minutes, she was sound to sleep.

I will never forget the emotions I felt and the healing taking place between the three of us and my guardian angel that night. When I left her room and stepped into the hallway, I walked slowly down the common areas in my house. Every step I took, I saw pictures, wall hangings, and mementoes that symbolized our lives together placed there by my wife to remind us of where we started, where we were, and, at the end of the hall, where we were headed. I realized I had the power to stop it all by placing the final sign that simply said "The End." On the other hand, I could run to my room, dig through my dresser, and pull out a large picture given to me by my mother-in-law that featured my children and me. On the back of the picture I wrote a message that stated, "Today I must make my first decision about the future of my family. That decision is to continue the journey called life and allow God to decide when it is time to put up the sign signifying it is now the end." I placed the picture in a new frame and hung it at the beginning of a new path down the lane of life.

After several months of making adjustments, we had made it through my son's birthday in October and Thanksgiving. Christmas was only four weeks away, and I knew this would be our most difficult time to handle as a family. Just the year before, we had enjoyed our best Christmas together ever as a family, and she was the reason why. A number of thoughts raced through my mind about how to get through this time. Maybe it was asking too much of my children to stay at home and get by the best we could. My wife's mom and dad told me I could bring the children out to their house and celebrate the day with them. We had several similar offers, but my daughter made the decision easy for me to make.

She came in my room one night and told me she wanted to have Christmas at our house just as we had done Christmas ever since she was born. She wanted the house decorated; she wants the three of us to go out in the woods and cut down a Christmas tree and decorate it just as we had done in the past. She wanted to go Christmas shopping on Christmas Eve and eat the candy she planned to make before we went to bed. "I want to wake up from my own bed and go down the hall to my brother's room and wake him up. I want this because I think it is the way my mom would want it to be. Many things have changed, and who knows, this could be the last Christmas with just the four of us: you, me, my brother, and our mom's memory."

We did it her way, and it was a day full of emotions, both sad and happy. Many stories were shared between the three of us about past Christmases and memories of their mother. I told the children we would do something special to seal the memory of this Christmas forever in time. We started a tradition that we continued for every Christmas since that last Christmas we had together as a family. I told the children I would continue the tradition as long as I could and they could join in when they could. During the Christmas holidays, primarily on Christmas Eve or Christmas Day, we took her a gift to her gravesite and we placed it on her grave. We also brought a gift for each one of us to open with her and share a special prayer that included the changes we had experienced during the previous years. On this Christmas, I decided to make a wreath from the vines in our yard and line it with the evergreens from the blue spruce we had planted the year we moved into the house. This tradition has kept the memory of her and her love for Christmas alive in spirit and in our hearts.

Fifty-Eight

UNEXPECTED EMOTIONS

We were trying our best to set good priorities on our time and continue the healing process we so very much needed. My daughter asked if we could attend a local tap and ballet presentation. One of her best friends was performing and she wanted to be there for her. Dance was something she and her mother enjoyed doing together. I remembered her first dance recital and watching her mother bob and weave with every step she took.

At intermission, she told me she was glad we came and that the dancers were all excellent. She went through the rest of the program brochure with me to highlight the dance routines being performed by some of the top-level dancers at the recital. She said she could not wait for the next curtain call. Her friend was in the group of dancers coming up next in the program. To be very honest, I was not a connoisseur of the fine arts and really did not know one dance step from another. My son knew only two things about dancing. He did not like it, and he was bored and ready to leave after the first dance. I did appreciate the athleticism of the performers and knew convincing your body to bend and stretch in the positions needed to perform the dance took a lot of time and practice.

The final performer of the night was a young artist. She was extremely talented and had a very impressive resume, which highlighted her amateur career. She was destined for greatness and clearly a future star on the big stage someday. I noticed that while she was performing, the people sitting around me looked like scouts and could not stop taking notes and pointing at every incredible jump and turn she made. They were obviously from places like New York, Chicago, and Los Angeles. When she finished her dance, the audience jumped to their feet with a long standing ovation. She received several curtain calls and, I must say, deserved them all. During the last call, something strange happened. When I look back on it, I think Soul was sending me a message. For no apparent reason, the dancer paused for a second and made direct eye contact with me. Both of us froze in time for a split second, which Soul had done to me in the past. On the other hand, she may have been acknowledging one of the scouts sitting directly in front of me. I just thought, *What a strange sequence of events.* Once the performance was over, we exited the auditorium, and I never saw the girl or her family. My son said, "Thank God it finally ended; let's go get something to eat.

Fifty-Nine

CHANGE IS IN THE AIR TONIGHT

In late March, Soul reminded me it was time to get back out into the community and call to order the first tee ball meeting of the year. I told him I planned to coach my son and daughter's teams and nothing else. I said I had paid my dues, and it was time for me to step down and let someone else run the league. He said, "But you have not fulfilled your purpose. You are not doing this for your children or me—not even for God or all the other angels who held your hand the past two years. I told you from the first day you called the first meeting this mission had a particular purpose and it would have nothing to do with tee ball. When your season ends, you will experience another life-changing moment."

I said, "Soul, you are confusing me about this mission. The league has never been in better shape. I cannot imagine how much more you think my heart can handle. I completed my calling with the terminally ill children as a counselor at the Kentucky Easter Seals cancer camp. Later, I cleared the path for my baseball player to do it his way. I was with my wife and held her hand to the end. I have been a good father to my children to help heal their pain from the loss of their mother. At this point in my life, I feel so blessed to have my children and family doing as well as we are doing. Right now, I need to schedule my time wisely and not lose sight of my responsibilities.

Soul, you know firsthand how much time it takes each day to actually operate the league."

Soul paused for several minutes. I think he was seeking guidance from his boss before he responded to my decision to step down and not be on the board of directors. I went outside to shoot some hoops and relax before it was time to put my children to bed.

Soul finally said, "God said to you, 'Losses are a test of your faith in yourself and in me. You will forever be tested on earth and in heaven. I promise the sadness you feel in your heart today because of a loss will heal as time moves on. It gets better when you can accept the fact you are still here and your life is not defined by one single event or point in time. It is a journey that has no defined boundaries or limits. This means you will always have within yourself what it takes to turn losses into victories if you choose.' He is giving you a chance to turn your loss into a victory. There is a lonely heart out their tonight who needs your help and can help you turn your loss into a victory if you just give this a chance. She will help you complete your mission and you will help her complete hers. He said you had to do it for her. If you go to the meeting, she will come."

I said rather disgusted, "Soul, please do not play matchmaker for me. I know what true love feels like, and I will make my own choices." He said, "But if you quit now, her life will never be the same and she will not fulfill her destiny. You will be cheating yourself and your children out of a fantastic journey. You will not fulfill your plan on earth; it is right at your fingertips, and all you need to do is reach out and take a chance. He said you have to trust me. The night at the pavilion was the beginning of your healing process. It was also a test to see if you could do all the things you promised your children. You have done it all and more. I cannot tell you anymore. My job is to show you the path; it is up to you to walk down it.

"God told you that sometimes things would happen that make no sense at the time. Well, this makes no sense to you right now. However, it will, I promise if you do the one thing I am asking you to do one more year. My friend, you are standing on the one-yard line. Time is running out, and all you need to do is reach the ball out across the goal line and victory is yours."

Finally, I was ready to take my last shot of the night. I told Soul, "If this ball goes through the hoop without touching the net, I will do it. If it does not, I am not going to help run the league. When he said, "Deal," which I knew he was not allowed to do, it became apparent he was up to something. It goes without saying that by the time Soul finished stretching out the net, two basketballs would have fit through without touching it. Soul looked down at me from the top of the backboard and said, "Nice shot."

"The free throw also never hit the rim the night I came back to you from Vietnam. I am not sure what your fiancée saw or heard, but it never touched the rim." I said, "Let it go Soul." He quickly responded in a very assertive tone of voice, "I am your guardian angel, and it is my job to let it go when it is time to let it go and not a second before."

Then he said to me in a solemn, soft tone of voice, "This will be a calling like none other you have experienced. It will be your biggest challenge, and your life is about to change yet again. It will not be easy or simple, but out of all the people God could choose for this mission, he chose you." I said, "Please Soul, do not take any more of my loved ones out of my life. I cannot handle another loss like the last one." He just smiled and said, "We are not taking anyone out of your life, but just the opposite, and you will enjoy the journey if you can be patient."

I rushed home from work to fix supper for my children. The meeting was at 7:30, and I had just enough time to drop them off at my sister-in-law's house on Boone Road.

I met my friend Tooter outside the meeting place and we talked about a few rule changes we would like to see made. We had spent the last five years making changes, and we had just come off our best year.

I was standing beside my car, and a young woman pulled up and parked between Tooter's car and mine. She stepped out of her car and our eyes made contact. I could tell she wanted to drop her head and walk on by, but it was impossible for her to do. She said, "Thanks for saving me a parking place." I had not felt those feelings for many years, but I knew what it meant. I was just curious if I was getting a little help from my guardian angel.

I asked Tooter to give me a minute so I could close my trunk on my car. I walked behind my car and told Soul if he caused these feelings to happen I was going to kick his butt when we got home. I am not sure how one would go about kicking their guardian angels butt, but I knew I had time to figure it out latter. He said, "We only show you the path and turn on the lights. What you see and feel in your heart is completely up to you."

She went on inside the American Legion Hall. I asked Tooter who she was, and he told me what he knew about her. Tooter had grown to be the person in Carrollton who knew everybody, and everybody knew him. He said she had divorced several years ago and had two children. She was in a relationship, but it had ended and she was focusing on raising her two children. Word on the street was she did not intend to date another man for the next several years. She was a member of the Carrollton Christian church. I began thinking about what Soul had said about my mission and how if I went, she would come. Soul knew I knew exactly what true love felt like; it was not something I had to think about for very long.

Tooter said, "She is way out of your league, son. Do not even think about her; get her out of your head right now." I said, "I thought you told me those same words standing in the hall just before we went into biology class several years ago. I told you then I was going to marry her someday and I did. How about two for two my friend; I am going to marry her someday as well."

He laughed aloud and said "No way, not again, this could not happen two times in one lifetime. It is impossible, improbable, and this time I will bet you my last dollar it will not happen. If you ask this girl out on a date, prepare yourself for your first big disappointment back out in the real world of single women and heartbreak. You two people grew up on opposite ends of the bridge of life. She is a city girl and will always be a city girl the way you will always be a country boy. She is a good fairy with the majestic wand used to change a frog into a prince, and you, my friend, are not a prince. You would wrestle a bear taking honey from a bees nest. It will not work—never has, never will, my friend." He swung his head from shoulder to shoulder and placed his finger on his right hand, symbolizing "No, no, no."

I just smiled and said, "Better get your money out son." He could not hold back. He said, "This girl is a model; she is athletic and was a member of one of the top high school dance teams in the state. Her ex-husband was the son of one of the most thoughtful and kind men to have ever lived in Carroll County. He was a state representative, and I can assure you she was the prettiest woman at every social and political public event he ever attended. She has spent most of her adult life giving back to the community in supporting numerous charities and fund raising events for those in need. Just last year, she helped raise enough money to give a terminally ill young man his last wish. She and her friends actually went to the airport in Louisville and presented the young man with gifts and well wishes from the entire county. She has friends way up in state government she can reach out to and get things done. She has socialized with governor's wives and fills her dance card at the governor's ball each year. She will never dance with you! No! No! No! Never! I will tell you again my friend, leave this one alone; she is out of your league." Soul always did like Tooter but was growing a little perturbed with him. He said quickly, "Do not judge a book by its cover. You make your own choices."

It was time to go inside the meeting hall and begin the meeting. I noticed her sitting by herself in the back of the room. She never made eye contact as I walked by to take my seat in the front of the room facing the audience.

The league president called the meeting to order and stated that the floor was open for nominations for league president. The board chairperson read off the responsibilities of the next president. The president read off the list of returning officers and then opened the floor for nominations for president.

Someone nominated me right at the start and before I could decline, and a woman in the back of the room seconded the nomination. I interrupted the proceeding and thanked both for their support. I said, "All of you know my situation at home, and I think it would be a disservice to the league for me to take on the role of president. However, I am willing to be the vice-president." The president started to take a vote but then said, "Who is kidding whom. Congratulations Mr. Vice-President." I looked out into the audience and saw the same people who helped start the league. I could feel the love and compassion flowing through the hearts of each person in the audience. They missed my wife almost as much as I did.

The president said the floor was now open for president. Soul was about to jump off my shoulder trying to nominate the woman in the back of the room. He said, "You will not get this chance again; you had better go for it." I made eye contact with Tooter and gave him the sign to nominate her for president. Tooter just shook his head, smiled, and nominated her, and she accepted the nomination. Soul said, "Yes, yes! Now we are back."

The president asked if there were any other nomination before he opened the floor for a vote. Soul was growing impatient and asked, "What he is waiting for; it's time to vote. We do not need any more nominations." I said, "Down boy, procedures require him to ask this question. Please just be patient."

The president closed the nomination and asks for any discussion before taking a vote. A woman located in the back of the room stood up and ask some very direct questions about the nominee's capability to be president of the association. The organization had grown to several hundred children, and we had sixteen teams in each league. I think this woman really wanted to be president but no one had nominated her.

Soul stooped down on one knee as if he was the coach about to explain to his team the next play to run. He said to me, "Listen to this big boy." The woman asked Tooter's nominee why she felt she was capable of being president of our organization. The current president stated that it was a fair question, and since no one in the room really knew much about my nominee, he asked her to answer the question.

She told the group she had been president of several very prestigious community organizations. She was currently president of the Younger Women Club, Fair Board Chairperson, and the president of the female's version of the Jaycee's. She was on the board of directors of the local Tobacco Festival Committee, and her responsibility was managing the parade. She had recently chaired a team that raised enough money to establish a county park for our community.

Then the woman asks about her experience in running a youth baseball league, I think Soul would have had a heart attack if I had not spoken up and helped her through the question. It was the first time I would stand by her side. I told the group I would do all of the detail work and she could do the management of the association. She certainly sounded qualified, and she said she wanted to help lead the league so her son could have an enjoyable summer. I seconded the nomination. The vote was unanimous to award her the presidency of one of the largest children's summer leagues in the state. The league championship game the year before had over four thousand people in attendance. That was twice as many fans as the Little League World Series drew for its championship game.

Once the meeting was over, I moved to the back of the room to where she was sitting and welcomed her to the board. She asked if we could have a meeting the following Tuesday night to review the budget and sign-up schedules. We all agreed on the date and time to meet. As we were leaving the meeting, she put her hand out to shake mine. When I took her hand, I felt her nervousness. I could hear her heart beating in perfect rhythm with a message I could not ignore. The message was, "Please God, let this be love." I kept hearing Soul's words repeatedly in my head: "If you go to the meeting, she will come." I told her good night and that I would see her the following Tuesday night.

I went straight home, helped my children with their homework, and tucked them both into bed. My children had spent some time talking about our family, and my daughter told me she hoped I would find someone to love someday. I told them both at the time that I knew what true love felt like, and when the right person came along, I would know.

They both knew how their mother and I met and that the probability of that happening again, especially in a small town, would be astronomical. Soul told me not to be so quick about ruling the opportunity out because he had a good feeling.

After they both went to sleep, I went outside and shot hoops for several hours. I spent the time thinking about where I wanted my life to go. I was very lonely, but really had not spent much time thinking about dating. I always loved being married, and I knew it would happen in time.

I had a thousand questions in my mind, and I was going through them one by one until Soul said in a very loud and assertive voice, "Stop it, stop it! I said, stop it! You do not need to ask these questions. You already have the answer to the most important question. Man, you could spend twenty years trying to find the answers to questions you do not need to ask. I know what is on your mind, but as you told me earlier, it is time to let it go. God showed you she was in heaven doing her job just as it is supposed to be with every person who believes in him. It is time for you to travel down a different road."

I knew Soul was right, but in my mind, I felt, that if I allow another's love into my heart it meant I would have to let go of her love. He screamed back at me that I was wrong and that God would never have let this girl into my life if that would happen. "You think you have all the answers, but you are a fool." I took my basketball and threw it with all of my strength over the trees and deep into the woods surrounding my house. I broke down in tears and told Soul he was attacking my innermost area of my heart. "I gave it to her and I am not sure if I can give you or God what you want by giving it up."

Soul dropped his head and put his hand on my shoulder. He said, "You have to understand that you are no longer lost, my friend, you have been found, and you need to embrace your gift." Soul, for one of the few times in his life with me, said "I love you." He said, "I wanted you to know the day she took her last breath; I hurt just as bad as you did. I cried just as many tears and felt just as lost as you did. My father in heaven gave me the same advice as your father on earth gave to you."

I calmed down and lay down on my court and looked up at the heavens above. I located the star in the clear sky above that my wife had proclaimed one night as our star. I knew she was looking at the star from heaven as I made a wish for our star to help me find the peace in my heart I needed to move on with my life. I know how unbelievable this may sound but our star was suddenly brighter than before and it appeared to move to a new location in the sky. I saw this as a sign from her, it was time to let go and let Soul and God show me the way. I lay there on the court for a couple of hours and finally got to my feet and walked out into the woods to locate my basketball. As I walked with Soul, he said, "God, on this night, blessed you with his finest gift. You should not question it or have doubts about it. You should embrace it and enjoy the blessing. I know the most important thing you must consider is how this will affect your children's life. Please, just draw strength from your faith, draw knowledge from your experiences, and God will light up your path to follow. Remember what God said to you: 'Sometimes you will suffer grief and loneliness and ask how I could allow this to happen. The loss of a loved one is never easy to accept or understand. My only advice to you is if you truly love someone, make sure you appreciate the time you have with him or her every day. Make sure they know how much you care about them in whatever way is appropriate. For every person born on earth, there is a plan for his or her eternal life in heaven with me. The love you have in your heart and the love you share is my gift to you. It has a place and a time and a purpose on earth and in heaven.'" I said, "I remember, and it is time for me to share." Soul smiled and said, "Think you can hit one from here?" as I picked up my ball. I said if you help me, I know I can.

Even though I did not want to acknowledge it, I knew in my heart the second I took her hand, I had beaten the odds and the woman I had met three hours earlier stole my heart.

The week was passing at a snail's pace. I could not wait for Tuesday to come. I left work early to figure out exactly what I was going to wear to the meeting. I told my children I was going to a meeting and that I would be home in a couple of hours. I felt like a teenager getting ready for my first date. I got to Carrollton a half hour early and just drove around the block until it was time for the meeting. On my 56th trip around the block, I notice that only one of the parking spaces near Legion Hall was still available. Then I realized her car was not in the group. I spotted her in my rear view mirror coming down Main Street. I knew I had to drive right by the open parking space and attempt to find a space two streets over. I parked my car and sprinted two blocks to arrive just in time to open the door for her to enter Legion Hall. The meeting was business as usual. Nevertheless, for some reason, I lost focus more than in past meetings.

After the meeting, I walked her to her car. Most of the conversation was about the meeting that had just finished. She offered to give me a ride to my car, but I declined. We finally ran out of words and just stood and looked off into the distance. I could tell she had something on her mind but wanted to search for just the right words. When I said, "Well, I need to be getting home," she turned and ask me if I was going to the big dance on Saturday night. I had to confess to her that I had not been traveling in social circles and I really did not know anything about the dance.

We spent the next half hour talking about our families, and mostly our children. I told her about losing my wife the previous August and how I spent most of my time working and taking care of my children. I asked her if she planned to go to the dance, and she said yes.

I was hoping Tooter was right about her plan not to date for a couple of years. However, I also realized this young woman was an 11 on a 10-point scale in the eyes of men. She was very petite with lovely hair and a gorgeous smile. She was in very good shape physically, and I was betting she was a long-distance runner. I was preparing myself for her to let me down easy by telling me she already had a date.

She said she planned to go down to the Carrollton Inn, have dinner with her friends, and then attend the dance with them until the dance was over. I think she sensed it was time to clear the air and let me know the friends she would be meeting were all female friends.

She said she had her heart broken a few times since her divorce and the next person she dated would be her true love.

She asks me if I would come to the dance. She said, "I will promise you the first dance of the evening if you do the same for me." I immediately thought about Tooter and collecting his last dollar. I told her it would be an honor, but first I would need to find a sitter for my children. I assured her it would be my pleasure to be the first to sign her dance card Saturday night. She said she would be there at 8:00. I told her I actually preferred to meet her at the dance and to not consider this a date. She said she understood and she could not wait for the big night.

Another week passed by at the same old snail's pace. However, it gave me time to think about what Tooter had said about the difference between her and me. I knew I had the confidence and intelligence to pull this off, but what about all the other stuff he pointed out? I knew I could handle a slow dance, but what if it was a waltz, another ballroom dance, or a modern dance I could not do? People for some reason in the nineteen seventies and eighties decided they wanted to dance and dance often. We had disco, line dancing, slam dancing, street dancing, flash dancing, and many others I had never done. On my way to work one day, I noticed a sign advertising the dance as the "Spring Fling Sweet Hearts Dance."

I got up early Saturday morning and told my daughter I was going to town for a few minutes. When I returned with a bag, she asked me what I had purchased. I told her it was just a few clothes. She opened the bag, took the clothes out, and said, "Dad, it was about time you joined this decade. At least you will not look like a dork tonight—oops," she placed her hand over her mouth, "and embarrass yourself." I did not acknowledge the tonight comment she made and changed the subject. I spent the rest of the day cleaning my new special edition solid-red Pontiac Trans-Am I had bought the week before right off the showroom floor. I wanted to get a Buick, but Soul begs me to buy the sports car.

I took my children to their grandparents' house and told them they would be spending the night.

When I got to the dance, I put my tee-tops back in place in my sports car, just in case it decided to rain. I spent five minutes combing my hair and making sure I looked my best. I went to the dance, but she had not arrived, so I sat for a few minutes and was growing very nervous. I took a quick peek at my watch and realized it was only seven-o'clock. Then I realized the only people there was the team setting up the tables and decorating the dance floor. Someone finally asked if I could get a ladder and help hang some of the decorations from the ceiling. I said, "Sure, why not, it is what we are here for right?"

The music started, and I found myself sitting in a crowd of people I did not really know, but most seemed to know me. One of my friends asks me where my date was and that he would love to meet her. He said Tooter had told them all about the date and how he had played matchmaker and introduced the two of us. I told him we were going to meet later and that she had another engagement before she could attend the dance. When the old clock hit 8:15 PM and she was a no-show, I was ready to leave. I went over to visit a couple of people I knew from work and talked to them until 8:30 PM. I decided it was time for me to take my dejected heart home and help it understand I was not ready for this in my life. As I was walking out the exit door, she and her friends came in the entry door. We made eye contact, and when she realized I was leaving, I saw sadness in her face for the first time. I was almost to my car when Soul got my attention. He said something I never thought I would ever hear him say. He said, "I cannot make you stop, but for the first time in my life, I am begging you to stop, turn around, and go back in the building. Please do not give up on her; give her a chance to explain her lateness. I think you will find it was not her fault. You are one of the most fortunate people on earth to know what true love feels like. The woman you just walked past had never felt true love until last Tuesday night."

Soul convinced me to swallow my pride and go back inside the armory.

I located her table. She was sitting with her friends, and from the expressions on their faces, they were doing what friends do to console a friend.

One of her best friends saw me come in the door leading to the dance floor. She hurried over to where I was standing. She was emotional and wiped away her tears. "Please let me explain why we were late. Do not give up on her! She is a special person and you are a special guy. You two belong together whether you realize it or not. Please sit with me and hear me out."

I knew who she was, but I had not seen her since we graduated from high school together. I decided to sit beside her. She told me it was her fault they were late for the dance. They ordered their food, but the restaurant was unusualy busy due to large crowd that would be attending the dance after they ate.

"If you leave tonight, you are crazy. I have been her best friend for many years. I was there when she went through the divorce and every time she had her heart broken since that day. She has experienced the lowest level a broken heart can go and continue to beat. I know when your wife took her last breath your heart was broken to the lowest level a man's heart can break and still live." I think when she said those words, Soul could no longer hold back his tears. "I hope you can see this is destiny, and destiny is a path to travel and never question. Someone somewhere lined up the stars in the universe tonight and they belong to you and her. She called me last Tuesday night after the meeting and told me she had found true love. She said when she stepped out of the car her eyes met yours and she felt an emotion she had never felt. Her heart started racing and she could barely make it to her seat. She was not sure why it happened or what she was going to do with it, but she knew for the first time in her life what true love felt like. She felt healthy, confident, and happy for the first time in a very long time. She said she was going to pray every day and ask all of her friends to pray you felt the same about her. You do know you could have asked her to marry you last Tuesday night standing in the parking lot and she would have said yes.

"I have known you since we were little kids, and I have known her for many years. If you walk out of here tonight, it will be your biggest mistake. Please do not break her heart tonight over something that was not her fault. She has so much love in her heart to give you, and she will stand beside you and support you if you just give her a chance.

"The day your wife died, a piece of every person you two had touched in your lives from every corner of the earth died with you. My family and I cried a thousand tears that day. We reached out to you and your children with our prayers and our love.

"Only you know when it time to reopen your heart and love again. There is no timetable or chart to follow. It is all right here," she said as she placed her hand on my heart. "I will promise you this: when you are ready, even if it is years instead of days, she will be there by your side ready to accept your hand."

She smiled and said, "I know what true love feel like and looks like. For the first time in her life, she has felt true love. When it happens, you cannot stop it. It is one of Gods gifts he makes us search for, and when we find it, we know it and we do everything we can to protect it. People search for years and never find their true love. When it happens, it happens, and it becomes your best day."

I told her thanks and that she truly was a great friend. Then I said, "I got this from here." I walked over to her table, and suddenly all of her friends had something they needed to do right away. Within a few seconds, we were all alone. I took her hand, looked in her eyes, and told her I was sorry for leaving so abruptly. I said, "I am usually never like this, but when you did not show up, I was so disappointed I just needed separation—not from you, but from this space and this time. Mostly I questioned if my heart was ready for another round of hurt. I went out in the parking lot to find the answer. Fortunately, I met a good friend out there who convinced me to take a chance and come back in." Soul just smiled a big smile. "Please find it in your heart to accept my apology. It will never happen again." She said, "He must have been a great friend, and someday I want to get to know him." I said, "You will in time, I promise you." I think the both of us had found in each other what we needed to complete our recovery. We didn't say another word for ten minutes. I just kept my eyes on her eyes and she did mine. I held her hand and she gently touched my face with her soft hands.

I ask her to excuse me for a second. The leader of the band was a good friend and a previous softball associate of mine, and he knew my story. I asked him to play a song named "Lady" and make it last as long as he could. He just smiled and looks out in the crowd at her and said, "Wow. To get you here and to request this song, she must be special." I went back over to where she was standing and asked her for the next dance. She said yes, and I took her hand and led her out to the center of the dance floor. The bandleader announced, "This next dance is for one of my good friends and his date, please feel free to join them on the dance floor." When the song started, the first words were, "I am your knight in shining armor and I love you." She placed her head on my shoulder, and I think our feet left the floor. It felt like we were floating across the dance floor. Our movements were as deliberate as if we had danced this dance a thousand times. I finally opened my eyes and found we were the only couple on the dance floor. The rest were sitting, smiling, and holding hands with their loved one and watching us move so gracefully around the dance floor.

When the song ended, the bandleader said he was not sure what had just happened, but he had never sung the song as beautifully as he did that night. I never told anyone, but I knew from the first words sang it was not him singing the song. It was the same incredible voice I heard at the old wooden cross in Vietnam. It was Soul. For him to do this for me after the way I had treated him was truly amazing. It was a test, and we both passed. It was a symbol of our shared belief that sometimes things will happen we do not understand but if we keep our faith in God and heaven above, we will remain strong and resilient all the way to the pearly gates and beyond.

After all we had been through, it would have been easy to give up. However, giving up would have ended the journey God had planned for us to travel on earth and possibly in heaven. For us, giving up was never one of our options, it never crossed our minds.

The night turns into a magical night, as we danced every dance to the wee hours of the morning. As it turns out, the dance was sponsored by the Carrollton Younger Women Club, in which she was president. When the lights came up and the crowd cleared, it was time to put up the tables, clean the floor, turn off the lights, and lock the doors.

Sixty

Book II, I Took Soul to Church

Well, the first thirty years of my life with Soul were very eventful. You can only imagine what the next thirty years have been like. In the next book, we will describe our continued efforts to find a mate, raise our family, continue my career, and deal with multiple natural and manmade disasters. We suffered the first attack on our homeland since the British, and the only constant was the unrest in the Middle East. The latest world development is Russia's decision to convince territories who defected from the rule of a dictator to rejoin Russia. It is apparent that the younger generation does not understand what the rule of a dictator can be like or the fall of the Russian Empire in the seventies. We can only pray we are not moving toward World War III, fought for the same reasons as the last world war. Just the thought makes Soul very uneasy. I think he sees the suffering when those two nuclear bombs exploded.

To give you a glimpse of the next thirty years, I will fast-forward to an incredible story of survival of a little girl not supposed to live more than a few minutes after delivery.

Sixty-One

COME ON ABBY, YOU CAN DO THIS

The day started out with the thought that we would be attending an event that could only be defined as one of our happiest or possibly one of the saddest, darkest days of our lives.

We were early getting to the hospital that morning and decided to spend a few minutes in the chapel. We had so many things to pray for, it was difficult to figure out which one to bring up first. I decided to take a walk outside the hospital and wandered into the courtyard. We had transferred the family to this hospital because they appeared to be the best of the best for delivering children with Holoprosencephaly (HPE). As I walked around the perimeter of the hospital, I had a strange feeling we had made an excellent choice.

The hospital is the Medical University of South Carolina's Medical Hospital. It is a teaching hospital, and one of the staffers was doing some great work with children born with the disability my granddaughter was apparently about to be born with. As I strolled around the park connected to the hospital, I noticed the beautiful flowers in the gardens. The daffodils were as yellow as the morning sun we witnessed on our walk over to the hospital. The magnolia trees were just starting to bloom, and it looked like a great year for this particular species of flowering tree.

I remember thinking, *How could such beautiful morning lead to such a terrible day*. It turns out the day would be full of emotions, hope and a major miracle before I would step foot outside the hospital twenty hours later.

We were there to provide support to our oldest son's family; his wife was delivering twin daughters. One would be born healthy and ready to face life's challenges and opportunities. The other daughter would probably not live more than a few minutes. She had been diagnosed with HPE. Typically, with this disease, the child lives just long enough to give the father and mother a chance to say hello and goodbye. My wife and I had raised our four children together and we had indeed celebrated our share of good times.

This time I knew I would need to help my wife deal with this moment in a way we had never experienced in our twenty-plus years of marriage. This was our third youngest male child. I think it is evident that boys are always closer to their moms and daughters are closer to their fathers. I had spent the night before holding her and doing everything possible to give her the strength to make it through this day.

The delivery room doctor told us what to expect as the babies were delivered. The one we called Sydney would be born first and would be transferred to the viewing room once she was ready. The second, named Abby, would move to the room occupied by the mother and father for them to have as much time as possible with her before she passed. The son told the doctor he wanted his mom and me in a room with them. I knew he wanted his mom there because he loved her so much. He wanted me there to be a coach and to help support my wife and to help him deal with the four broken hearts that would fill the room when his daughter took her last breath. The doctor agreed, and the babies were delivered within a few minutes.

We spent about twenty minutes with Abby, and she appeared to be in pain, so her mother asked the doctor if there was anything he could do. It was her first motherly decision for her babies, and even though it was a difficult question, she did not want her child to suffer. The doctor told her he could move the baby to the neonatal room and she would be more comfortable there. He cautioned her that only mothers, fathers, and immediate grandparents could visit her, and only one at a time. Her mother agreed, and we all lined up to kiss her one more time before she was moved over to the neonatal unit. I knew I was not her biological grandfather and this would likely be my last kiss. Just as I told her I loved her, she barely opened her left eye as if she recognized my voice and wanted to get one last look.

She transferred to the unit, and the biological parents and my wife took turns visiting her. I took the role of coach in the waiting room and held my wife each time she returned from the unit. I had seen her with a broken heart, but I had never witnessed anyone hurting so badly. I knew my wife, Abby's grandmother, would have made a deal with the devil if she could have kept Abby alive.

A man dressed as a security officer approached my wife and ask why I was not taking a turn to visit the baby. She explained I was not the biological grandfather and that I would follow hospital rules. The security guard left the room, and within a few minutes, he brought me a gown and told me to follow him. My son was just leaving the room, and the security guard told him to show me how to prep to enter the neonatal room. My son said, "Gladly," and walked me through the sterilization procedure. We never saw the security officer again.

When I entered the room, Abby's private nurse greeted me and told me where to stand next to Abby. The neonatal nurse explained to me what the medical monitors connected to Abby and the rest of the critically ill children were telling her about each of the babies. She said she was due to deliver her first child in about a week and asked if I minded if she sat down at the nurses' station a few feet away. I told her how much I appreciated the chance to visit Abby and that everybody just calls me coach.

As I held Abby's little hand and started talking to her in a soft gentle voice, I noticed something was happening.... Her vital signs were improving. Her heart rate moved up to close to normal and her temperature increased to within a few degrees of where it was supposed to be. I looked at the neonatal nurse with a look of bewilderment. "Is this it for her? Is she about to die? Or is it something that needs the nurses immediate attention?" She just smiled at me and told me she had witnessed this happen on occasion, but very rarely did it happen so quickly. She said Abby was communicating with me and she liked what I was saying. I asked the nurse if she needed to get a doctor or at least my son in the room to see this.

She said she would tell my son and the baby's mother what was happening, but that I should just continue to talk to her. She said, "She recognized your voice and she knows you are the person everyone calls Coach."

I will assure you I have experienced some intense moments in my lifetime, but this was the most unusual. The nurse said, "If her vitals continue to improve over the next two hours, I will alert the medical staff. Maybe, just maybe, this one is not ready to leave us just yet." When the nurse said Abby might have a chance to live, she might as well have challenged me to climb the tallest mountain in the world. I would have attempted to scale up the steepest side of the mountain in the middle of a snowstorm to save this baby and give my wife the thing she wanted most in the world.

I felt Abby wrap her little hand around my little finger. Her fingers were so small they could not make it all the way around my finger, but I did feel the pressure. She was using all of her strength to send me a signal that her life was not going to end this day. She did not care what the doctors had to say. I asked the nurse if I could take her out of the incubator and hold her in my arms in a rocking chair next to her bed. The nurse said yes and helped me move all of the monitors and machines close to the seat. We had to keep her as warm as possible, so the nurse wrapped a warm blanket around the two of us.

The song came to my mind, and I just kept repeating the words in my head. Finally, I started singing the song to Abby. I told Abby I would stand by her, dry her eyes, and fight her battles if she would not give up. On the start of the second verse, I felt this little baby relax and open both of her eyes and look into mine for the first time. No one will ever convince me I did not see her smile. It was a look that said, "Thank you Coach for believing in my plight and my will to live."

Abby's daddy entered the room and asked what was happening. I pointed at the monitors measuring every heartbeat, her temperature, and every breath she was taking. The nurse explained to him what the normal readings should be and then pointed to where Abby started and where she was at that second. He asked the nurse how it was possible and reminded the nurse what the doctor had said. The nurse said, "This is amazing, and if she keeps improving this will be the miracle of all miracles."

I will never find the words to express what I saw in this young man's face. All I can say is that at that second he became a father willing to do anything possible to save his child's life. He asked the nurse what he needed to do, and she said, "Just let Coach keep rocking and talking to her." He looked at me and all he could say was, "Thanks, Coach." I told him, "I will be sitting right here until this baby's numbers matches those of the average child." I told him to go tell his wife, his other baby, and his mother what was taking place. I asked him how Sydney was doing, and he said she was beautiful and he hoped she would get a chance to know her little sister.

I told him he should start planning on that to happen because Abby was not going anywhere. He reaches over my shoulder to touch his daughter's hand. He left the room, and within a few minutes, I saw six eyes and three smiles pressed up against the neonatal room window. I told Abby she would not believe it, but she had an audience watching her, consisting of her mom, dad, gammy, and her twin sister watching her monitors.

I spent the next several hours telling Abby about her entire family, starting with her dad's family first. She seemed most interested when I told her about our family and how I met her gammy and how her dad and mom met.

At one time, I looked around the neonatal unit and noticed five nurses had pulled up rockers and were listening to my stories. I talked to Abby about her life to come and all of the things she would get to enjoy about being a girl. Sometimes I made the nurses laugh when I talked about dating and going to dances. Other times when I talked about God and how he could help make life the most incredible venture on earth, I saw the nurses pull the babies they were caring for a little closer to their bodies.

Once her measurements reached normal, the nurses and doctors stepped in and began doing what these incredible people do. She continued to improve as the days went by, and the photo moments increased. I still think the best of the best are the photos with the four of them sitting side by side as a family.

Abby has now celebrated her fifth birthday, and she has struggled at times to make it to the next milestone, but she somehow has found the strength to fight the fight.

A few days ago, I watched Abby and Sydney have a tea party together. I realized she had made it to the first thing I had told her about in the first few hours of her life. I told her she would have fun playing with her twin sister someday.

I can only pray that somehow she gets to do all of the things we talked about someday. If she does, she will have outlived us all. I know Abby has the gift millions of ordinary people wish they could have. This gift allows her to find another way to continue when most people give up and accept defeat. I know this gift when I see it, and I have witnessed it many times in her life up to this point. I remember sitting and holding Abby while we were watching a football movie one day. It was a movie filled with the emotions of winning and losing. I watched Abby's reactions and feelings to each of the scenes in the movie. I felt her sadness when the film began, demonstrating hate, bigotry, and racism within a small community in Virginia. The next scene took place in summer camp, involving a group of high school athletes who had to make a choice. They could continue to hate one another or find a way to let the past go. I felt her team spirit kick in when the two sides came together and decided to work hard and help each other to become champions regardless of the color of their skin. I think Abby sees the world through my eyes. She sees a time when she will have the ability to tell her mother how she feels and what her needs really are. She envisions a day when she can get up out of the restricted seat she has today, walk into her room, and close the door—a time when she and her twin sister can share a cup of tea she made from scratch—when she can read, write, and count the number of candles on her birthday cake. Maybe one day she can schedule a meeting with all of her HPE friends and lead a discussion that starts out, "Do you remember when." I know in my heart the feelings she has; she is full of determination, and until a cure is found, she will continue to fight her way through the obstacles in her way to live another day.

I was finishing a story one day and I heard my youngest grandchild tell several of the children in the audience she was going to grow up and become a doctor so she could find a cure for HPE.

Well, only time will tell if this story will ever come true. Nevertheless, I will tell you this; if she does find a cure, it will be an incredible accomplishment. Abby, along with the other tens of thousands of children with HPE will be forever grateful for her gift. If it happens, it will become the I took Soul to Church Today 3rd edition.

For more information about Abby's life, go to www.runformecoach.com and please donate to support the charities. For more information about HPE and the Families for Hope charities located in Indianapolis, Indiana please go to *www.familiesforhope.org.*

Families for HoPE, Inc.
1219 N. Wittfield Street
Indianapolis, IN 46229
888-533-4443
Contact us via email at Info@FamiliesforHoPE.org

The End

Other Great Books by This Family of Writers

Book Titles	Author	Release	Access
I Took Soul to Church II	Dennis Ray 'Coach' Clifton	2016	Most Major Book Stores, Amazon.com, Printed in many Languages
My Family Emergency Preparedness Plan	Dennis Ray 'Coach' Clifton	2015	Most Major Book Stores, Amazon.com, Printed in many Languages
My Health & Wellness	Dennis Ray 'Coach' Clifton	2015	Most Major Book Stores, Amazon.com, Printed in many Languages
My Family Task Management Plan	Dennis Ray 'Coach' Clifton	2015	Most Major Book Stores, Amazon.com, Printed in many Languages
My Safety Plan 'Home & Work'	Dennis Ray 'Coach' Clifton	2015	Most Major Book Stores, Amazon.com, Printed in many Languages
The Annual Employee Safety Plan For Commercial & Industrial Businesses	Dennis Ray 'Coach' Clifton	2016	Most Major Book Stores, Amazon.com, Printed in many Languages
Hunt Gather Grow Eat First Edition	Jason Akers	2013	Amazon.com
Gardening with Insects	Jason Akers	2014	Amazon.com

Hunt Gather Grow Eat Your Guide to Food Independence	Jason Akers	2013	Amazon.com
The Scrounged Homestead	Jason Akers	2012	Amazon.com
Building Pastured Poultry Pens	Jason Akers	2013	Amazon.com
The Garden Creature Compendium	Jason Akers	2013	Amazon.com
Planting Trees the Low Cost Easy Way	Jason Akers	2013	Amazon.com
Start Hunting Now!	Jason Akers	2012	Amazon.com
The Process Oriented Gardener	Jason Akers	2011	Amazon.com
The Self-Sufficient Gardener	Jason Akers	2012	PODCAST